THE GHOST WRITER

John Harwood grew up in Hobart and studied literature and philosophy at the universities of Tasmania and Cambridge. He has published biography, political journalism, satire and poetry. *The Ghost Writer* is his first novel.

John Harwood

THE GHOST WRITER

VINTAGE

Published by Vintage 2005

2 4 6 8 10 9 7 5 3 1

First published in Great Britain in 2004 by
Jonathan Cape

Vintage
Random House, 20 Vauxhall Bridge Road,
London SW1V 2SA

Random House Australia (Pty) Limited
20 Alfred Street, Milsons Point, Sydney
New South Wales 2061, Australia

Random House New Zealand Limited
18 Poland Road, Glenfield,
Auckland 10, New Zealand

Random House (Pty) Limited
Endulini, 5A Jubilee Road, Parktown 2193,
South Africa

The Random House Group Limited Reg. No. 954009
www.randomhouse.co.uk/vintage

A CIP catalogue record for this book
is available from the British Library

ISBN 0 099 46082 3

Papers used by Random House are natural, recyclable products made from wood grown in sustainable forests. The manufacturing processes conform to the environmental regulations of the country of origin

Printed and bound in Great Britain by
Bookmarque Ltd, Croydon, Surrey

For Robin and Deirdre

Margaret Adams
200 Michigan Av
Sturgis, Michigan

Bought in Dublin
Ireland
5/3/05

PART ONE

I FIRST SAW the photograph on a hot January afternoon in my mother's bedroom. She was asleep – so I thought – in the sunroom at the other end of the house. I crept in through the half-open door, enjoying the feeling of trespass, breathing the scents of perfume and powder and lipstick and other adult smells, mothballs for the silverfish and insect spray for the mosquitoes our screens never quite managed to keep out. The net curtains were drawn, the blind half lowered; there was nothing to see through the window except the blank brick wall of old Mrs Noonan's place next door.

I stole across to my mother's dressing-table and stood listening in the dim light. The house was silent apart from the muffled ticking and creaking which my father insisted was the iron roof expanding in the heat, not someone creeping about in the dark cavity above the ceiling. One by one I tried the drawers, three on each side. As always, only the bottom left-hand drawer was locked. There were wooden panels between each layer, so you couldn't see what was in the drawer below by pulling out the one above. Last time I had searched through the litter of tubes and jars and bottles crammed into the uppermost drawer on the right. Today I started on the next one down, rummaging through a shoebox crammed with packets of needles and carded buttons, reels of coloured cotton and hanks of wool, the loose ends hopelessly tangled.

To see if there was anything behind the shoebox, I tugged at the drawer. It stuck, then shot right out of the dressing-table and hit the floor with a thud. I tried to force the drawer back in, but it wouldn't go. Any second now, I expected to hear my mother's footsteps hurrying up the hall, but no sound followed. Even the ticking in the ceiling had died away.

There seemed no reason why it wouldn't fit. Except that something cold and hard was stuck to the underside, right at the back. A small brass key. I had prised it loose, peeled away the tape and opened the locked drawer before the enormity of what I was doing had begun to register.

The first thing I saw was a book, whose title would elude me for years afterward. *The Carillon*? *The Chemillon*? *The Chalmion*? A word I didn't know. The grey paper cover was crumbling at the edges and pitted with rust-coloured spots. It had no pictures and looked grown-up and boring.

I couldn't find anything else. Then I saw that the brown paper lining on the bottom of the drawer was actually a very large envelope. It had a typewritten address and stamps on it, and one end had been slit with a knife. Another disappointment: just a thick bundle of pages with typewriting on them, tied together with rusty black ribbon. As I drew out the bundle, a photograph slid into my lap.

I had never seen the woman in the photograph before, and yet I felt I knew her. She was young, and beautiful, and unlike most people I had seen in photographs she did not look straight at you, but gazed away to one side, her chin tilted slightly upwards, as if she did not realise anyone was looking at her. And she did not smile, at least not at first. As I went on staring at her I began to think I could see the faintest trace of a smile, just at the corner of her mouth. Her neck was amazingly long and slender, and though the picture was in black and white, I felt I could see the changing colours of her skin where the light fell across the back of her neck and touched her forehead. Her hair, masses and masses of it, was drawn back behind her head and wound up in a long plait, and her gown – as I felt sure a dress as wonderful as hers must be called – was made of a soft dark velvety material, with shoulders gathered like the wings of angels.

Boys, I had learned from somewhere, were supposed to think their mothers were beautiful, but I suspected mine was not. She looked older and thinner than most of the mothers at my school, and worried about everything, especially me. Lately she had been very worried indeed. There were dark pouches under her eyes; the lines across her forehead and around her mouth seemed to be cutting deeper into the skin, and her hair, which used to be dark brown, had grey streaks running through it. I worried that I had worn her out by not being good enough; I was always meaning to be better, yet here I was burgling her secret drawer. But I also knew that the anxious, haunted look could descend when I had done absolutely nothing wrong. Whereas the woman in the photograph was calm and beautiful and *alive*, more alive than anyone I had ever seen in a picture.

I was still kneeling in front of the drawer, lost in the photograph, when I heard a hissing sound from the doorway. My mother stood rigid, fists clenched, nostrils flared. Tufts of hair stuck out from her head; the whites of her eyes seemed to be spilling out of their sockets. For a long, petrified instant she didn't move. Then she sprang, hitting and hitting and hitting me, screaming in time to the blows that fell wherever she could reach until I broke away and fled wailing down the hall.

From old Mrs Noonan I learned that if you shivered for no reason it meant that someone was walking over your grave.

Mrs Noonan was thin and stooped and had twisted papery hands with strange bulges around the knuckles; she smelt of stale lavender and felt the cold even in summer, especially when she took her first sip of tea. My mother didn't like her saying it, so Mrs Noonan took to shivering silently when she was drinking tea in our kitchen, but I knew what she meant. When I wasn't being bad, I used to imagine that someone had found out my mother's grave, a man in dark clothes with a dead white face who dodged behind a tombstone whenever he saw you coming, so that you could never catch him doing it. That was why her anxious look came down for no reason at all. Some days you could tell that he was tramping back and forth, back and forth, over and over her grave.

We would sometimes drive past Mawson cemetery, but I'd never been inside because we had no relatives there to visit. My father's parents were buried in Sydney, and he had a married sister in New Zealand who wrote every Christmas, but they never came to see us. All my mother's relatives were buried in England, and that was where I imagined her grave must be.

Mawson is an overgrown country town sprawled along the edge of the Great Southern Ocean. It used to be called Leichhardt, after some luckless explorer who never returned from the dead heart, until, so my father explained, the council decided to change it to something more cheerful. Beyond the remnants of the old town centre there's nothing much to see except shopping malls and filling stations and mile after mile of sprawling identical suburbs. Beaches to the south, hills to the north; the dead heart beyond. That was where you ended up if you crossed the narrow strip of farmland beyond the hills and kept driving north through the endless sandy scrub and saltpan into the desert. In summer when the north wind blew, clouds of fine red dust covered the town. Even inside, you could feel the grittiness of it between your teeth.

My mother's stories of growing up in the English countryside were full of things we didn't have in Mawson, chaffinches and mayflies and foxgloves and hawthorn, coopers and farriers and old Mr Bartholomew who delivered fresh milk and eggs to their house with his horse and cart. When she wasn't away at boarding-school, she lived with her grandmother Viola, and a cook and a maid, in a house called Staplefield which had staircases and attics and more rooms than you could count, and she had a best friend called Rosalind who was allowed to come and stay for the summer holidays. My mother could describe their favourite walks so vividly you felt you were there, provided you didn't interrupt. There was one I especially liked to hear about, which led across fields full of friendly cows to something called a wicket gate, up through an oak forest, where if you moved very quietly you might easily see a hare or a badger, and out into a clearing, where they would find – somehow it came as a complete surprise every time – a pavilion, which my mother once drew for me. It was like a smaller version of the bandstand in our Memorial Park, but freshly painted, cream and blue and dark green, with cushions for the polished wooden seats. No one ever disturbed them, so they would stay for hours, talking or reading or looking out over the countryside below, so far they could almost see the ships anchored away to the south in Portsmouth harbour.

At Staplefield, my mother and Rosalind could go anywhere they liked in complete safety, whereas boys who wandered away from home in Mawson would be dragged into cars by strange men and taken away and murdered, if the street gangs didn't get them first. Our house was a red brick bungalow on the edge of the old town, but double brick, as my father never tired of saying, not like the shoddy brick veneer they're building nowadays.

Like every other house in our street, it sat squarely on a quarter-acre of dead flat ground. There was one step up to the front porch and into the hall, which was always gloomy once the door had closed. We had plaster walls, cream with an odd brownish tinge, and dark green patterned carpet that smelled faintly of dog, even though we'd never had one. To the right was my mother's bedroom, the largest of the three, then the sitting-room (never to be called 'the lounge'). To the left was my father's bedroom, then mine, then the kitchen with its grey linoleum, green-painted plywood cupboards, Laminex table and chairs, and an old yellow fridge which opened with a pull handle. At night I could hear the wheeze and rattle when the motor started up. You went on through a doorway to the bathroom and laundry and a tiny alcove we called the study, on the left opposite the sunroom. The sunroom itself was a lean-to extension made of cement sheet and hardboard, the only room in the house where it was light all day.

As I grew older the paddocks at the end of the street became development opportunities and then subdivisions as the shoddy brick veneer suburbs rolled over us, but we stayed put. Instead of mayflies we had Portuguese millipedes, uncountable armies of them, coming up out of the leaf litter when the autumn rain set in, armoured, segmented, swarming towards the light. In winter, if my father forgot to spray the paths, the inside walls would turn black overnight. You had to get the broom, sweep them off the walls, gather up the writhing mess with a brush and pan and carry them out by the bucketload. They were quite harmless but my mother hated the damp, clammy feel of them. And if you squashed even one, the bitter pungent smell seemed to follow you around the house.

In summer the millipedes went underground and the ants came in, an endless black column that no amount of poison would keep out of the food cupboard for more than a few hours. Kitchen ants were not supposed to bite but if you stood too long barefoot near one of their trails you would feel the nip nip nip of tiny jaws. Outside in the yard we had fierce orange bull ants whose bite was like a red-hot needle; and, for a season, two nests of the dreaded inchmen. Half a dozen of those could put you in hospital; if you slipped and fell against the mound you were as good as dead. Likewise if you were foolish enough to leave an open can of soft drink unguarded: a wasp would climb in through the hole, sting your throat as you swallowed and you would choke to death. Funnel-web and redback spiders lurked in the woodpile behind the shed; you had to wear heavy rubber gloves to gather firewood until we changed over to bottled gas, and stamp very loudly as you approached in case a deadly brown snake like the one that killed Mrs Noonan's cat was sharing the woodpile with the spiders.

At Staplefield they did not need flywire and could leave their windows open on summer nights. We had fine mesh screens on all the doors and windows, to keep out the small black flies which rose in clouds around the back door when anyone approached, clogging your eyes and nostrils and crawling into your ears, and the huge lumbering blowflies that according to my mother vomited whatever they had last eaten over your food as soon as your back was turned. But no wire, however fine, would keep out the flying ants that swarmed on the first hot night in spring, worming through the mesh to form a dense cloud around the light bulb. In the morning, feebly twitching bodies lay in a drift of severed wings.

If it hadn't been for my mother's stories, perhaps Mawson – street gangs, millipedes and all – would have been simply home to me. But for as long as I could remember, I had wondered why we didn't go to live at Staplefield. Asking her for reasons, though, did not just break the flow of recollection, but sent it into reverse. It wasn't simply that Staplefield had been sold to other people long ago, or that we couldn't possibly afford a house like that today. England too had come down in the world. Where once the chaffinches had sung, mountains of garbage now accumulated on every street corner, breeding giant rats which ate babies and thrived on the strongest poisons. No more long, cloudless summers; now it rained for eleven months of the year, and you could not get coal or electricity for weeks at a time. By the time I was seven or eight, I had learned not to ask, but the questions remained. Nobody in our street had an upstairs room, let alone a cook, and it was hard to see why you would need a whole extra person just to grill chops, boil vegetables, and open tins of fruit. Nevertheless, I could not help seeing our lack of staircases and servants as one more consequence of the obscure misfortune which had landed us in Mawson.

All afternoon I stayed hidden behind a stack of timber in the garage, expecting another beating. But she did not call, and eventually hunger and thirst drove me inside to face a long interrogation. No, I told her several times – 'Look me in the eye, now, Gerard' – I had not done *anything* except look at the picture of the woman. I wanted to ask who she was, but I didn't dare, then or afterwards.

'Prying into other people's private things is a terrible sin,' she said finally – 'sin' was a word she seldom used – 'like opening their letters or reading their diaries or listening at doors. Promise me you'll never, never, never do anything like that again.'

I promised, which did not prevent me from sneaking into

her bedroom at the first opportunity, only to find the drawer locked again, and the key no longer in its hiding place.

By the end of the summer holidays my mother had apparently forgotten my trespass. But something had been lost between us, something I could not identify until I realised that since the day she caught me with the photograph, she had not once mentioned Staplefield or Viola. I tried again and again to draw her out, in vain; at the merest hint of an approach, she seemed to suffer an attack of deafness, assuming a look of blank incomprehension until I changed the subject or slunk away.

It seemed a double punishment. Talking of Staplefield had been the one thing more or less guaranteed to soften the lines of worry etched into her forehead. Now I had not only proved myself too wicked to re-enter that enchanted world; I had deprived her of the comfort of talking about it. I crept about the house, trying to be good, or at least appear good, but it made no difference. My father kept even more out of the way than usual.

Gradually, I came to realise that my mother did not love me any less; indeed as I moved on to high school and adolescence, she seemed to become ever more anxious on my behalf. Unlike some of my schoolfriends, I had never been allowed to roam freely, but nor did I really want to; the world beyond the local shops a few hundred yards away was a sinister place, fraught with unseen menace of which funnel-webs, street gangs, and plausible well-dressed men who preyed on wandering boys were merely the outward and visible signs. Even the man from the Department of Statistics who knocked at the door one evening was a potential kidnapper in her eyes. If my father hadn't been home, she'd have refused to answer a single question. She needed to know where I was, every minute of every day; if I got home even half an hour late from school, I would find her hovering beside the telephone table in the hall. I knew myself to be the centre of her existence, but on the subject of her past – not only Staplefield, but her entire life before she arrived in Mawson to marry my father – the habit of silence grew between us.

We had photographs of my father's parents, of his sister and her husband and children, but of my mother nothing before her wedding day, and very little after. The wedding photograph, taken on the steps of Mawson Registry Office in May 1963, is in black and white, just the two of them, no confetti. My mother is wearing a skirt and jacket and the sort of shoes that used to be called sensible. Thirty-four years (as I would learn from my own birth certificate) – thirty-four years of being Phyllis May Hatherley have just ended without trace, at the side of Graham John Freeman. My father's left arm is crooked for her to hold, which she does awkwardly. His clenched fist presses against his ribs. The top of her head is level with the handkerchief projecting from his breast pocket. His dark suit doesn't fit properly; the sleeves are too short, the shoulders droop. You could easily mistake him for the father of the bride, though he's only eleven years older. The lower half of his face has already taken on the shrunken, slightly simian look that makes you think someone isn't wearing their false teeth. And despite my mother's insistence that the sun was shining, they both look cold and undernourished, as if it's really a winter's day in England, a decade or more earlier, with rationing still in force.

I don't think my father ever knew any more about her life before they met than I did. He seemed to have been born without the faintest vestige of curiosity. His own father had come from an engineering family in Southampton, emigrated to Sydney in the 1920s, married, survived the Depression and war service as a mechanic in the RAAF, and set up his own machine shop. Dedicated to perpetuating the finest standards of British craftsmanship, with a portrait of the reigning monarch on the office wall. So far as my father was concerned, his entire family history could be expressed in micrometer readings, expansion coefficients, and the ability to work to tolerances set not merely in 'thou', but within a few ten-thousandths of an inch. As a draftsman, he must have been fluent in the new metric system, but we spoke only imperial at home. Whatever they might believe at Mawson Junior High, I knew that reality was measured in pounds and ounces, feet and inches, chains and furlongs and acres and miles and strange biblical quantities like cubits.

Outside of his workshop, my father's only apparent aim was to get through life as quietly and inconspicuously as possible. As far back as I could recall, my parents had slept apart, though they must, presumably, have shared a bed at least once. His room was as bare as a monk's cell. Board floor, single bed, bedside locker, wardrobe, chest of drawers. And one upright chair. No secrets there. On top of the chest of drawers he kept a framed photograph of my mother, one of the few we had, standing on the front porch in her twinset and sensible shoes, doing her best to smile. As if she were on the other side of the world instead of across the hall. They called each other dear, and never quarrelled within my hearing. Every morning he would collect the lunch she had packed for him and set off for the Land Surveys Department. He dug the vegetable garden, serviced the car, and did the household repairs. The rest of his time he spent with his trains.

They were nominally mine at first: 00 gauge electric, on a six by four baseboard in a corner of the garage. An oval track with an inside loop, a siding, two stations, and a tunnel through a papier mâché mountain. I was bored within hours; he doubled the outside track; after a few more hours I lost interest again. We all went on speaking of 'Gerard's trains' for years as the baseboard expanded and the tracks tripled and quadrupled below the signals and gantries and water towers, and the engines and rolling stock multiplied until our car was eased out into the carport, never to return despite the threat of rust. He bought an old kerosene heater for the winters, then a second-hand air conditioner for the ferocious summer heat. The baseboard grew until there was only a narrow walkway down each side to his stationmaster's quarters at the far end, where he had his workbench and his electric jug, an old brown leather swivel chair, and row after row of switches and levers and dials, all labelled according to a code that he carried around in his head. Everything on the board was electrified: not just the trains, but lights, points, signals, level crossings, even miniature bells. He bought his components – boxes of relays and solenoids and rheostats and endless coils of coloured wire – at army surplus sales and government auctions, swap meets with other train men. When the air conditioner wasn't running you could hear the hum of the transformers.

Every line had its own timetable, and all of the stations had English village names like East Woking or Little Barnstaple, but the network wasn't a map or a model; it was a self-contained, perfectly ordered world, every tiny detail meticulously crafted to scale, except that it contained no human figures. Some train men have crowds of miniature people waiting on platforms, fields full of minutely hand-painted porcelain cows: my father's universe was populated only by trains. If it hadn't been for 'your mother's nerves', I think he might have moved into the shed altogether; as it was, he brought the last train into the depot at 10.27 each night and retired dutifully to his bedroom.

He and I were always going to have 'a bit of a talk about things' but we still hadn't quite got around to it on the night, just before my eighteenth birthday, when he didn't come in at 10.30, or eleven, and she found him dead in his stationmaster's chair, with a single train running at full speed, round and round the outermost track.

If I had seen pictures of Staplefield, they might have cramped my imagination of it, suffused with depths and subtleties of colour unknown in Mawson. Memories of Staplefield – my memories, as they truly seemed, for my mother's stories had left me with such an acute visual sense of the place that I could walk around it in my head, fix my attention anywhere I pleased, the forge in the village street, or Viola, upright, elegant and silver-haired, seated at her walnut writing-desk, the two attic bedrooms with their gabled windows and dark wooden floorboards and Persian rugs, the view southwards over the fields from the pavilion on the hillside, and see every detail plain – these memories became my principal refuge as the miseries of Mawson Junior High crowded in. Until I met (for want of a better word) my invisible friend, Alice Jessell.

The letter arrived on a hot, airless, overcast morning towards the end of the summer holidays. I was thirteen and a half. My last days of freedom were slipping by. For weeks it had been too hot to do anything except lie on my bed reading or just listening to the rattle and creak of the fan as it swung to and fro, alternately wishing the time away and willing it to slow down. Nothing to look forward to but another year trailing after the legion of the lost: the swots, the cowards, the hopeless at sport. I heard the tinny put-putting of the postman's motorbike through my window and slouched out to the letterbox, just for something to do.

Apart from the usual bills and circulars, my parents received very little mail, and nothing at all from overseas except the occasional invitation to join a book or record club. Until that day, I don't think I'd ever seen a letter addressed to me. This one had my full name on it: Master Gerard Hugh Freeman. I slid the letter into the pocket of my shorts just before my mother followed me out the front door, and handed her whatever else the postman had brought.

Penfriends International, it said in typewriting at the top. PO Box 294, Mount Pleasant, London WC1. By Airmail. Inside was a letter, also typewritten, beginning Dear Gerard, asking me if I would like a penfriend, and if so, whether a girl or a boy. All I had to do was write to the Secretary, Miss Juliet Summers, telling her something about myself to help her find me my ideal penfriend, and return my answer in the enclosed airmail envelope.

I knew exactly what my mother would say. But Miss Juliet Summers sounded warm and friendly, and I ended up writing her several pages – I even talked about Staplefield – asking her to find me a girl penfriend. I did the whole thing in a rush, knowing I mustn't give myself time to think, so that it was only on my way back from the post office that I realised my mother would almost certainly see the reply before I did.

Sure enough, when I got home on the Friday of the first dismal week of school, she was hovering in the hall, clutching an envelope. The skin around her nostrils looked taut and shiny.

'There's a letter for you, Gerard,' she said accusingly. 'Shall I open it for you?'

'No. Can I have it please, Mother?'

This would normally have been met with 'No *thank you, Mother*' – she hated 'Mum' and would not have the word in the house – and '*May* I have it please, Mother?' But today she just stood there, glancing from me to the envelope, which she was holding so that I could not see the writing on it.

Suddenly I understood that, for the first time in my life, the high moral ground was mine.

'Please may I have my letter now, Mother?' I repeated.

Slowly, reluctantly, she held it out to me. 'Penfriends International'. The envelope was crumpled where her finger and thumb had gripped it.

'Thank you, Mother,' I said, retreating towards my room. But she was not finished with me.

'Gerard, have you been giving anyone our address?'

'No, Mother.'

'Then how did they know where to send it?'

I was about to say, I don't know, when I saw where this was leading. Taking a letter from the box and answering it without telling her, even a letter addressed to me, would count as being sneaky and dishonest. I could feel the high moral ground subsiding beneath me.

'I – I saw it on a noticeboard at school,' I improvised. 'About the penfriends.'

'Did Mrs Broughton give you permission to write to them?'

'No, Mother, I just . . . wanted a penfriend.'

'So you *did* give them our address.'

'I s'pose so – yes,' I muttered, choosing what seemed the lesser evil.

'You had no right to do that. Without asking me first. And where did you get the stamp?'

'I bought it with my pocket money.'

'I see . . . Gerard' – in her take-no-prisoners voice of command – 'I want you to show me that letter.'

I was afraid that if I did, I would never see it again.

'Mother, you've always said that letters are private . . . why aren't I allowed to read my own letter?' My voice broke upwards into a squeak on the last word.

Her colour rose; she glared, turned on her heel and walked away.

The letter was typed, but it was not from Miss Summers.

Dear Gerard,

I hope you don't mind, but Miss Summers sent me your letter to read (she sent lots of others too, but yours was the only one I really liked), and you sounded so much like the penfriend I've been hoping for that I asked her if I could write straight back to you myself. Of course you don't have to answer if you don't like the sound of me!

My name is Alice Jessell, I'll be fourteen this March and like you I'm an only child, except that both my parents are dead, we were in a car crash together. I know maybe I shouldn't write this bit straight away but I want to get it over with. Anyway you might not want to read any more, so it's only fair, as long as you know that I'm definitely not looking for sympathy and I don't ever, ever want you to feel sorry for me, just to be my penfriend if you'd like to. So as I was saying my parents were both killed in the accident, which happened about three years ago. I survived because I was in the back seat, but my spinal cord was damaged so I can't walk. My arms are OK though – I only type because my writing's really hard to read, and already I can type much faster than I could ever write. And because we didn't have any relatives or anything I had to go into a home – I know how awful this must sound and of course it was unbelievably unbearably awful at first. But it's a really lovely place, in the countryside, in Sussex. The insurance money pays for me to be here, I even have my own lessons so I don't have to go to school, and a beautiful upstairs room all to myself, looking out over fields and trees and things.

So now I've said it. I really do mean it, about not wanting sympathy, I want you to think of me if you can – only if you want to be my friend of course – as a normal person who just wants to share normal things. I don't watch TV or listen to pop music I'm afraid but I love reading – it sounds as if you do too and I'd love to have someone my own age to talk about books with. (Most of the other people here are very nice, but much older than me.) And to sort of be part of someone else's life, and be their friend. Anyway that's enough about that.

There's snow on the fields right now, but it's a bright sunny day, there are squirrels running up and down the big oak tree outside my window, and three plump little birds on the windowsill, they're singing so loudly I can hear them over the clatter of the keys! Actually where I am sounds a little bit like the place where your mother grew up – a big red brick house in the countryside with woods and fields around it. Mawson sounds awfully dry and hot! Sorry, that sounds a bit rude, I mean I'm sure it's lovely, just so different from here.

Anyway I'd better stop and give this to Matron (she's more like an aunt, really) to send on to Miss Summers, that's because Penfriends International are a sort of charity, they pay the airmail postage. So if you want to, write to me care of Miss Summers, and then every time she sends on one of your letters to me, she'll enclose some reply coupons to post back to you – that way you won't have to buy stamps. Our letters will be completely private.

I really must stop right now. Before I panic and crumple this up for maybe making a complete idiot of myself.

Sincerely,

Alice

P.S. I think Gerard is a really nice name.

I lay on my bed and read Alice's letter over and over again. She sounded incredibly, unbelievably brave, and yet I realised I truly didn't feel sorry for her. Sympathy, yes; but even though being an orphan in a wheelchair did sound unbearably awful, her letter made me feel as if I'd come in out of the dark on a freezing night, not knowing how cold I'd been until I felt the heat of the fire.

Reading other people's letters is a terrible sin. But it hadn't stopped me from trying to open that drawer again. I looked around my room for a hiding-place. Under my mattress? On top of my wardrobe? Behind the books in my bookcase? Nowhere was safe. I thought again about how brave Alice must be, and felt suddenly ashamed of being thirteen and a half, starting second year high school and still too scared to tell my mother that yes, I did have a penfriend, and no, I wasn't going to show her my letter.

But facing the full blast of my mother's disapproval at dinner that night, I also had to face, for the thousandth time, the fact that I really *was* a coward.

'Mother I want to, I mean please may I – write to my um . . .'

'You will not be writing to *anyone*, Gerard. I'm still waiting for you to give me that letter.'

'Mother, you've always told me it's wrong to read other people's . . .' Again my voice betrayed me. My mother was visibly swelling. Sensing imminent meltdown, my father concentrated on his chop-bone.

'*I* am going to read that letter, because *you* are going to give it to me. Who is this penfriend, anyway?'

'She's – she's a—'

'A *girl*? You won't be writing to any girl, Gerard, not until I've seen that letter and written to her mother myself.'

'She doesn't *have* a mother,' I blurted. 'She's an orphan – in a home.' It felt like betraying Alice, but I saw where my only chance lay.

'And where is this home?'

'In – in the countryside.'

'That letter came from London,' she snapped.

'They send them on – Penfriends International – and pay the postage – for children who – children like Alice who don't have parents.'

'You mean it's a *charity*?'

I nodded eagerly. My mother was silent for a moment. She looked faintly uncomfortable.

'Oh. Well of course I'll have to write to them first . . . but I suppose . . . yes, go and get that letter please. And then we'll see.'

Just when I thought I'd wriggled off the hook.

'Mother –' I began hopelessly.

'It's his letter, Phyllis.'

My mother could not have looked more astonished if the fruit bowl had spoken on my behalf. Her mouth opened, but no sound came out. My father looked equally startled.

'I'll go and get the address,' I said in an inspired moment, knowing she would never let up until she had at least written to Juliet Summers.

My mother nodded dumbly, and I left them staring at each other in utter bewilderment.

After I'd dried the dishes I went out to the garage and asked my father if I could have a box with a lock 'to keep some of my stuff in'. He seemed determined to behave as if nothing out of the ordinary had happened, but he gave me a stout metal toolbox and a shiny new padlock and key, and we spent the rest of the evening playing trains. I felt sure he knew what I was really thanking him for.

I started my first letter to Alice that same night and continued most of the weekend, pages and pages written straight down as if I were talking to her, everything about my confrontation with my mother, about school and its miseries, all of my likes and dislikes, and much more about Staplefield, how much it meant to me and how my mother had refused to talk about it after I found the photograph in her room. I wrote compulsively, as if from dictation, knowing I mustn't re-read what I'd said, or let myself think about what I was doing. And spent the next fortnight in a torment of hope and fear, until her answer arrived and I knew for certain it would be all right.

My mother never told me whether she'd written to Juliet Summers. She acted as if the letters I would find waiting on my desk when I got home from school had materialised without her knowledge. Part of me longed to win back her approval, but I also knew that if I once spoke of Alice, I would never be able to stop until every last detail had been dragged out for inspection on the kitchen table.

So our silence over Staplefield came to include Alice. But now I had Alice to write to, and she never tired of hearing about Staplefield. Or, it seemed, anything to do with my life. It was almost as if she was writing *from* Staplefield, for the view from her window reminded me constantly of the landscape my mother used to describe: the formal garden below, with tall trees rising up to her window, then the patchwork of green fields, leading to steep wooded hills in the near distance.

Of course I wanted to know exactly where she was, so I could look it up in the atlas. But from the beginning Alice laid down certain rules.

Gerard I need you to understand why I don't want to talk about my life before the accident. I love my parents, I think about them all the time. Often I feel they're very close, watching over me, corny though that sounds. But to survive I had to let go of everything before the accident. My friends, all my stuff, everything. The only thing I brought with me was my favourite photo of my parents, it's here on my desk as I'm writing this. As if – this is going to sound awfully weird I know – as if I died with them and went on to a sort of after-life, only still here on earth, like a reincarnation only different. I knew if I tried to hide under a blanket of pity I'd smother. And to throw off the blanket I had to throw off everything.

Of course if I had brothers and sisters and relatives I'd have no choice. But then I'd be the family cripple, and I don't think I'd want to go on living. This way I'm just a girl who happens to need a wheelchair to get around. Not a cripple or a paraplegic or a disabled person, just me. I'm really mobile, I do everything for myself. And the people here are wonderful, apart from physiotherapy and stuff like that they treat you as completely normal.

But I have been very lonely and your letters make all the difference. They light up my life.

Now for the difficult part. I don't want to tell you exactly where I am, because . . . (there's been a really long pause here, I've watched a girl and boy, they look about our age, walking across the fields with their arms round each other, all the way from the footpath outside our garden wall to the edge of the forest, wondering how to say this the way I mean it) well for the same reason I don't want to send you a photo of me. (For a start I don't have any, but that's not why of course.) And it's not because I'm hideously disfigured or anything, I don't actually have any scars at all.

No it's because a picture would have to be a picture of me in my chair, or anyway of me not able to walk, and I don't want you to see me that way. I'm afraid you'll feel sorry for me. I do hope you'll understand, even though – this really is unfair, I know – I'd love to have a picture of you (and of your parents, and the house where you live, only if you'd like to of course). In exchange I'll try to honestly answer anything you ask me about how I look.

If by some miracle I get to walk again, then I'll send you a picture. But until then I want to be

your invisible friend

love Alice

PS This is really vain I know. But I just realised you might think I'm sixteen stone and covered in acne or something like that. In fact I'm only just seven stone and – well not totally hideous anyway.

PPS If I'm honest that's not the only reason – about not sending my photo I mean. I don't want to be fixed by a picture. However you want to think of me, that's the way I'd like you to.

I had been avoiding the subject of photographs, because the thought of Alice seeing my sticking-out ears and banded teeth was too humiliating to bear. So I assured her I did understand (which was only half true); and that I was sensitive about my bands, so could we both stick to word-pictures (hoping as I wrote this that she wouldn't ask any searching questions about ears, hair, spots, freckles, knees, teeth or indeed anything much to do with my physical appearance).

Far from pitying her, I often caught myself forgetting all about the wheelchair and the loss of her parents, contrasting the beauty of her surroundings with the drab suburban desolation of mine, wishing, passionately, that I could be there with her wherever exactly 'there' in Sussex might be. After those early letters, she wrote, for most of the time, as if her injury didn't exist, as if she were a young heiress living alone in a mansion, with her own private tutors, taking herself for outings, as she called them, whenever the weather was fine. They certainly had a wonderful library at the home, because no matter what book I mentioned, if she hadn't already read it she would have by the time her next letter arrived. Besides, our situations were, in many respects, remarkably similar. My parents had never had a television, didn't read magazines, and bought the local paper only on Saturdays, for the advertisements. They took no interest in politics, or news beyond the boundaries of Mawson. Occasionally, my mother would listen to classical music on the radio. But mostly she and I just read, in silence.

Which was exactly how Alice spent her days, when she wasn't having lessons or out in the garden: reading, and gazing out of her window. Even at fourteen, she seemed to have outgrown all the usual teenage interests, whereas I hadn't even started on them. Just before we met – the word she always preferred – I had been trying to develop an interest in rock music. But as soon as I learned that Alice didn't like any kind of pop music – she said anything with a beat made her feel as if she'd drunk too much coffee – I gave up the pretence. I stopped trying to fit in with anyone. Instead of trailing miserably round the schoolyard, trying to avoid being beaten up, I stayed in the library every lunch hour, doing my homework, so that I could spend the evenings in my room writing to Alice. Gradually, I became aware that I wasn't being picked on nearly as often; and despite the amount of time I spent writing to, and dreaming about, Alice, my grades actually improved.

My outdoor life was almost as constrained as hers, bounded by my mother's pathological dread of what would happen to me if I strayed from the narrow path that led from home to school (and post office) and back. But now that I had Alice, I no longer felt confined: gazing out of my own window, I would find myself staring through, rather than at, the rusty metal cladding of Mr Drukowicz's massive shed, to the woods and meadows of – as I would often catch myself imagining – Staplefield.

But of course I began to want more, much more: to see Alice, to hear her voice, to hold her. I told her that I prayed every day (even though I didn't think I really believed in God) that her spine would heal or that the doctors would find a cure. 'I'm glad you do,' she replied, 'but I mustn't think about it. They told me I'll never walk again, and I've accepted that.'

So I went on praying, and didn't mention it again. I would happily have spent my life savings on one short phone call, but she wouldn't allow that either. She didn't – at first – encourage any endearments or professions of love from me beyond 'Dear Alice' and 'Love, Gerard', and yet she told me, in almost every letter, that I was the closest, most important person in her life.

She did, however, keep her promise to answer honestly anything I asked about her appearance, even though she said it embarrassed her and she was very much afraid I'd think her vain. She admitted that her hair was long, and curly (she called it frizzy), and thick, and 'a sort of reddy-chestnut-brown colour', that she had very pale skin, dark brown eyes, and 'a nose that's really straight but looks as if it's just a little bit turned-up'. And though I'd been too shy to ask, she volunteered, 'just to get it over with', that her legs were quite long – and her waist quite small, 'and otherwise I suppose people would say I was quite well-developed for my age, and now I've embarrassed myself quite enough for one letter, my face is burning and I'm not saying any more'.

In other words, she looked like a goddess. A goddess who mostly wore jeans and T-shirts but sometimes, just for a change, put on one of her long dresses, 'like the one I'm wearing today, which is white and musliny and gathered at the waist, with small purple flowers embroidered over the bodice'. Apart from the obvious fact that she was stunningly beautiful, I learned, from her letters, the impossibility of capturing an individual face in words alone. My imagination of her remained both painfully vivid and tantalisingly blurred.

Then one lunch hour in the school library I found a book of paintings, mostly black and white but with a section of colour plates in the middle. They'd only just catalogued it, so the women in the pictures hadn't yet been equipped with beards, moustaches, monstrous breasts and grotesque genitals in livid Texta-Colour – you weren't allowed to borrow the art books, but that didn't save them. I turned over *The Last of England* and there was *The Lady of Shalott*, at whom I gazed, transfixed, for many minutes: this was surely Alice.

Before the afternoon bell rang I had discovered the Pre-Raphaelites, and found at least a dozen more Alices. She seemed to have modelled for the entire Brotherhood, but they weren't all equally good at painting her. Rossetti could do her hair, but he'd given her a mean mouth; Burne-Jones could do her face very well, but the hair wasn't quite right, and besides he'd painted her naked, emerging from a tree, for some reason, with her arms around an almost equally naked youth: I only dared glance at that one and pass hastily on, afraid that Mrs McKenzie the librarian would catch me. Millais's *The Bridesmaid* was close, but I kept turning back to *The Lady of Shalott*, and thinking that if only she could manage to look a little less tragic, the likeness would be perfect.

I told Alice that same night, and when at last her reply came it turned out that she already knew the picture, and yes, she supposed she did look a bit like the Lady of Shalott, except that she thought her hair was darker than the Lady's, and of course the Lady was much better-looking; whereas I felt certain the comparison was quite the other way round. I invested most of my savings in a book of Waterhouse's pictures, which I managed to smuggle home after one of our rare trips to Mawson Central Shopping Mall. Sex was not merely a taboo subject in our house; we had always lived according to the pretence – made possible by the absence of television and magazines – that no such thing existed. And even though Waterhouse's naked nymphs were Art, I knew my mother would not see them that way, any more than I did.

And then I had the dream. It was late summer, two years since we'd started writing. I woke – or so I thought – in bed in my own room, everything the same except that a full moon was shining through my window. A strange moon, because its light was soft and golden, like candlelight, and warm against my face. An impossible moon, because my window faced south and the sky was blotted out by the side of Mr Drukowicz's shed, but in the dream it seemed absolutely right and natural. I lay there for a little while, feeling the warmth of its rays, until I became aware that the source of the warmth, which was now filling my whole body, was much closer than the moon.

I turned my head on the pillow. Alice lay facing me, smiling the most enchanting smile, a smile of pure joy and tenderness and love. Her head was only a few inches from mine, her red-gold-chestnut hair rippling over the pillow in the candle-moonlight, our bodies not quite touching, and for a small eternity I just lay there, floating in perfect bliss. She did not look exactly like the Lady, or any of the women in the paintings; she was simply Alice, and beautiful, and the warmth of her body flowed into mine as our lips brushed and met and I woke in my wet pyjamas, alone, to the familiar patch of neon from the streetlight spilling across the wall of Mr Drukowicz's shed. It was 1.30 in the morning.

Always before, scrubbing at my pyjamas and sheets by torchlight, I'd felt nothing but shame and dread that this time – for the stains were always horribly visible in the morning – my mother would say something. But that night I went through the routine almost absent-mindedly, praying that I would float straight back into the dream, and Alice radiant beside me.

Instead I lay sleepless for a long time, struggling in vain to recapture her face as I had seen it, the glow fading until there were only the faces from the paintings left, and I buried my own face in my pillow and wept.

As I was finally drifting in and out of sleep, I had another dream, of myself as a very small child, being read to on my mother's knee, in lamplight on our couch at night. My mother was in her dressing-gown, which made it feel very late, and she was reading from a book with no pictures, a story I didn't understand at all, but I sat listening intently just the same, following the cadences of her voice. I was watching from outside, as if my older self were sitting invisibly on the couch beside them. Then I saw that my mother was crying silently as she read. Tears were streaming down her face and splashing over my pale blue sleeping suit, but she made no attempt to wipe them away; she just went on reading and the tears went on falling until I woke again briefly to find my own pillow still damp from the tears I had shed for Alice.

On the Saturday morning after the dream, I found myself alone in the house. My father was at a train men's swap meet on the other side of town; my mother had run herself late for the hairdresser. I came out into the hall when I heard the front door slam, and saw that she had – most unusually – left the door to her room open. As I moved closer my gaze fell upon the drawer I had opened on that stifling January afternoon.

My unspoken pact with my mother had kept me away from her room before this. I won't pry into your secrets if you don't pry into mine. But the door was open, and Alice was so fascinated by Staplefield, and Viola, and anything I could remember about the photograph I had found.

The drawer was still locked, and there was no small brass key in any of the obvious places. Then I remembered that the tongue – or whatever the bit that worked the lock was called – had been nothing more than a plain metal tag with a slot cut in the front end of it. So I went around the house collecting and trying keys from other pieces of furniture until I found one that fitted.

The lock clicked over. Kneeling in the half-light, breathing mothballs and insect spray and the faint doggy smell of the carpet, I saw my uneasy reflection staring from the depths of the dressing-table mirror. *Gerard is so like his mother.*

The envelope and the photograph had gone. The only thing in the drawer was the book with the faded grey paper cover, mottled with reddish brown spots. *The Chameleon* – I still didn't know what a chameleon was but I recognised the word – *A Review of Arts and Letters*. Volume I, Number 2, June 1898. Edited by Frederick Ravenscroft. Essays by Richard Le Gallienne and G.S. Street. Poems by Victor Plarr, Olive Custance, and Theodore Wratislaw. I tried to open it and discovered that the pages were joined together at the edges. Except for one section. 'Seraphina: A Tale', by V.H.

Seraphina

LORD EDMUND Napier liked everything about him pleasant and agreeable, and since he was rich, handsome, unmarried, and possessed of a splendid town house in Cheyne Walk, the world made haste to oblige him. Indeed it had been hastening – with one disagreeable exception, as we shall presently learn – almost from the moment of his birth some forty years before the afternoon upon which we find him gazing at a blank space on the wall of his private gallery.

Though the main entrance hall and staircase of his house were adorned, as might be expected, with portraits of Napiers past, this gallery was known only to Lord Edmund's most intimate associates. It was a long, vaulted, panelled room, reminiscent in its proportions of a place of worship, but lit so as to draw in as much natural illumination as possible while excluding any direct glare. The merest glance around the walls, however, would reveal Lord Edmund to be, as the phrase goes, a devotee of the female form, lavishly and variously illustrated by over a hundred canvases running the length of the gallery on either side, and supplemented by numerous pieces of statuary in bronze, marble, jade, ebony, and other precious materials; all, I hasten to add, in the finest of taste; the finest, indeed, that money could buy. But to describe Lord Edmund as a worshipper at the shrine of Beauty would be, if not precisely untrue, at least a shade discourteous. A gentleman predestined to adorn the very pinnacle of society cannot but be conscious of his own perfections; and it would be fairer to say that Lord Edmund and Beauty had long been on intimate terms. And this, paradoxical as it may seem, was the source of a certain discontentment on his side, and the reason why the wall at the northern end of the gallery, farthest from the great double doors which opened onto its vaulted length, the very space in which the finest flower of his collection ought to have been displayed, remained obstinately blank. He had, over the years, tried any number of canvases in the place of honour, but none had ever quite sustained that pitch of perfection he had, almost unwittingly, come to require of its subject.

Lord Edmund himself could scarcely have accounted for his single state, which nevertheless remained a topic of lively interest to every fashionable hostess with marriageable daughters at her disposal. Many a matron had fancied her favourite as good as engaged to his lordship, only to discover, just as she thought him safely landed, that the catch had unaccountably slipped the net, and so adroitly as to leave her without even the consolation of an action for breach of promise. In truth his lordship's heart had only ever been engaged on one occasion, and that many years ago, when he was but four and twenty. The match was impossible: Miss Eleanor Brandon, though undeniably beautiful and sweet-natured (and, it must be admitted, far more cultivated and better read than the youthful Edmund himself) possessed neither family nor fortune; worse, she nurtured artistic ambitions, accepting whatever was offered her in the way of scenery-painting and the like around the studios of Chelsea. She had, at the time of their meeting, an impoverished suitor some ten years older than herself, a portrait painter constitutionally incapable of fulfilling any of the few commissions offered him; to whom, nevertheless, she was on the verge of committing her affections. But youth and charm prevailed; so entirely that Edmund could not but be swayed by the force of her love for him. He did not – at least in retrospect – believe that he had explicitly pledged himself to her; but he did speak privately to his father, the earl, who forbade not only the match, but any further association with Miss Brandon.

Edmund was of age, and sole heir, and could have defied his parent, but severe financial constraint, and a great deal of unpleasantness, would certainly have followed. What was a fellow to do? He owed Miss Brandon, at the very least, the courtesy of an interview; but that would certainly upset her, and therefore him, so how could it benefit either? And if his father were to hear of it . . . no; a letter was the obvious thing; but it proved so devilish difficult to compose that he was forced to abandon the attempt. An emissary: now there was an idea; a good friend upon whose delicacy and discretion he could absolutely rely; indeed, he knew the very man for the task. But the very man was so far affected by Miss Brandon's distress as to charge his friend with cruel and unmanly conduct; which led, inevitably, to a breach between them, and left the matter still unresolved. Perhaps he really ought to see her, come what may . . . and if only his father's temper, uncertain at the best of times, had not been so vile of late, he really thought he would have gone.

So the days stretched into weeks without anything decisive being done, until one afternoon, when he had just concluded a painful exchange with his father on the subject of his expenditure, and was about to set forth in search of new distractions, a footman informed them that there was 'a young person' at the front door, refusing to accept that Edmund was not at home, and insisting upon an interview. With a sinking heart, he descended the stair, his father immediately behind him. Eleanor's pale, stricken face was terrible to behold; still worse, the momentary joy transfiguring her expression when she saw that it was he. She moved as if to embrace him; transfixed by the baleful presence looming at his back, he could only stammer and retreat, until the door was closed against her. That evening he learned that a young woman had flung herself off Battersea Bridge and drowned. It was Eleanor; and the coroner's jury, hearing that she was with child, brought in a verdict of suicide while the balance of her mind was disturbed.

Edmund's name was not connected with the tragedy. He was sent immediately abroad, where he remained for some months until his father resolved to settle all outstanding differences between them by dying of apoplexy. At first, his conscience troubled him sorely, but like other young men of wealth and title he learned to subdue it through the strenuous pursuit of pleasure, until everything about him was once again pleasant and agreeable. Eleanor's face, overlaid by so many others, faded from his memory, until he had only the vaguest recollection of her appearance. By the time of his fortieth birthday, she had not crossed his mind for years.

He would have counted himself the most fortunate of men, were it not for a certain restlessness, a—not precisely boredom, but a feeling that the world had lost something of its charm. Often, of late, he had found himself neglecting the manifest delights of his gallery in favour of the empty wall, as if by sheer intensity of scrutiny he could divine, beneath the faint sheen of panelled oak, those lineaments of face and form which yet eluded him. Such was his absorption in this pursuit that he would wake, as it were, to find that upwards of an hour had vanished, leaving him restless and unsettled, incapable of responding to the voluptuousness all about him, seeking only to escape from gallery and house alike and lose himself in the great city, walking away the hours until it came time to return and dress for his evening engagements.

So it was, on the afternoon in question, that Lord Edmund emerged from his front door, turned, as was his invariable custom, left into Cheyne Walk, and set off mechanically towards Royal Hospital Road, vaguely intending to stroll up Ebury Street and take a turn around Green Park. It was a bright, clear, spring day; a light breeze, cool and invigorating, ruffled the surface of the river. Still brooding on—he knew not exactly what—he had almost reached his turning when his attention was caught by a solitary figure on the other side of the Embankment, some fifty paces ahead of him and moving in the same direction. A tall, slender, female figure, evidently youthful to judge from a certain sinuous freedom of movement, clad in what appeared to be a soft pale gown, trimmed with dark blue or purple, and crowned by—plain even at this distance—an extraordinary cloud—no other phrase would do for it—an extraordinary cloud of auburn hair which seemed to swirl and float about her as she moved.

Not, it must be admitted, for the first time in such a circumstance, Lord Edmund abandoned his intended route and quickened his pace along the Embankment, meaning to come up with the young woman on his side of the road and then—see what might be made to follow. But despite his best efforts, and without any visible acceleration on her part, the distance between them unaccountably refused to diminish. She betrayed not the slightest awareness of his interest; such was the abundance of the auburn cloud that he could not tell where her attention was directed, but she certainly had not turned her head towards him. She maintained, to all appearances, the same easy, sinuous, unselfconscious gait, and yet by the time they passed Chelsea Bridge he was stumbling between a rapid walk and an undignified trot; flushed, overheated, and altogether captivated. So they continued all the way along Grosvenor Road to Vauxhall Bridge, onto which, to his surprise, she turned, proceeding across the river at the same deceptive pace, still so surrounded by the radiant cloud of hair that despite the altered angle of vision he could see nothing of her face.

Lord Edmund now crossed over, and made his way in turn onto the bridge, noting as he did so that the tide was very low. To his perplexity and dismay, he saw that the distance between himself and his quarry had, if anything, increased. Had they been alone, he would have broken into a run, but there were other persons on the bridge, and, indignity aside, the spectacle of a gentleman in hot pursuit of an unaccompanied young lady might lead to worse humiliations. Yet, even hastening as fast as he dared, he could see all too plainly that his cause would soon be lost. He was not half-way over, yet there was her dwindling figure almost at the far side; he absolutely could not reconcile her unhurried rhythm of movement to the speed with which she was now eluding him. And what on earth could prompt her to turn, as her choice of descent began to indicate, in the direction of Lambeth, surely a most unsuitable destination for one such as her?

The auburn cloud vanished from sight, and a bitter desolation, sharper and more painful than any emotion he could recall, overwhelmed him. No; it was not to be borne; he must and would see her face, would speak to her. He looked wildly around for a hansom, but there was none in sight. Heedless of curious glances, he began to run. As he crossed the farther bank of the river, he thought—no, he was certain—he saw her disappearing into Vauxhall Walk. Thus began a chase which drew him further and further into noisome lanes and unfamiliar alleys, lured ever onwards by what was surely a flash of pale muslin, a swirl of bright hair floating like flame upon the unwholesome air, but always deceived until at last, winded, footsore, and defeated, he found himself leaning against a blank wall at the end of a dim, cobbled cul-de-sac. As the pounding in his ears subsided, he became aware of an uncanny stillness around him. There was not the faintest sight or sound of any inhabitant, not even the distant barking of a dog; the ragged crowds through which he had lately forced his way might have been a hundred miles off. The doors and windows along both sides of the alley were barred and shuttered; all but one, on closer inspection: a dingy shopfront above whose recessed doorway hung the triple symbol of the pawnbroker's trade.

Wearily, he pushed himself upright and made his way

towards the shopfront, hoping at least to secure a cab, and perhaps find something palatable to quench his thirst. His footsteps rang loudly on the cobbles; the silence was really quite uncanny. Coming up to the shop window, he saw that it was so heavily layered with grime as to be entirely opaque. The door, however, stood slightly ajar. He pushed, expecting the stillness to be broken by the scrape of a lintel or the jangling of a bell, but it swung smoothly and noiselessly open.

He paused, irresolute at the threshold, willing his eyes to penetrate the gloom within. In the light from the open door he could discern the outlines of chairs and tables and other articles of furniture crowded and heaped high, one upon the other, so as to fill both sides of the room, leaving only a narrow central passageway receding into darkness. Scents of ancient timbers and musty fabrics, of decaying paper and chill metal, of dust and rot and mould, floated about him. It was not as he had imagined a pawnbroker's shop should be; there was no counter, no sign of a proprietor; only the heaped and crowded furniture and the artificial passage, scarce wide enough to admit him, into whose Stygian depths he continued vainly to peer. Lord Edmund was, of course, a man accustomed to command; in his natural surroundings it would never have occurred to him that his smallest wish would not be instantly and silently gratified, with scarce need of utterance on his part. But this was not Cheyne Walk, nor Napier Hall, nor even one of those more boisterous parts of town where gold could buy the service of any man—or woman. He stood mute, incapable either of advance or retreat, unmanned by darkness and silence.

How long he remained thus he could not tell, but a light

began to glow dimly at the far end of the passage, or tunnel, as he perceived in the brightening gleam, for the aperture was not only framed but roofed over by the heaped furniture. Like a man under mesmeric compulsion, Lord Edmund found himself drawn into and along the passageway, which extended a surprising distance, given the mean proportions of shopfront and alley. As he emerged from the confinement of the tunnel, he was at first dazzled by the light of a single lantern held aloft by a motionless figure a few paces off to his left.

"Pray step forward, sir," said a grave, unexpectedly cultivated voice, "and let me know how I may be of service to you."

The figure resolved itself into a man of indeterminate age, somewhat below Lord Edmund's height, and slighter of figure, clean shaven, clothed in a plain dark suit like a manservant's. The lamplight fell upon a long, pale, melancholy face, indefinably wasted as if by prolonged illness or suffering, the eyes shadowed beneath a high forehead, the nose thin and aquiline, the lips almost bloodless. It was evident, despite the encircling gloom, that the man posed no threat to his lordship, who was about to inquire after hansom cabs and refreshments when his attention was caught by a large rectangular structure, a little to his right and taller than himself. As if anticipating a request, the proprietor—for who else could he be?—bore the lantern towards it, making, as he went, some adjustment which caused the light to brighten further. Lord Edmund, following, saw that the object was in fact a canvas, resting upon a frame; indeed a picture at least six feet in height. As the light came full upon it he caught his breath.

It was not like any picture he had ever seen, for the illusion of seeing *through* the frame, exactly as one looks through an open window to the view beyond, was, in the lamplight, absolute. He was staring at, or rather into, a woodland pool surrounded by dense foliage, and from this pool, with arms outstretched towards him, was emerging a marvellous naked woman of that preternatural beauty he had long despaired of encountering. Still more marvellously, her hair, though damp from recent immersion in the translucent waters that swirled about her waist, and thus falling dense about her shoulders rather than floating like flame upon the air, was of the exact, miraculous shade he had but lately pursued and lost. Whether this was the very same woman he could not tell; that she was *the* woman he had so long sought he had not the shadow of a doubt. Her expression seemed, at first glance, solemn and spiritual; but subtly endowed with the faintest of smiles, a hint of tender mockery, almost of invitation. He felt that he could gaze for ever into the fathomless depths of those dark eyes, upon the light caught in the minute droplets of water clinging to her lustrous flesh—but surely she breathed? Was that not a faint pulse in the delicate blue vein at her throat? Aroused, entranced, and altogether forgetful of his situation, even of the silent presence bearing the lamp, he stepped forward to claim his prize—and found himself confronted by unintelligible swirls and textures of pigment. He stepped back, and the miracle repeated itself; approached once more, and again the vision dissolved before his eyes.

"Who is she?" he inquired in a tone of wonder, more of himself than of his companion.

"Seraphina," replied the sombre voice at his back. The

lamp silently approached and descended, illuminating a small bronze plate set into the base of the frame and engraved with that name in plain italic lettering.

"And—in life?" asked his lordship, still unable to take his eyes from the picture.

"There I cannot help you, sir."

"But surely she must . . . who then is the artist?"

"There too, sir, I am unable to enlighten you, save that I understand him to be deceased, and this to have been his only finished work."

"Then how . . . pray tell me, is it for sale?"

Lord Edmund had meant to pursue his inquiries further before raising the matter of purchase, but anxiety and impatience, a dread that he might not after all take possession of his heart's desire, had overmastered him.

"It is, sir."

"And—the price?"

"Twelve guineas, sir."

His lordship's jaw dropped in astonishment. He knew full well the dangers of judging a work by artificial light, but here was no question of authenticity, only an anonymous miracle of brushwork; had the man said twelve thousand, he would have called for an emissary to secure a draft from his bankers by return.

"Twelve guineas!" he repeated incredulously. "You are sure . . . ? That is to say, yes, I will take it. Now, if you please; in fact I have that sum about me." Lord Edmund was not one of those noblemen who count it an indignity to bear the currency of the realm upon their person; he took, rather, the view that an adventurous spirit never knew when a little gold might not come in handy.

"Very good, sir. If you would care to step this way,

perhaps you will allow me to offer you some refreshment whilst I make the necessary arrangements."

Scarcely able to drag his gaze away from the picture, Lord Edmund reluctantly allowed the man to conduct him, not via the passage through which he had entered, but in the opposite direction, over what he vaguely perceived to be a flagged stone floor, past various shrouded objects, down another corridor and into a small office, into which a little natural light was filtering by way of a dusty pane. There were, of course, a dozen, a hundred more questions to be put, but somehow he found himself alone, settled in a chair with a glass of brandy in his hand before he had done more than—at his own insistence—complete the transaction and take possession of his receipt. In a remarkably short time, as it seemed to him, his reverie was disturbed, not by the proprietor, but by a man of coarser aspect entering via the street door—it seemed that the establishment spanned the entire distance between one lane and the next—to inform him that his purchase was secured and ready for conveyance. Lord Edmund looked out through the other door, whence the proprietor had left him; called several times, but received no answer. The silence remained unbroken; no trace of light appeared in the darkness of the corridor. He called once more, took a few ineffectual steps into the gloom, retreated, and gave it up. He had the picture safe, that was the main thing, and would return to satisfy his curiosity on the morrow.

On the way home, however, Lord Edmund was beset by fear that the picture might prove a disappointment, or worse, a complete delusion, for the strangeness of the afternoon's experiences did not fully manifest itself until they were jogging briskly along the Albert Embankment. It was only by an extreme effort of will that he restrained himself from signalling the cabman to stop, that he might tear the wrappings from the picture in full view of the street. By degrees he grew calmer, though he could not entirely rid himself of the sensation of having stumbled through a dream and back into the waking world, and it was with a pounding heart and a swimming sensation about his head that he watched the parcel transferred from the cabman's care into the gloved hands of his own servants. He had already resolved that, if he were not deceived, none but he would ever set eyes upon Seraphina again; she would be his, and his alone. Accordingly, he directed his men to hang the picture, still in its wrapping, in the place of honour at the head of his gallery, and withdraw, leaving him in sole possession—but of what? With trembling fingers he tore at the intervening knots, but was forced to employ a knife, in terror lest a slip of the hand should damage the picture. He was near fainting as he drew away the last of the wrappings and stepped away from the canvas.

He was not disappointed. Indeed, though he would have thought it impossible until that moment, the enchantment was stronger than before. All consciousness of his surroundings faded as his senses were once more ravished by Seraphina. Once more the sensation of gazing upon a living, breathing woman grew upon him; he could swear that the water rippling about her slender waist was actually moving; once again his senses impelled him forward; once again she vanished as completely as if a curtain had fallen swiftly and silently between them. He moved closer still, bewildered by the inscrutability of those ripples and swirls of pigment. On minute inspection, the surface of the picture was really quite uneven; in some places the weave of the canvas was plainly visible; in others the paint seemed to be thickly and crudely spattered in parti-coloured daubs, betraying no trace of the extraordinary, nay, the unprecedented skill that must have directed the artist's hand. How on earth was it done? He fixed his eye upon a dab of colour and moved slowly backwards. One pace . . . two . . . three, and the surface remained opaque; four, and the canvas seemed to dissolve seamlessly into rippling water, a verdant depth of forest, and lustrous Seraphina stretching out her arms as if to entreat him into her embrace with that faint but irresistible smile of invitation. Lord Edmund forced himself to take another pace back, and then another, but she did not vanish; the illusion of seeing beyond the frame as if a window had been let into the gallery wall remained as strong as ever, no matter how far, or at what angle, he retreated.

It was not until he stumbled and almost fell against a plinth, upon which stood a diminutive Aphrodite he had always thought especially pleasing, even by the exalted standard of his collection, that he was able to take his eyes from Seraphina and regain some awareness of his surroundings. One thing was instantly plain: she outshone everything else in the room as the full moon outshines the faintest stars. The canvases he had once admired were now revealed as drab and tawdry; beside the perfection of her flesh, his most delicate pieces of statuary, such as the Aphrodite he had nearly toppled, seemed coarse as sandstone. On the instant he knew what must be done. The gallery must be cleared, and forthwith. He would not look again upon Seraphina until it was done, until the last trace of her least rival (though even to speak of rivalry was absurd; as well ask whether a gas-lamp could rival the sun) had been effaced, and then, perhaps . . . he knew not quite what . . . He shook his head in an effort to clear it. To shroud her again in those coarse wrappings was not to be thought of. He would call for a length of the finest velvet, drape her as reverently and securely as he might, then set his entire staff to work to clear the gallery with the utmost possible speed. But where should he instruct them to store the contents? Well, it hardly mattered; the ballroom would do for the present; he would not be giving any more dances now that . . . again his head seemed to blur and spin. Perhaps, after such excitement, he needed a little air; as soon as the picture was suitably draped, he would give his instructions, and take a turn along the river while they were carried out.

The cool evening air did, at first, clear his head wonderfully, and he was swept along on a tide of self-congratulation. But the prospect of the Embankment, and the tranquil river beyond, brought him back to the afternoon's pursuit with the full force of recall. That flaming hair and sinuous grace; the uncanny speed with which she had eluded him . . . "she" must, surely, be the model for Seraphina, for how else could she have led him to the very place where the picture awaited him? Though he could not, on reflection, claim with any certainty to have been led; beyond the entrance to Vauxhall Walk he could not positively swear to having traced her. Was it after all, merely a strange coincidence? Or had he been, in some mysterious way, practised upon? No; that made no sense; he had the picture safe . . . though he did not seem to be thinking so clearly after all; perhaps his adventures had taken a greater toll of his faculties than he had yet realised. At any rate, the thing to keep in mind was that the picture, however miraculous in execution, was nevertheless no more than a canvas which must, indubitably, have been painted from a living, breathing model; yes, surely the woman he had followed that very afternoon. All that remained, therefore, was to find her, and the obvious beginning was—to do at once what should have been done before he carried away his prize: resume his interrogation of the proprietor. He stepped into the road and secured an approaching hansom.

Here, however, a difficulty presented itself. He had assumed that the address would be inscribed upon the receipt which he had folded, without a glance, into his pocket-book. But on inspection it proved to be a crudely printed docket, devoid of any particulars save "Received for: 'Seraphina'; The sum of: Twelve guineas"—to which was appended an entirely illegible signature. Lord Edmund's journey proved altogether fruitless, despite the expenditure of more gold than had been laid out upon the picture itself, the enlistment of, as it seemed to him, half the population of Lambeth in the search, and the cabman's express willingness to drive all night, and investigate every cul-de-sac in the district, if it would please his lordship. But as night wore on the futility of proceeding impressed itself more and more firmly upon his lordship until, thinking himself wearier than the long-suffering cab-horse, he instructed his driver to turn for home.

Some two months later, at a little before twelve on a mild midsummer's night, Lord Edmund might have been observed slipping quietly away from a palatial residence in Hyde Park, having made his excuses on the ground of headache and general indisposition. All too visibly true, but utterly inadequate to the haggard and ghastly countenance illuminated by the street lamp, the fixed, sunken glare of the eyes, the frame from which all flesh appeared to have been stripped. Seraphina still awaited him in his gallery, poised for the hundredth, or was it the thousandth time, to ravish his senses until he could not but believe she lived, could not but take the fatal forward step, like a man drawn by vertigo to the very brink of a precipice and over, betrayed once more by those indecipherable whorls and ripples of pigment. Again and again he would find himself drawn into this dance of torment, and yet no matter how often he was compelled to perform its steps, he remained wholly in thrall to the conviction that *this time* he would at last take possession of warm, breathing flesh, feel the pressure of those perfect lips upon his own; and so his senses were wrought to a pitch of raging deprivation that Tantalus himself could scarcely have endured.

Lord Edmund was not, of course, quite in the position of a man dying of thirst in a desert, but he might as well have been, for beside Seraphina, all other women had become hateful to him; at the mere recollection of some of his former conquests, he would shudder like a man racked by poison. And when at last he could tear his gaze from hers, and flee from his denuded gallery out into the Embankment, he would instantly be seized by the contrary conviction: that the radiant vision he had just quitted was a mere painted shadow of the flesh and blood Seraphina who was surely, certainly, to be found somewhere close by. Never again, in waking life, had he so much as glimpsed the sinuous figure with the flame-coloured hair whom he had so long ago—as it now seemed to him—pursued. Instead he had become a figure of ridicule, the butt of jests and the subject of wagers, on every thoroughfare in Lambeth. He could fairly claim to have quartered every inch of ground, questioned every stallholder, visited every pawnbroking establishment in the district and far beyond, in vain; as vainly he had scoured his memory in the effort to recall the route he had taken on that fatal afternoon. Only in dreams could he retrace his steps, and then always, at the very doorway in the dim and silent alley, he would sense her presence at his back, and turning as she vanished, resume the chase, until his cries of "Seraphina" called him back into the waking world—and to his gallery.

Even so, he could not hate her, for she was too entirely beautiful to hate; but the force of his desire was equalled only by his detestation of the crudely pigmented surface he had so often and so fruitlessly examined. It seemed to grow uglier and cruder by the day; to become ever more completely the antithesis of the radiant perfection it concealed. More than once, Lord Edmund had caught himself in the attitude of a beast coiling itself to spring, with fingers bowed like talons eager to rend and tear the canvas. Only the terror of losing her for ever restrained him, for all the extremity of his torment, but he knew that he must very soon go mad, or die.

On the midsummer's night on which we rejoin him, some residual instinct of self-preservation had goaded him into fulfilling an engagement to dine, as he had not done for many weeks. In any ordinary sense, the evening had proved disastrous: he had felt himself to be the object of universal and horrified concern, even repulsion, and could scarce summon so much as a phrase on his own account; his head had begun to ache from the moment of his arrival, and by the end was pounding as if a band of steel had been clamped around it. Nevertheless, the occasion had so heightened his awareness of his plight as to spur him to a desperate resolution: he would go directly home, enter his darkened gallery and destroy the picture, for no matter what torments might follow, they could not, surely, be worse than those that now assailed him.

He had intended to take a cab, but the prospect of confinement proved intolerable to him, and so he set off on foot. The night was at first overcast, but as he turned into Royal Hospital Road the moon broke through the clouds, and by the time he reached the Embankment it was shining full upon the tranquil surface of the river. His headache had not so much diminished as changed character, as though the steel band clamped about his temples had been drawn into a red-hot wire, strung through a point just above his right eye and tautened until the inside of his head rang with a high, shrilling note. As he reached his front door, it rose to an intolerable pitch. Seizing an antique dagger from a rack in the entrance hall, he stumbled towards his gallery and, shielding his eyes with one upraised arm, pushed open the great double doors.

He had imagined that the gallery would be entirely dark, but beneath the shielding arm he could see moonlight gleaming on the marble floor. His knees trembled as he approached the dais set before the painting; knowing that one glimpse of Seraphina would be his undoing, yet more appalled with every step by the enormity of what he was about to do. No, he could not; one last glimpse he must have; he lowered his arm.

By moonlight, the conviction that he gazed upon a living woman was more instantly compelling than ever. He *saw* the slight rise and fall of her breast, the subtle change in her expression as she caught sight of him; he *knew* her outstretched arms were opening to embrace him. The waters parted at her waist; the dagger slid from his hand and clattered upon the marble floor; he stepped forward. As he did so the moon passed behind a cloud, or so it seemed to him; at any rate the light momentarily failed. Something caught his foot; he fell; scrambling on all fours, he threw himself, as he prayed, towards her. But yes, at last, he was through; the miracle had happened; there she was arising like Venus from the water, with no intervening frame between them, though further off than he could have imagined from the other side. Unable to take his eyes from her, he missed his footing and plunged down a rocky slope. No matter; she was still there, closer now; he could see moonlight rippling on the water all around her. The shrilling in his head had softened into a high, sweet note, like that of a violin perfectly sustained, exquisitely drawn out. Her smile had never been more entrancing. Ascending to the very peak of passion, he reached the edge of the pool and leapt, unhesitating, into her embrace. But what was this choking taste of mud, and why could he not breathe? He tried to ask her to release his arms, but cold black water filled his lungs, and drew him down into the waiting dark.

At the inquest, a cabman told the coroner that he had seen a gentleman racing, hatless, across Battersea Bridge, from which, about half-way over, he had vaulted into the river. The tide was running strongly, and by the time the witness had reached the edge of the embankment, there was nothing to be seen. The body was washed ashore several hundred yards downstream, entangled in a piece of netting. In deference to Lord Edmund's high position in society, the jury, despite some contrary evidence, accepted the argument that his lordship might have been deceived by moonlight into thinking he had seen some person in need of rescue, and returned a verdict of accidental death.

It only remains to add that, when his lordship's executors were ushered into his private gallery, they were quite bewildered as to why its late owner should have banished so many fine works in favour of a single canvas of no visible merit whatsoever. Certainly its title gave no clue as to its subject; indeed, it proved impossible even to determine what the artist had sought to depict. One member of the party ventured that it had been meant for clouds; his colleague said it put him in mind of a dense fog; the youngest and most suggestible of the trio thought that he could just discern, in the upper half of the canvas, the impression of a woman's features, with perhaps the faintest of smiles playing across her lips, but agreed that he could easily have been mistaken.

I READ THE story in an intense, nervous rush, crouched beside the open drawer, and went straight back to my room, as soon as *The Chameleon* was safely locked away again, to tell Alice about my discovery. But somehow the letter never got sent. Seraphina's resemblance to Alice as she had appeared in my dream was so disturbing that no matter what I wrote, it sounded as if I were subtly accusing her of something – I didn't quite know what – and the longer I left it the more difficult it became to explain why I hadn't mentioned the story before.

The morning after the dream, I had woken early and told Alice everything I could remember (except its sticky aftermath), and that I loved and adored her and could not live without the hope of seeing her as soon as I could earn the airfare and persuade my parents to let me go. And when, a fortnight later, I tore open the waiting envelope and saw 'Dearest Gerard' for the first time, I thought for a moment I had won.

Dearest Gerard,

Your dream of me was wonderful, I'm so glad you told me and there's more I want to say about how happy your letter made me and how much it means to me. And before anything else: yes, I love you too, I really do. And think about you, and dream of you – in fact I had a dream of you, like yours of me, only a little while ago, but I was too shy to tell you. Now I will, but first

This always happens when I come to a difficult bit, I've been staring out the window for ages, at the last of last week's snow melting where the field slopes up towards our hill, the one where the pavilion would be if this really were Staplefield. From inside my warm room it looks wonderfully inviting this morning, blue sky and bright sunlight, you can see very fine mist floating just above the wet grass, and I can hear cows lowing – mooing always sounds so – I don't know – too dumb and farmyardy, I think cows have such expressive eyes

Gerard you're forgetting I'll never be able to walk. I don't ever doubt your love for me but

there's a girl riding a horse along the footpath, wearing really smart riding clothes, beautifully cut, all fawns and tans and creams, she's really good-looking which sort of leads in to what I have to say

Sooner or later you're going to meet, I mean fall in love with a girl who can walk and run and swim and dance with you – and not just one, maybe lots of girls. I know you don't think so, you believe you'll always love me, but we have to be sensible, realistic. All those hateful words . . .

If I were braver I'd try to pretend to feel less, to make it easier for you. But I'm not that brave. I do love you, Gerard, and I know I'll be jealous when you fall in love with someone else. In fact I'd rather you didn't tell me when it happens – see, I'm already preparing myself – because I don't want us to stop writing whatever happens, and if I knew you were in love with another girl I might stop writing out of jealousy.

Now it sounds as if I'm telling you to lie to me, which isn't what I wanted to say

I'll try again. If you could see me, you'd see the girl in the wheelchair, the paraplegic, the disabled person. All the labels. I don't think that's how you think of me now, but if you saw me you wouldn't be able to help it. It's not really sympathy I'm most afraid of. It's your disappointment. Us meeting and then breaking up. I couldn't bear that.

Do you know what happens to the Lady of Shalott, in the poem? She lives alone in her tower, quite content, weaving her magic web of colours. But she has a magic mirror that shows her the road to Camelot, knights and ladies and young lovers coming and going, and one day she sees Lancelot riding by, the handsomest of all the knights, and falls in love with him. The magic mirror cracks, the web breaks, she lies down in her boat and floats along the river to Camelot, singing until she dies.

Maybe my window is my magic mirror. I just think if we can be content with what we have, we might keep it for ever. You'll say – anyway you'll think – I'm a coward and maybe I am. But please try to understand, and go on loving me as we are.

Now I'll tell you my dream. It was after lunch, I was really tired, so I lay down on my bed and went to sleep. Then I dreamed I woke up and could move my legs – I often can, in dreams – and you were lying beside me, looking so beautiful – that's the only word that feels right – and so overjoyed to see me. Then we started kissing, and suddenly I realised that neither of us had any clothes on. This is why I was too shy to tell you before, but in the dream I wasn't shy at all, it just felt absolutely right. It felt wonderful, to be honest, so wonderful I – well anyway, then I woke up and cried for ages because you weren't there any more.

I do hope you'll understand. I'll always be, with all my heart,

Your invisible lover,

Alice.

P.S. My dream might even have been the same day as yours, only mine was in the afternoon and yours was at night. Wouldn't that be amazing?

And a fortnight later:

. . . How silly I forgot to say, I was so worried about the other part of that letter. Yes it was, it <u>was</u> Tuesday the 3rd of March when I had my dream – <u>our</u> dream – and of course you're right about the time being different, three o'clock in the afternoon for me was about half-past one the next morning for you. That's just so magical. I truly am, with all my heart

your invisible lover

Alice

At first I thought she was only waiting for me to persuade her. How could the wheelchair make any difference once we were lying together as we'd been in the dream? She must know how utterly I adored her. Gently, lovingly, she met every entreaty with the same reply. As things were, our love for each other was free, equal, and absolute, but if I were to meet the girl in the wheelchair it could never be truly equal; and if I ever fell out of love with her, I might stay, out of duty. And so on.

But in my daydreams and fantasies, Alice refused to stay in her wheelchair. It might begin at the door of her room; or I might come in through the formal garden, along the gravel path, up the front steps, between two great wooden doors standing open. There was never anyone else around: the house was always shrouded in tense, expectant silence. Along the echoing hall, up flight after flight of stairs until I reached her door, which like the front entrance was always open when I arrived. There I would see her sitting at her desk, which I knew was old and made of glowing red cedar, very like the colour of her hair, with a soft green leather top on which her typewriter sat. She would be gazing out of her window, a tall bay window with the desk in the centre of the alcove, wearing her long white dress with the embroidered purple flowers, her chin resting on the palm of her left hand, so absorbed that for a moment she wouldn't notice me standing quietly in the open doorway. And then she would push her wheelchair back from the desk, turn towards me with that enchanting smile I had struggled so often and so vainly to recall, and rise gracefully, effortlessly to her feet . . . and very soon, if I was safely alone in my room, we would be lying in each other's arms on the snowy white counterpane of her bed, her long legs entwined with mine in transports of bliss, and on to the inevitable solitary conclusion.

I tried everything, even blackmail. Didn't she long to see me and hold me and kiss me as much as I longed for her, to be lovers physically instead of only in dreams? Yes of course she did, but then we'd no longer be free, equal . . . and besides, she added, subtly turning the tables, did I really feel that we'd 'only' been together in dreams, when for her it was utter, blissful, ecstasy? Didn't I feel the same?

By the time I was seventeen she had taught herself a technique called 'directed dreaming': you started by learning to visualise your hands in dreams, and to do simple things like clasping them and touching your face, and gradually you developed the ability to move around consciously in your dreams, and eventually to fly wherever you wanted to go. It was like astral travelling, she said, only you didn't have to believe in silver cords or astral bodies or anything like that, you just practised the mental exercises whenever you were going to sleep until you could do them while you were actually dreaming. Soon she and I were making rapturous love in her dreams – in which she was always healed, moving with complete freedom - whereas I practised and practised and got nowhere at all.

With the dreaming, that is. Instead, I was using her dreams to script my sexual fantasies about the composite Pre-Raphaelite goddess I imagined as Alice – I had never been able to recall her as she had appeared to me that one magical night – meanwhile pretending that I'd learned to dream as she did. Not knowing what else to do, I modelled my letters on hers, which were never physically explicit, but tenderly, ecstatically, erotic. I dared not confess my abject failure at directed dreaming; I knew the words they used at school, and felt myself sinking into the coarse, fallen world of shame and guilt and bestial obscenities on lavatory walls, whilst Alice soared higher and higher into the golden light of heaven, in pure, innocent, orgasmic bliss.

Which she believed we shared. The thought of losing her trust was unbearable, yet I knew I no longer deserved it. Until then, my letters had flowed as effortlessly as speech: whenever I felt I hadn't said what I really meant, I'd just keep on writing until I had. Now I began to labour over them, re-reading anxiously, tearing up whole pages as I had never done before, my mind more and more frequently as blank as the sheet in front of me. And all too soon, she noticed.

I feel there's something wrong, your letters aren't as long as they used to be, and they seem – I don't know – a bit stilted? – anyway something's changed in the feeling of them. Please tell me. I'd hate it if you felt there was anything you couldn't say to me – even that you'd fallen out of love with me – I do mean that, truly. Trust me. I'll always adore you with my whole heart.

Your invisible lover,

Alice

I agonised over and destroyed one reply after another as the days slipped remorselessly by, and there was nothing left to do but tell the truth, at least as much of it as I could bear to confess. So I told her the dreams I'd been describing were really daydreams, though they still said how much I loved and adored her – I just hadn't been able to do the dreaming, hadn't dared tell her because I thought she'd think I didn't love her as much as she loved me, whereas I loved her truly, madly, desperately. And that I was unhappy because I really, really needed to be with her, couldn't go on living so far from her, and so – assuming she didn't decide to break it off right now, which I knew I deserved – if she did still love me would she please, please say that we could be together one day, I didn't care how long I had to wait. And so on, for several more scrawled, incoherent pages which I posted in utter despair, and dragged myself home in the spirit of a prisoner on his way to the condemned cell.

Over the next fortnight I learned the meaning of anguish. My face was numb and stiff with misery; I could scarcely speak. My appetite had vanished, my tongue sat in my mouth like some bloated alien substance, and yet the black gnawing hole in my stomach made me feel continuously sick. My mother pleaded with me to tell her what was wrong. My class teacher phoned my parents; the family doctor was summoned; I fended them all off with the adolescent's listless 'nothing', whilst wondering how I could find out how many aspirins you needed to swallow to die a painless death, and whether inhaling bottled gas would knock you out and kill you before the smell of it made you vomit. Alice's letters continued to arrive, even after she had answered the last of mine but one, wondering anxiously, tenderly, if I was sick or unhappy, telling me that she would always love me no matter what happened. Unable to write, I re-read all of her letters from the beginning several times over, waiting for the end.

When the letter finally arrived it took me an hour to summon the courage to open it.

Dearest Gerard,

I'm so, so sorry, I've been selfish and insensitive, too wrapped up in my own happiness – the happiness you give me – I should have realised. You're so brave to have told me, I would have done exactly the same if it had been the other way round. Can you ever forgive me?

And I haven't been completely honest, either, because I haven't always been asleep. When I've imagined making love with you, I mean. I was afraid you'd be shocked. I'm such a coward, I should have trusted you the way you've trusted me.

But now at least we know that neither of us needs to be shocked or embarrassed about wanting to make love. I really did mean what I said before, that nothing between us could ever be wrong, and to prove it to you . . . every day from now on, at half-past one, I'm going to lie down and close my eyes and imagine myself into my dream-body, and make love with you. And if you were to do the same, at ten o'clock at night, in your bed, then you can tell me exactly how you'd like to make love with me, on a special day, say in four weeks' time, so I can write back to you, and then we'll both know, on that day, that everything we've said is really happening.

And then . . . well how much can distance really matter, when I'll be as close to you as your dreams, your heartbeat?

Your invisible (but very passionate) lover

Alice

And so we became, in our strange and solitary way, lovers. She taught me not to be ashamed of what we were doing together – as she always insisted we were – but I lived in terror of my mother steaming open one of her letters until I discovered that for a few dollars a year I could have my own post office box with my own key. Gradually, subtly, tenderly, Alice taught me about her body – the body I had never seen – what she liked, what she loved, what she adored. Yet sometimes, afterwards, as I lay awake, staring at the side of Mr Drukowicz's shed, she seemed further away than ever. And no matter how eloquently I pleaded, she remained adamant that until she was healed – at least she had begun to say 'until' – we could not meet. I couldn't accept, or even understand, but I did come to see that my entreaties were only distressing her. I gave up pleading and kept my plan to myself. As soon as I had saved enough for my fare, I would be on the plane for England; I would search the length and breadth of Sussex until I found her. In my darkest imaginings, I would see myself being turned away with a stern 'Miss Jessell does not wish to see you.' But I went on saving every cent I could muster towards my airfare, and praying that I would not die without having seen Alice Jessell face to face.

Towards the end of my third year at Mawson University College, I set about applying for a passport. I was still living at home with my mother, banking the extra money I earned from shelving books in the college library, along with every cent I could save from my library studies scholarship, but still over a thousand dollars short of the sum that would take me to England and Alice.

For almost seven years now, my mother and I had maintained the pretence that Alice's letters were as invisible as Alice herself. At first, whenever I got home from school to find a letter waiting on the desk in my bedroom I used to examine the envelope closely for signs of tampering. (I had read about steaming open letters, though I'd never seen it done.) But I never found any. I knew that I was causing my mother pain, and if she had once broken her silence over Staplefield, I would have felt much worse about doing to her what she had previously done to me. Her 'nerves' had grown steadily worse, even before my father's sudden death. She hated being left alone after dark. Even now, if I got home more than half an hour late from my evening shift at the library, I would find her haunting the telephone table, wondering when to start ringing the hospitals.

Without Alice's letters, life at home would have been intolerable, but without Alice I wouldn't have been living there. Or in Mawson. My grades had been high enough to get me a place in one of the big eastern universities, but – apart from confronting my mother's pathological fears on my behalf – that would have made saving for England impossible. Whereas the Grace Levenson Memorial Library Studies Bursary paid all my fees and a living allowance, and would, I hoped, get me a job in England in just over a year's time.

And it pleased Alice to know that I hadn't abandoned my mother. Soon after we began writing, Alice and I had vowed that no matter what happened, we would never betray each other's secrets, or let anyone else read our letters: apart from the postman, no one outside our house even knew that Alice existed. She now had photographs of my parents, our house and its surroundings, and even, more recently, of me, to illustrate the day-to-day chronicle of my life in all its sameness and tedium; though Alice frequently assured me that nothing about me, however trivial, could possibly be boring to her. But she was troubled by the estrangement between my mother and me, and too perceptive not to see that she herself was partly the cause of it. At the same time, she understood my fear that if I broke the silence on my side, my mother would keep pushing and pushing until she had forced me into another confrontation. 'I know it's hard,' Alice had written recently, 'but you must cherish her, Gerard, you won't know how precious she is until she's gone. I only wish she could understand that I'm no threat: the last thing I want is to take you away from her.'

Alice was entirely sincere in this, because she still clung to her conviction that, short of a miraculous healing, we must never meet. But I had other plans.

Until I assembled my passport application, I had never seen a full copy of my own birth certificate. The short version I had used until then had told me nothing about my mother except that her maiden name had been Hatherley. Now I discovered that Phyllis May Hatherley had been born on 13 April 1929, in Portman Square, Marylebone, London W1. Father George Rupert Hatherley, occupation Gentleman; mother Muriel Celia Hatherley, neé Wilson.

It ought not to have come as a shock. She had never actually *said* – at least I could not recall her ever saying – that she had been born at Staplefield, which after years of fruitless searching of atlases and reference books, I thought I might have found. Collins' Road Atlas of Britain showed a tiny village – the only Staplefield in the index – on the southern fringe of St Leonard's Forest in West Sussex. Just a minute black circle on a yellow by-road called the B2114, but it looked and felt right, though by no stretch of the imagination could anyone have expected to see ships at Portsmouth, fifty miles away to the south-west. Alice thought it would be quite common for a big country house to have the same name as the nearby village. Yet I still hadn't asked my mother about it – or anything else in her life before Mawson. Why had I always believed that her own parents had died when she was very young? Had she actually told me that, or had I simply imagined it? Why, above all, had I accepted her silence for so long? Didn't I have a right to my own history?

That evening, in our sitting-room after dinner, I handed her the certificate. She took one look, and thrust it back at me.

'Why did you get this?' Her voice was ominously taut.

'I'm applying for a passport.'

'Why?'

'Because I'm going to England. As soon as I can afford to.'

My mother's attention was apparently fixed upon the unlit gas heater in our old fireplace. I could not see her face clearly because of the standard lamp between our armchairs, but its light fell upon her clasped hands, suddenly reminding me of old Mrs Noonan's, fingers clamped around swollen knuckles, blotched purple and livid white, the nails suffused with blood.

'You mean to stay,' she said at last.

'I don't know yet, Mother. If I did, I'd want you to come and live there too.'

'I can't afford it.'

'I could help.'

'I wouldn't let you. Anyway, I couldn't stand the winters.'

'But you hate the heat, Mother.'

'The cold would be worse.'

She was speaking mechanically, as if hardly aware of what she was saying.

'Mother, I didn't show you that to upset you. But it's time we talked – again. About your family. Because it's mine, too.'

The silence dragged out until I could bear it no longer.

'Mother did you hear what I—'

'I heard you.'

'Then tell me—' I broke off, not knowing what to ask. 'I – look, I still remember everything you used to tell me, when I was – before I – everything about Staplefield, and your grandmother, and I want to know – why you stopped talking about it, why I don't know anything –' I heard my voice beginning to quaver.

'There's nothing to tell,' she said after another long pause.

'But there must be. Your own parents. What happened to them?'

'They both died before – when I was a few months old. I don't remember anything about them.'

Her hands had dropped out of sight, below the arm of her chair.

'So – so did you live with your grandmother – Viola – was she your father's, or your mother's—'

'My father's. I told you everything I could remember, when you were a small boy.'

'But why did you stop after I – was it her picture I saw that day?'

'I don't remember any picture.'

Her voice sounded flatter and more disembodied with each reply.

'You *must* remember, Mother. You were so furious. The picture you caught me with, that afternoon in your bedroom –'

'You were always poking about in my bedroom, Gerard. You can't expect me to remember every single time I caught you in there.'

'But – but –' I could not quite believe this was happening. 'After that day you never mentioned Staplefield again –'

'All I remember, Gerard, is that as you grew older you stopped asking. And a good thing too. We can't live in the past.'

'No, but why won't you talk about it?'

'Because it's *gone*,' she snapped. 'There was – there was a fire. After we left. During the war. The house burned to the ground.'

'You never told me that!'

'No . . . I didn't want to disappoint you. That's – that's why I stopped talking about it.'

'Well I wish you had told me, Mother. All these years I've been hoping, hoping to . . .' I couldn't go on.

'Gerard, you didn't think it was *ours*?'

'No, of course not. I just wanted to see it.'

But of course I had thought of Staplefield as mine, without ever quite admitting it to myself. The long-lost heir, stranded in Mawson, waiting for the family solicitors to call him home. Ridiculous, absurd. My eyes were stinging.

'I'm sorry, Gerard. It was very wrong of me. I wish I'd never mentioned the place.'

'*No*, Mother. I wish you hadn't stopped. Why did you leave? What caused the fire?'

'It was – a bomb. We – I was away at school. In Devon. Away from the bombing.'

For a moment she had seemed genuinely contrite. Now she sounded evasive.

'And Viola?'

'She looked after me. Until she died. Just after the war. Then I had to go out to work.'

'But it was a big house, you had servants. Wasn't it insured? Didn't Viola leave you anything?'

Another long pause.

'It all went in death duties. There was just enough left to pay for my typing course. She did everything she could for me. That's *all*.'

'Mother it is not all and you know it. What about "Seraphina"?'

'I don't know what you're talking about.'

'Viola's story. In the drawer with the photograph.'

'I don't remember any story.'

I opened my mouth to object, and realised I couldn't push it any further.

'*Why* don't you want to talk about your past?'

'For the same reason you never talk about your – *friend*, I suppose. It's no one else's business. Not even yours.'

For the first time in seven years, my mother had acknowledged Alice's existence.

'No, it's not the same. Alice isn't – she's nothing to do with you—'

'She's taken you away from me.'

'That's not fair! Anyway, I'm almost twenty-one, people leave home and get married—'

'So you're getting married? Well thank you for mentioning it—'

'I didn't say that!'

'Well are you or aren't you?'

'I don't know yet!'

We were both almost shouting.

'I don't want to talk about her, Mother,' I said more quietly.

'But you're going to see her.'

'I – I just don't want to talk about her.'

'Gerard,' she said heavily, after a long silence, 'I know you think I'm jealous. A jealous mother who won't let go. Nothing I say will make any difference. Just remember: I tried to keep you safe.'

'Safe from what, Mother?'

But all she said was, 'I'm going to bed now.'

'Tell me one thing, then,' I said, 'I won't ask you any more. Where exactly was Staplefield? The house, I mean. Was it in Staplefield village?'

Her chair creaked. She stood up and moved stiffly towards

the door. I thought she would leave without speaking, but in the doorway she turned, light flashing from the lenses of her spectacles.

'Going to look for Staplefield would be a complete waste of money. There's nothing left. Nothing.'

She flung the last word over her shoulder. It hung in the air like the smell of charred paper as her footsteps receded along the hall.

I HAD ALWAYS imagined the dead heart as a featureless, Saharan expanse of sand. From thirty-five thousand feet, I watched the patterns unrolling beneath the wing, fantastic whorls and cross-hatchings and striations, ochreous yellows and earth-browns and purples and deep rust-reds, until the hostess asked me if I would mind closing my blind so the other passengers could watch the movie. I did mind, never having been in a plane before, but I closed it anyway and sat holding my unopened book.

Twenty-two hours to Heathrow. I didn't seriously believe – did I? – that after eight years of undying adoration Alice would have me turned away at the door? Her letters were as tenderly passionate as ever. I had written to tell her I would be at the Stanhope Hotel, Sussex Gardens, London W2, which sounded leafy and grand, despite being called 'budget' in the brochure. Admittedly it was January, so there might not be many leaves, but there was sure to be a letter waiting when I arrived. From the hotel I would ring Penfriends International, who were bound to be in the phone book, though I still had only their box number. Maybe I should have written ahead to Juliet Summers, but I'd been over and over that. Much better to plead my case in person.

Since I had stopped pleading with Alice to change her mind,

neither of us had mentioned the possibility of our meeting. Her view of my coming to live in England was seemingly unchanged: she would love to feel that I was so much closer, but only if I could persuade my mother to join me. Alice and I were pretending to believe that, while it would be wonderful to be in the same country at last, the purpose of my trip was to look around for places where my mother might be persuaded to settle. And to see Staplefield, assuming my mother really had invented the fire. But how could Alice possibly doubt that I'd come looking for her? And since she hadn't made me promise not to, she must – mustn't she? – be waiting for me to find her.

The businessman in the seat next to me had put away his papers and fallen asleep. I knew already that I wasn't afraid of flying. So why did I feel so numbly apprehensive, as if something cold and leaden had lodged in the pit of my stomach and refused to dissolve, not just since take-off but for days beforehand?

Perhaps I was more anxious about my mother than I was willing to admit. She had been behaving as if I had a terminal illness rather than a three-week excursion fare to London. Not to mention a job as an assistant librarian at Mawson University College, starting in February. I couldn't imagine how I would tear myself away from Alice, but three weeks was all I could afford; I would have to come back to save more money and apply for permanent residence. If my mother couldn't bear the thought of life without me, she would just have to overcome her pathological fear of return, or travel, or whatever it was. It didn't matter how often I repeated that I was a thousand times more likely to die in a car than a plane crash; she treated all of my attempts at reassurance as irrelevant interruptions. I noticed that she had grown even more intolerant of noise; she could not bear the radio on, and reacted to the ringing of the phone as if it were a fire alarm. She seemed to be listening to – or for – sounds inaudible to anyone else.

Since the night, just over a year ago, when she told me Staplefield had burnt down, she had not once referred to Alice. Our day-to-day life had gone on as before, as if the no-go areas did not exist. I had learned to cook in spite of her protests, though she still would not let me near the washing-machine or the iron, or accept any money for board. But the balance between us had altered. Now it felt as if she was the one on the defensive. I won't mention your *friend* again, her silence seemed to say, so don't ask me any more about my past.

I was shocked by my reaction to the loss of Staplefield. My rational self stood helplessly by while I grieved for the place as if I had watched it burn with everything I loved inside it. Knowing that these feelings were utterly illogical didn't seem to help in the slightest. Until one night, in the middle of a letter to Alice, it struck me that in all my happily-ever-after daydreams, we simply took over Alice's room, whereupon it was magically incorporated into Staplefield, to which I was of course the rightful heir. And now we couldn't live there, because it had burnt to the ground. Even after this disturbing recognition – which I did not mention to Alice – I was troubled by a kind of waking nightmare in which I stood alone at her window looking out at a charred, blackened landscape, feeling that I was somehow responsible for the devastation.

Yet at the same time – and this made my distress seem even more irrational – I still suspected my mother of inventing the fire on the spot, to block any further approach to Staplefield, for reasons I couldn't begin to fathom. Alice, for all her reluctance to join in any criticism of my mother, plainly thought I was right. 'Perhaps', she had written,

> there was some sort of family quarrel, after your great-grandmother died, and your mother was disinherited – of course she couldn't possibly have done anything to deserve that. But I know how it feels, having to let go of everything you love. Perhaps it's easier for your mother to say the house went up in smoke than to admit that other people are living in it. And surely she'd have said something about the fire, when you were little, so as not to get your hopes up? I mean, of living there one day. Perhaps when you were small she still hoped Staplefield might come back to you, and then something happened, something final that meant it could never be hers, or yours, and that's why she stopped talking to you.
>
> Actually that reminds me of something.
>
> Later: I've just been reading through your letters, the very first ones you ever wrote me, and I just found this: 'Mother said we can't go and live there because it was sold a long time ago and we don't have enough money to buy it back.' Perhaps she was still hoping, when she said that, that one day you <u>might</u> be able to afford it. Before whatever happened that made her abandon hope completely. What do you think?

I thought it made perfect sense. It also reminded me of the photograph I had found in my mother's bedroom. I'd always assumed that she had stopped talking about Staplefield to punish me. Perhaps the two things were unrelated: maybe the bad news just happened to arrive at about the same time. Maybe . . . but that Medusa-like fury . . . No, there had to be a connection. Perhaps catching me with the photograph had caused my mother to make some enquiry about Staplefield, something that brought on the bad news, whatever the news might have been? No point asking her. 'Photograph, what photograph?' More to the point: whose photograph? Not Viola's, surely: my mother had only ever spoken of Viola with affection. Wouldn't Viola's picture have been displayed on our mantelpiece, at least when we were still talking freely of Staplefield?

And I still hadn't said anything more to my mother about finding 'Seraphina', so I still didn't even know, for certain, that 'V.H.' was my great-grandmother. I had opened the drawer one more time and found it empty. Then as I learned more about the library, I realised I could order *The Chameleon* on inter-library loan, photocopy the story, present it to my mother as if I had no idea who 'V.H.' might be, and see how she reacted. Only one problem: there wasn't a copy of *The Chameleon* to be found anywhere in the southern hemisphere. From the British Library Catalogue I learned that it had run for just four numbers, from March to December of 1898. The only way to see them was to secure a reader's ticket; I had my letter of introduction in my pocket.

Seraphina's resemblance to Alice still sometimes troubled me. Rationally speaking, I knew there was nothing in the least uncanny about it. Of course Viola would have been to exhibitions of Pre-Raphaelite painting. She might perfectly well have seen the Lady of Shalott herself when the picture was first exhibited at the Royal Academy. Only Seraphina hadn't reminded me of the Lady, or any of the faces I'd borrowed from Burne-Jones, Millais, Waterhouse and company, but of Alice as I'd seen her in the dream. The memory had faded as quickly as it had come, but I had never quite shaken off a superstitious fancy that in opening the drawer for a second time I had accepted the terms of an inheritance, with no idea of what that might entail.

The plane shuddered and rattled like a bus crossing a stretch of gravel road. Twenty-one and a half hours to go. The dull weight of subdued, half-anaesthetised anxiety had not diminished. Maybe reading would dislodge it. I picked up Henry James, *The Turn of the Screw and Other Tales*.

'Where, my pet, is Miss Jessel?' The phrase repeated itself over and over, through the cramped, interminable night aboard QF 9. The engines played endless rhythmic variations on the words: dum dadadda dada, dum dadada dum, dum dadadadadada. They didn't care that Alice spelled her surname with two 'l's. Every so often they would lift the tempo to Miss Jessel Miss Jessel Miss Jessel Miss Jessel, just to make sure I was still awake enough to hallucinate. Where, my pet, is Miss Jessel? Waiting in Alice's room of course. I knew I would never get the name out of my head. I had once looked it up in the Mawson phone book. Not a single Jessell, whichever way you spelt it. Alice would take one look at me and know that something was appallingly, irrevocably wrong. I wouldn't be able to look at her without thinking of Miss Jessel. Miss Jessel with her dead white face and long black dress. Like the man in the churchyard, tramping over my mother's grave, and were you aware sir, that your late mother was in a highly disturbed state, while out in the garage the trains still ran on time, round and round and round Miss Jessel and where Miss Jessel is my pet, waking with a thump to the runway lights of Heathrow and rain streaming over the wing.

I hadn't realised that it would still be dark when the Airbus deposited me outside Paddington station. Or that the Stanhope

– when they eventually agreed to let me in – would be a claustrophobic warren, smelling of wet animal hair, stale fry-ups, and mould. The stairs creaked at every tread, and the only window in my room, or rather cell on the second floor, opened into a so called lightwell and a view of blackened walls and rusting fire escapes.

And no letter from Alice, though I had sent her the address a fortnight before I left. Struggling to shake off the depression which seemed to be gathering around me like thick black mist, I stumbled back down the stairs to the payphone in the foyer.

From Directory Enquiries I learned that Penfriends International had an unlisted number. There were dozens of entries for Summers, J., in the phone book, but none of them gave the Mount Pleasant box number as their address. And when it finally occurred to me to phone Mount Pleasant post office, they would only confirm that Penfriends International were indeed at Box 294. All other details were strictly confidential sir, I'm sorry there's nothing more I can tell you, more than my job's worth, sorry sir but there it is, can't help you any more.

I dragged myself back up the creaking staircase, lay down on the bed, and slipped head-first into a pit of darkness.

It was all true, everything my mother had said, there really were mountains of black plastic bags spewing garbage on to the pavement wherever you went. Ragged beggars lined the underpasses, wrapped in sodden cardboard, lying in pools of unspeakable filth. I couldn't walk two blocks through the rain and sleet without getting lost, or stop to wrestle with my *London A–Z* without being jostled into the gutter by seething crowds. Half frozen but rabidly adhesive dogshit lurked beneath the slush. The chaffinches had all mutated into scrofulous pigeons.

Each morning until the postman arrived, I hovered in the Stanhope's reeking foyer, waiting for a letter which never came. Then I would set off for the British Museum in grey half-light, to haunt the Reading Room until closing time, searching for some trace of Alice. I knew that I ought to be overwhelmed by the sheer scale of the Museum: the immense stone columns, the rainswept forecourt seething with tourists, the Babel of unknown languages rising from the front steps, the Reading Room itself, into which the whole Mawson College Library building would have fitted quite comfortably. I would stare up into the blue and gold dome above the tiered galleries and try to feel something, anything, but it was like looking at the sun through a thick pall of smoke. I would feel eyes following me up and down the aisles; several times I felt certain I had caught people staring at me with horror, as if they could actually see the fog of black depression that enveloped me.

Some of my fellow readers were in no better shape: the little old woman in the filthy grey raincoat who sat all day in row L, with half a dozen tattered shopping bags clustered at her feet, muttering at the partition in front of her; or the wild-eyed, white-haired man at the far end of row C, who shielded his book with both arms when anybody approached him. And once a tall, emaciated old lady, who smelt strongly of mothballs and wore a black veil so impenetrable you could not see even the outline of a face beneath, came and sat next to me for two hours while I worked my way through a pile of directories. She had *The Times* open in front of her, but I felt she was watching me all the time.

On the third day I braved the slush down Kingsway to Catherine House, where the records of births and marriages were kept. A gloomy concrete bunker, dank and cold, smelling of greasy folios and sodden clothing. The quarterly registers – huge steel-reinforced volumes, red for births and green for marriages (deaths were kept on the other side of Kingsway) – were housed in rows of battered metal shelves. Grim-faced searchers swarmed over every row, fighting for position, slamming the massive volumes on and off the shelves. Couples fought and shouted in the aisles; the noise was deafening. I hovered politely beside the 1960s for a few minutes before trying to insinuate myself into the scrum. Someone rammed the metal corner of a register into my kidneys; an elbow jabbed my ribs; an anonymous hand snatched 'J–L Jan.–Mar. 1964' from over my shoulder and carried it off. Finding Alice's birth certificate, I realised, would contribute absolutely nothing to my search for her. Cowed, shivering, I surrendered without a fight.

In the relative tranquillity of the Reading Room, I scoured directories for lists of nursing homes in Sussex and poured pound after pound's worth of coins into payphones: no Alice Jessell anywhere. Alice didn't want to be found.

On the fifth day I woke with a thick head and a rasping throat, but rather than lie staring into the darkness of the lightwell I dragged myself back to the Museum.

In a Sussex directory for the 1930s, I looked up the entry for Staplefield. There was a Staplefield House listed, but the owner was a Colonel Reginald Bassington. No Viola, or any Hatherley was listed as a resident, there or in any of the neighbouring villages or towns. There was no Viola Hatherley in the main catalogue either. I ordered the four numbers of *The Chameleon*, thinking as I did so how horribly prophetic 'Seraphina' had turned out to be.

But of the four numbers only the fourth and last was delivered: the slips for the other three came back marked

'Destroyed by bombing during the war'. Without much hope or even interest I glanced through the table of contents. *The Chameleon*. Volume I, Number 4, December 1898. Essay by Ernest Rhys. Story by Amy Levy. Poems by Herbert Horne and Selwyn Image – and 'The Gift of Flight: A Tale', by V.H.

The Gift of Flight

The Reading Room of the British Museum is not, I think, the first place in which most of us would seek refuge from a consuming grief, especially not in winter, when fog creeps into the great dome and hangs like a damp halo about the electric lamps. Nor are one's fellow readers always the most desirable company, some being less than fastidious in matters of dress and personal cleanliness, whilst others, seemingly on the verge of madness, conduct whispered conversations with phantoms, or crouch motionless for an entire afternoon, glaring at the same unturned page. Others again lie sprawled in attitudes of abandoned despair or exhaustion, snoring away the hours with their heads pillowed upon priceless volumes until the attendants come to turn them out. There are of course many industrious souls deep in concentration or copying busily, so that the dome seems to echo, at times, to the faint sound of a hundred nibs scratching in unison, but to a troubled mind that sound can too easily suggest the fingernails of prisoners clawing upon stone.

So, at least, it seemed to Julia Lockhart, and yet she was drawn back there by the conviction that the library contained one particular book which would speak directly to her sorrow. It would be like finding a new friend, one whose perceptions were so subtly and delicately attuned to hers as to see further into her heart than she herself was capable of doing. But since she had no idea what kind of book, or by whom, she spent a great deal of her time idly turning the pages of the catalogue, or gazing sightlessly into the black leather surface of her desk, or wandering the circumference of the labyrinth—the image that came most frequently to her mind, given the catacombs filled with shelf upon shelf of books that she imagined stretching away into darkness beneath the floor.

It had been many months since she and Frederick Liddell had parted, and yet the pall of grief had in no way diminished; instead, it had darkened into something quite beyond her experience. A thick veil seemed to have fallen between her and the world; she felt estranged, not only from friends and family, but from herself. She could not work, for all power of concentration had left her. Her husband kept his accustomed round between his chambers, his club, and his chair by the fireside, tranquilly unaware that anything was wrong; her daughter Florence was away at school in Berne; and the chatter of friends, in which Julia had once joined so enthusiastically, now seemed like the gibbering of dead souls in limbo. Yet to all outward appearances she had merely done what so many women yoked to indifferent husbands had done before her. She numbered amongst her own acquaintance women who moved cheerfully and lightly from one lover to the next, and knew of cases in which the children of such unions were accepted by the said indifferent husbands without apparent protest. The code seemed to be that so long as appearances were more or less maintained, women as well as men could do as they pleased. Whereas to Julia the taking of a lover had seemed an altogether momentous step. She had yearned for an intimacy to which she could bring her whole heart, which would release something trapped within her, free a door in her imagination which seemed to have swollen and stuck fast; but until the day she met Frederick Liddell she had come to believe she would die without ever having found it.

Marriage to Ernest Lockhart had been the great disappointment of Julia's life. Yet she had nothing to say against him, beyond an entire absence of passion, and even there, he had not deceived her; she had deceived herself. At twenty, she had allowed herself to be overborne by the romance of marrying a man sixteen years her senior, so assured and cultivated beside, say, young Harry Fletcher who had blushed and stammered every time he spoke to her but who, as she realised far too late, had plainly adored her. Her parents had not forced her; on the contrary, she could still recall her father asking her very earnestly if she was quite sure, and hear herself saying blithely yes, airily convinced that Ernest Lockhart's reserve concealed an answering force of passion. And then to discover her husband so . . . well, so inept and lifeless, yet so wedded to the shows and forms of marriage, and so incapable of comprehending her unhappiness. Had it not been for her daughter, born within a year of the wedding, she would have left him; as it was, she had worked at her writing and entertained her friends, unable in the end to hate her husband for being what he was, and feeling, as her thirtieth birthday receded, only a dull subterranean anger at the inexorable waste of life.

And then, on a warm spring afternoon at the house of a distinguished man of letters, she had been introduced to Frederick Liddell, whose latest volume of poems she had read only the week before, and very soon found herself deep in conversation with him in a quiet corner of the distinguished man's garden, where they sat upon a bench in the shade of an oak and talked until she had lost all consciousness of time. He was not much over thirty, and looked even younger, for his complexion was as fair and soft as a woman's, and his dark eyes capable, as it seemed to Julia, of a quite feminine subtlety. Even his wavy brown hair seemed expressive in its unruly abundance, brushed across a broad, high forehead, the face narrowing markedly to a strong, rounded chin. His enthusiasms chased one another across his features; in repose, his most characteristic expression was one of gentle melancholy, a mild sadness which Julia found quite irresistible, all the more so because Frederick seemed utterly devoid of guile. She was used to fending off the attentions of practised seducers such as her unhappy friend Irene's husband Hector, with whom, it was said, no woman could safely be left alone for five minutes, but whose oily countenance invariably reminded Julia of Mr Chadband. But she was quite unused to being listened to with such responsive absorption. By the time she discovered that he had read and admired the one tale of hers that had so far been published, Julia felt certain she had made a friend for life.

They spoke a great deal that afternoon of religion, or rather of the impossibility of either believing in any of its prescribed forms, or living without some aspiration beyond the material, without coming to any definite conclusion save that their feelings seemed to be in entire agreement. In poetry they were divided by Julia's preference for Keats against his for Shelley, but this only opened the happy prospect of their reading their favourite passages to one another on some future occasion. From there they progressed naturally to dreams, and Julia found herself telling Frederick of a dream she had had on perhaps half a dozen occasions. It usually began in soft summer twilight, in an open field, a gentle slope covered in long green grass. She would begin to run down the slope, taking longer and longer strides until she could feel her feet just brushing the tips of the grass and remember, with a great rush of joy, that she had been born with the gift of flight. Then she would extend her arms and soar above the fields, feeling utterly at home in the air until the awareness that she was dreaming began to press itself upon her. Always she would struggle to hold onto the dream; for one magical, exhilarating moment she would believe that she had woken and yet continued to fly, until the world dissolved beneath her and she was left alone and bereft in darkness, like the knight-at-arms waking upon the cold hill's side. This was something she had never disclosed to anyone, for fear that if she did not keep it secret, the dream would never come back to her. Yet she spoke of it quite spontaneously to Frederick, and when she had done so, saw that he was greatly moved.

Some years ago, he said, he had fallen in love with a dancer named Lydia Lopez—not her real name, for she had been born and bred in London, but the only one he had ever known her by, just as he had been left only one memento of her, though he did not say what it was. He had gone every night to the theatre where she performed, and sometimes taken her to supper afterwards. Frederick did not describe Lydia very distinctly, other than to say that she was very small and slightly formed, so much so that she could easily have been taken for a child of twelve or thirteen.

One particularly elaborate scene—a favourite with the audience—called for her to be equipped with wings and to soar, suspended from a wire, high above the stage. Frederick had been in the front row on the night when the wire gave way and Lydia fell from the painted heavens; he could still, he said, shuddering at the memory, hear the dreadful thud of her body striking the boards. The curtain was instantly drawn; yet to everyone's amazement and relief, she came out half an hour later, looking a little dazed but apparently uninjured, and took a bow, drawing rapturous applause from the house. But the relief was premature; a few hours later she lapsed into unconsciousness, and she died two days later of a haemorrhage to the brain.

Before Lydia, Frederick confessed, he had fancied himself in love with a different woman every week, but he had never since been able to care for anyone as he had cared for her. 'I did not know how much she meant to me until she was gone,' he said, gazing into Julia's eyes with such open, unaffected feeling that her sympathy went out to him entirely; so much so that she found she had taken his hand in both of hers. She felt, if anything, strangely reassured by this disclosure; and he accepted her invitation to tea at her house in Hyde Park Gardens with such eagerness, and told her with such warmth how delighted he was to have met her, that she went home happier than she could remember being since she had first held her infant daughter in her arms.

Julia knew herself in love with Frederick from that first afternoon, but it was many weeks before she dared hope that her feeling might be returned, for when she saw him next in company she wondered if he were not exactly the same ardent, attentive listener with everyone of his acquaintance. Yet he accepted all of her suggestions for meeting, despite the demands upon his time—he had a small private income, supplemented by a great deal of reviewing—with such eagerness that her imagination would insist upon running far ahead of her. She dared not invite him too often to her house, for she could not bear the thought of their relations becoming the object of common gossip, and so they met in galleries and parks, and sometimes in the Reading Room, always maintaining the pretext that such-and-such would be an interesting thing to do as soon as they found the opportunity. There always seemed to be more to say than they had time for, and as the days lengthened he spoke less often of Lydia; but it was not until spring had passed into summer that she arrived, with a rapidly beating heart, at the entrance to a mansion block towering above a narrow Bloomsbury street, in response to his first invitation to tea.

He had warned her about the stairs, apologising for his preference for living as high above the street as possible, but she was still surprised by how many flights there were, and though the day was cool and cloudy, she was quite dazzled by the light when he ushered her into his sitting-room. There were tall casements on either side of narrow French windows, through which Julia glimpsed the iron railing of a small balcony. The room was not large; two armchairs and a sofa arranged upon a Persian carpet took up much of the floor, and there were bookshelves ranged along the other walls. Julia would have liked to look around, but Frederick immediately invited her to be seated; his manner was more formal than usual, and his constraint affected her, so that instead of the sofa she took the right-hand armchair, whereupon Frederick excused himself to make the tea, and left her alone in the room.

From this she deduced that she was, as she had hoped, to be the only guest, and sat willing herself to feel less agitated and more at ease. As her eyes adjusted to the brightness she became aware that she was not, after all, quite alone, for on a desk at the window nearest to her chair stood a framed photograph, a head-and-shoulders portrait of a young woman who could only be Lydia. She was both like and unlike the Lydia of Julia's imagination: at first glance the face appeared rounded and child-like, especially in the set of the lower lip and chin, but there was also a subdued sensuality which became more apparent the longer one looked into the dark eyes that gazed so directly back, the eyes of a woman fully aware of her power to charm—or mesmerise. "For ever wilt thou love, and she be fair!": the words echoed suddenly in Julia's awareness, and left her wishing she had not recalled them.

She was still absorbed in contemplation of Lydia's portrait when Frederick returned with the tea-tray. But he did not seem to notice, and instead launched into an account of how he had that morning read and reviewed four three-decker novels without cutting a single page, delivered his copy, and sold all four in pristine condition in Fleet Street in time for lunch. Julia felt a certain pang at the thought of judgement being passed so lightly upon all those months or years of hard authorial labour, but reminded herself sternly that Frederick was obliged to earn most of his own living by his pen, and had not the luxury of Ernest Lockhart's twelve hundred a year, which prompted a pang of quite another sort. They started several other topics, but none of them seemed to catch fire; perhaps it was the effect of Lydia's cool, steady gaze, which Julia could neither dismiss entirely from her consciousness nor allude to directly; at any rate the constraint seemed to grow between them until she sat miserably wishing she had not come. The room, too, was very close; she could feel herself becoming flushed and overheated as her unhappiness increased, until she was obliged to ask Frederick to open a window. He sprang from his chair in a welter of apologies and threw open the French windows, letting in a welcome draught of air. Unable to bear the pressure of Lydia's regard an instant longer, Julia rose and went to join him in the doorway.

She had never been—at least she felt she had never been—so high above the ground. The balcony appeared to her no larger than a window-box, with a small semicircular floor of pressed metal, and two hooped black horizontal railings curving out into empty space. The higher of these was only a little above her own waist. Even standing in the doorway, she seemed to be looking straight down into the abyss. Julia had stood close to the edge of a precipice without feeling anything like the fear that gripped her now; the sheer, vertiginous chasm beneath her feet seemed to be drawing her irresistibly towards the brink; in another second she would surely pitch head-first over the rail and into the void. All of these impressions raced across her mind in the space of a single glimpse, during which she was also aware of Frederick turning towards her and opening his mouth as if to speak, but ridiculously slowly, so that he reminded her of some great bird ponderously opening its beak. With the same absurd slowness, she saw herself reaching for his arm to save herself from falling, suspended between terror and a strange impulse to laugh at Frederick's gathering her in such a leisurely fashion into his embrace that she seemed to have time to reacquaint herself with every nuance of his expression before feeling, at last, the pressure of his lips upon her own. The sensation of vertigo remained; perhaps they had indeed fallen, but it did not seem to matter, for she felt quite weightless, and might as easily have been floating up as down.

That evening she walked alone around the banks of the Serpentine and felt the world to be a blessed place. She knew, dimly, that the gulf between her present situation and the life she imagined herself living with Frederick might prove impassable, but she could not give him up now; perhaps her husband would bow gracefully to the inevitable; in the meantime she felt perfectly content in the warmth of the sun's diminishing rays and the certainty that Frederick loved her, and would tell her so again before tomorrow's sun had set. But with the next morning's post came a note which said only: "Dear Mrs Lockhart, I very much regret that I shall be unable to keep our appt this afternoon; I can only plead the most pressing and unexpected business, and pray that you will accept my most abject apologies. Believe me, yours very sincerely, Frederick Liddell."

Julia had always appreciated his tact and discretion, but the note's formal brevity, and worse, the absence of any indication as to when, or even if, she might expect to hear from him again, chilled her to the bone. In vain she struggled to reassure herself with the thought that Frederick had, after all, to earn his living as best he could;

for if such demands had never before prevented him from seeing her, how could they possibly have done so now? The rest of the day crawled by beneath an ever-darkening cloud of apprehension and despair. After a sleepless night of torment, Julia could bear no more; as soon as her husband had departed for his chambers she sent Frederick an unsigned note saying she would call at his rooms at three o'clock.

He was waiting at the street door when her cab arrived. One glance at his face confirmed her worst fears. In silence they trudged up flight after flight of stairs to the room that had witnessed such extremities of rapture. As the memory flooded back to her, Julia turned towards Frederick as if praying to be woken from a nightmare. To her horror, he actually recoiled before checking himself with a forced, mechanical courtesy that set the final seal upon her humiliation. Bright sunshine streamed mockingly through the tall casements; the French windows were closed.

"Frederick; tell me what has happened."

Her lips were so numb with misery that she could barely utter the words.

"I fear—I find I am not free," he stammered, "that is to say . . . that my affections are after all engaged . . . I had hoped to overcome . . . that it would not . . . but I find I cannot . . ." He trailed off hopelessly.

"Do you mean—that there is someone else?"

"Yes." His eyes looked like the eyes of a dead man.

"Then why did you not tell me so before?"

"I did. But I had hoped . . ."

She did not understand until she realised that he was gesturing towards the portrait by the window. For a long moment Julia stood transfixed by Lydia's cool, implacable gaze, unwilling to comprehend what she had just heard.

"She is dead, Frederick. Whereas I . . ." But she could not go on.

"To the world, yes, but alas, not to me."

"And you feel you have betrayed her," said Julia bleakly.

"Yes," said Frederick. "I am most dreadfully sorry . . ."

Her tears would no longer be denied; she went blindly from the room and left him to his self-recrimination.

As the months passed, Julia felt herself more and more irretrievably exiled from the life she had formerly led. The longing to speak of her sorrow remained as acute as ever, but there was no one, not even her closest friend Marianne, upon whose discretion she could absolutely rely. Perhaps it was pride that made the idea of being talked about so intolerable to her; more particularly, the idea that anyone should know that her life had been laid waste by a rejection that, to some women of her acquaintance, might have meant little more than a loss at croquet. Julia was herself bewildered by the extent of the desolation that had befallen her; it was like wandering through the abandoned ruins of a once-thriving city. Yet so far as she could tell, most of her friends were scarcely aware of the change in her. It was very strange to look in the mirror and see the same face and form that Frederick had once called beautiful, thinner and paler, but otherwise unaltered.

Her dream of flight had not returned; instead she had been several times visited by a nightmare of finding herself high up on a shattered wall of stone, like the ruin of some great abbey whose roof had long since collapsed. Far below, mounds of fallen brickwork and rubble lay heaped upon the outlines of foundations and the remnants of other walls, with grass and weeds growing over them. At first the top of the wall on which she knelt would be relatively broad, though jagged, but in seeking a safe way to descend she would find the way becoming narrower and more precarious, the stone crumbling beneath her hands until she saw that she had crawled to the very end of a broken arch where she could only cling to a rotten tongue of stone, petrified by fear of plummeting down amidst great shards and fragments of masonry, feeling the very fabric of the world dissolve within her grasp.

Doubtless if she had been able to speak openly to anyone, she would not have come to haunt the Reading Room, or to believe that somewhere in the labyrinth was hidden that one book, whatever it might be: not a work of philosophy or theology, for Julia had had little taste for abstract thought even in happier days, and could now make no more sense of philosophical discourse than she could of Sanskrit. She imagined a voice speaking plainly and directly out of the wilderness into which she had stumbled; for someone must have crossed it before her, and found exactly the wisdom she so painfully lacked.

To be entirely candid with herself, she was also drawn to the Reading Room by the hope of seeing Frederick. But the hope had so far proven vain. Recently, while consulting the catalogue, she had overheard an exchange between two men, evidently acquaintances of Frederick's, the one remarking that Liddell had become a complete recluse these days, to which his companion replied that poor old Freddy must be immersed in the composition of some great work. They had laughed at this, in a way that Julia found very troubling, so that she had returned to her place and sat for an indefinite time gazing sightlessly at the volume before her.

The truth was that she still loved him, though she wished she did not. She had tried to hate him and failed; she could not even hate Lydia, for how could she blame a dead woman for what had happened? Indeed she felt herself increasingly surrounded by people who preferred the company of the deceased to that of the living. Her husband, as he had grown older, had become ever more fascinated by his departed forebears; then there was poor Aunt Helen who had spent the greater part of her life going from one séance to the next, constantly receiving messages from her adored fiancé Lionel who had been lost to fever in the Crimea nearly half a century before. Julia had lately accompanied her aunt to a few of these gatherings, and had been depressed by the mingled accents of credulity and fraud, not to mention the thought of all those others thronging the great city in pursuit of phantoms. And now there was Frederick, lost to the memory of Lydia; and Julia herself was scarcely in a better case. She had often selfishly wished they had fallen from the balcony that afternoon; she would have died in bliss instead of being condemned to linger in a world where, as it seemed to her, so many of the living moved like ghosts among the seekers of the dead.

Such were her thoughts on a sombre afternoon late in February, when the fog hovering in the dome seemed thicker than usual. Julia was on the verge of packing up to leave when a book was delivered to her place; she did not see by whom. It was not, however, the edition of Clare's poems for which she had earlier lodged an application, but a plain octavo volume with black boards; so plain, in fact, that it bore neither a title nor an author's name upon its spine. Puzzled, she opened it, to be confronted only by the heading, "Chapter One"; yet there was no sign of damage or missing pages. It appeared to be a novel; indeed a novel set in Bloomsbury, for it began with a description of a furious altercation between two cabmen in Great Russell Street. One of the men wore a dirty red kerchief, the other a white; as the dispute grew yet more heated, the two men descended from their respective boxes and fell to pushing one another about the pavement, and then to blows, whereupon both were forced to give way by "the approach of an immense woman, dressed entirely in black and bearing in her arms what appeared from its shape to be a child's coffin, incongruously wrapped in brown paper and tied with string"—but when Julia went to turn the page she found that it had not been cut. Curious to know how the narrative would proceed, she looked about for an attendant. At once a tall, nondescript man whom she could not recall seeing before approached; he had evidently observed her difficulty, for with a murmured "Pray allow me, madam" he took up the volume and disappeared through a side door.

Julia sat for some minutes waiting for him to return, but he did not, and her faint curiosity dwindled away to nothing. The pall of melancholy settled once more about her; she collected her belongings and left the Reading Room. Outside, the sky was dark and lowering; it looked as if rain, or even snow, might begin to fall at any moment, so she hastened across the courtyard and requested the constable at the gate to secure her a cab. None were in sight as she stepped onto the pavement of Great Russell Street, but then she saw two appearing round the Montague Street corner. She heard the constable whistle; the cab at the rear swung out and attempted to pass the one in front;

the vehicles seemed to touch, and the next moment the two cabmen were embroiled in a furious exchange of oaths. One leapt down from his box; the other followed; Julia thought she saw a flash of red at the latter's throat, but it was not until a vast woman, clad in voluminous layers of black, emerged from a doorway bearing a large, strangely shaped parcel in her arms and forced the struggling cabmen to part, one on each side of her, as she set out across the road, that the full import of what she was seeing struck Julia like a physical blow. In the same instant she heard the constable addressing her and, half turning, saw that a third cab had emerged from Museum Street and drawn up immediately behind her.

"Best get in, ma'am," said the constable. "I'll 'ave to see to that there embrocation."

Numbly, Julia obeyed. As her driver turned his horse, she had just time to see the two cabmen retreating towards their vehicles at the approach of the constable, and the woman's immense back departing in the direction of Southampton Row.

Ten o'clock the next morning found her once again at the Reading Room, though she had never before arrived so soon after opening time. The day was raw and foggy, the heating barely sufficient to dispel the bone-numbing chill of the journey, but Julia was conscious only of her need to recover the anonymous black volume, which meant finding the man who had brought it to her, for she could not recall even seeing a press-mark. Since waking early from a troubled sleep she had been prey to increasing doubt as to whether she had actually read the account of the scene in the street, or had merely been confused by an especially striking instance of the experience the French term *déjà vu*. Like others of her acquaintance she had occasionally found herself, for the space of a few sentences, in the midst of a conversation which seemed oddly familiar, but nothing remotely like yesterday's experience had ever befallen her.

The search for the tall, nondescript attendant proved, however, hopeless. She found herself entirely unable to describe him with any accuracy, save that he was tall and had been clad, she thought, in a grey suit of some kind; her memory simply refused to summon him as anything more than a blurred outline of a man. The attendants on duty did their best to accommodate her; three possible candidates were summoned from the nether regions for her inspection, but without result. They were however adamant in maintaining that the delivery of a volume without a press-mark was an impossibility; author and title might conceivably be dispensed with, but a book without a press-mark, madam, would be like a soul without a name upon the Day of Judgment: it could never arise, and would be lost for all eternity. Julia could see the force of this; she could see, too, that to persist would merely confirm their evident belief that the book had been delivered to her only in a dream (she had, of course, said nothing about what had followed in the street) and so she returned, bewildered, to her place.

Sitting in the same seat as she had occupied the previous afternoon dispelled the doubts that had gathered overnight; the book had certainly been delivered to her; she could visualise the words at the foot of that first page, see herself trying to turn to the next and finding the opening uncut. Several times she walked the circumference of the room, searching for the attendant in grey, but with no success. The fog hanging about the dome seemed even thicker than it had yesterday, and readers unusually scarce; apart from a motionless figure several seats away to her left, she had a whole row to herself. To quieten her mind, she set about writing a full account of her experience, and became quite absorbed in the attempt to recall and record every detail. The damp air grew closer and stuffier; she could feel the warmth rising from the heat-pipe beneath the desk as she wrote on, half mesmerised by the steady scratching of her own pen. After an indefinite interval, she became aware, as she reached mechanically for the inkwell, that the scratching of her pen had become the only sound within her hearing; and she looked up to find herself entirely surrounded by fog.

Her first thought was that someone must have left a door or window open, but that was plainly absurd: she had never seen fog of this intensity inside a building before; it must be some freak of nature. She sat within a little cocoon of light shed by the electric lamp above her place; there was only the usual faint halo about the shade, but the edge of the fog-bank swirled to within two feet of her on either side, and overhead. Cold wisps of it curled across her desk, bearing a strange, ashy, sulphur-salt smell, as of a huge sea-creature suddenly emerging from the depths. She was—or had been—perhaps two-thirds of the way out from the central circle where the catalogue was kept; all she had to do was get up and make her way carefully to her left, and then left again around the circumference of the room until she reached the main entrance. But what would she do then? The fog must be even more impenetrable outside, and besides, there was something profoundly unnerving about it, something that made her very reluctant to leave her small circle of light. Perhaps she should call out; but why could she not hear anyone else calling for assistance? There had been other readers in neighbouring rows; and was it not the attendants' duty to go about and reassure those who might otherwise fall prey to panic? Yet still there was no sound other than the faint, muffled susurration of the fog-bank.

But surely fog did not *make* any sound? That soft rustling away to her left was not the fog; it was someone coming stealthily up the row towards her. Julia held her breath, listening. The rustling came closer, and ceased; the swirling wall of fog remained utterly opaque; then she heard the faint scrape of a chair—it sounded like the chair immediately to her left—being drawn out, followed by the almost inaudible creak of the seat as someone, or something, settled themselves upon it.

Silence returned. Julia tried to tell herself that it was only another reader, lost in the fog and deciding to sit down until it cleared. But the trembling of her hands belied her. Very slowly, keeping her eyes on the fog-bank between herself and her invisible companion, Julia began to ease herself off her chair, hoping to slip away silently in the other direction, towards the catalogue. Her chair creaked loudly, and as it did so the wall of fog to her left rose up like a curtain.

In that first glimpse, Julia was relieved, though startled, to discover that the chair beside her was occupied by a child, a little girl of no more than eight, with golden curls and pink cheeks, dressed in a starched white frock and petticoats. The reassurance lasted only an instant. There was something fixed and unnatural about the bright, smiling face turned towards Julia, and especially about the eyes, which had been slightly downcast, but suddenly opened wide with an audible click. They were the shoe-button eyes of a doll; the face looked as hard and rigid as porcelain; and yet the creature was alive, for it was swinging its legs around with the evident intention of sliding off its chair and coming over to Julia.

All of Julia's hair stood on end; or such was the sensation. The "click" of those eyes snapping open seemed to lodge in her own body with a visceral jolt of terror such as she would not have believed a human being could endure. If the smiling doll-creature touched her, she knew she would die; she could not cry out, for the fear was choking her. Its satin shoes touched the floor; Julia sprang up, knocking over her own chair, and backed away into the wall of fog. Blundering from chair to chair, with still no sign of another human being, she retreated until she collided painfully with what felt like the circular bookcase which housed the catalogue, groped her way along its edge, and lurched into what she hoped was another alleyway of desks, where she stopped and tried to hold her breath and still her pulse enough to listen for the rustle of her pursuer's dress.

From the moment Julia left her seat, the fog had closed impermeably about her. If she held her hand so close that her fingers actually touched her face, she could see the outline of it, but beyond that distance she might as well have been immersed in cotton wool, through which filtered a dim, uniform, yellow-grey light. Even in normal circumstances, the Reading Room has a labyrinthine aspect; some have compared it to a spider's web; but because it is possible to see over the tops of the rows of desks and across the central bookcases, these sinister possibilities lie mostly dormant. If all light were to be extinguished, one might imagine that the regularity of its construction, with the rows of desks radiating out from the centre like the spokes of a wheel, would still render escape relatively straightforward. But in fact, merely by pausing to listen, Julia found that she had lost all sense of direction. The strange sea-creature smell confused her senses, and the blood would not stop ringing in her ears. She could not hear, yet she knew that to run blindly would be fatal; the noise of her flight would give her away. Besides—she tried to suppress the realisation, but could not—the creature had found her in spite of the fog. Julia began to tremble uncontrollably.

Noise might be fatal, but to remain waiting for a porcelain hand to insinuate itself into hers was quite unbearable. She took a slow step backwards and bumped against a chair, which scraped; set off in what she thought was the right direction and encountered a cold, vertical surface which she could not identify at all, and from there veered into empty space, losing even her sense of up and down. She felt herself falling; reached out to save herself and clutched at a narrow ledge or flange, which seemed at first solid but suddenly gave way with a rasp, shot from her hand and fell at her feet with a dreadful smash. The creature would be upon her any second; Julia stumbled back into the void, and this time managed to hand herself from chair to chair along the entire length of a row. The noise was frightful, despite the muffling effect of the fog; several chairs fell behind her, but she kept on, and when nothing met her hand after the expected interval, threw herself forward with both arms outstretched until she collided with what, she prayed, was the bookcase that ran right around the circumference of the Reading Room. Instinct told her that if she were to follow the curve around to her left, she would eventually arrive at the main entrance, where help must surely be at hand.

Julia stopped again to listen, but her breathing would not slow. Terror had left no room for any thought beyond the desire for escape; she set off again, as fast as she dared, with her right hand brushing along the curved bookcase and her left stretched out before her. In a surprisingly short time she came to an opening, which, she told herself, must be the entrance; she felt her way through, stumbled for some distance in another void, and collided with a wall. No, a door, for it swung away under her weight, and she went on through, quite unable to visualise the foyer in sufficient detail to tell whether she was in it or not. She took a few steps forward, but the floor did not feel right underfoot; it had a hollow, skeletal quality about it; then she brushed against a cold, vertical metal surface, which certainly did not match her recollection of anything in the foyer. Running her hand across the metal surface beside her, Julia realised that it was the end of a bookshelf. Reaching around it, she disturbed a volume which fell over with a thud, and all at once understood where she must be. This was the Iron Library, a maze of shelves crammed with books in their numberless thousands. If she could not regain the door through which she had entered, she would be utterly lost.

But perhaps help was closer at hand than she had thought, for was that not the faint sound of voices? And quite close by; perhaps it was only the muffling effect of the fog that made it sound like whispering. She took a step forward, keeping one hand on the metal surface to her left, and now the sound was even clearer, though oddly repetitive in its cadence, as if someone were whispering the same word over and over. Her hand slid off into space and across to the end of another shelf: and yes, the voice was coming from the aisle between the shelves; it seemed to be rising up from the floor as the fog once more lifted to reveal the doll-child's upturned porcelain smile, the shoe-button eyes opening wide, painted fingers reaching towards the hem of Julia's dress, and the rosebud mouth opening and closing mechanically, whispering "Julia . . . Julia . . . Julia . . ."

Thus began a fearful game of hide-and-seek which drove Julia ever further into the gloomy depths of the Iron Library. The fog had thinned somewhat, so that she could see from one end of an aisle to the other, but that only worsened the terror of seeing the painted smile appearing from around a stack or worse, coming up behind her as she paused, wondering which way to flee. Though the creature's head came no higher than Julia's waist, the thought of turning upon it, or trying to kick it out of her way, only prompted a further spasm of horror; she knew she could not endure its slightest touch, and so could only retreat until she ran up against an iron staircase spiralling up into the foggy darkness overhead.

Her pursuer was not at that moment in sight, but there was no other way back. Shuddering at the image of the doll-child lurking in wait for her, Julia began to climb. But she could not keep the staircase from sounding beneath her feet; her footsteps rang out over the fog-bank which now rolled back below her, so that she could neither see nor hear whether the creature was following. She passed an exit onto a narrow metal gallery and kept climbing higher and higher, with the fog still rising so that it swirled continuously just below her hurrying feet.

Soon she could go no higher; the last turn brought her out onto another gallery, whose floor, like the others in the Iron Library, was a sort of grid, so that one could see through it to the fog drifting just beneath. On one side of her was a sheer dark wall, on the other a handrail, through which, as she paused wondering which direction to take, she could feel a faint rhythmic drumming, as of footsteps coming lightly and rapidly up from below. Julia began to retreat along the gallery as fast as she dared, glancing frequently over her shoulder. There was no sign of the doll-child yet; but she saw that she was coming to a dead end; there was nothing ahead of her but an end-rail, and no more stairs.

A cold gust of air rose about her; the wall of fog rolled back and seemed to dissolve upon the instant, and Julia found herself looking down from a great height, at row upon row of skeletal iron floors plummeting away into darkness. Vertigo seized her as it had on the brink of Frederick's balcony. Simultaneously, the doll-child emerged onto the gallery and trotted purposefully towards her, the painted smile broadening, its tread sounding heavier with every step. Caught between the terror of falling and dread at the creature's approach, Julia pressed herself against the wall. The porcelain arms reached out; the eyes clicked wide open. As a cry of repulsion rose ungovernably in Julia's throat, her fingers found a handle. Part of the wall gave way with a crash, flinging her out upon another gallery, beneath a vast, windowed hemisphere which took up her cry and sent it ringing and reverberating across the Reading Room, high above a sea of upturned faces.

The following afternoon found Julia, somewhat to her own surprise, back in the library. Her interview with the Chief Attendant had been long and humiliating: he had looked at her so strangely when she first mentioned the fog that she spoke, thereafter, only of taking a wrong turn and finding herself lost in the Iron Library. When asked why she had climbed the stair, she could only reply that she had mistaken it for the way out. But he was plainly not satisfied: she had, he said sternly, broken several regulations, ignored numerous notices, created a disturbance in the Reading Room, and placed herself in serious danger. The Trustees would have to be informed, and might well decide to suspend her ticket.

What had actually occurred remained unfathomable. Julia had been followed onto the Reading Room gallery, not by the doll-child, but by an attendant who had noticed a woman ascending the staircase in the Iron Library. The only rational explanation she could conceive of was sleepwalking, but she could not quite believe it. There was, of course, the darker possibility that her mind had given way under the strain of prolonged grief. Yet she could not shake off the sense that the anonymous black book and the terrifying encounter in the fog were in some way connected. Besides which she had discovered, in the course of another troubled night, that fear of the doll-child's renewed attentions had followed her home. Until she could discover the meaning of these events, she would not feel secure, and instinct told her that the answer must be sought in the Reading Room, to which she accordingly returned, heavily veiled and in other ways disguised as far as possible.

The afternoon outside was bright and clear, the dome filled with light and entirely free of fog, which at least implied that she would be safe from a renewal of yesterday's terrors. But although an inspection of the upper gallery confirmed that she had been too high above the readers' desks for her features to be easily discerned, Julia felt most conspicuous and ill-at-ease. To inquire any further after the anonymous black book was obviously impossible. But wait: there was, after all, a section of the catalogue devoted to anonymous works, and she might as well look through it as sit uncomfortably wondering whether the voices murmuring on the other side of the partition were murmuring about her.

"Anon", however, proved far more prolific than Julia had anticipated. She had begun her search on the principle of the child's game of "warm or cold", filling out an application for any title which looked remotely promising. But mindful of the notice discouraging readers from requesting numerous books at any one time, and of her already uncertain standing in the Reading Room, she found her progress—or lack of it—so slow that the light was fading from the dome before she had surveyed even a fraction of the titles beginning with "A". It would clearly take weeks or months, with no likelihood of success . . . but what was this?

A Full and True Account of the Strange Events leading to the Death of the Poet Frederick Liddell, Esq., on the night of Thursday 2nd March, 1899. 8vo. London. 1899.

The date given was today's, or rather tonight's: an impossibility, but there it was, starkly presenting itself to Julia's uncomprehending gaze. The printed entry slip, which looked as if it had only just been pasted in, was set out in the usual fashion, and accompanied by a press-mark which, together with the first few words of the title, Julia had numbly copied onto an application slip and deposited at the issue desk before the import of the words had even begun to sink in. It must be another Frederick Liddell, an inner voice kept repeating, but she knew this to be false; she had looked up his name in the catalogue too often, formerly for the pleasure and latterly for the pain of seeing it printed there. Almost any other reader, confronting the same entry, would have attributed it to clerical error, or at worst an elaborate and distasteful hoax; to Julia, the words emblazoned upon her inward vision seemed like a declaration of the inevitable.

Fifteen minutes crawled by, and then a half-hour. The electric lights came on; the windows in the dome darkened steadily; Julia waited in growing apprehension with her thoughts revolving as upon a treadmill. Should she not go to his rooms and see if he was there, to warn him? But warn him of what? To know exactly where and when the danger lay, she would have to see the book . . . but then the rational part of her mind would rise up in protest, only to be subdued in turn by a vivid recollection of the immense woman bearing the coffin-shaped parcel, so that she sat paralysed between these warring inner factions until an attendant came to inform her that no record of any such volume could be found. Julia returned at once to the catalogue; she could visualise the position of the entry quite clearly, in the top right-hand quarter of a right-hand page, but realised, when it did not appear in the expected place, that she had absolutely no recollection of its surroundings. Because new entries were constantly being pasted in, their order was not always precisely alphabetical, but she searched many pages in either direction without finding what she sought. This, however, only heightened her sense of foreboding. It was black night outside; she could delay no longer, no matter what humiliation might follow. But if she were not home soon, even her husband might become anxious enough to initiate a search. Hastily scribbling a note to say that she would be dining with Marianne, Julia gathered up her things and rushed from the Reading Room.

The night air was damp and still, with a hint of mist about the street lamps, as Julia rang the bell at the street door below Frederick's rooms. There was a long wait, made even longer by the combined weight of foreboding and painful recall, before the door was opened by an ancient porter.

Her apprehension increased with every one of the seemingly endless flights of stairs, and she was obliged to pause even longer than was necessary to recover her breath before she could summon the courage to knock at Frederick's door. All had been silent within; at the sound of her tapping the silence seemed only to deepen; then there was a muffled thud, followed by the sound of rapid footsteps and a clatter of locks and bolts being undone. Almost worse than the dread of what she might encounter was the resurgence of a hope so long repressed, a hope that flared wildly at the first sight of his face, so pale and gaunt and worn, suddenly radiant with an answering joy. She had crossed the threshold and flung her arms around him—feeling at once how dreadfully thin he had become—and kissed him with all the passion of her resurrected love, before the name he was so tenderly murmuring resolved itself as, undeniably, "Lydia".

Julia disengaged herself and drew back, searching the well-remembered face for some sign of recognition. It was, and yet was not, the Frederick of old: unshaven, clad in a crumpled shirt and trousers and a pair of old carpet slippers, with a frayed green dressing-gown over his shoulders, his hair even longer and more disorderly, but lacking its former lustre. His adoring expression did not change, but he seemed to be gazing through rather than at her face. For a moment she feared that he was blind, until he evidently noticed the open door, which he reached out and closed behind her. As it clicked shut, an expression of bewilderment crossed his face; he looked from her—or rather, from the person he evidently saw in her place—to the door and back again.

"It is finished, and you have come," he said in a strange abstracted tone, "but I expected . . . I thought you would have . . ."

He trailed off, glancing towards the French windows, which Julia saw were open to the night. Despite the fire burning in the grate opposite, she felt the chill draught from the balcony. She did not want to understand his implication, nor did she wish to believe him mad. Might he be sleep-walking? And if he stood, as it were, in the midst of a dream of Lydia, might he not be woken . . . ? But even as she opened her mouth to cry, I am Julia, not Lydia, the futility of it overwhelmed her. Dreaming or waking, Frederick had given his whole heart to a dead woman, and there was no room in it for the living; that love was ashes, and would arise no more.

Besides, she had somewhere read or heard that sleep-walkers should not be woken abruptly, but coaxed back to bed and watched until they fell into a true sleep, from which they would awaken with no recollection of the previous night's encounters. There flashed upon her the conviction that she understood the omens of recent days, for had she not come to him tonight, Frederick might well have plunged heedlessly to his death. The first thing, therefore, was to close the French windows; no, first get him safely into bed, then secure them.

"Frederick," she said, gently taking his arm, "you are very tired, and must rest now."

"Yes, I am very tired," he repeated. "But—you will not leave me, Lydia? Not now?" His voice rose and quavered on the last words.

"No, Frederick," said Julia sadly, "I will not leave you. But you must go to bed now, and sleep."

With that she led him slowly across the room, staying as far as possible from the dark doorway opening onto the night, and along the passageway to his bedroom, now dreadfully stale and disordered. He stood obediently, like a child, while she straightened the bedclothes as best she could and turned back the sheet; like a child he sat on the edge of the bed and removed his slippers and dressing-gown, then immediately lay down and composed himself for sleep. His eyes had closed before Julia had settled the bedclothes about his shoulders, and within the space of a minute the rhythm of his breathing had slowed and deepened. She watched him for a few minutes more, recalling how often and how ardently she had yearned to watch over Frederick whilst he slept. Now her prayer had been answered, and all she could feel was a profound weariness of spirit. His breathing slowed still further; Julia would have liked to open the window, but was afraid of disturbing him, and so turned down the gas and went back to the sitting-room.

She had meant to close the French windows immediately, but the staleness of the bedroom seemed to have followed her down the passage, and it was not, after all, especially cold; she would close one side and leave the other open for the moment. But on her way over, her attention was drawn to the desk beneath the right-hand window. A lamp burned beside the portrait of Lydia, placed so that it also illuminated a loose sheaf of papers, which were secured by a crystal paperweight. Julia was uncomfortably reminded of a votive offering. The uppermost sheet bore two stanzas in Frederick's small, precise hand:

The midnight moth besieg'd the lamp,
The magic casement opened wide;
I heard at last the soft wing-beat
Of my returning bride;

And, as I lean'd still farther out
Upon the unresisting night,
Saw my beloved hovering near,
Enraptur'd with the gift of flight.

❦ ❦ ❦

The ink looked quite fresh, as if this were the final page of a fair copy which had not yet been put into its proper order. Julia drew out the chair and sat down, meaning to examine the rest of the manuscript, but found herself intimidated by Lydia's cool, proprietorial stare, which in the lamplight seemed unnervingly watchful. She stretched out a hand to turn the picture's eyes away from hers, but as she leaned forward, her foot thudded against something hollow beneath the desk. There was, indeed, scarcely enough room for her feet, and she bent down to see what the obstruction was. A window-box? No; too low, and she had felt it move. But its proportions were somehow familiar. A black, rectangular box, about three feet long: some musical instrument, perhaps? Curiosity impelled her to set aside her chair and draw the thing out from beneath the desk. It proved surprisingly light for its size. No doubt it would be locked; but the first of the three silver catches snapped open when she touched the knob; the other two followed suit, so there could be no harm in raising the lid.

Whatever it contained was, however, concealed beneath a purple velvet covering. Julia was kneeling alongside the box, and as she reached in to draw aside the covering, she overbalanced so that her right hand slid beneath the purple velvet and encountered something hard. There was a flash of white; she tried to snatch her hand away, but something caught it fast with a hot, piercing sensation, and the doll-child sat up and opened its eyes.

The porcelain fingers gripped like the needle-sharp teeth of a serpent; with her free hand, Julia tried to fend the creature off, but it seemed to leap from its box as she recoiled through the French windows and fell heavily against the balcony railing. She felt the creature dragging her over; for one dreadful instant it hung, smiling, in mid-air before its grip upon Julia's hand was broken and the doll-child went whirling down into the void; whole seconds seemed to pass before Julia heard it smash upon the pavement.

She remained, clinging to the railing, until the worst of the shock had subsided. But the piercing sensation in her right hand did not diminish; one of the serpent-fingers must have lodged in it. Shuddering, she lifted her hand to the light and discovered that the source of the pain was, in fact, a hat-pin, driven deep into the side of her palm. Bunched beneath the head of the pin were several torn folds of white material. Clenching her teeth, she drew out the pin and dropped it over the rail; then she stood up and leaned over to see if she could discern the fragments of the doll by the light of the street lamp below. She was too far up to make anything out, but as she watched, a small figure shuffled into the pool of light and seemed to be stooping over something in the road.

Julia became suddenly conscious of where she was, but vertigo did not follow. She felt she could stay here, leaning on the rail, for as long as she liked. But there was nothing to stay for, and her hand was throbbing painfully. She returned to the sitting-room, closed the doors, restored the empty box to its place, and exchanged a final glance with Lydia's portrait. The eyes had lost their wariness; indeed the picture seemed to have faded, to have become simply a photograph of a young woman seeking to make the most of her beauty for the camera. Julia wondered, as she turned away, if she would ever see the poem in print, but it was addressed to Lydia, not to her; all that was left for her to do was to ensure that a doctor would be summoned. Looking in upon Frederick for the last time, Julia saw that he was smiling faintly in his sleep. She left him dreaming of the dead, and went wearily down the stairs to rejoin the world of the living.

I EMERGED from the story with the sensation of waking from a dream in which I was Julia, and dreadfully cold, and the Reading Room had slipped its moorings and floated out to sea. The dome was palpably revolving; I could feel the sway of the waves as I struggled up from the depths, only to find that I was already awake, with a burning forehead and a deep, shivering ache in every bone. Walking back to Russell Square tube station, I was shaking so hard I had to clench my teeth to stop them chattering. From amongst the press of bodies in the lift, a desolate male voice announced to the world at large, 'Ah'm not happy. Ah feel bad. Ah'm depressed.' 'Aren't we fuckin' all,' muttered a man behind me. Crammed into our filthy metal cage, steeped in the farmyard stench of sodden clothing, we sank in silence into the earth.

For the next ten days I shivered and sweated and coughed, drifting in and out of dreams in which the doll-child appeared several times. Worst of all was a recurring nightmare in which I pursued a fleeting figure, who might or might not have been Alice, through a maze of deserted streets and derelict buildings. Usually she would vanish; once I cornered her in a blind alley and she turned to me with a face of stone. Outside the rain pelted down upon the icy slush, through which I slithered to the chemist for more drugs, or to the nearest cheap restaurant for another oily Indian meal. The Westland affair fizzled and died. The space shuttle blew up. The Iron Lady went on and on.

Three days before I was due to leave, I thought about taking a train from Waterloo to Balcombe, a village about three miles north-east of Staplefield. The least I could do was see the village and ask around. But as I looked again at the tiny black circle marked on the B2114, all I could feel was 'what's the point?' I tried to summon the old sense of wonder and refuge, but it was like feeling for a lost tooth. Without Alice – by now I had convinced myself that I would never hear from her again – Staplefield was dead and gone.

On my last day, a Saturday, a watery sun came out. I took a bus to Hampstead Heath and walked up to the top of Parliament Hill, where I did at last feel some sense of awe at the great sweep of the city below. But the wind was keen and biting, and so cold my fillings began to ache. I descended to the swimming ponds, shuddering at the sight of the icy green water in which some madwoman was actually swimming. Dodging pushchairs and bicycles, I wandered the muddy gravel paths as far as the Vale of Health, and came back along the boundary road.

I hadn't imagined I would welcome the heat and glare of a Mawson summer. When I emerged from customs, my mother hugged me as if I had returned from the dead.

'But you're so *thin*, Gerard. What's happened to you?'

I told her about the flu, and agreed I should have gone to a doctor. There didn't seem to be much else to say. After breakfast we sat with our coffee under a flowering gum in the back yard. Crimson filaments drifted across the lawn; the sky was a dazzling blue. Breathing the dry, pungent scent of eucalyptus,

I couldn't help thinking that it was better to be desolate and warm than desolate and frozen.

'– were you too ill to do anything at all, dear?' my mother was saying.

The only thing I could think of was my walk on Hampstead Heath. Idly watching a pair of rosellas as I talked, I was unprepared for the outburst.

'How *could* you be so reckless, Gerard? You might have been murdered!'

Her forehead was beaded with sweat, though it had been dry a moment before.

'It was a Saturday afternoon, Mother. There were people everywhere.'

'People get dragged off those paths, all the time. And never seen again. I've read about it. Anything could have happened to you.'

I tried to reassure her, but she would not listen, and shortly afterwards she said she was going inside to lie down.

* * *

c/o Penfriends International,
Box 294, Mount Pleasant PO,
London WC1
31 January 1986

Dearest Gerard,

I'm so sorry, I've only just got your letters (the ones you wrote while you were here) because I've been in hospital. Don't worry, everything's fine now – wonderful in fact. There's a real chance that in a couple of years' time I'll be walking again! I've been on Mr MacBride's waiting list – he's a neurosurgeon – for ages, and I thought it would be months more, but then he had a cancellation on New Year's Day and they whisked me off to Guy's Hospital in an ambulance. Only I didn't know where you were staying because your letter from Mawson with the hotel address in it must have been delayed in the post – it was waiting with the others when I got back yesterday.

I would have written much sooner, only there were complications with the dye they injected into my spine for the X-rays – God, those endless hours lying in the scanner, trying not to move, or even breathe – anyway I got terribly sick and spent two weeks on a drip because I couldn't keep anything down. I had a monster headache that never stopped, and my eyesight went so blurry I thought I was going blind – this often happens, apparently, with spinal injections – it's almost back to normal now. I thought of you all the time but I was just too ill to write.

I would have told you about the tests only I just couldn't bear to raise our hopes – you know how superstitious I am – until I knew for certain there was something to hope for. And there is, there truly is. Mr MacBride is working with a new laser technique for splitting healthy nerves to replace the damaged ones, and he thinks that in a year or two – it just needs one more breakthrough with the lasers, he says – he'll be able to operate with a ninety per cent chance of success!

This must go now to catch today's post; I've told them to send it express. I'm so sorry about the mix-up with letters and that you had such a miserable time in London – I'll make it up to you, I promise.

More, much more, tomorrow.

I love and adore you with all my heart, and I'm longing to hear from you.

Your invisible lover

Alice

If Alice had told me then that I would have to wait another thirteen years . . . but it was never going to be thirteen years, only 'another year or two at the most'. And the longer I waited, the more I had to lose by not waiting just a few months longer. Alice finished her degree with the Open University and took up teaching English by correspondence to disabled students. Somewhere around the five-year mark, she promised me that we would be together after the operation, even if it failed. Then why not now? 'I want to run into your arms,' she would say, 'and now that we've come so far, please, please can we wait just a little longer?' By the time I persuaded her to go on to email, we had exchanged over four thousand letters through Penfriends International.

I had a life, of sorts, and friends, up to a point. But never any real intimacy; sooner rather than later, every friendship ran up against the wall behind which Alice lay hidden. So long as I keep her secret, I would tell myself, she will be healed, we will be together. As in those fairy tales in which all will be well so long as a certain question is never asked, or a prohibition disobeyed. Never enter my chamber during the hours of darkness.

In all this time, my mother and I kept to our undeclared agreement: she didn't ask about Alice, and I didn't ask about her past. It never seemed worth moving out of the house because I never meant to wait thirteen years. Everyone at the library assumed I was gay, but too timid to leave the closet – at least that was what I assumed they assumed. Quiet, polite, still living at home with his mother, never seems to go out, never talks about himself: no one, I imagined them saying, could possibly be that boring. Not even Gerard. I went on working at the library and staying at home with Mother, while the longed-for breakthrough in microsurgery shimmered on the horizon, always just another year away.

Not leaving my mother alone with her legion of terrors became part of my bargain with God – a God I didn't believe in, but a bargain nonetheless: I'll look after Mother if you'll make sure Alice is healed. Looking after Mother meant, above all else, not leaving her alone at night. Her conviction that the danger was *out there*, like the snake in the woodpile, had never wavered. She had endured, rather than lived, nearly four decades in Mawson, but I had never seen her bored; she had been too absorbed in her vigil, too intent on catching the slightest whisper of snakeskin over bark. Call it paranoia, chronic anxiety syndrome, obsessive compulsive disorder or common-or-garden neurosis; no matter how many labels you stuck on it, the serpent had been real to her. As her seventieth birthday approached, I noticed that she was losing weight and colour, and that her skin had taken on a greyish tinge. But she refused to see a doctor. She went on listening to inaudible sounds until the tumour had grown too large to ignore.

A fortnight after the oncologist told me there was nothing more he could do, Mr MacBride put Alice on his waiting list. I said nothing to my mother. In just under two months, if all went well, Alice would walk out of the hospital. In the last week of July, about when my mother was expected to die.

* * *

'You've been a good son to me, Gerard.'

I did not feel like a good son. I had resented her devotion too often and too bitterly for that. We were speaking as usual in clichés, the tireder the better. The silence between us had always been more profound than anything we had managed to say to each other. Now it filled the house like the hum of defective wiring.

She was propped up on the daybed in the sunroom, her book face down on the blanket, looking out over the garden. Drifts of fallen leaves had gathered around the trunks of trees, against the garage wall, along the back fence. This time last year, she would have wanted them all swept away. Afternoon sunlight slanted across the floor; I had already closed the window against the encroaching chill.

I was home on leave from the library, doing what little cooking was required. Now that she needed morphine to sleep at night, my mother would accept nothing solid, only soup and fruit juice and hot drinks. When darkness came, I would help her up the hall to her bedroom. She could still walk, with difficulty.

I reached across from my chair beside the head of her bed, and touched her hand. She did not turn back from the window, but her cold fingers closed over mine, and we stayed like that for a while, watching the crimson leaves stirring beneath the flame tree. It struck me, not for the first time, that she might have been happier with no son at all.

Her fingers twitched; she was drifting into sleep. I reached over with my other hand and picked up her book, so that it would not slide off and wake her. A battered Pan paperback: Josephine Tey, *To Love and be Wise*. She must have read that one a dozen times. From bargain tables and goodwill stores she had amassed a vast collection of detective stories, all English and nothing after the 1950s: Agatha Christie, Dorothy Sayers, John Dickson Carr, Marjorie Allingham, Josephine Tey, Freeman Wills Crofts, Ernest Brahmah, J.J. Connington and more. She would alternate these with anything from Daphne Du Maurier to Elizabeth Bowen or Henry James, but beyond 'I think you'll like this, dear', or 'not as good as so-and-so, I thought', she never discussed her reading, which – or so I sometimes imagined – had come to revolve more and more around the lost country-house world of her childhood with Viola at Staplefield.

The sun was sinking into the canopy of our flowering gum, the tallest of all the trees we had planted. I could remember our back yard as a summer dustbowl, the year the town's reservoirs threatened to run dry and hoses were banned. The dead grass had blown away with the topsoil before the end of the holidays. Our parched saplings, surrounded by cylinders of wire netting to keep off the rabbits, were kept alive by surreptitious buckets of water. My mother would sometimes doze in here in the afternoons, blinds drawn against the glare, pedestal fan rattling in the doorway; she used to say it might be hotter out here, but it wasn't as airless as her bedroom.

The fingers clasping mine twitched again. Her face was still turned away from me. As it had been that afternoon when I tiptoed up to the door to see if she was safely asleep. Sitting here beside my mother, day after day, I had tried several times to recall the face in the photograph. Sometimes I felt sure I was remembering perfectly, the light falling across her neck, the mass of dark brown hair – but how could I know that when the picture had been black and white? Then the certainty would dissolve and I would be left with only the memory of vividness, not the face itself. As with Viola and Staplefield – there had been a tall house, and a pavilion on a hill, a friend called Rosalind, a picturebook village – and that was all I could recover. Oh and a wicket gate, whatever that looked like. And a walk through some woods with badgers and some other creature – rabbits? hares? – and an old man with a cart who delivered . . . milk, eggs? Surely there must have been more, far more?

And then the stories had ceased. She had looked ten feet high in the bedroom doorway, Medusa hair flying, incandescent with fury. But why, Mother, why? Why would you never talk to me about Viola?

'I loved her,' said my mother's voice.

The hair on the back of my neck bristled. Her face was still turned away from me. Had I spoken aloud? Was she talking in her sleep?

'You loved Viola?' I asked, keeping my voice low and my hand still in hers.

'Yes . . . loved me too.'

'Then why – why couldn't we talk about Viola, you and I?'

The papery fingers tightened a little.

'I had to keep you safe.'

'Mother I am safe; I'm here with you.'

She stirred; her head turned slowly towards me. Her eyes did not open; her expression remained calm.

'Then talk to me now,' I said after a pause. 'About Viola –' but what could I ask her? My mind had gone blank. 'Tell me – did she always live at Staplefield?'

Unease crept over her face. I sat very still and waited until her expression grew calm again.

'Viola wrote stories. Tell me about them.'

'Ghos' stories. She wrote ghost stories.'

The voice had grown more animated. Her eyes flicked open, stared directly at me, and closed again.

Then she said something that sounded like, 'one came true'.

'Did you say, one came true? How? What do you mean?'

No answer.

'Mother, what came true?'

Her grip on my fingers tightened. Her eyelids fluttered, her breathing quickened. Again no answer.

'Mother, who was the woman in the photograph I found? Was it Viola?'

Her eyes shot open, glaring.

'NO!' It came as a hoarse shriek. She sat bolt upright. The unseeing eyes settled on my face.

'Gerard? Why are you here?'

'Mother, come back – you're having a bad dream –'

'You shouldn't be here. *She'll see you* –'

Her face was convulsing again.

'Mother, wake up!'

Recognition came back. She sank down amongst the pillows.

'Gerard.'

'You were dreaming, Mother.'

She lay silent for a while, breathing harshly.

'Mother – what did you mean, in your dream, she'll see you?'

A quick, uneasy glance.

'How did you know?'

'You were talking in your sleep.'

'I dreamed you were asking me questions, like you used to when you were – what else did I say?'

'You said – you said the woman in the photograph wasn't Viola. Who was she?'

She didn't reply. A different kind of horror was creeping into her expression. As in that moment when you still can't believe you could possibly have done something so appalling. The gas left full on, a child alone in the house.

'Gerard, I'm very tired. I want you to take me back to my room now.' She spoke the words stiffly, through a mask of dread.

'Is the pain very bad?'

'Yes.' But it didn't look like physical pain. We made our slow way up the hall.

'Gerard,' she said when I had settled her into bed, 'bring me the kitchen steps.'

I looked at her, nonplussed.

'The kitchen steps. In case – in case I need to get up.'

'Mother, you've got the buzzer, how can they possibly help—'

'*Just bring them.*'

'If you insist. But you must promise me—'

'*Gerard!*'

Bewildered, I went to fetch them: three aluminium steps with a vertical handle to grasp as you climbed up.

'Thank you, dear. Leave them next to my bed-table.'

Her bed was still where it had always been, its headboard centred against the boarded-up fireplace. Floor-to-ceiling cupboards had been built into the alcoves on either side of the chimney. Her bed-table was on the right-hand side of the bed, nearest the door.

'Mother, if there's anything you want me to get down for you—'

'No, dear. What I'd like, if you're not too tired, is for you to make us some more of that nice vegetable soup. I'll have a sleep now. Close the door as you go out.'

She did look utterly exhausted. Reluctantly, I left the room. For several long minutes I hovered outside the door. Not a sound. I eased the handle open and looked in. She was breathing heavily through her mouth. I stood there watching for what felt like many minutes more, but she did not stir.

Something must have alerted me, because I was already through the kitchen door and running when the crash came. I found her on the carpet beside the overturned steps. The topmost cupboard door was half open.

At the hospital they told me she had a depressed fracture of the skull, just above the left eye. All they could do was put her on a drip and wait to see if she recovered consciousness. I sat beside the bed with her hand resting in mine and talked to her as the nurses came and went and the night hours crawled by. Once or twice I thought her dry, rice-papery fingers twitched very slightly in response. Towards morning I must have dozed off, for without any perceptible interval I became aware that her hand had grown colder, and that the only sound of breathing in the room was mine.

A week after the funeral, I was sorting through the papers in the study. The furniture had not altered since my father had died: a five-drawer olive green army surplus filing cabinet, a very small three-drawer desk and a wooden chair filled the entire space.

I was still on leave. Friends from the library would phone and ask if they could call by, and I would make them tea or coffee and agree that it must be very hard for me having been so close to my mother, and what a wonderful person she had been, and feel guilty about counting the days until I could be with Alice.

All of my mother's clothes and shoes had already gone to the goodwill shop. The books were packed and stored. As soon as probate was granted, I would put the house on the market. I had worked my way from the front rooms, starting with my mother's bedroom, right through to the sunroom, without finding a single fragment of her thirty-four years in England. But something of her would be making the return journey. I had decided to scatter her ashes – her 'cremains', as the funeral director insisted on calling them – at Staplefield. I was trying to persuade Alice to be there too, but she thought this was something I should do alone.

On returning from the hospital, I had gone straight to my mother's room to find whatever it was she had died trying to reach. But there was nothing in the top cupboard except the dust of years and the desiccated shells of millipedes. Each of the enclosed alcoves had a wardrobe-style door from floor to head height opening on to hanging space, and a smaller rectangular door to the high cupboards above. The high cupboards were simply enclosed storage boxes. I looked in the one opposite, but that too was empty. I found nothing on the floor or under the bed, and nothing but clothes in the wardrobes on either side. Or in the bottom drawer of her dressing-table, where I had seen the photograph, and later 'Seraphina'; I had found it unlocked and empty. If she had managed to remove anything from the cupboard before she fell, she must have swallowed it.

I had deliberately put off opening the filing cabinet in the study, saving it until last; so long as I hadn't looked, I might still find something. There were papers here all right. Masses of them. My father had evidently filed every piece of official correspondence he had ever received, receipts for every bill he had ever paid; and my mother had followed his example religiously. Thirty-six years of electricity bills, stamped and receipted and filed in strict chronological order. A folder full of notices dating back to 4 January 1964, warning the householder that the supply of electricity would be interrupted on such and such a day. Ditto for water and council rates, insurance, tax returns, car service, registration, driving licences, medical bills. Receipts, instructions, guarantees, and full service history for every appliance they had ever owned. All of my old school reports. On and on. It looked as if the only papers my mother had not kept were personal letters, assuming she had ever received any. Or anything that might indicate she had ever lived anywhere but Mawson.

I moved on to the desk. Writing paper in the top drawer, pens, pencils and rulers in the second, envelopes in the third. And at the back of the envelope drawer, a packet of unused aerograms so ancient they belonged in a museum. Australia. 9d. Slipped in amongst them was a stiff blue envelope, unsealed, which also looked very old; the dark brown glue on the flap was cracked and flaking.

Inside the envelope was a black and white photograph of my mother with me, only a few months old, perched on her knee in one of those miniature flying suits that babies wear, beaming up at her and waving one chubby hand in obvious excitement. I didn't recognise the room, or the sofa she was sitting on. She was smiling at me, looking amazingly youthful, far younger than she appeared in her wedding photograph. And different. For a start, her hair was much longer than I could recall; longer and curlier and more abundant. Her dress – I didn't know enough about fashion to say exactly, but it was more stylish than anything I could remember her in; and sleeveless, which she didn't usually wear, even in summer.

And there was something else unusual, apart from her looking so extraordinarily young and carefree. In the albums in the sitting-room we had innumerable photographs of me at every possible stage of development, but nearly all of them were of me and my father, or of me alone. My mother's dislike of being photographed had extended even to being photographed with me; in the ones in which we both appeared, she was invariably looking away from the camera so that you could not see her face. Of all the photographs of her – of us – I had seen, this was by far the most joyful. So why had she hidden it away at the back of a drawer?

I went through the packets of envelopes much more carefully, but there was nothing else in the drawer. Taking the photograph with me, I wandered out of the study and up the hall to her bedroom, not really knowing why. I went over the dressing-table again, removing all the drawers and checking the underside of each one. Nothing but dust, and a reel of white thread which had fallen down inside the cabinet.

The kitchen steps were still where I had left them, beneath the right-hand cupboard. Could she possibly have been looking for this photograph? I remembered the horror creeping over her face, that last afternoon in the sunroom.

I had to keep you safe.

From whom? Or what?

You shouldn't be here. She'll see you.

Who would see me? I caught myself glancing uneasily towards the door. Not Viola, surely? I couldn't recall the very last thing she'd said.

Take me back to my room, Gerard. Bring me the steps. Go away and make the soup.

I climbed up for another look at the top cupboard. There were faint marks like scratches on the dusty floor of the cupboard. But the dust was otherwise smooth and undisturbed. The floor was just a sheet – no, two half-sheets – of plywood, the underside presumably forming the top of the wardrobe. I pried at the edge of the right-hand half and it lifted out of the frame.

Only I was not looking down through the wardrobe, but

into a shallow recess. In which lay a large sealed envelope. Inside was a thick wad of typewritten sheets. 'The Revenant'. Below that, in the lower right-hand corner of the title page, 'V.H. 4 Dec 1925' in a clear, spiky hand. I checked the envelope again and found a small printed slip: *With the author's compliments.*

Still standing on the top step, I began to leaf through the typescript. As I turned to descend, a photograph slid from between the pages and fluttered to the floor.

I had imagined that if I ever saw her again, recognition would be instantaneous and complete. But it was not quite like that. The dress with shoulders gathered like the wings of angels, the swan-like carriage of her head, chin slightly lifted, gazing off to the left, the dark mass of hair drawn back in what I now knew was called a chignon – all seemed exactly the same, yet I felt sure something had changed. Well of course she looks different, I told myself, *I've* changed. I was ten when I last saw her. I hadn't heard, then, of chignons, or fine bones, or classically proportioned features: we didn't talk like that at Mawson Primary. Nor had it struck me that she wore no jewellery at all, neither necklace nor earrings. The back of her dress was secured at the neckline by a plain velvet bow.

Of course I hadn't met Alice then, either. This woman didn't look like my imagination of Alice; she was beautiful, but in a more spiritual, less sensuous way. Yet she reminded me of someone; someone I'd seen very recently.

The photograph in the blue envelope. Side by side, the family resemblance was clear; a resemblance that must have faded very quickly, for I couldn't see it in any of my memories of my mother. And since the woman in the studio portrait was, just as clearly, not my mother, who else could she be but the young Viola?

I turned over the photograph and saw that there was writing on the back: a faint inscription in pencil.

'Greensleeves'
10 March 1949

Greensleeves? If that was the date it was taken, it couldn't be Viola after all. But I couldn't imagine this face inspiring horror in anyone. Not even my mother. All these years I'd assumed she had beaten me for looking at the photograph. But she'd never actually said so. And since she'd already disposed of *The Chameleon* (unless it was hidden somewhere else in the house), I picked up 'The Revenant' again and went through it more carefully. But there was nothing else hidden between the pages. It was just a plain typescript, a fair copy on quarto paper with no corrections or annotations.

One came true. I took the typescript over to the window and settled down on the floor, my back against the wall, with the story my mother had died trying to keep me from reading.

The Revenant

Part One

THOUGH ASHBOURN House stood only a few hundred yards from the village of Hurst Green, the surrounding woodland was so dense, and the trees so tall, that Cordelia had often imagined herself living deep in an enchanted forest. As a child, perched high above the lane in her favourite window-seat, she had dreamed away whole days as Mariana, the Lady of Shalott, and other melancholy heroines of romance. No handsome prince had so far appeared, possibly because the sign at the village end of the lane made it look like a private drive. Just beyond the house, to the left, the lane diminished to a muddy footpath. It was, in fact, a right-of-way through the wood, but the villagers seldom used it, and not simply because of the mud. According to local legend, as Cordelia had later discovered, the house was not only unlucky, but troubled by the apparition of a veiled woman in black: the ghost of her own grandmother, Imogen de Vere.

It was a tall, tower-like stone house, perhaps a hundred years old, evidently built, as Cordelia's Aunt Una was fond of complaining, by someone with a passion for climbing stairs. From the rear of the house, the land sloped downwards, and from the upstairs windows you could look out across the garden and above the treetops, over green pastures and wooded hills. But at the front, there was only a narrow forecourt of gravel and then the lane, beyond which the trees grew even higher than the house. By the time she was sixteen, Cordelia had advanced from the window-seat to the sill of the second-floor sitting-room window, where she liked to read on summer afternoons. Aunt Una could never see her leaning against the frame of the open window, so close to the edge that she could look straight down the long vertical fall to the gravel below, without an involuntary squeak of dread. But Cordelia was not in the least afraid of heights.

About ghosts she was not so sure. When she was seven or eight, she and her sister Beatrice had spent many days happily playing at ghosts with the aid of a worn-out sheet begged from Mrs Green the housekeeper, creeping along gloomy corridors and lurking in empty rooms, sending one another into paroxysms of pleasurable terror, until one afternoon it occurred to Cordelia to surprise Beatrice by dressing up as Grandmama's ghost. All she could recall of Grandmama, who had died just before her fifth birthday, was a silent, veiled figure, sitting by the fireside or moving about the garden. It was not polite to mention the veil. As Aunt Una had privately explained, Grandmama always wore it because she had once been very ill, and light was bad for her skin.

Grandmama's room had not been disturbed since the day of her funeral. The door was always locked. But Cordelia had recently discovered that the keys to the bedroom doors were interchangeable. Thinking that her father was safely downstairs in the drawing-room, she stole into the room, which smelt strongly of camphor, and began opening chests and closets to see what she could find. In the bottom drawer of a clothes-press, she came upon Grandmama's black veil, neatly laid out all by itself. She lifted it out and pressed the cool material against her face, breathing in camphor, and some other medicinal smell, and a very faint fragrance of perfume. When she put it on, the front of the veil came right down to her waist, whilst the back – it went all around, like a headdress—almost touched the floor. She could still see, though dimly, but when she looked in the long mirror her face was quite invisible, and because of the angle it seemed as if the veil was hovering of its own accord.

Panic seized her, and she fled into the corridor, only to confront a huge, dark figure blocking the way to the stairs. Her own shriek was drowned by a hoarse yell of terror, booming and echoing around her as she tore at the constricting veil and saw that the dark figure was in fact her father. Worse than her own fear, worse even than the beating that followed, was the memory of that cry, and of his face, momentarily frozen in horror before rage came to his rescue. Later he told her that he was sorry to have beaten her; he had lost his temper, he said, seeing her in Grandmama's veil. Though he was usually very indulgent, Cordelia found the apology troubling; she knew she had been terribly wicked, and deserved her punishment, and it seemed to her that Papa was trying to convince her—and perhaps himself—that he had not been frightened. She knew that Papa, a soldier, was as brave as a lion; Aunt Una was always saying so, yet she dared not ask what had so alarmed him. There were no more games of ghosts, and she was plagued for many months by a nightmare in which she was pursued and finally cornered by a malevolent, shrouded figure, who appeared in many guises but always became, in the instant before she woke in terror, her grandmother in the act of raising her veil.

She was, at the same time, fascinated by the portrait—the only surviving likeness of Imogen de Vere—which had hung on the second-floor landing for as long as she could remember. It showed a woman of great beauty, apparently in her early twenties, though she must have been about thirty-five when it was painted, against a dark, indistinct background. Her face, lit from above, was partly in shadow, accentuating the darkness of her large, luminous eyes. She wore an emerald green gown, cut high at the neck; her heavy, copper-coloured hair was loosely pinned up, with a few escaped strands curling across her forehead. The artist (who had not signed his name to the portrait) had captured some elusive quality in her gaze—an intense serenity, or perhaps a serene intensity of feeling—which compelled your eyes to return again and again to hers.

Though Cordelia did not doubt that the woman in the picture was, or had become, her grandmother, she found it curiously difficult to associate the face that so compelled her imagination with the veiled figure of memory—or nightmare. By the time she was fully grown, Cordelia had only to pause in front of the picture to feel that she was resuming a wordless intimacy which had accompanied her all through her childhood. Somehow her sense of communion with the portrait had become entwined with her feeling for her lost mother, whom she had never known: Frances de Vere had died of puerperal fever a few days after giving birth to Beatrice. It was not a matter of physical resemblance, for the photograph on Cordelia's dressing-table was of a shy, fair-haired girl, smiling tentatively at the camera.

She looked about sixteen years old, and had died before her twenty-fourth birthday.

Imogen de Vere herself had died when she was not much more than fifty. Over the years, Cordelia had gradually assembled fragments of her grandmother's history; she had deduced that Imogen must have separated from her husband at about the time of the onset of her illness, and with her only child Arthur (Cordelia's father) who was then twelve or thirteen years old, come to live at Ashbourn House with her cousin Theodore Ashbourn and his sister Una. The illness—a mysterious and virulent disease of the skin, which no doctor had ever been able to diagnose—had plainly been far more severe than Cordelia had once believed. Imogen de Vere had spent the last fifteen years of her life at Ashbourn, permanently veiled and in constant pain. She slept badly, and would roam about the house in the small hours. Uncle Theodore had sometimes seen her wandering the garden by moonlight; she seemed to find relief in movement, and had walked miles every day until her final illness. So it was hardly surprising that many of the inhabitants of Hurst Green would swear to having seen a veiled figure peering from an upstairs window, or gliding amongst the trees of Hurst Wood, long after Imogen de Vere had been laid to rest in the village churchyard.

On a chill, grey afternoon late in February, soon after her twenty-first birthday, Cordelia was standing in front of the portrait, lost in sombre reflection. Beatrice had declined, reasonably enough in view of the weather, to come out for a walk, but then a little later Cordelia had seen her disappearing along the lane in waterproof and Wellingtons. As children, they had played together constantly, but their intimacy had not survived the death of their father, who had fought unscathed through four years of war only to lose his life a month before the Armistice. Cordelia, who was then thirteen, had tried to comfort her sister, but Beatrice had refused all consolation. She would not speak of her father, or remain in the room if his name was even mentioned, and if she wept for him, she did so alone. Nor would she tolerate any inquiry as to her feelings, which seemed to alternate between listless apathy and a sullen, silent anger at everyone and everything around her.

Thus she had remained for many months, and it seemed to Cordelia that her sister had never entirely recovered; or at least, that relations between them had never been the same. Perhaps they had simply grown apart, even in small things: both, for example, were avid readers, but Cordelia would always set her book aside for a chance of conversation, whereas Beatrice, who read only novels, had become even less tolerant of interruptions. In the game of animal comparisons Cordelia liked to play in the privacy of her own imagination, her sister had always been a cat. Beatrice had inherited their mother's almond-shaped eyes; her face narrowed markedly to a small, determined chin, making her cheekbones look more prominent than they really were. Now, at nineteen, she was more than ever the cat that walks by itself: watchful, silent, aloof, disdainful of petting, the kind that will settle only on the lap of its own choosing. Cordelia had sometimes accused herself of clinging to a romantic ideal of sisterly intimacy; yet she could not shake off the feeling that a door had been closed against her at the time of Papa's death, and never reopened.

Beatrice would not concede that anything had altered

between them, but there was something about the very adroitness with which she had learned to evade her sister's overtures that seemed to say: "You have wounded me very deeply, though you profess not to understand what you have done; so I will not quarrel; there would be no point; of course we shall stay friends, but I shall never completely trust you again. As for the door you accuse me of closing, you are quite mistaken; it is you who have closed it; or perhaps there never was a door, only a blank wall, which is no more than you deserve." Cordelia had racked her memory and her conscience; she had privately asked her aunt and uncle, whether they knew of anything she had done to offend her sister, but no, Beatrice had said nothing against her. "You must not take it personally," Uncle Theodore had said only recently. "Your sister's nature is very different from yours; she turns inward, away from others, as you turn towards them. I don't think she has ever got over your father's death. You must not blame yourself for what is none of your fault."

His words came back to her as she stood on the chilly landing. The mention of her father—and a certain unease in Theodore's tired, kindly, slightly bloodshot eyes (a beagle's, or a bloodhound's; she had never quite decided)—had stirred an old, obscure suspicion that his death was somehow the cause of the estrangement. As if summoned by Imogen de Vere's intent, shadowed gaze, her thoughts were drawn along a path from which she had always turned uneasily aside, as she had once avoided the corridor that led past Grandmama's bedroom.

Papa had blamed Beatrice for their mother's death. Not consciously, she felt sure; and perhaps "blame" was too strong. He would have been shocked, no doubt, if anyone had confronted him with the idea. But just as she had always known that she was Papa's favourite, so she had become aware of a certain constraint in his manner towards Beatrice. Whenever he came home on leave, the two girls would be allowed to wait, if they were not at school, at the front gate, and run along the lane to greet him as he appeared at the turning. Cordelia, being the elder, would always reach him first, and fling herself into his arms, and he would swing her high into the air and onto his shoulder. But with Beatrice he was never quite as spontaneous; sometimes he seemed almost to recoil for an instant, though the shrinking would be as swiftly checked, and it seemed to Cordelia that he never sought Beatrice out, whereas he would often come looking for her when he wanted a game (which was how he had caught her wearing Grandmama's veil that afternoon). Everyone else in the house, including Mrs Green, had made a special pet of Beatrice, and yet Cordelia had never felt any the less loved; on the contrary, she was proud to be included in a sort of adult conspiracy to spoil Beatrice (though nobody had put it quite like that), especially when Papa was away with his regiment. They had kept up the conspiracy through four anxious years of war, until the arrival of the letter from the War Office, the dark winter of grieving, and Beatrice's retreat into sullen, resentful silence.

The suspicion that her father had, however unconsciously, held Beatrice responsible for the loss of their mother, did not begin to trouble Cordelia until after his death. The more she struggled against the idea, the more firmly it took root, until she felt compelled to question her aunt. But instead of offering the hoped-for reassurance, Aunt Una had looked very grave, and talked of how deeply

Papa had loved their mother, and how he had married her as soon as they had both turned twenty-one and no longer needed their parents' consent—though Grandmama, she added hastily, had given them her blessing; they had been married from Ashbourn House . . . and of course it had been a terrible blow to Papa, losing their mother so young, but Cordelia must always remember that he had loved both her and Beatrice very dearly, and try not to think such troubling thoughts.

Years later, she had learned from Uncle Theodore that the reason they had never seen their grandparents on Mama's side, and the reason Papa had never so much as mentioned them, was not because they were dead, but because they had never forgiven him for the death of their only daughter. They had blamed him, in other words, just as he had blamed Beatrice.

But why should Beatrice have turned against her, Cordelia, on account of their father's death? For that was what had happened, she was sure of it. That subtle note of accusation . . . as if Cordelia had somehow betrayed her sister; but how? By having been his favourite? Or had Beatrice divined the reason behind Papa's reserve and taken the burden of Mama's death upon herself?—and then assumed that Cordelia blamed her too? Such a heavy burden . . . but why should she assume that? And spurn all reassurance? *It is not fair; why does she hate me so?*

Cordelia again became conscious of her surroundings, realising that she had spoken the words aloud. The face of Imogen de Vere seemed to coalesce out of its dark background, glowing as if lit from within. "No, it is not fair," she imagined the portrait replying; "do you think it was fair that I lost my beauty overnight?" Of course not, any more than the loss of Papa had been fair; but knowing that half the families in the kingdom had lost fathers, husbands, sons, and brothers had not made their own loss any easier to bear. It had not been fair of Mama's parents to hold Papa responsible for her death. Or to refuse to acknowledge their own granddaughters because of it. "Unto the third generation . . ." But Papa had not sinned; and besides, the last of her belief—at least in the omnipotent God of the Scriptures—had died with him.

Aunt Una and Uncle Theodore had done their conscientious best, making sure that she and Beatrice had been christened and confirmed, but Cordelia felt that neither of them really believed. Even Mr Gathorne-Hyde, the present vicar, did not sound as if he believed his own sermons about God's mysterious ways and the gift of free will. A poisoned, maleficent gift, that allowed men to slaughter one another wholesale. Or a single child to starve. Beatrice had refused to enter a church since the day the War Office letter arrived. Yet Cordelia still occasionally attended. More often, she would slip into St Mary's when it was empty and stand for a while in the dim silence, which seemed to echo even when the church was completely still, breathing the smells of ancient timbers and stone, musty cassocks and snuffed candles and dried flowers, "hoping it might be so"—without even knowing what "it" might be.

Last autumn, she had gone with Uncle Theodore to visit Percival Thornton, the father of one of Papa's dead comrades. Robert Thornton had died only a few months before Arthur de Vere, and the families had kept in touch. Their visits, though inevitably painful, meant a great deal to Mr Thornton, a widower who lived quite alone. Each time they saw him, he looked thinner, greyer and more stooped; his grief was visibly consuming him. Robert's medals, brilliantly polished, were displayed in a mahogany case in the parlour; his dress uniform, immaculately brushed, hung beside his bed in his old room, and the house was crowded with photographs of Robert at every stage of his short life, most of them taken by Mr Thornton.

There was a settled ritual to these visits. They began with an inspection of various mementoes, followed by tea, which Cordelia always insisted on preparing, and then a stroll in the garden if the weather was fine. But on this occasion, it seemed to Cordelia that he was striving to conceal an unwonted, almost feverish anxiety. She noticed, too, that since their last visit his hands had become curiously blotched and stained. As they were finishing their tea, he asked, rather hesitantly, whether he might show them a photograph.

They were naturally expecting yet another portrait of Robert, but the picture he brought out showed only a vacant bench which stood against the hedge at the rear of Mr Thornton's garden, beside an ornamental fountain—a tiered array of stone dishes, each wider than the one above, with a cherub at the top, though the water had long ceased to flow: the dishes were filled with autumn leaves. Dappled sunlight, evidently filtering through the branches of an overhanging tree, was falling upon the bench.

Cordelia had moved over to sit on the arm of her uncle's chair; Mr Thornton remained hovering on the other side. She could feel his agitation increasing as the seconds passed, and neither she nor Uncle Theodore could find anything to say.

"Don't you see him?" said Mr Thornton at last, in a

voice of desolate appeal. A blotched and trembling finger indicated the end of the bench nearest the fountain. Peering more closely, Cordelia suddenly saw that if you took a semicircular splash of light, falling roughly where the head of a seated person might have been, to be the lower half of a human face, the confusing patchwork of light and shadow beneath could form the suggestion of a body—a man's body, if you took the shadows of (presumably) two vertical branches for legs . . . and if you then went back to the "face", there were indistinct patches of shadow which would do for his mouth and nostrils, and yes, two faint specks of light more or less where his eyes ought to be . . . and below, glimpses of a collar, a shoulder, a lapel . . .

Robert Thornton, as she had last seen him nine years ago, in his officer's cap, uniform jacket, breeches and boots, materialised upon the bench. The back of her neck prickled; she glanced at her uncle, whose bewildered expression had not altered; then up at Mr Thornton's anxious, imploring face, and back to the picture.

The figure had vanished. There was nothing but the empty bench, and the dappled shadows of leaves and branches. Again she fixed her eyes upon the "face", but she could not summon the illusion a second time; it remained simply a patch of sunlight on the hedge. Something drew her gaze away from the picture, to the framed photographs ranged along the mantelpiece; there was a gap near the end to the left, where last time, she was sure, there had been a picture of Robert Thornton, in uniform, seated on this same bench.

She heard a quavering intake of breath. Mr Thornton's gaze had followed her own.

"It is true then. He was there." He was smiling, and tears were streaming down his cheeks.

"Yes," she said, unhesitatingly, though the figure—or rather the memory of the other photograph—had not returned, and Uncle Theodore was looking as bewildered as ever. "Yes, I am sure he was."

Cordelia stood up and embraced the old man, who was almost sobbing with joy and relief.

"I thought I should move . . . the other . . . so as not to influence you. It was his favourite place in the garden, you see," he added, beaming down at Uncle Theodore, who could plainly see nothing at all.

"It is Robert, uncle," said Cordelia, hastily resuming her place in order to indicate where the "face" had been, "here on the bench, by the fountain."

"Oh—er—yes, yes of course. I am sure I see him now. Tell me—er—when was this taken, Percival?"

"Last week, dear friend."

"Last *week*? I mean—er, how extraordinary; that is to say, how wonderful . . ."

"Yes," said the old man. "I had not quite dared to believe it until Cordelia saw him too. I feared I might be deluding myself. And after so long . . . I had almost given up hope."

He moved slowly across to a cabinet on the other side of the room, and returned with a file-box which he set before them. It was full of photographs. Looking through them, Cordelia saw with something like horror that they were all of the empty bench, all taken from the same angle, in every degree of brightness from full sunlight to near-darkness, hundreds and hundreds of them.

"I read about it here, you see." Mr Thornton, his eyes still wet with emotion, passed them a large book.

Photographing the Invisible, Practical Studies in Spirit Photographs, Spirit Portraits and Other Rare Phenomena, by James McIntyre. "The camera, as you see, can sometimes detect what the naked eye cannot." To Cordelia, leafing through the pages, it seemed that a great deal of what the camera had detected was plainly fraudulent: ghostly faces, conveniently shrouded in a sort of soap-bubble haze, floated behind group portraits, or bobbed about on staircases with no visible means of support. She could tell that her uncle was struggling to hide his scepticism. Yet her own illusion had been utterly lifelike. Despite knowing what had caused it, the memory was still so vivid that she understood Mr Thornton's reaction only too well.

"I do all my own developing now," he continued. "Mr McIntyre says—or at least implies—that commercial developers are not always to be trusted. The Church, you know; they don't approve. And I had almost despaired, after so many attempts. But now . . . I am so happy, now you have seen him too."

Soon after, they went out into the garden. Though it was a mild, tranquil autumn day, Cordelia could not repress a slight shiver as they approached the now-celebrated bench. I don't think I could ever sit there again, she said to herself; it would seem—like trespass, or tempting fate. Yet why should I find it sinister? I should simply be delighted for poor Mr Thornton.

But as the extremity of their host's emotion subsided, she became aware that he was not as happy as he professed to be. His earlier anxiety reappeared; he asked them several times whether they were completely certain they had seen Robert in the photograph. With each repetition, Uncle Theodore's assurances sounded less convincing, her own more forced. Her spirits sank lower as the afternoon wore on, until the pressure of Mr Thornton's haunted, beseeching gaze became quite unbearable, and despite the warmth of their farewells, she left with the dismal feeling that their visit had done him more harm than good.

"I wish he had never seen that book!" she said passionately, as they were walking back to the station. "What he really wants is for Robert not to have died in the war; to have him back alive and warm and breathing, and he can't have that, and can't bear it, and the photograph only torments him."

"Indeed. But—er—how did you know, my dear, exactly what he wanted us to see?"

She explained about her illusion.

"I see—or rather, I didn't. So you think it was simply your memory of the other photograph?"

"I suppose it must have been," she replied uneasily, remembering that Mr Thornton had not actually brought out the earlier picture for comparison, "only just for that instant, I really did see Robert, sitting there in his uniform . . ."

Cordelia was startled out of her recollection by the awareness that Uncle Theodore was standing beside her on the landing, contemplating the portrait on which her own unseeing eyes had been fixed.

"I am so sorry, my dear. I did not mean to alarm you. You seemed so deep in thought, I didn't like to interrupt."

"No, I'm glad to be interrupted. I was remembering our last visit to poor Mr Thornton."

Uncle Theodore, when agitated, had a habit of running

his hands through his thick, unruly silver-grey hair; today it was sticking out wildly in all directions. Small and wiry (at five feet seven, he was only a little above Cordelia's height), he had always looked years younger than his age. But today he seemed to be feeling the burden of his sixty-seven years; his face had taken on a greyish tinge, making the lines scored vertically down his cheek seem more than ever like fine scars or claw-marks. And there was a lurking indecision or anxiety in his bloodhound eyes that reminded her suddenly of Mr Thornton.

"Is something troubling you, uncle?" she asked, when he did not immediately reply.

"Not exactly—the fact is, my dear, I have something to say to you, and I don't know where to begin."

"Well," she smiled, "you should take the advice you always used to give me: begin at the beginning, and go on until you come to the end."

"Ah, the beginning . . ." he murmured, his eyes upon the face of Imogen de Vere. "Did you know," he continued, as if irrelevantly, "that your grandmother and I were once engaged to be married?"

"No, I didn't," said Cordelia, surprised.

"Ah. I thought perhaps Una might have said something."

"No, she hasn't."

"I see."

He paused, as if seeking guidance from the portrait.

"As you know, I grew up mainly in Holland Park; we only came here for the summers, then. Her father's house was only a few hundred yards from ours, but much grander. He was a City man—stocks and shares and directorships, all that sort of thing—and did very well out of it. Whereas we were in tea, as you know; perfectly comfortable, but by no means rich."

He lingered for a while on familiar ground, rehearsing the slow decline of the importing house founded by his grandfather, and the growth of the friendship between himself, his sister (Una was two years younger than Theodore), and Imogen Ward.

"Imogen and I were so slow to realise that we were in love—it was mutual—that I couldn't tell you when it began. We must have been eighteen or nineteen before anything was declared between us. But once we had spoken, we were quite certain—that is to say I was quite certain—that we would be married as soon as she had turned twenty-one.

"We knew that her father wouldn't like it. Horace Ward didn't approve of me, for a start; he thought, quite rightly, that I lacked ambition; and then, aside from the difference in wealth, he was violently opposed to marriage between cousins. We were second cousins, not first, and the relation was on our mothers' side, not his, but it made no difference. Any degree of relation was too much for him. From the day she first sounded him out, I was banned from their house, and she from ours, under threat of disinheritance. To do him justice, he was very fond of her; I think he genuinely believed that if he'd consented, he would have been making a sort of human sacrifice of his only daughter, for whom some princes mightn't have been good enough—quite apart from their habit of marrying their cousins. Anything she wanted was hers for the asking; anything except me."

Theodore was still speaking as if to the portrait of Imogen de Vere.

"Why must you be so reasonable, uncle?" said Cordelia tenderly. "He sounds absolutely horrible."

"It's a sort of failing, I suppose, always to see the other side. There are times when you should simply act . . . If I had known what I know now, I'd have waited, and asked her to run away with me on her twenty-first birthday. We went on meeting in secret, but inevitably, word got back to him; there were more scenes, and more threats . . . it was a terrible strain for her . . . until I began to fear that I really was ruining her life. In the end we agreed, Imogen and I, that I would go out to Calcutta as my father had hoped, to look after the business there, and stay two years, and then, if our feelings hadn't altered . . . She had just turned twenty when I left.

"Her letter telling me that she was engaged to a forty-year-old banker named Ruthven de Vere arrived about three months before I was due to come home. I stayed for fifteen years."

He turned away from the portrait, towards the window at the head of the staircase, studying the wintry fields. Traces of last week's snow still clung to the highest of the hilltops beyond.

"But uncle, I don't understand. How could she come to live with you, after all that?"

"Do you mean, because of the impropriety?"

"No, no, I mean, how could she accept, after what she'd done to you?"

"You mustn't be angry with her, my dear. Not on my account. She was seriously ill; both her parents were dead; de Vere had charge of all her money, what was left of it; she had nowhere else to turn. We'd kept in touch, you see.

Another excess of reasonableness on my part; doubtless many would call it lack of spirit."

"I wouldn't. She was very lucky, to have such a generous spirit to turn to," said Cordelia, taking his arm. "But why did she leave her husband, just when she became ill? Did Papa ever see his father again? Why would Papa never speak of him? Or Aunt Una? Even you? Did you ever meet him? Ruthven de Vere, I mean?"

"No, my dear. You must remember, I was away in India until the year before—it happened; if my mother had lived longer, I wouldn't have been here at all. And Imogen's letters had been mostly about Arthur. I had heard that they had a grand house in Belgrave Square—it was one of the first in the square to be equipped with electric light—and entertained very elaborately, but she hardly mentioned any of that. Or her husband. I wrote, of course, to let her know I was back, and she replied that she would love to bring Arthur to see us, and how sorry she was to hear about my mother.

"That was the last I heard from her, until I got her wire . . ."

He turned back to the portrait, wincing at some painful memory.

"Why on earth did she marry him in the first place?" cried Cordelia angrily.

"Because she was in love with him, I presume. He was handsome, and cultivated, and charming, as even Una—who attended the wedding only at my insistence—was forced to concede. And a most attentive husband—everybody agreed about that—"

"Uncle, will you *please* stop trying to defend him? You don't believe a word you're saying. The way you said 'attentive' made my flesh crawl; you're only making me loathe him even more."

"My dear, you misunderstand me. I'm not defending him, I assure you, not in the least; only trying to show you how the marriage must have appeared in the eyes of the world. Even at the end."

"I don't care what the world thought, I want to know what really happened. Why he never saw Papa again. Why Papa never once mentioned him. Uncle, have you all been hiding something you think is too horrible for me to hear? I'm twenty-one now, I'm a grown woman. Besides, it couldn't be worse than some of the things I've imagined."

"Are you quite sure of that?" he asked quietly, his eyes still fixed upon the portrait. Something in his tone set her skin crawling again, though she tried not to show it, and for a little while neither of them spoke.

Struggling to reconcile her anger at the woman who had betrayed a true and faithful lover to marry for money (for surely she wouldn't have accepted de Vere if he'd been poor?) with the familiar face before her, Cordelia found that she simply could not do it. This woman—the Imogen the painter had seen and rendered with such compelling subtlety—was surely incapable of deceit, cruelty, or greed. She looked so . . . *untouched*, that was it . . . so entirely self-possessed . . . that calm, accepting gaze that gave you the impression she understood exactly what was in your heart . . . a perfect stillness, yes, but living, vibrant, trembling on the edge of speech. "Thou still unravished bride of quietness": the words came to her unbidden; and with them the awareness that her anger had melted away.

"I see why you could not be angry with her," she said at last.

"I am glad you see that, my dear. It is a true likeness. His name was Henry St Clair—the painter, I mean."

"But you've always told me, uncle, that you didn't know who painted it."

"I said it was by an unknown artist, which was, and remains, true. But yes, I equivocated. When your dear father died, I resolved not to burden you with anything of—of which we must now speak—until it became necessary to do so. But now you are indeed twenty-one, and a grown woman, the necessity is upon us."

Once more he took counsel from the portrait.

"She met him—Henry St Clair—in a gallery in Bloomsbury. At a small exhibition of landscapes, including one of his, which she happened to be admiring while he was there. This is what she told me, you understand, on the one day we spoke of it. She described him very vividly: freckled and wind-burnt from a recent sketching tour—on foot, sleeping under trees; he couldn't afford so much as a bed in a village inn—slender, with one of those fresh, boyish faces that makes a man look years younger than he really is, brown eyes, curly brown hair which he wore quite long—a sort of animated brown study, she said, because he was wearing a brown velveteen jacket, somewhat paint-stained, and brown corduroy trousers.

"She bought the picture; they left the gallery together, and walked all the way up to the Heath, where they sat and talked for hours. That first afternoon, she said, was like emerging from a dark cavern into sunlight; there was a radiance about his personality . . . you needn't frown for my sake, my dear; I encouraged her to speak freely.

He warned her that he was constitutionally vulnerable to melancholia, but throughout the time she knew him, he remained in this sunny, upland mood. And if it hadn't ended so appallingly, I would have been simply glad, I assure you . . . but I must not run ahead of myself.

"He had his studio above a restaurant in one of the back streets of Soho; I believe the family who ran it spoke almost no English. He told her he liked being surrounded by people talking in languages he couldn't understand; he found the noise of the kitchen cheering, and could eat downstairs for practically nothing. And after years of living hand to mouth, a modest legacy from a remote relative had—or so he assured her—lately freed him from the daily struggle for survival.

"The picture she bought—for two guineas; he would accept no more than the gallery's asking-price—was the first he had ever sold. He had been in London for several years, working relentlessly at his painting whenever he was not out earning his living (work, he said, had always been the best anodyne for his melancholia), never satisfied with what he produced, always striving to surpass himself. He had exhibited canvases before, during fits of enthusiasm, but had always removed them when the inevitable darkening of his mood followed, and his tendency towards merciless self-criticism regained the upper hand. But their—friendship was the word she insisted upon—their friendship, and the reprieve it brought from his despondency, gave him the impetus to work towards an exhibition of his own, and to begin the portrait you see before you.

"He had worked at portraiture as hard as he had worked at his landscapes, using various members of the restaurant-keeper's family for models, but every attempt before this had been painted over or scraped out. At first she worried about his devoting so much time to the picture, which obviously couldn't be shown. She came to his studio as often as she could, whenever her husband was—as she thought—safely occupied in the City. But as the weeks passed, she watched him becoming calmer, more confident, more assured, until, she said, the subtle transformation taking place in him became as absorbing as the progress of the portrait itself. Whilst he was working, they hardly exchanged a word, but those days of silent communion were, she said, amongst the happiest of her life—"

"It was not fair of her to say such things, to you of all people!" said Cordelia.

"Very little in life is fair. What Imogen Ward was to me, Henry St Clair was to her. We don't choose such attachments, my dear; they choose us. She came to me at the worst moment of her life; that was reward enough. I wanted, above all, to understand. And as you will shortly realise, there were things it was necessary for me to know.

"As to her relations with her husband; there was much that she withheld, but the truth was plain enough. Ruthven de Vere was not—or had not been—a cruel or negligent husband; on the contrary, he took enormous pride in her appearance; but there was an essential coldness at the heart of his regard; he valued her as a collector would value a rare and precious stone.

"It was clear that she had ceased to love him, and that matters between them had come to a crisis, long before she met Henry St Clair. De Vere, you see, had been her father's protégé in the City. Horace Ward trusted him entirely, and so the terms of the marriage settlement allowed him to do more or less what he liked with Imogen's fortune, and, a few years later, with everything that came to her under the terms of her father's will. De Vere had always allowed her whatever she asked, but in such a way that almost everything she had ever bought was, at law, his property, even her clothes and jewels, as she discovered when she first asked him for a separation. If she left him, he assured her, she would leave with neither her money nor her son—in whom de Vere took very little interest; he seemed, she said, quite devoid of fatherly feeling, which made the threat even worse. And so she stayed.

"Until the day she met Henry St Clair, she had gone on playing her part with a sort of compliant indifference, waiting until Arthur would be old enough for her to leave. But from that day forward, she was playing for her life. When she was with St Clair, she never thought beyond the moment; away from him, her mind swarmed uncontrollably with plans, imaginings, hopes, longings, fears. Yet outwardly, as she knew from the compliments of her acquaintances, she had never looked more serene.

"Her husband, as she thought, suspected nothing. It was, she said, like tiptoeing around a sleeping gaoler, day after day, always managing to creep back into her cell before he stirred. Everything, she felt, must wait upon the completion of the portrait. Throughout that spring and summer, she was sustained by the conviction that if only St Clair could finish the picture before they were discovered, all would be well.

"In September, she was obliged to go away with her husband for a fortnight at some great country house. The day after their return to town—it was a Sunday, but she could wait no longer—she slipped away to the studio, where she found Henry St Clair contemplating the finished portrait. She was standing before the picture, with his arm about her waist, when something made her glance over her shoulder. Ruthven de Vere was standing in the doorway.

"She heard herself say, with perfect coolness, though she knew it was hopeless: 'Ruthven, this is Mr Henry St Clair, the artist, who as you see has just completed my portrait. I was keeping it as a surprise for you. Henry, my husband, Mr Ruthven de Vere.'

"St Clair stood paralysed. De Vere did not, by so much as the flicker of an eyebrow, acknowledge his presence. He offered his arm to Imogen as if they were quite alone. She allowed herself to be led from the room, down the narrow rickety stairs and out to a waiting cab, without another word being spoken.

"They reached Belgrave Square, still in silence. She had resolved to answer no questions, respond to no threats, volunteer nothing. But with Arthur—still only thirteen, though thankfully away at school—as hostage, her resolve soon crumbled. Besides, she was in fear of her life. If he had raved and ranted, she thought she could have resisted, but de Vere's constraint was terrifying. There was a sibilance about his speech that reminded her of steam escaping from an engine, and when his spittle touched her cheek, it burned like acid.

"That one glimpse from the doorway of the studio had fired a train of suspicion that burned through hours of question and accusation, towards an insane conclusion. They were alone in his study; he had ordered the servants to admit no one, and to remain below stairs. Treating every denial as an admission, he forced the date of her meeting

St Clair back and back through the years until he had persuaded himself that they had been lovers before he, de Vere, had even met her; from whence it followed inexorably that Arthur was not his child.

"She had refused, until then, to admit that she and St Clair had been anything more than friends. Now she saw, too late, that her denials had spurred her husband toward the most dangerous delusion of all. In that extremity, she believed that the only way to save Arthur's life was to surrender her own: if her husband strangled her, or beat her to death, then surely the police would lock him up and Arthur would be safe.

"So she told him the truth—exactly what truth, she did not say, and I did not ask—expecting him to strike her down. Instead he grew quieter; but still he pressed and pressed for an admission that St Clair had been her lover throughout the marriage until, goaded past endurance, she said 'No, but I wish he had been'.

"He was standing over her as she spoke. She waited for the blow to fall, but without another word, he turned and walked out of the room, locking the door behind him.

"She rang repeatedly, but no one answered. Hours passed; she paced the room, rehearsing every imaginable horror. It was close on midnight before he returned.

"'I have decided,' he said, 'that you will leave this house tomorrow morning. You will take your son away from his school—he will no longer be welcome there—and do with him as you please. But there are conditions.

"'First, you will sign over to me all of your property: every farthing not already assigned to me by your father; every jewel, every trinket, everything but the clothes you stand up in.

"'Second, you will sign a paper confessing to your adultery with St Clair.

"'Third, you will sign an undertaking never to see or communicate with St Clair again.

"'Fourth, you will undertake never to communicate with any of our mutual acquaintance. You will leave London and never return. I wish it to appear that you and your son have vanished from the face of the earth.

"'Defy me in any particular, and you will lose your son. I fear you have spoiled him, but it is not too late to remedy that. You will also be branded in court as an adulteress, and I will bring an action against St Clair for alienation of affection which will bankrupt him.'

"'Why should I trust you?' she asked. 'Since you intend to be merciless in every other respect, why not keep Arthur, and make my punishment even more cruel?'

"'Because as long as you have your son, you will live in fear of losing him. As you surely will, if you do not keep to the letter of our agreement. As for trust, you must rely upon my word as a gentleman—and hope that I will be more scrupulous than you have been about your marriage vows.'

"He had already prepared the papers. One by one he set them before her. She signed mechanically, fatalistically, scarcely bothering to read what he had written, and then declared that she would leave the house at once. But he insisted she remain that night, alone in her bedroom, to give her 'time for reflection'. The bell, he said, had been disconnected, but she would find a cold supper waiting for her.

"Dizzy with fatigue and hunger, she dragged herself up to her room and bolted the door. There was also a connecting door between her bedroom and her husband's, opening into her room. It was locked already, but the key was missing.

"Despite her exhaustion, she had no intention of sleeping, but within minutes of eating her supper she felt overcome by an irresistible drowsiness. The food had been drugged. Fear lent her enough strength to drag a heavy chest across the connecting door. She collapsed onto her bed and sank into an abyss of darkness, from which she emerged the following morning with the sensation that her head was on fire. In the mirror she saw that her face and neck had turned a livid shade of purple.

"Her first thought was that her husband had exacted a terrible revenge. But the door into the corridor was still bolted on the inside; the chest stood where she had dragged it, blocking the connecting door; the window remained fastened on the inside, and from the sill to the area below was a sheer drop of thirty feet. The room was undisturbed, her pillow unmarked. Even if a corrosive spirit had somehow been introduced into the room, it could not have injured her so terribly without damaging the bedclothes.

"Then it occurred to her that she might have been poisoned as well as drugged. Apart from the burning sensation, she felt well enough, but how long would this last? Sick with horror, she dressed, put on a veil to hide her face, and despite her husband's threats, gathered up a few pieces of jewellery left to her by her mother, as well as all the money she had in her room.

"Thus far, she had not heard a sound from her husband's room. Listening at the other door, mustering the courage to open it and confront him—for surely he would be lurking outside—she became aware that the usual morning bustle was absent. Very quietly she undid the bolt and peeped out. The corridor was empty, the house completely still. All the way down to the front door she expected him to pounce, but no one appeared; for all the signs of life, the house might have been deserted. She let herself out into the street and secured a cab."

Theodore fell silent. He had become so absorbed in his own narrative that he continued to stare at, or rather through the portrait until Cordelia took his arm; then he turned slowly towards her like a man waking from a dream.

"I am very sorry, my dear. I fear I have said far more than I intended. The fact is, I was back in the drawing-room downstairs, thirty years ago, listening to Imogen. Even her voice was altered—by the illness, I mean—I had remembered it as a vibrant contralto; now she spoke in a hoarse, whispery monotone, all expression lost . . ."

"Uncle, why do you call it an illness? He *must* have poisoned her."

"I know, I know; and so your father always believed. But I asked a specialist privately, and he assured me there was nothing in nature that could produce such an effect. One man thought it might be Saint Anthony's Fire; another said it resembled a severe case of scalding, but her condition grew worse, not better, for weeks afterwards; we had a nurse here, all the time. Drugged or not, she would have woken instantly if she had been burnt . . . besides, there was no possibility of physical attack. No one could have got into that room."

"Uncle, why did you say 'physical attack' like that? Do you mean she might have been attacked in some other way?"

"Not unless you believe . . . but no, no . . . I think we

must put it down to a rare and horribly malignant infection, brought on by the strain of events."

Cordelia wanted to ask what he had been going to say, but the recollection was plainly so distressing that she did not like to press him.

"And Henry St Clair?" she asked. "Did she see him again? I suppose she must have, when he brought the picture here."

"No, my dear, she did not. And it was not St Clair who brought it here. Which brings me to the part that concerns you."

Cordelia's feet were numb with cold; her breath was clouding the chill air, but she did not want to break the thread. Serene, untouched, untroubled, Imogen de Vere gazed back at her while Uncle Theodore collected his thoughts.

"Of course she was desperate to let him know what had happened. Against my advice, she wrote to him the day after she arrived here, but at my insistence she did not give him this address. De Vere knew nothing of me, and I feared that even this minor breach might bring him down upon us. I tried to get word of Henry St Clair by indirect means, but without result, and soon she was too ill for us to think of anything else.

"For at least two months—it seemed a lifetime—she was delirious with pain, for all the doctors could do for her. But as she began to convalesce, I could tell that anxiety about St Clair was preying upon her mind, and so I agreed to go up to London and seek him out.

"It was midwinter by then, bleak and dismal. I took a cab from Victoria and sat wishing I had never heard of Henry St Clair as we jolted and slithered through the frozen slush, and the streets grew darker and narrower. At the restaurant—which was dim and narrow, and smelt strongly of garlic—I was told that Mr St Clair had gone away, weeks ago, nobody knew where. I thought perhaps they were protecting him until, with the proprietor's daughter acting as interpreter, I learned that all of St Clair's belongings, including the entire contents of his studio, had been carried off by the bailiffs. I spent the rest of the afternoon confirming what I feared. St Clair had been in debt to various moneylenders; the 'legacy' he claimed to have received had evidently been only the latest in a series of loans. De Vere had bought up all of his debts and called them in, bankrupting St Clair and seizing everything he possessed, including the portrait."

"Then how did it come here?" asked Cordelia. "Did you buy it from him?"

"No, my dear, I did not. I attempted to trace St Clair, without success. Nothing more was ever heard of him; he simply vanished from sight. All I ever told Imogen—I should have said, by the way, that all she wanted was to know that he was alive and well; quite apart from the risk to Arthur, she knew by then that the disfigurement would be permanent . . . I told her that the restaurant people had lost his forwarding address. She never learned what de Vere had done.

"Your father, as you know, was privately tutored here. By the time he turned sixteen, he was already so well-grown that de Vere would not have dared touch him; and if Imogen hadn't made Arthur swear never to approach his father, I think there would have been some sort of reckoning.

"But I must come to the point. Imogen lived—that is to say endured—the rest of her life here, without once going beyond the parish boundaries. We never heard from de Vere, or any of her former acquaintances—it must indeed have seemed as if she had vanished from the face of the earth. At her own request, we placed neither a death nor a funeral notice in any of the newspapers. Your father's army friends knew that his mother had died, but if news of her passing ever reached her old circles, nothing came of it.

"Now of course poor Imogen had nothing to leave your father. He had his commission by then, but a junior officer's pay is small, and my own fortunes had taken a turn for the worse. The business was on its last legs. I had taken a mortgage on this house, and was paying the interest out of what remained of the principal. It looked as if we should soon have to sell up and move to something exceedingly modest. With your father's help, I managed to hold out for another year, but the ground was slipping from under us.

"And then came the letter telling us that Ruthven de Vere had died, leaving his entire estate in trust to Arthur.

"It looked, at first glance, like belated repentance. But doubts very soon crept in. Nowhere in the will—which had been drawn up only weeks before de Vere's death—was Arthur acknowledged as his son: the income from the trust was left simply to 'Arthur Montague de Vere of Ashbourn House, Hurst Green, Sussex'. It was disturbing to learn that he had known where we lived. But the condition was far more so.

"In a nutshell: the income from the trust (about five hundred a year; the estate had been much depleted) would come to Arthur, provided that he agreed to take charge of the contents of a particular upstairs room in de Vere's house. The will did not specify what these contents were;

I shall come to that in a moment. The income would continue so long as these contents were maintained, together and intact, at Arthur's 'principal place of residence'. If anything were to be removed, sold, abandoned, destroyed or given away, the income would go to a distant relative in the north of Scotland. Otherwise it would pass, on your father's death, to his eldest child, and then to that child's eldest child—"

"—unto the third generation," said Cordelia softly.

Theodore looked at her with something like fear. "How could you know that?"

"Know what, uncle?"

"That those were the words of the will."

"I didn't. They just came to me, a while ago, when I was thinking about— something else. So what is to happen, at the third generation?"

"The trust descends to your eldest child. When that child dies, the income passes to the descendants of the remote relative in Scotland. As would already have happened if Arthur had not had children."

"And—the contents of the room?"

Theodore did not reply. Instead he moved towards a door in the panelling a few paces to the left of the portrait. Because of the arrangement of the stairwell, the landing extended quite some distance, from the window in the end wall to the entrance to the corridor which led to the girls' bedrooms. The door her uncle was now attempting to unlock stood immediately to the right of that entrance. This was the door to 'the storeroom'; Cordelia passed it several times a day, but had long ago concluded that, since it was never opened, nothing of interest could be stored there.

The lock snapped over; the hinges groaned; her uncle pushed the door wide and ushered her in.

Grey afternoon light filtered through two very grimy windows in the wall to her right. The room was perhaps fourteen feet by ten, but so crowded that it looked much smaller. The centre of the floor was taken up by various items of furniture, heaped against each other so as to make the most of the available space. A bedstead and a table, both standing on end, formed the backbone of the stack. From the doorway, Cordelia could make out the backs of two chairs, a wooden locker, a tin trunk, several other boxes, and various irregularly shaped bundles piled one on top of the other. Paintings hung from the picture rails all around the room, jostled together in no sort of order, some on board, some on canvas; below these, half-finished works, sheets of board, empty frames, rolls of canvas and other remnants stood propped against the walls, leaving a narrow aisle of dusty floorboards between them and the furniture piled in the centre of the room. The air was surprisingly dry, laden with odours of varnish and pigment, timber and canvas, leather and horsehair and traces of something sweet and aromatic that reminded her of a long-abandoned beehive.

"You see before you," said Theodore, "all the worldly goods of Henry St Clair. I took the liberty of opening the shutters this morning."

Cordelia took a few steps into the room. Dust lay thickly everywhere, stirring in small puffs as she moved, settling about her feet as she paused before a canvas depicting an expanse of tranquil waterway, stretching away into hazy distance, with several small boats in the foreground and the dim shapes of others farther off, a low green promontory or headland away to the right, and the great vault of the sky sweeping up from the far horizon, a dome of the palest blue, shot through with skeins and filaments of cloud. The artist had perfectly captured that quality of light which seems to float just above the surface of rippling water. Everything was held in suspension, even the foreground detail soft and blurred, yet somehow suggesting a delicacy of outline beyond the most exacting draughtsmanship.

"But this is beautiful, uncle. Why have you kept it locked away all these years?"

"We must come to that soon. But look around first."

The canvas beside it was very different. It showed a woodland path in dim, greenish moonlight, winding beneath tall, skeletal, overarching trees. About half-way along the path, a solitary figure, slightly hunched, was approaching. You could not quite decide whether it was man, woman, or child, or make out its features in the pale light, but its whole posture was expressive of profound unease, of someone trying to hurry without appearing to do so. Perhaps twenty yards further back, on the very edge of the path, something humped and hooded—or was it only a bush? or a small rocky outcrop about the height of a man?—seemed to be detaching itself from a thicket.

"*This* is his too?"

"I believe so."

Moving around the room, Cordelia saw at least a dozen landscapes strongly reminiscent of the tranquil waterway she had so admired. These, even at a cursory inspection, were the work of a man fascinated by the play of sunlight on water in all its manifold forms, not only liquid, but ice and frost, vapour and mist, haze and fog and every variety of cloud, a man in pursuit of some celestial vision in which air and fire, light and water were as one. But interspersed amongst them were at least as many pictures which could only be described as works of darkness: as melancholy, even malignant in feeling as the daylit scenes were joyous, a world of dark woods and crumbling, labyrinthine ruins, fraught with insidious menace.

"Imogen told me that he painted those when his melancholia was at its blackest," said Theodore as she examined another moonlit scene. "He called them exorcisms."

This one showed a series of high stone arches, some complete, some partly collapsed, each framed by the one in front, receding into the far distance over rubble-strewn ground. Shattered remnants of whatever they had once supported lay all around; the light gleaming on the debris had a greenish, phosphorescent tinge. Cordelia could not look at it without feeling that she was being drawn vertiginously into the picture. Again she found it difficult to believe that the canvas next to it, a study of sunlight on a fog-bank at dawn, had come from the same hand. Even in that grey, wintry light, the luminosity of the fog was extraordinary.

"I don't understand," she said at last. "If Ruthven de Vere hated him—Henry St Clair—so much, why did he keep his things? And why leave them to us? I thought 'the contents of the room' would be something horrible, from the way you spoke."

"So did I, my dear, when I read that will. It was written as if the bequest were a trap—or a curse—with the annuity as bait. That was why I went to see Mr Ridley, de Vere's solicitor, on Arthur's behalf.

"By a fortunate coincidence—one of the few in this dark affair—Mr Ridley's father and mine had been friends; we had never met, but it gave me an opening. And I could tell from the outset that he hadn't liked de Vere, and was himself uneasy about the will.

"It was a cold day, and he had a fire burning in the grate in his office. Rather than speak to me across his desk, he invited me to take a chair by the fireside, and very soon we were talking like old friends.

" 'I can't tell you what you most want to know,' he said, 'that is to say, the precise purpose behind the condition, because he didn't reveal it to me. But I'm afraid you're right in suspecting him of malign intent.'

"Then he asked me what I had made of the report of the inquest. I said I didn't even know there'd been an inquest into de Vere's death. And after a little self-inquisition, he told me everything he knew."

The mention of a fire had made Cordelia aware that she was shivering with cold. They locked up the room and hastened along the gloomy corridor to the sitting-room at the other end, where the coals of an actual fire were still smouldering.

"After the separation," Theodore continued, once they had got a good blaze going, "de Vere kept up his accustomed round of dinners and grand receptions. He let it be known that Imogen had suddenly resolved to make a religious retreat, and wanted no further contact with the world. The boy was being privately educated in the country. De Vere was even heard to say, 'She has taken the veil'—profoundly disturbing, even in retrospect; I was glad not to have known it at the time. No doubt his chivalrous behaviour was much admired.

"So he went on for another decade or more, until people began to notice that he was not as charming or attentive as formerly; he seemed troubled, abstracted, preoccupied. It was rumoured around the City that de Vere was losing his grip; he was certainly losing money. By the time of Imogen's death—of which, according to Mr Ridley, he certainly knew—he had sold his interest in the bank, withdrawn entirely from society, and discharged all but three of his servants. His appearance, too, had altered profoundly. Once the epitome of elegance in all matters of dress and grooming, he now, in these last months of his life, received Mr Ridley at Belgrave Square in a crumpled suit, carpet slippers, and with a grease-stained dressing-gown draped about his shoulders. His white hair—which only recently had been iron-grey, and immaculately trimmed—was long and scanty; he had lost most of his teeth, and his face had fallen in upon itself. He was sixty-seven, and looked twenty years older.

"I asked Mr Ridley if he thought de Vere had been of sound mind when the will was drawn.

"'Sound,' I remember him saying—he made a steeple of his fingers, like this—'sound, now that's a very broad church indeed. In the eyes of the law, yes: he knew the meanings of words; he knew exactly what he wanted, and he insisted on having it. Further than that I shouldn't like to go.'

"There was malice in him, Mr Ridley told me, malice but also fear, a morbid pressure of anxiety as palpable as the ill-will. De Vere had his chair hard against a wall, opposite the door, and all the time they talked, his eyes were darting about the room. And that was the last Mr Ridley saw of him until—as the executor—he received a note from the attending doctor, saying that de Vere had died in a fall from an upstairs window, and inviting him to step round.

"The room from which de Vere had fallen was the room containing everything that had once belonged to Henry St Clair.

"As de Vere's valet—though he can't have had much to do in the way of valeting—would later tell the inquest, St Clair's possessions had remained undisturbed, so far as anyone knew, in the upstairs boxroom until about a year before, when he had happened to see Mr de Vere unlocking the door. From then on, his master had visited the room more and more often until he was spending hours there every day, or rather night, for it was at night that he mainly went there, always with the door locked. Mr de Vere had made it clear from the outset that he was not to be disturbed during these visits. As to why he spent so much time in the room, or what he did there, the valet—whose name was William Lambert—could not say. Sometimes when he passed the door he would hear bumping and scraping noises, as if things were being dragged about, but mostly there was no sound at all.

"On the night of his death, de Vere had locked himself in the room at around ten o'clock. It was late in the autumn, a still, cold night. At about midnight William was dozing, fully clothed, in the attic on the next floor up—his master was in the habit of demanding refreshments in the small hours, and then sleeping very late—when he was woken by a splintering crash, followed by a thud in the area below. He ran downstairs and found Mr de Vere lying dead on the flagstones.

"The doctor, suspecting foul play, had the police summoned and the boxroom door forced. But there was no one within, no possible means of escape, and no sign of a struggle beyond the shattered window through which

Ruthven de Vere had made his last exit. Closer examination suggested that he had run full tilt at the closed window, and dived head-first through the glass.

"According to the servants, he had not received a single visitor since the signing of the will. The maid and the housekeeper spent most of their time below stairs, and so the valet was the principal witness to the final weeks of de Vere's life. William told Mr Ridley privately that he had sometimes watched unobserved as his master approached the boxroom: it had seemed to him that de Vere was drawn to it almost against his will, like a man defeated by his craving for drink, or a murderer compelled, as popular belief has it, to return again and again to the scene of his crime. This never came out at the inquest, at which the coroner, for reasons best known to himself, cut short the valet's halting attempts to characterise de Vere's mental state, and prevailed upon the jury to bring in a finding of death by misadventure.

"In Mr Ridley's view, the verdict should have been suicide while the balance of his mind was disturbed. I pressed him further on the matter of de Vere's sanity at the time the will was drawn.

"'If you're thinking the terms might be challenged on that ground,' he replied, 'I can't hold out much hope. The man's instructions were precise; he questioned me closely about the effect of the wording; there was nothing capricious or repugnant—that is to say, inconsistent at law—in the terms he required. Speaking privately, I am sure his intention was malign, but it was also founded upon a delusion: namely, that in bequeathing Mr St Clair's effects to your nephew, he was visiting some sort of evil upon him and his descendants. So there's really nothing to object to:

the intent to harm was no doubt real enough, but the danger is almost certainly phantasmal.'

"I asked why he had said 'almost certainly'.

"'Professional caution, I suppose. One never quite knows . . . there are more things . . . I suppose I had wondered whether the man might have concealed something dangerous amongst St Clair's effects. What sort of danger, you ask? Well, to cite another authority, it would cease to be a danger if we knew the answer to that. Most improbable, of course. A thousand to one the man was simply deranged. Of course, if you *were* to discover anything dangerous amongst the contents of that room, it would be a nice point, at law, whether the trust could require it to be left *in situ*. But if I were your nephew, I should accept the bequest, take the income, lock everything away securely, and think no more about it.'

"If we hadn't needed the money so badly," said Theodore, "your father would certainly have refused it. He loathed the idea of gratifying his own father, even in death, and insisted on having the entire income paid direct to me until you should reach the age of twenty-one; it is what we have lived on for the past seven years. I comforted myself with the thought that we were, in effect, recovering money that should have been Imogen's. But now that you are twenty-one, the income, and the responsibility, are yours alone."

"I should like things to go on just as they are," said Cordelia without hesitation. "Only . . . you haven't said why you brought out the portrait, and left all the other pictures shut away."

"Simply because I could not bear to think of her—her picture—locked away in the dark. As for the rest, it was your father's preference."

"And, did you do as the lawyer suggested, look to see if he—I suppose I must call him my grandfather—had hidden something dangerous in the room?"

"Well, I watched while St Clair's belongings were brought up from the cart—your papa had taken you and your sister out for the day—and saw nothing sinister. But it was not my place to examine things closely."

Cordelia stirred the fire reflectively.

"I think I should like to bring some of the other pictures out," she said after a while. "Am I allowed to do that? Would the trust stop me? How would they know?"

"The trust is three elderly gentlemen in the City. Mr Ridley's successor, a Mr Weatherburn, acts on their behalf; Mr Ridley retired soon after I met him. You are supposed to write to Mr Weatherburn once a year and assure him that the conditions have not been breached. He or his representative may appear at any time and demand to see that everything is in order. In fact we have been visited only twice: once soon after everything had arrived here, and again after I wrote to tell them of your father's death. Once you have made your own decision, I imagine they will send someone down: there are papers you will have to sign. You could ask whoever they send."

"I have already decided, uncle; I will accept. But—just supposing I said I didn't want the money, what would happen to the pictures?"

"Everything would be taken away, and stored by the trust until your eldest child reached the age of twenty-one; then the same offer would be made to him. If he declined, the entire contents of the room would be burnt to ashes—that's the actual phrase—under the supervision of the trust. As will happen in any case, when the line dies out or upon the death of your eldest child."

"How horrible! That makes me even more determined to bring them—well, perhaps not the exorcisms, but all the others—into the light where people can admire them. And—what if Henry St Clair is still alive? How old would he be now?"

"About sixty, I suppose."

"Then—shouldn't we try to find out? I mean, they are his things, really; my grandfather stole them, just as he stole Imogen's money. Though of course, if we gave them back, we would lose the income, wouldn't we?"

"Not only that, my dear. In law, those pictures are the property of the trust; supposing we found St Clair and returned them to him, we should all be charged with theft."

"What an evil old man! I hate to think of him as my grandfather. I suppose that's how Papa felt, only worse . . . So there is nothing we can do, in the long run, to save the pictures from being burned."

"I fear not, my dear."

"And Beatrice?" said Cordelia after a pause. "How much should I tell her?"

"That is for you to decide."

"It will only make her dislike me more," said Cordelia despondently.

"I know," replied Theodore with unusual candour, "but we must do the best we can. I will tell her, if you like, that the administration of the trust that supports us—if you are quite sure about that—"

"Quite certain."

"—has passed to you as the eldest. She need know no more than that, until you decide otherwise."

"Thank you, uncle. Tell me—and please don't pretend—why do *you* think she dislikes me so?"

"Envy, I fear—don't tell your aunt I said so—she envies you your good nature, your affectionate disposition, and—to be entirely frank—your having been your father's favourite."

"I don't think my nature is as good as you make it out to be, uncle. But even if it were . . . it is not fair of her to blame me for that. I couldn't help being born first . . ."

She broke off, hearing again the echo of her complaint—so long ago, it seemed—upon the landing. Uncle Theodore leaned over and caressed her shoulder, but otherwise made no more reply than the portrait, and they sat for a long time in silence, watching the coals pulse and flicker while darkness gathered at the window.

PART TWO

SOME TWO months later, at about three o'clock on a warm spring afternoon, Cordelia was sitting at her accustomed windowsill high above the lane, affecting to read but really watching out for a visitor. Though the lane was already in deep shadow, she herself was bathed in sunlight so dazzling she could scarcely see beyond the forecourt. But, as she was doubtless aware, it also enhanced the creamy whiteness of her dress, and the lustre of her thick fair hair, which she had washed only that morning. She had learned from Mr Weatherburn's clerk that the trust would be represented by 'young Mr Beauchamp', whom she hoped to charm into letting her bring out more of the pictures. Uncle Theodore had obligingly taken Aunt Una and Beatrice up to London for the day, and so she had the house entirely to herself.

Beatrice had declined, predictably enough, to hear anything about the business from Cordelia: Uncle Theodore, she declared, had told her all she needed to know. She would not even enter the room in which 'Cordelia's paintings', as she insisted on calling them, were stored. (Aunt Una, too, had declined to view them, but only because of the stairs; she had recently moved her bedroom from the first to the ground floor.) Aside from the familiar pain of rejection, Cordelia had been forced to admit to herself that she was relieved; she could not help feeling proprietorial about the room. Unlocking the door and letting herself in when no one else was around still gave her a childish thrill of pleasure, like rediscovering a secret hiding-place. She felt perfectly at home there, especially in the mornings when the room was bright with sunlight. Indeed the more time she spent in it, the harder it became to think of the contents as the property of the trust. She was eager to set out some of the furniture as it might have been thirty years ago, when her grandmother first visited Henry St Clair's studio, but thought she should at least ask before doing so. In the meantime she had cleaned the windows, and dusted and swept as thoroughly as she could without disturbing anything.

A figure emerged from the shadows at the end of the lane and crunched across the gravel. A man—a young man—though he did not look in the least like a lawyer, for he wore a blue open-necked shirt and had a small canvas bag slung over his shoulder. But when he caught sight of her, he waved so cheerfully that she could not help waving back, or bounding down the four flights of stairs despite Aunt Una's warnings about loose carpets and broken necks, so that she opened the front door a little out of breath.

His attire looked even more informal at close quarters. The blue shirt was distinctly faded; he had on brown corduroy trousers and battered brown walking-boots in need of polish. As well as the knapsack, he had a khaki greatcoat, with rows of brass buttons embossed with eagles, draped over his arm. He was slender, not much taller than Cordelia herself, with reddish-brown curly hair, a ruddy complexion, and a long, humorous face which lit up with an irresistible smile at the sight of her. She felt an immediate attraction, and a strange, slightly unnerving sense of familiarity; as if some inner voice was saying, *I know you*, even though she knew she had never seen him before.

"Miss de Vere? I'm Harry Beauchamp, from Weatherburn and Hall."

"Oh yes, do come in. But you must call me Cordelia."

"Then you must call me Harry. You are—this is a delightful house. You would never guess it was here. I thought I must have got your directions wrong, until I came out of the wood and there you were in your window, waving down at me."

"You waved first, I think. Will you have some tea?"

"I should love some, but might we look at the pictures and things first? If you've time, that is. Then I'll feel I've earned it."

"Oh yes, I've lots of time," said Cordelia, blushing slightly at her own eagerness. "Come this way. I must say, you don't look at all like a lawyer."

"So my uncle—he's Hall, you see—is always complaining. You told our clerk it was a bit of a muddy walk from the station, so I thought it would be all right—I say, I hope you don't mind."

"Oh no, not at all, I was hoping you wouldn't be someone stuffy."

"To tell the truth," he continued as they set off down the hall—he moved, she noticed, with a slightly uneven gait, rolling a little to the right—"I'm much more interested in pictures than I am in the law. That's another reason Uncle Timothy despairs of me. I wish I could say I'm here because I know something about pictures, but to be honest it's because he thought even I couldn't make a mess of checking things off against an inventory and asking you to sign a few papers."

"Well I'm glad," she replied, "because I care for the pictures, and I hope you will too."

As they started up the stairs, she saw that his left knee did not bend properly, so that he had to check himself momentarily at every second step in order to swing his leg up to the next.

"Legacy of the war," he said, as if in reply to her unspoken question. "Entirely ignominious, I'm afraid. I was late getting back to barracks one night, and took a spill on my motorcycle. Spent the rest of the war on crutches, doing staff work in London. Otherwise I probably wouldn't be here. None of my friends are. From before, I mean."

"Yes. I lost—we lost our father, a month before it ended."

"How awful. Makes it worse, somehow, to have come so close . . . sorry, tactless thing to say."

"No, not tactless, it's true. I don't think truth ever hurts—well it shouldn't, anyway," she added, thinking of Beatrice.

"I say, who's this?" he exclaimed as they reached the landing and stopped in front of the portrait.

"Imogen de Vere, my grandmother."

"It's very fine. Very fine indeed. Who was the artist?"

"Henry St Clair—don't you know the story?"

"You mean this belongs to the *trust*? Good God. No; all I've read is the deed. A very odd bequest . . . quite mad, if you don't mind my saying so. Why on earth . . . ?"

"Yes, I think he was mad. And bad." Repressing a temptation to pour out the whole story, she said almost nothing about Imogen, confining herself to Ruthven de Vere bankrupting St Clair "in a fit of madness" and hiding away the pictures. Harry Beauchamp listened attentively while studying the portrait. Once or twice he glanced at Cordelia, as if comparing faces.

"So really," she concluded, "morally, I mean, they belong to Henry St Clair, though I know the law doesn't agree."

"No, unfortunately—but I see what you mean. The more I look at this, the more I feel I *should* have heard of him. Extraordinary eyes . . . may we see the others?"

Though the room was now familiar, she still could not cross the threshold without a shiver of anticipation. Ushering her first visitor through the door—especially one as personable as Harry Beauchamp—prompted an additional *frisson*, and she was not disappointed in his reaction. He began by making a slow circuit of the room, moving from picture to picture, while she watched from the doorway, remembering her own progress that first wintry afternoon. So absorbed was he, by the time he passed her and began a second circuit, that he might have been walking in his sleep. At last he stopped before the first of the "exorcisms"—the solitary figure hastening through the moonlit wood—and turned to face her.

"I'm sorry," he said, "I had no idea . . . until I saw that portrait, I was expecting a roomful of amateur watercolours or something of the sort. But these are quite remarkable. This, for example, reminds me a lot of Grimshaw—do you know him?—No, he's not much thought of these days. Went in for moonlight in a big way. Fine painter. But there's a menace about your man here . . ."

"He called them exorcisms," said Cordelia, coming over to join him. "For his melancholia."

"I see . . . Now this—" moving on to another moonlit scene—"why, it's a sort of joke!"

To the untutored eye, there was nothing comical about it. The upper half of the canvas showed a tall, gaunt house framed by a tracery of bare branches. Orange light shone from an upstairs window, accentuating the dark outlines of the casements in a way that gave an unnerving impression of bared, grinning teeth. Leaves and twigs were strewn thickly over a flagged path: the place had an overgrown, desolate air. The path led down, by way of a series of steps, to a gateway between stone pillars. But there the semblance of normality ended, for just beyond the pillars, the ground ended in a sheer, vertical fall of rock, plunging to infinite depths. Flagstones hung precariously over the lip of the precipice, which ran like a jagged tear right along the front wall of the house. Torn earth and foliage gleamed in the moonlight.

At first, the precipice that dominated the lower half seemed almost featureless. Cordelia had gazed at it before, without discerning anything more than vague outlines. But now impressions began to form, as if her eyes were growing accustomed to the dark. She was looking into the mouth of a great cavern, thronged with dim figures which might or might not have been human, their eyes materialising into tiny points of reddish light, as if reflecting the fiery glow in the window far above.

"Extraordinary, isn't it?" said Harry. "You know, that house is pure Grimshaw, and yet—look at this." He indicated something that Cordelia had taken for a hairline crack in the canvas: a thin, forked line of pure white darting across the mouth of the cavern.

"Lightning, wouldn't you say?" he continued. "Mad Martin to the life."

"I'm afraid I don't—"

"Sorry, I shouldn't call him that. John Martin. Early last century. It was his brother who was mad, poor chap. Huge apocalypses—I saw one in a sale not long ago. It went for ten pounds; I'd have bought it myself if I had anywhere to hang it. But putting them together like this, it's a sort of comedy of excess. Remarkable execution. And what are these?"

He moved on to a series of canvases, all seemingly versions of the same scene: a water-bird's-eye view of a dense forest of reeds along a riverbank, done in deep greens and browns and flashes of silvery light, painted so that the reeds looked as tall as trees. Lurking amongst them were a number of dark, mottled purplish shapes which might have been crustaceans, or jellyfish, or the shadows of creatures hovering above the frame. Cordelia could not tell what they were, and yet they drew her eye: whenever she tried to focus on some other aspect of the scene, there was a disconcerting impression of movement among the reeds.

"These don't remind me of anyone," said Harry. "Are you sure they're by the same . . . well, here's his signature, anyway. Extraordinary. And this—" turning to a picture, at least four feet by two, of pairs of naked lovers floating in a firmament of blue, dozens or even hundreds of them, some no larger than gnats, but all intricately detailed—"looks like somebody else entirely. But here's his signature again . . . did you say he might still be alive?"

Moving away from the lovers, who were making her blush, Cordelia told him everything she could recall about Henry St Clair, without mentioning the affair. Not, she realised, because she would actually mind Harry Beauchamp knowing about it, but because it seemed too intimate a topic, alone in the house together; and she was having quite enough difficulty with her colour already.

"You know," he said thoughtfully, "rather than hanging them here and there around your house—though that would be quite all right; the deed doesn't say that everything has to be kept in the same room—you could make a sort of exhibition in here, or in another room, if that suited you better. The stuff in the middle could go somewhere else, if you've space for it, and then . . . just imagine if Henry St Clair *is* still alive. And if we were able to find him. At least he could come and see his pictures, and know they were safe—though not for ever," he added, his expression darkening. "But if we could find him—I mean just supposing there'd been something illegal about the way your grandfather bought up those debts, we might just be able to save the pictures and . . . I say, I'm terribly sorry, I've no right at all . . ."

"No, no, please go on, this is a wonderful idea. But . . . surely you're not supposed to try and save them?"

"Oh no," he said cheerfully. "My uncle would sack me on the spot, if he heard me talking like this. But the pictures are more important, don't you think? There's nothing in the trust that actually prohibits us from trying to find him; and besides, I'd be doing it in my own time, not the firm's. If you approve, that is."

"Oh yes, absolutely," said Cordelia, restraining a wild impulse to throw her arms around him.

"Then—er, could I come back, do you think, for a longer look? There's bound to be something here that will help us . . . it would have to be on a weekend, if that's all right . . ."

"Oh yes, absolutely," she repeated, blushing more than

ever. "And you could easily stay, there's loads of room. I know my uncle won't mind."

"Wonderful . . . would this Saturday be all right then?"

"Oh yes, absolutely, perfect . . . gosh, do excuse me for a moment," she blurted, and ran from the room.

What is happening to me? she thought as she splashed her burning face. Despite their relative isolation, she had fended off the attentions of enough young men to think of herself as entirely level-headed in these matters. She had never met anyone so attractive, or so interesting, as Henry—no Harry Beauchamp; it was such a relief not to have to apologise for liking books and paintings, and the limp didn't matter at all, she wasn't so keen on dancing or tennis that she couldn't happily . . . You must stop this, you don't even know he likes you, she reproved herself. But her heart refused to listen, and she hastened back along the corridor, to find him examining an imposing black folio volume which he had evidently extracted from the materials heaped in the middle of the floor.

"I hope you don't mind," he said, "but this looked interesting. Have you ever opened it?"

"No, I didn't like to touch any of those things."

"Well, as the trustees' representative," he said, with a charming smile, "I'm delighted to inform you that you can look at anything you like, whenever you like. There's nothing in the deed that says you can't."

He had also unearthed a tall wooden stand, like a portable lectern, on which the folio was now resting. It was, she saw, no ordinary book, but a stack of boards or plates of some kind, sandwiched between thick hide covers and secured by a tarnished metal clasp. There was no lettering visible anywhere on the cover or the spine.

He tugged at the clasp, but it would not budge.

"I can't see any keyhole," he said. "Must be a trick to it . . . ah, that's got it . . . damn."

The catch sprang open with a loud snap and he recoiled, with drops of blood forming across the fingers of his right hand.

"Shall I get you a bandage?" she asked, with concern.

"No, it's only a scratch." He wrapped his handkerchief around the injury and picked up the book, which was evidently very heavy.

"Can we take it out onto the landing? I think we may need the room."

He carried the book outside, and set it down on the floor. "Here, let me," she said. Heedless of dust, she knelt beside him, opened the cover, and lifted out something that looked like a blue frieze made up of interlinked panels. It had to be done very carefully, because the panels seemed to unfold from the bottom of the pile, so that she had to carry the whole gradually diminishing bundle across the landing, with Harry following as the work extended.

At first the panels seemed more or less identical: nothing but surging, blue-grey water, viewed from just above the surface of the ocean so that entire sections were filled by the slope of a single wave, streaked with foam, and occasional glimpses of a low, swirling sky. The sections themselves appeared to be made of very thin board covered in cloth, the hinges so carefully wrought that, as the work extended across the floor, the joints were scarcely visible. But as the scene unfolded, a lurking presence just below the surface began to reveal itself: a long, pale shape, distorted and sometimes hidden by the seething water, but becoming more palpable with each new opening.

Behind what appeared to be the final opening was another panel, secured by two small sliding clips. She released it and recoiled, stifling a cry of horror. The face of a drowned man, life-size, teeth bared, eyes wide open and staring, glared up at her. Water poured from his open mouth as a wave bore him upwards; his hair was thickly matted and choked with seaweed. The lurking shape beyond resolved itself into glimpses of naked torso, trailing limbs, and a dead-white hand, its outstretched fingers grasping at emptiness.

A young man's face: or so she thought at first. But when she moved to look more closely, the drowned man's expression altered. Not only his expression, but even the shape of his face, which seemed to age as she leaned further over the panel until it had mutated into that of an old man, gaunt and toothless and quite bald: the "hair" was all seaweed; only the agony was the same. She leaned back again, and the transformation reversed itself.

"Remarkable feat of *trompe-l'oeil*," said Harry, crouching awkwardly beside her. "Something in the paint, I think; see the way it catches the light from different angles?" He moved back along the length of the frieze, examining it closely.

"Look at this."

She saw that he had freed a blank page, like a flyleaf, which had evidently been sticking to the back cover. Inscribed on the endpaper beneath, in archaic black lettering, was "The Drowned Man".

"Interesting. You can't see it—or you'd be very unlikely

to—until after you've seen the work itself," he went on. "And you know, this is the only thing I've seen so far with a title."

"Do paintings have to have titles? I mean, is it a rule?"

"Well, not a rule, but it's rare to see a whole collection without any. And—" he crouched down, moved awkwardly back along the length of the work, and began to fold up the panels, examining the back of each one as he did so—"apart from being the only one with a title, it's the only thing so far without a signature. At least, I can't find one."

He laid the frieze out for a second time.

"What do you think that means?" she asked.

"Well . . . it certainly looks like his work, speaking on a very brief acquaintance, of course. But the book itself, the whole thing, apart from the actual design, looks far too old. Eighteenth-century, I'd have said, though I've never seen anything quite like it. Could he have found it blank, I wonder? Painted his own design, added his title . . . but then why didn't he sign it?"

He fell silent, staring at the drowned man's contorted features.

"And you're really sure you'd like me to come back, and try to find out some more about him?" he said at last, as if to the drowned man.

"Oh yes, absolutely."

"I'm glad—No, please, let me."

He began to fold the panels away again. When he had got them all together and secured the clasp, he bore the heavy volume back into the room, and replaced it reverently on the lectern. As if it were a prayer book, she thought, but her unease was swept aside by the warmth of his smile as he asked, "And now, does your offer of tea still stand?"

"Of course. Would you like to look around for a little and then come downstairs?"

"No, do let me come and help—well, at least talk to you while you make it."

The kitchen, unlike many of its kind, was bright and cheerful, its walls crowded with pots and pans and crockery. French windows opened onto a flagged courtyard, with an expanse of grass and shrubbery beyond. She made Harry sit at the scrubbed wooden table in the centre of the room, and took down an apron, thinking, he may as well get used to seeing me in it. The words passed through her mind so naturally that it took several seconds for the implication to surface.

"I say, this is very jolly," said Harry. "Er—do you do everything for yourselves?"

"We do all our own cooking, since Mrs Green died. She was our housekeeper for ever and ever, practically one of the family. Molly—a girl from the village—comes in to help with the washing and cleaning; and Mr Grimes does the garden."

She answered his questions almost mechanically while she worked, shaken by the speed with which her emotions had run ahead of her. Yet it did no good to tell herself, *But I hardly know him*, or, *We've only just met*: already she felt as if they had been intimate for a long time. She carried the tray out to her favourite seat at the far edge of the lawn, where she learned that he had grown up in Plymouth and had one sister, who was now married and living in Canada. His father had died before the war; his mother five years ago; he had lived in London ever since, and was sharing rooms with a friend in Coptic Street, close by the Museum. He was just thirty years old, and—according to every indication she could divine—quite unattached. Her own history seemed to lead quite naturally into that of her grandmother, and so, while the shadows lengthened around them, she came to tell him almost everything she knew about Imogen de Vere and Henry St Clair and the evil that had overtaken them, and the strange story of the bequest, praying, every so often, that Uncle Theodore was giving Beatrice and Aunt Una dinner in town. Though it was after sunset before Harry Beauchamp said reluctantly that he supposed he really must be getting along, the air was still warm as she walked with him to the station, where they continued talking through the open window of his carriage until the train pulled away from the platform.

Cordelia was quite unable to conceal the fact that something momentous had happened, and before Harry's return she had confided her feelings to her aunt and uncle (though not to Beatrice, who, to her immense relief, would be spending the weekend in London with an old friend from school). To distract herself during the interval, she spent a great deal of time in the room with the pictures, thinking about how Henry St Clair's studio might have looked when he was painting her grandmother's portrait in the summer of 1896. Uncle Theodore, with some misgivings, despite her assurance that the trustees would not object to the bequest being housed in two adjacent rooms, agreed to let them store some of the furniture in the empty bedroom next door. He was plainly troubled, not only by her having formed an attachment to the lawyer representing the trust, but by her determination to—in her own phrase—restore the studio.

"I just feel this is something I must do," she said to him, struggling to explain why it seemed so important. "It will be—it will be like Henry St Clair painting his exorcisms. The room has always been left as Ruthven de Vere would have wanted it—everything cluttered in a heap and shut away in the dark. If we make it look as if—well as if Henry could come back and work in it—light and airy and clean—then de Vere will have lost his power over us."

"But my dear—you don't *expect* him back, do you?"

"If we can find him—I mean if he is still alive, yes. Don't you think it would be wonderful? And then we would have undone some of the wrong my grandfather did him. Just to restore the studio will be a start."

"I fear that only trouble will come of it. This Henry Beauchamp—"

"Harry, uncle—"

"Harry, then—seems to be taking a very cavalier view of his responsibilities to the trust. If we lost—that is to say, if you lost your income through some breach of the trust—well, we should have to sell this house."

"I know Harry would not put us at risk, uncle; you will see for yourself when you meet him. And please, please promise me that you will do your very best to like him."

"I shall, my dear, for your sake. But I wish you would leave that room alone."

Walking back with Harry from the station on Saturday morning, Cordelia was quite overcome with shyness; he too seemed ill at ease, and she performed the introductions wishing she had never said a word about him. Though she could tell he was making a good impression upon her aunt and uncle (she had intimated to Harry that the subject of the pictures had best be left until later on), her discomfort grew worse in their presence, so much so that she was compelled, several times during lunch, to hide in the kitchen on the pretext of arranging dishes she had actually prepared beforehand.

Yet as soon as they entered the studio, their intimacy was restored as completely as if no time had passed since they left it four days ago. Harry seemed to understand, without her having to explain any further, exactly why she wanted to restore it, and to agree entirely with her intuition as to what ought to go where. And he did not try to prevent her from lifting things, but worked alongside her on equal terms. Getting covered in dust and grime while hauling furniture about also helped to disguise her renewed attraction to him; it was natural that her colour should be high, and that they should touch frequently; and as the afternoon went on, she felt increasingly certain that all of her feeling was returned. At one point she caught herself thinking that if they were to marry and live in London, the pictures would go with her. A few moments later, Harry had remarked, seemingly out of the blue, "of course if you were ever to move to London, the pictures would come with you; you could have a room like this, you know, your own private gallery, and invite people to see them. There's nothing in the trust to prevent it." He spoke with such warmth that she felt sure his thought was running beside hers.

By the end of the day, they had sorted through everything that had been stacked in the centre of the floor. The bed now stood beneath the windows; Cordelia had been amazed to discover that the bedding, despite thirty years in storage, had escaped the attentions of moths, silverfish, and damp, and was only a little musty. She had placed the table and two upright chairs between the bed and the door, and a small sofa against the wall to the right of the doorway. An empty easel stood in the middle of the room, with Henry St Clair's palette-tray attached to it. The tubes of colour had, of course, long since dried up, but she set them out anyway, along with his brushes and palette knives and other implements. Some of the unfinished or scraped-out pictures, along with pieces of board and canvas and framing were still stacked along the other two walls, so that it would look as much as possible like a real working studio.

They had made a preliminary selection of about twenty finished paintings for display, so that the pictures would no longer be jammed together. Cordelia had wanted to consign all of the exorcisms to the room next door, but Harry persuaded her that even the darkest aspects of his vision ought to be represented, and so several of the night scenes remained, along with "The Drowned Man", resting on its lectern in the corner opposite the door.

With everything swept and polished, and light filling the room, she felt that the malignant spirit of Ruthven de Vere had at last been banished for good. They had looked through every box and bundle and found nothing sinister; other than bedding and linen, the various boxes and bundles yielded only more painting materials, including a set of carpenter's tools, presumably for fashioning frames. Aside from "The Drowned Man", the only object that Cordelia had felt slightly uneasy about retaining was a box—or rather a cube, since there seemed to be no way of opening it—made up of panels of dark polished wood, about fifteen inches square. It was not very heavy, and clearly hollow. The panels gave slightly when you pressed them, and if you rocked it to and fro, you could hear—at least Cordelia was half-persuaded she could hear—a very soft rustling noise. But it was so elegantly made that she decided to keep it in the corner nearest the sofa.

After she had bathed, and put on a dress of apricot silk which especially suited her colouring, she went downstairs to fetch her uncle and show him what they had done. Harry, now clad in a surprisingly elegant suit, had come down before her and was chatting to Uncle Theodore as if they were old acquaintances.

It was close on sunset, and in the fading light the transformation seemed even more remarkable; it really did feel as if they were stepping back thirty years. The illusion grew stronger still as Cordelia lit the candles she had already arranged. There was no electric light in the room; St Clair's belongings had been stored here long before the house was electrified, and Theodore had preferred not to disturb them. It occurred to her, as her uncle stood contemplating the results of their labours, to ask him if he recalled seeing electric lights in the restaurant in Soho on that dark winter afternoon.

"No, my dear, I don't think I did. In fact I'm sure there were none; I remember a gas-lamp on the wall. Electric light was still a luxury, you know; they would have been far too poor. And you're sure," he added, to Harry, "that the trustees would approve of this?"

"Entirely sure, sir. After all it's our—that is to say, your—duty to ensure that everything is well cared for, and this could only be seen as an improvement."

Uncle Theodore asked several more questions along these lines, and seemed reassured by the replies, which encouraged Cordelia to make the request that had been shaping itself in her mind.

"Uncle . . . would you mind terribly if we were to bring Imogen's portrait in here and put it on the easel? We could have another key made—I don't think Beatrice would care, she never looks at it—so you could come in and see it—I mean, any of the pictures" (remembering she had told Harry nothing of her uncle's love for Imogen de Vere) "whenever you like."

"You don't have to ask my permission, my dear; it's for you to decide. But why do you want to?"

"I shan't unless you approve, uncle. I'd like to because . . . because then the room would look just as it did before."

"Before?" he prompted.

"Well, before everything went wrong," she floundered, realising this was delicate ground.

"I see . . . You can't undo the past, you know."

"I know that, uncle. I just feel it would be the right thing to do."

"Well my dear, I shall trust your feeling, and accept your offer of a key."

She could tell that he was uneasy, but felt sure of persuading him once the portrait was back in its rightful place. One of Henry St Clair's luminous daylight visions could take its place on the landing.

At dinner that night, Harry insisted upon acting as her assistant, and between them they made a game of waiting upon her uncle and aunt. In Cordelia's private bestiary, her aunt had always been, in the nicest possible sense, bovine: large, placid, gentle, utterly without malice or guile. She could not walk very far, these days, because her legs tended to swell, and her heart was not strong. But tonight she wore her best dove-grey silk, and beamed upon Harry as if he and Cordelia were already engaged. Uncle Theodore brought out a couple of bottles of his best wine, and as the evening unfolded it seemed to Cordelia that everything in the room took on a deeper and richer glow. Harry and her uncle did most of the talking; she was perfectly content to sit and gaze at her beloved, bathed in a radiance so entrancing she felt she had never seen candlelight before.

Given that Henry St Clair's entire property had been seized without warning, they had expected to find papers, letters, perhaps even a diary. Harry—to his uncle's displeasure, as he cheerfully acknowledged—had spent much of the interval inquiring after the painter, without result: no one in any of the established galleries or salerooms had ever heard of a St Clair, let alone seen the man himself. Nor, thus far, was there indication that he might have continued working under another name. They began their search of his belongings with high hopes; but late on Sunday afternoon they were compelled to admit defeat. There were no books, no keepsakes, no photographs, no papers of any kind. The sole clue to his identity was his signature on the paintings.

"I don't understand," said Cordelia, when they had put away the last box and returned to the studio. "If they let him keep everything personal, why not his painting things?"

"I think," Harry replied, "that de Vere" (Cordelia had told him that she disowned her grandfather) "must have destroyed everything of that sort."

He was standing at the lectern, examining the face of the drowned man, as he had done several times that morning; it seemed to hold a particular fascination for him. By leaving off the clasps that secured the last panel, he could display the final opening without having to lay out the rest of the work.

"But then why would he leave everything else?"

"Well . . . madness aside, it does look as if he removed anything that might have given us a clue to St Clair's whereabouts. Which suggests to me that he wanted to make sure nobody *did* find St Clair. So perhaps there *was* something illegal in the way he got hold of the pictures . . .

"And suppose . . . suppose you hadn't been interested, just left them locked up; then in due course the whole lot would have been burned by the trustees without anyone ever having seen them. De Vere really would have managed to erase all trace of St Clair's existence. 'Here lies one whose name was writ in water' . . ."

He paused, still gazing at the drowned man's face.

"But even now, if we could only find him—and somehow I feel sure he's still alive—we could change that, and perhaps save his pictures as well. For ever, that is."

"I see what you mean," said Cordelia. "But supposing we did find him, and it turned out that everything really did belong to him, the income would stop and my uncle would have to sell this house. I'm not saying we shouldn't try—we must do what's right—but it will make him terribly anxious. He loves Ashbourn—so do I—and I should hate to be the cause of his losing it."

It crossed her mind that her uncle and aunt would not always be here—and what would happen to Ashbourn after that?—but this was a train of thought she did not want to pursue.

"On my reading of the deed that wouldn't necessarily follow, not at all. Besides, St Clair would surely be happy to see his pictures here; he wouldn't want to do anything to harm you, of all people. And to recover possession of the pictures, he would have to bring an action against the trust, which could be very costly. No, my idea is that we would look after them for the life of the trust, but if we could establish St Clair's claim, then we ought to be able to persuade the trustees that the pictures shouldn't be burned; if they went to the nation, nobody could be accused of profiting from the change."

It seemed to Cordelia that this chain of reasoning depended on a great many "ifs", but she was too delighted by "we would look after them" to care. Warm scents of blossom drifted in through the open window, where she was perched, in her usual fashion, on the sill with her feet upon the counterpane of the bed. The portrait of Imogen de Vere, serene and luminous as ever, rested upon the easel as if the artist had just laid down his brushes. Yes, she thought, we really have banished the last of the evil; the intended curse has turned out to be a blessing. Without the pictures I would never have met Harry; now this room will be our special place until we have a house of our own. Harry had accepted Uncle Theodore's invitation to join them again the following weekend, so eagerly that she really could not doubt it . . . and perhaps, one day soon, they would find Henry St Clair and bring him here, and show him that his work had not, after all, been lost. If only Imogen were still alive, everything would be perfect. It was a pity, too, that Henry St Clair had not painted a self-portrait; but she could picture him so vividly, it scarcely mattered. He would have looked very like Harry . . . who was once again absorbed in contemplating "The Drowned Man", moving his head in the way that caused the face to metamorphose from youth to age and back again.

"What is it that fascinates you so?" Cordelia asked.

For a second or two, when he looked up, he seemed not to know who she was.

"I don't know . . . it draws me, that's all. The way it changes . . . it's like being reminded of something, and not being able to remember what it reminds you of . . ."

He folded away the panel and closed the cover, and seemed to come fully awake again.

"Shall we go for that walk now?" he asked. "There's still plenty of time before the evening train."

"Oh, yes," she said eagerly, and the uneasy moment was forgotten.

Beatrice came home the next day. Though Cordelia strongly suspected Uncle Theodore of taking her aside and enjoining her to be on her best behaviour, Beatrice betrayed no awareness that anything out of the ordinary was afoot; she did not even ask what had become of Grandmama's portrait. Walking back from the station with Harry the following Saturday morning (now with her arm in his; the lane was obligingly slippery after several days of rain), Cordelia warned him that her sister was inclined to be cool and distant, so that he must not be hurt if she seemed aloof, or even hostile. But on this occasion, Beatrice behaved quite out of character; her normal self-possession vanished when she was introduced to Harry, and she became quite bashful and tongue-tied. At lunch, Cordelia noticed that her sister was very pale; she ate almost nothing, and spoke even less than usual, but followed the conversation intently, her eyes darting constantly between Harry and Cordelia. And then, as she helped clear the table, Beatrice surprised her sister still more by asking, quite humbly, whether she might be allowed to come up to the studio with them to see the pictures.

Not wanting to appear ungenerous in front of Harry, Cordelia agreed, hoping she would have seen all she wanted in fifteen minutes. But Beatrice stayed nearly two hours. She asked so many questions, and listened so attentively to the answers, that before she left she had elicited much of what Uncle Theodore had revealed two months before. Yet she did not seem to be making a set at Harry. Her behaviour throughout was that of a young girl grateful for the attention of an admired older sister and her accepted suitor. She praised Cordelia's arrangement of the studio, and admired the pictures one by one, displaying every appearance of genuine curiosity, until, despite her suspicions, Cordelia began to wonder if perhaps she did not know her sister nearly as well as she had imagined.

Beatrice seemed especially interested in "The Drowned Man", at whose face she gazed intently for some time before asking Harry to explain how the strange metamorphosis between youth and age might have been achieved. While they were talking, Cordelia, who was standing a little way behind them, found herself glancing from Beatrice to the portrait—as Harry had done that first afternoon with her. It was not a likeness in the ordinary sense—Beatrice's face was narrower, her eyes differently shaped, her hair a smoky brown rather than copper-coloured—rather, something in the carriage of her head, an aura, an atmosphere. Cordelia felt as if a veil had been lifted, not from the portrait but from Beatrice, who was listening with her whole attention to what Harry was saying, intent, receptive, with no trace of her usual watchful self-awareness. But for the most part, she addressed her questions to Cordelia while Harry watched and listened, becoming visibly more perplexed as he saw how much of the family's history was new to Beatrice. As he said to Cordelia later, when she had finally got him away for a walk in Hurst Wood, if he had not known otherwise, he would have sworn that she and her sister were the best of friends.

That evening, Beatrice (who usually preferred them to take turns at the cooking) offered to help Cordelia prepare the meal, and did so with perfect amiability. But then she came down in a striking dark blue gown which Cordelia had not seen before. Perhaps she was simply obeying her uncle's instruction to be on her best behaviour—but it seemed to Cordelia that Harry's eyes were straying rather too often in her sister's direction, and she lay awake most of the night, alternately fearing the worst and hating herself for giving way to jealousy and suspicion. On Sunday morning during another walk in the wood (Harry insisted that exercise was good for his injured leg, and refused to coddle it), she fought down the impulse to tell him just how uncharacteristically Beatrice was behaving, observing instead, "My sister is very beautiful, don't you think?"

"Indeed she is," he replied, "almost as beautiful as you", and with that he kissed her—or perhaps she had kissed him, she was not quite certain, afterwards—in a way that left her in no doubt as to his feelings for her.

A casual observer would have concluded, as the week went by, that Beatrice was reverting to her usual manner. The hoped-for reconciliation did not eventuate; each day she seemed a little more withdrawn, but it was a different sort of retreat: preoccupied, abstracted, self-forgetful. It was as if the wall between them had finally collapsed, only to reveal that there was no one on the other side. Her demeanour throughout Harry's next visit was so much more constrained that he asked Cordelia several times if he had done anything to offend Beatrice. Cordelia could only assure him he had not; her intuition of the cause was not something she wished to confide to anybody, least of all him.

Beatrice remained, so far as Cordelia could tell, in this melancholy frame of mind for the next few weeks, as summer approached and Harry's weekend visits became a settled thing. Then, early in June, Beatrice went up to London to spend a few days with her friend Claudia in Bayswater. On the evening of her return to Ashbourn, she announced to her uncle and Cordelia (Aunt Una had already retired to bed) that she wanted to learn typewriting, with a view to earning her living in London.

"Miss Harringay's academy in Marylebone will take me, and Claudia's mother has said I am welcome to stay with them. I can go up to town on Monday morning and come back each Friday. I wish to earn my living, especially now that Cordelia will soon be married—"

"He hasn't asked me yet."

"I'm sure he will, very soon. And then you will need the money from the pictures—"

"No I shan't," said Cordelia sharply. "Uncle knows that the income will stay with him; he has cared for us all our lives, and I shouldn't dream of taking a penny of it."

Cordelia and her uncle had already spoken of this. He wanted her to take at least her share of the income when (as everyone now assumed) she and Harry were married, but she had declined absolutely. The securities in which the trust's capital was invested had declined in value, reducing the income to less than four hundred a year, only just enough to maintain her uncle and aunt at Ashbourn with the extra help they would need if she and Beatrice were to leave. She loved Ashbourn, and did not want to see it sold, any more than her uncle did. Of course now that Beatrice would be leaving . . . it came to her suddenly that her ideal would be to live here with Harry, and that when, as must eventually happen, Ashbourn descended to her and Beatrice, she might be able to use the income to buy out Beatrice's share of the house. But then Harry was very much attached to London, and if, as she hoped, he were to give up the law, and seek a position in one of the galleries or auction houses, it would be even less practical for him to leave.

"Beatrice was just saying, my dear, that it will cost three guineas a week, all in all, for her to attend this academy; and that the training will last about twelve weeks. So the question is, whether you approve?"

"If you mean about the money, uncle, it is for you to say; speaking for myself, of course I approve."

"We can just afford it," said Theodore, "but we shall have to make some economies."

"Then let us make them," said Cordelia. It struck her as she spoke that Beatrice would be only a mile or two from Harry throughout the week, while she would be very much tied to Ashbourn by the need to look after her aunt. But it was too late to call back the words, and besides, it was only for three months; though of course, if Beatrice were then to find work in town, could she really leave her aunt and uncle to manage alone? Cordelia tried her best to appear enthusiastic for the rest of the evening, but these depressing speculations followed her up to bed.

Cordelia had always imagined a proposal of marriage as a sort of magical transformation: one minute, perhaps, you were still wondering whether he really did care for you; the next (provided you adored him) you were the happiest woman on earth. By the time Beatrice announced her intention of leaving home, Harry was talking as if their future together was already a settled thing; of what "we" might do with the pictures in "our" house in London, for example; or how wonderful it would be if Henry St Clair should reappear and become "our" friend; and so forth. He would say these things quite unselfconsciously, but despite constant encouragement he had not come to the point of proposing, and she had not liked to ask him directly.

Oddly enough, it was Harry's continuing fascination—she was beginning to think of it as an obsession—with "The Drowned Man" that brought about their betrothal. Whenever they were in the studio, and he was not actively engaged in conversation, or studying one of the other pictures, he would begin to drift towards the lectern, there to sink once more into half-mesmerised contemplation, swaying slowly back and forth. She was reminded of the way in which she used to lose herself in her grandmother's portrait; but to lose yourself in the face of a corpse, locked in its final agony, with bloodshot eyeballs straining from their sockets, and weed and water flowing in and out of its gaping mouth . . . It was all the more troubling because, when she ventured to distract him, she would sometimes detect a flash of irritation, even hostility, before his features resumed their normal cheerful cast. Away from the studio, he would agree that his fixation might be unhealthy, but she could tell that he did not like to speak of it. The face reminded him of something, he would repeat, something he felt sure would help him in his search for Henry St Clair, if only he could draw it to the surface. But many hours of concentration seemed to have brought him no nearer to understanding what that something might be. She had asked him twice if he thought it might be a despairing self-portrait, painted after he had lost Imogen. Possibly, he replied, but that was not what drew him to it. Nor, thus far, had his inquiries around the galleries, or his researches in Somerset House, Chancery Lane, the Reading Room of the British Museum, and other repositories of records and documents, yielded the slightest trace of Henry St Clair's existence.

On the Saturday after Beatrice's announcement, Cordelia and Harry were once more in the studio, at his instigation. He wanted to look again at one of the waterscapes (as she liked to call them) to see if he could establish where it had been painted. To Cordelia this was no more than a pleasant game of speculation; without benefit of title it was plainly impossible to identify any location, even on the remote chance that the place was one you had visited yourself. But she agreed readily enough, hoping she could lure him away for a walk in the wood before "The Drowned Man" could ensnare him. It was a perfect summer afternoon outside, and there was a particular spot she had in mind; a grassy bank beside a stream where they had lain side by side and he had fallen asleep, so that by insinuating herself closer she was able to embrace him while he slept. And then when he had woken he had kissed her for quite some time before saying that perhaps they ought to think about getting back. Although she loved him for being so protective of her virtue, she would happily have stayed there for ever; it was like receiving the keys to paradise, and then being told you could only go there for a few hours every week.

The room diagonally below that in which Henry St Clair's pictures were stored had been "Harry's room" from the first; his things were scattered around it, and throughout the summer his khaki greatcoat had remained on the hook behind the door. Theodore's bedroom was at the other end of the same first-floor corridor (one of the intervening rooms being that in which Grandmama's things were still gathering dust, undisturbed). The two girls slept on the next floor up; Cordelia next to her favourite sitting-room, and Beatrice about half-way along the corridor. To reach Harry's room undetected, Cordelia had only to tiptoe past her sister's bedroom, along the landing and down the staircase, carefully avoiding the treads that creaked. Several times now, always while he was away during the week, she had stolen into his room at night, wrapped herself in his khaki greatcoat and curled up on his bed, wishing she had the nerve to do so when he was actually there. Really there was nothing to prevent her (Uncle Theodore was a heavy sleeper) except the fear that Harry would be shocked, and think her "fast". And why should he not? A well-brought-up girl was not supposed to creep into a young man's bedroom in the middle of the night, however passionate her longing to see, and touch, and above all embrace him: the most startling thing about these newly discovered desires was her inability to feel ashamed of them.

The picture Harry wanted to study hung immediately to the left of the doorway: the rippling waterway, bearing a few small boats in the foreground, a dim green promontory in the distance, the great sweep of the sky overhead. He had said several times that he was sure he had been somewhere exactly like this; but today's scrutiny brought him no closer to deciding where.

"Shall we go now?" Cordelia asked. "It's much too beautiful to stay indoors."

"Yes, of course," he replied, moving towards the lectern, "I'll just . . ."

"Please don't. Wouldn't you rather be . . . ?" She broke off, not wanting to sound imploring.

"Yes, of course," he repeated. But his feet carried him another pace closer.

"What *is* it that draws you?"

"I must . . ." His voice sounded muffled, as if by a strong wind.

"No, you must *not*. *Please look at me*."

He turned, reluctantly, to face her. Again she had the eerie impression that he did not recognise her. "Like a man defeated by his craving for drink"—that was what de Vere's valet had said. She was suddenly afraid of him, and then very angry.

"I think you care more for that hideous face than you do for me. It is enslaving you, and you know it, and yet you . . . you would rather look at a corpse . . ."

Tears choked her, and she ran from the room and down the stairs. But then to her relief she heard footsteps echoing across the floorboards, followed by the irregular rhythm of Harry's tread as he too began to descend. She did not look back, however, but continued on down, praying she would not meet anyone, especially Beatrice, out through the kitchen door and around into the lane, out of sight of the house. There she waited until he caught up with her, gasping out apologies and assurances of devotion, and took her in his arms.

"I am so sorry," he said a little later. "You're quite right; it's bad for me; we'll put it away in the other room and I shan't look at it ever again."

"I'm sorry too, I didn't mean it. Only, I wish you would tell me—what do you see? what do you feel?—that compels you so?"

"I can't . . . it goes, like a dream, when you wake in the night and you're sure you'll never forget, and then in the morning it's gone . . . all you can remember is that you meant to remember, and can't."

Cordelia suspected that he was withholding something, but from there they progressed to the grassy bank beside the stream, where they lay down and embraced as she had hoped, and where, a little later, he asked her to marry him, and the drowned man was quite forgotten.

On a stifling, overcast evening towards the end of summer, Cordelia was once again watching from her old place in the upstairs window, waiting for Harry to appear at the turning of the lane. A scrawled note in yesterday's post had told her he would be arriving late on Friday, some time between five and seven-thirty, depending on when he could get away from the office.

The day had been exceedingly hot, the sun too fierce to venture out in; it had been a relief, at first, when the clouds came over. But still the heat pressed down like a blanket. The air was heavy with the perfume of the climbing roses on the porch below, mingled with that of a dozen different flowers, scents of foliage and bark and leaf-mould, warm stone and woodwork and paint still soft from the heat of the sun. She turned once more to look at the clock on the mantelpiece. Eight minutes past six.

For the first few weeks of their engagement, Harry had seemed perfectly content. A long spell of fine weather had enabled them to spend a great deal of time out of doors, including several paradisal hours on the riverbank. But even then, the intervening days had passed very slowly indeed. With Beatrice in town all week, Cordelia was effectively tied to Ashbourn, partly for reasons of economy, and partly because Aunt Una, after visiting a London heart specialist, had been ordered to avoid exertion, and rest for several hours every day. And since the house had no telephone, and Harry was, as he cheerfully conceded, hopeless at letters, she would usually have heard nothing from him since the last farewell.

He was also constitutionally incapable of catching a specified train, being always liable to slip into the Museum, or a saleroom, "just for five minutes" and emerge an hour and a half later. And then at Hurst Green he might be drawn into conversation with the stationmaster, or someone he met in the village street, and lose track of yet more time before he came into view of the house, waving as enthusiastically as ever. So she had got into the habit of settling herself with a book in the upstairs window at the earliest possible time, though she seldom did much reading. Her imagination was too active, her emotions too keen; and all too often, especially once the expected hour had come and gone, morbid anxieties would begin to flit about her mind. *The train has been delayed. He has accepted another invitation and forgotten to tell me. He has simply forgotten. He no longer loves me. He has met someone else. There has been an accident. The train has crashed. He is injured . . . he is dead. I shall never see him again . . .* all in the most vivid detail. It was like waving away midges at twilight: as fast as you drove one off, another would dart in and stab, on and on interminably, until they were banished by the familiar wave and greeting from the lane below.

For those few perfect weeks, that first embrace had seemed to her the purest essence of joy: she would twine herself around him, only wishing she could hold him close enough to annihilate all distinction between them. Until—she could not say exactly when; the more she brooded upon where the first shadow had fallen, the further back it seemed to stretch—she had become aware that his passion no longer matched her own. She had tried persuading herself that he was merely embarrassed by excessive displays of ardour in public, but even since she had learned to be more restrained, he was likely to say "Here, steady on, old thing", and glance nervously up at the windows. And then he had begun to say such things in private. Her conviction that she must be perfectly, blissfully happy had carried her along, as if she had set out for a walk on a cloudless day, too absorbed to notice the fine, tell-tale streaks of vapour overhead, the gradual weakening of the light, until quite suddenly she had looked up, and shivered, and realised that she had been cold for a long time.

She shivered in fact, though there was nothing chill about the present evening. The house was completely silent. Aunt Una would be lying down in her room; Uncle Theodore was no doubt reading in his study; Beatrice had not yet returned from town. Her lessons at Miss Harringay's were normally over by two o'clock each Friday, and she was supposed to come straight home. But perhaps Harry had got in touch, and suggested she travel down with him, though this had never happened before. At Uncle

Theodore's insistence, Beatrice had always taken the first train up each Monday morning, rather than returning with Harry on the Sunday night. Theodore had told Beatrice, when she began at Miss Harringay's, that he wanted her to impose as little as possible upon her friends in Bayswater; but Cordelia suspected that he had understood how she would have felt to see Beatrice and Harry setting off together, and was grateful to him. She had not realised until too late just how much she was giving up for Beatrice's sake. The four happy years she had spent at Ashbourn since leaving school now seemed to have vanished in a sort of contented sleep; she too wanted to be out preparing to earn her living, as she meant to do when they were married; and in London she could have seen Harry every day.

Beatrice, to do her justice, had not once suggested that Harry should escort her. Her manner towards him had grown still more constrained, but that was capable of more than one interpretation. Cordelia had not been able to stop herself asking Harry, every so often, whether he had seen anything of Beatrice in town; he always assured her he had not; but on the other hand, he had never asked whether she thought he ought to, which suggested he knew better than to ask. And once she had begun to doubt the strength of his feeling, her anxieties had multiplied and swarmed. Until, after tossing and turning for hours on the previous Saturday night, she decided to go down to the kitchen and make herself some cocoa (and perhaps, if she felt bold enough, look in at Harry while he slept). As she approached the room in which they had stored the remainder of Henry St Clair's belongings, she saw light shining from beneath the door.

Unlike the studio, which had its own special lock, this

door opened to the same key as all the other rooms in the corridor. Had somebody left the light on? But why? She had not entered the room for many weeks; not since they had put away "The Drowned Man" and turned the key on it. She listened, holding her breath. No sound came from within, but it seemed to her that there was a very faint, rhythmic pulsation in the pool of light around her feet. Which would be worse: to look and see, or lie awake with her imagination running wild? She took hold of the handle and softly opened the door.

Harry—still fully dressed, though it was two in the morning—stood facing her over the lectern, swaying slowly back and forth. She had last seen it in the far corner, draped in a cloth. Now it stood in the centre of the floor, directly beneath the light. If he had glanced up, their eyes would have met, but his entire attention remained fixed upon the lectern. She could see the glitter of his shadowed eyes, and it seemed to her that he was very faintly smiling. She waited, willing him to look at her, until the suspense became unbearable.

"Dearest?"

The rhythm of his breathing faltered like that of a sleeper on the verge of waking, but his concentration did not waver. How long had he been creeping in here at night? Dust was already thick upon the floor, and on the furniture, and yet the lectern, what she could see of it, looked spotless.

She took another step into the room, her hand still on the doorknob. But the hem of her dressing-gown caught on an empty frame and brought it clattering to the floor.

His head jerked up. For a dreadful moment, he glared as if he had come face to face with his worst enemy; he seemed to be gathering himself to spring. Slowly, recognition returned; now, he looked like her imagination of a burglar caught red-handed. He lowered his eyes, closed the panel, and slunk out from behind the lectern.

"I . . . I must have been sleep-walking," he muttered.

"Please don't lie to me. If you must look at it, at least trust me enough to tell me so."

"I didn't want you to know."

"To know *what*?" she cried.

But his reply was cut off by the sound of footsteps padding towards the room. It was Beatrice, a green dressing-gown thrown over her nightdress.

"What's the matter?" she asked.

"Nothing," replied Cordelia. "Harry—thought he heard a burglar, that's all. I'm sorry we woke you."

"Yes," said Harry. 'Er—false alarm. Sorry. Anyway, good-night both." He kissed her hastily, and made for the stairs.

Cordelia lay awake until dawn, then overslept, and came down very late with a headache. A contrite Harry immediate proposed a walk in Hurst Wood—something he had not done for weeks—and they set off towards the river-bank. He hadn't exactly been lying about the sleep-walking, he explained as they walked along; he had fallen asleep in the armchair in his room, and dreamed that he was looking at "The Drowned Man", and in the dream he had seen, at last, what the face had been trying to tell him. Then he woke, still with the sensation of understanding, but the substance had gone. And so he had taken his key and gone upstairs, hoping to recapture it.

"And did you?" she asked, longing to believe him, but not quite convinced.

"No . . . I thought . . . but no. I lose myself in it, and

then—then it goes, like that dream, when something calls me back."

"When I knocked over the frame, you looked as if you hated me." Her voice quivered as she spoke.

"I am so sorry . . . I was not myself."

"Then who were you?"

He glanced at her uneasily. "I meant, I didn't know what I was doing."

She stopped in the middle of the path, put her hands on his shoulders, and turned him towards her.

"Harry, look at me. There's no burden, nothing I wouldn't happily bear for your sake. But I can't marry you if you won't trust me."

He threw his arms around her and launched into a stream of apologies. He had learned his lesson; they would lock "The Drowned Man" away in a stout box and she could keep the only key of it, if she liked, but in any case he would never, never look at it again; he loved her, adored her, could never live without her . . . all very gratifying, but at the end of it she was no closer to understanding the cause of his strange compulsion. And when they reached the riverbank, she found herself drawing back from his kisses, and searching his face for the absolute assurance his words had somehow failed to provide, while her headache grew worse and worse until she was compelled to return to the house. Neither aspirin nor rest would subdue the pounding in her head, and by the time she came down again he was gone, leaving only a note to say that he had not wanted to disturb her.

The following afternoon, Cordelia went up to the storeroom and carried "The Drowned Man" and its lectern back to its former place in the studio. If he could not resist it openly . . . she did not know what would follow, only that she could not bear the idea of his creeping back to it in the night; and besides, her uncle held the only other key to the studio.

The day was cool and bright; a light breeze came through the open window, causing one of the pictures hanging on the opposite wall to sway and tap very lightly against the panelling. She finished sweeping the floor, then turned the easel so that it faced the light, sat down on the bed, and tried to lose herself in the portrait. Glowing, vibrant, perfectly composed, Imogen de Vere regarded her with intimate understanding. It struck Cordelia, not for the first time, that an observer might easily assume that the portrait was to her what "The Drowned Man" was to Harry. She had spent another restless night, and much of the day, brooding upon the possible causes of its power over him. Was it related, somehow, to his unflagging determination to locate and befriend Henry St Clair? Harry had yet to uncover a single scrap of evidence beyond what was stored in these two rooms, but his conviction that St Clair was alive and, as it were, waiting for Harry to knock on his door, remained unshaken.

It would have been better if they had left everything alone; this had all sprung from her idea of restoring the studio. She had felt so certain that the evil had been banished . . . but then she did not—did she?—truly believe in the power of curses. Not on a sunny afternoon like this, and besides, it made no sense. De Vere had not painted "The Drowned Man"; St Clair had. And even if you believed in—the sort of thing that came to you, lying awake in the dark, recalling, all too vividly, the story of de Vere's last days—there was nothing else in the room that could possibly . . .

Except the polished wooden cube in the corner at the foot of the bed.

It was much heavier than she remembered—of course, Harry had helped her lift it—and though there was no discernible rustling this time, she thought that something moved or shifted very slightly inside it as she set it down on the bed. You could not tell which way up it was supposed to go, if there was a right way: the six side panels looked exactly the same. Each had been overlaid with a plain strip of polished wood—cedar or mahogany, she thought—around the outside, so that the actual panel was recessed, with an elaborately carved rosette, about the size of a florin, in the centre. As she turned the box from side to side, she found herself coming back to one particular rosette, until it occurred to her to count the carved petals. All of the others had twelve petals; this one had thirteen. Gingerly, she tried pressing, and then twisting the rosette, and felt it turn very slightly. What might it be? Surely nothing could still be alive in there? A vision of huge, veinous eggs had her leaping away from the bed, almost knocking over the easel. Should she call her uncle? He would tell her, quite rightly, to leave it alone. Yes: put it back in the corner, or better still, lock it away in the room next door. But already those eggs had begun to hatch in her imagination. What if it sprang open, like a jack-in-the-box, as soon as she picked it up? Far better to leave it for Harry to move next Saturday; but that would mean five days of picturing monstrous spiders swarming about the studio, for the lid might fly up as soon as she locked the door . . .

An altercation of blackbirds in a nearby oak subdued these fearful visions sufficiently for her to seize the broom. Without giving herself time to think, she twisted the rosette with her other hand as far as it would go and sprang away again.

A dark line had appeared along the edge of the panel. She waited, straining to listen over the thudding of her heart, but nothing more happened. Holding the broom at arm's length, she tried to work the bristles into the crack, but her hand trembled so violently that she dislodged the panel completely, and it slid down onto the bed.

Nothing came out. Edging closer, she saw that the top of the box was tightly packed with crumpled-up sheets of newspaper. She began to dislodge these with the broom, which compelled her to move closer to the box as she worked down through the layers of packing until she began to uncover something green—a hard, rounded object about the size of . . . a turkey's egg . . . wrapped in a fine emerald green velvet cloth . . . no, an emerald green *gown*, she could see from the stitching . . . and the thing inside couldn't be an egg, because it had a dome-like protuberance at one end, with some sort of spike, perhaps, beyond that, and when she tapped it very lightly with the broom handle she could hear a muffled ringing sound. Gently, she prised up the bundle so that it lay on top of the packing. Whatever was inside could not weigh very much. She tapped with her fingers; too hard to be an egg. It felt like glass.

She lifted out the bundle, set it down on the bed, and began, very cautiously, to unwrap it. The object had been placed inside the waist of the gown, with the rest of the fabric folded around it. Not liking to reach inside, and trying not to stand too close, Cordelia began to lift the gown away. But her hands were seized by a sudden tremor; the thing slid out very suddenly, and before she could stop it, rolled off the edge of the bed and smashed to fragments.

All she retained was the impression of something like a distended electric light bulb, with long thin tubes or spikes of glass at both ends. There was one of the broken-off glass spikes, with a needle-like wire emerging from the end of it . . . and part of another; and a small square of thin dark metal, curved like a curling leaf, . . . and a third fragment of glass tubing, connected by wire to another metal square, the same size, but flat, and silvered like the back of a mirror.

Her curiosity was blotted out by the realisation of what she had done. They could lose the income, and the house; and Harry, for all his loyalty, was the last person she could tell. She must wrap up the fragments, put everything back in the box, and pray that nobody ever opened it again. As she moved to drape the gown over the bed, she saw that it was, undoubtedly, the gown that Imogen de Vere was wearing in the portrait.

And now she would have to sweep up all of the broken glass, and bundle it up in the gown . . . which she found she was holding so as to measure it against herself; it looked exactly her size. Though terribly crumpled, it was only a little musty. And the jagged edges would tear the velvet . . . no; she could not. The packing had been so flat, when the lid came off; it had surely never been disturbed. She draped the gown across the bed and unfolded one of the pieces of paper. *The Times*. Friday, 3rd December, 1896. Which would have been, from her recollection of her uncle's narrative, either just before, or shortly after Henry St Clair's things had been seized by the bailiffs.

But he would never have treated the gown with such contempt, assuming Imogen had left it at the studio. This was de Vere's work . . . all the more reason not to do his bidding. That green dress she had not worn for ages would do perfectly well to wrap the fragments. Meanwhile, it struck her that the safest place for the gown would be in the closet in Grandmama's room, which she had not entered since the day Papa had caught her wearing the veil; nor, so far as she knew, had anyone else. But if Uncle Theodore happened to go up to his room, two doors along from Grandmama's . . . she decided to hide the gown in her own closet for the time being, and wait until the coast was clear.

When she had swept up the glass and got the lid back on the box, she came downstairs and established that her uncle was dozing in his study. Then, without quite knowing why, she went back up to the first floor and let herself quietly into her grandmother's room.

Dust swirled as she crossed the floor and drew open the curtains. The stale, musty air was still warm from the previous day's heat. The furniture seemed to have shrunk; the swing mirror no longer towered over her. A faint odour of camphor greeted her as she opened the closet door, along with a vivid memory of playing at ghosts with Beatrice. Several dresses hung from the rail, all in sombre colours, and all "sensible", like the stout shoes on the floor. Imogen, she reminded herself, had arrived here in the clothes she stood up in. What had happened to the magnificent wardrobe she must have had at Belgrave Square? Her jewels? Books, letters, keepsakes? De Vere must have sold or destroyed everything else.

As she wandered about the room, Cordelia was struck by the realisation that her habit of thinking of Imogen de Vere and Grandmama as two separate people was in no way fanciful. Whether or not he had caused the illness—"his spittle burned like acid", she recalled Uncle Theodore saying—Imogen de Vere had died to the world, and perhaps even to herself that night, and woken as Grandmama, condemned always to wear a veil . . . which Papa must have returned to the bottom drawer of the press, for there it was, laid out exactly as she had seen it last.

Breathing again the scents of camphor and some sort of salve or balm, mixed with the faintest hint of another fragrance, Cordelia felt a sudden powerful urge to put it on, and for the second time in her life, she drew the black veil over her head and turned towards the mirror.

The verse about seeing in a glass darkly came to her. No wonder she had given herself—and Papa—such a fright. Her dress looked strangely incongruous below the veil, as though her own head and shoulders had been replaced with those of another person whose outlines could be glimpsed, in the stronger light from the window, floating in a black mist of gauze.

A floorboard creaked in the corridor outside. She drew off the veil and held her breath, listening, but there was no further sound beyond the faint thudding of her heart, and when she opened the door cautiously and looked out, the corridor was empty. Feeling that it would be safer in her own room, she folded the veil and carried it upstairs, where she hid it away in her closet, beside the emerald green gown.

The mantel clock chimed the half-hour. The clouds had sunk even lower, merging into a uniform, leaden grey like the underside of a fog-bank which hung, seemingly motionless, just above the treetops across the lane. If he had arrived on the six o'clock train, he would surely be here by now; there would be at least another hour to wait.

Why could he never be on time? She would have run all the way from Bloomsbury to Victoria rather than sacrifice an hour in his company. Suddenly angry, she slid down off the window-ledge and made for the stairs. She would walk as far as the village, just in case, and then circle back to the stream, where she could at least bathe her feet in cool water.

The light beneath the trees was very dim; there was still not a breath of wind. She had gone about a hundred yards when she heard the sound of voices, and stopped beneath the deeper shadow of an oak.

Harry and Beatrice appeared at the next turning, some thirty yards away. They were walking slowly, close together and deep in conversation. Should she wave, or call out? As they approached, still without seeing her, though she was dressed in white—the same creamy-white sleeveless dress she had worn that first afternoon—Cordelia began to feel distinctly uncomfortable. They had come within a few paces when she stepped out into the middle of the lane.

(*Here the typescript broke off at the foot of a page.*)

PART TWO

HATHERLEY. DESCENDANT anxious to trace family history. Would anyone with any information about the early life and antecedents of Phyllis May Hatherley, granddaughter of Viola Hatherley, born Marylebone, London, 13 April 1929, married Graham John Freeman (1917–1982) in Mawson, South Australia, on 4 May 1963, died 29 May 1999, please contact her son, Gerard Freeman . . .

* * *

c/o Lansdown and Grierstone
Commissioners for Oaths
14A Bedford Row
London WC1N 5AB
12 June 1999

Dear Mr Freeman,

I am writing in reply to your advertisement in this morning's *Times*. I am afraid I am not equipped to reply by fax or email as you suggest, and hope that you will be able to decipher my arthritic handwriting! I hope, too, that you will accept a stranger's condolences on the recent death of your mother.

To come straight to the point: in 1944 I was moved, due to the upheavals of the war, to St Margaret's School in Devon to complete my education. My new form mistress (who believed in order above all things) did not allow personal preference to determine the seating arrangements in her classroom. Desks were assigned alphabetically by surname, and so I was placed next to a girl called Anne Hatherley, who soon became my closest friend.

Anne Hatherley and her younger sister Phyllis (whom I never met, though we once spoke on the telephone) were brought up in London by their grandmother, Viola Hatherley, and their aunt Iris, Viola's unmarried daughter. I felt certain, therefore, as soon as I saw your advertisement, that your late mother and my dear friend's sister must be one and the same person. To make doubly sure, I re-read some of Anne's letters this morning, and established that Phyllis's birthday was the 13th of April. Anne was born on the 6th of March, 1928, and since Phyllis was just a year younger than her sister, the dates match perfectly.

Viola Hatherley died just after VE Day, and Anne was of course obliged to leave school immediately and return to London. I remained at home in Plymouth, but Anne and I wrote constantly for the next four years, and saw each other whenever we could. Her Aunt Iris died in the autumn of 1949, and soon after that Anne's letters abruptly ceased. I never heard from her again.

I shall, of course, be only too pleased to help you in any way I can. Do please write to me by sealed enclosure, c/o my solicitor, Mr Giles Grierstone, who handles all of my affairs, including my correspondence. I wonder – and I do hope you won't be offended by this – whether you would mind providing him with formal proof of your own, and your late mother's identity, including, if possible, photographs. Anything you send him will be treated in the strictest confidence.

Though you do not mention Anne in your advertisement, I do hope you will be able to tell me what became of her; I have never ceased to wonder.

Yours sincerely

(Miss) Abigail Hamish

c/o Lansdown and Grierstone
Commissioners for Oaths
14A Bedford Row
London WC1N 5AB
27 June 1999

Dear Mr Freeman,

Thank you very much for your kind and most informative letter. I do appreciate all the trouble you have gone to in providing Mr Grierstone with so much documentation, and so promptly. The photograph of your mother in the full bloom of youth, nursing your infant self, is most touching – I can certainly see a resemblance to Anne as I remember her. An aversion to being photographed must have run in the family, for Anne steadfastly refused to give me even a single snapshot of herself.

It was indeed a shock to learn that your mother always

spoke of herself as an only child. Yet I was not wholly surprised, for reasons I could not divulge until we had established beyond doubt that your mother was Anne's younger sister. I fear that what follows will prove distressing, but you have urged me to be frank, and I shall do my best.

There is very little I can tell you about your mother's childhood. Like your mother (perhaps it will be easier if I call her Phyllis), Anne almost never spoke of the loss of her parents; she herself was only two years old when the accident happened. They were brought up by their grandmother and their aunt Iris, in very comfortable surroundings; they had a nurse, and a cook, and a maid, and later a governess, and had never known any other life. By the time I met her, Anne had come to believe that her childhood would not have been nearly as happy had her parents lived. Whether Phyllis felt the same, I simply don't know. The war of course brought great upheaval: the girls, like so many children, were sent away from London when the bombing began in earnest. Iris and two of her spiritualist friends – she was a devout believer in séances and ouija boards and so on, despite Viola's scorn for such activities (odd that Viola, who wrote ghost stories, should have been the sceptic) – but I see I am getting into one of those parenthetical muddles that Miss Tremayne (the form mistress who believed in order above all things) was always warning me against.

Iris, I was going to say, took a cottage at Okehampton so as to be near the girls, but Viola refused to leave London, even at the height of the Blitz. The Germans, she declared, were not going to drive her out of her house. Though I never met Viola, Anne took me to tea with Iris on two or three occasions. 'Auntie's very sweet,' I remember her saying, 'but she will talk about her spirits as if they're real people you ought to be able to see. I've never minded, but it gets on Filly's nerves.' All I can recall of Iris is that she was tall and slightly stooped; my memory for faces is usually very good, but hers won't come to me as anything more than a vague impression of kindness. I have a feeling she may have been very short-sighted. Anne told me later that Iris lost her fiancé in the Great War and never got over it – but I am wandering from the point again.

The reason I never met Phyllis was that she left St Margaret's a few months before I arrived, to study typing and shorthand, I'm afraid I don't know where. I do know that she was working for a firm of solicitors in Clerkenwell soon after the war. Viola, you see, believed that girls should be able to earn their living, regardless of expectations. Anne had hoped to go on to Oxford, but Viola's death changed everything. Iris went quite to pieces, and because she and Phyllis did not really get on, much of the burden necessarily fell upon Anne. Of course they had no idea, when Viola died, that Iris had only a few years left to live.

As I think I mentioned in my previous letter, I was obliged to remain with my family in Plymouth. My own father was ill – he had served as an engineer with the Eighth Army, and his lungs were badly affected by diesel fumes – and I was needed to help look after him. Perhaps that was part of the bond with Anne. Our circumstances then were surprisingly similar. Viola's estate had been much reduced by the war, and if she had lived much longer, they would have had to sell the house to pay the punitive death duties that came in with Mr Attlee. And of course we were all coping with the exigencies of rationing, the constant shortages and so forth. We went on writing, and Anne came down to Plymouth several times to stay with us. My father was very strict, and would not allow me to go up to London on my own, much as I would have loved to.

I still remember those visits as the happiest days of my life. Anne was (or so I have always thought) an exceptionally beautiful young woman, quite without vanity – she had a lightness about her, a natural freedom from self-consciousness, or perhaps I mean self-absorption – but I must get on.

In the spring of 1949, Anne met a young man called Hugh Montfort. She was uncharacteristically reticent about him – perhaps fearing that I would be hurt by this new attachment – but as the weeks went by his name began to appear more and more frequently in her letters. It was plain that he was spending a great deal of time at the house. On the 30th of July she wrote to tell me he had asked her to marry him. She wanted to bring him down to Plymouth to meet me as soon as he could get away for a few days. But she never did. By the 20th of September it was all off. 'I promise I'll tell you everything, Abbie,' she wrote, 'but not just yet.'

Then on the 1st of October I got a hurried scrawl. 'The most awful thing has happened,' she wrote. 'Auntie and Phyllis have had the most dreadful set-to, I can't say what about, but Filly has run away. She packed two suitcases and left in a taxi, we don't know where she's gone, and Auntie has sent for Pitt the Elder' (Mr Pitt, their solicitor, it was a family joke) 'and I'm afraid she means to change her will. We're all at sixes and sevens – I'll write as soon as ever I can, love always, Anne.'

On the 8th of October she wrote a brief note to tell me that her aunt had died suddenly, of heart failure. Iris was only sixty-two. Of course I pleaded with my father to let me go up to town, but he would not allow it. I telephoned the house several times (from a call box – we did not have the telephone at home) but there was no answer, and no reply to my letters.

At last I resolved to defy my father. I took the money from my post office savings, caught the train to Paddington, and made my way, with much trepidation, to Ferrier's Close in Hampstead. The house, I should have said, was built by a bachelor uncle of Viola's. She was his favourite, and he left it to her outright. It was right on the edge of the Heath, in the gloomiest corner of the Vale of Health – or so it seemed to me. Anne had described the house so often and so vividly I felt I had been there, but in her descriptions it was always sunlit. On that bleak, cheerless November day, it looked more like a prison. The brick wall at the front was topped with broken glass, and so high that I could only see the upstairs windows. The blinds were down, the curtains drawn. No smoke rose from the chimneys. The only entry was through a wooden door in the front wall. Anne had told me that this door was always kept unlocked during the daytime, if there was anyone home, but it would not open. I stood shivering in the lane for nearly an hour, until all I could think to do was leave a note in the letter-box and begin the long journey home.

My parents, when they had got over their anger, took the view that it was none of our business. Of course Anne couldn't have stayed there alone, they said; she must have gone to relatives or friends. It was sheer selfishness on my part to expect her to write at a time of such grief. I could see the sense of this, but I was not convinced. Eventually I summoned the courage to look up Mr Pitt's address – I could think of no one else to approach – and write to him. He replied by return, to say that he had heard nothing from Anne for three months – it was now February – and would I please call at his office in Holborn as soon as was convenient?

Mr Pitt's letter was alarming enough, but nothing could have prepared me for the shock that followed. On the 26th of October (a fortnight before my own fruitless visit to the Vale of Health), Anne had come to see him in his office. Aunt Iris had indeed changed her will a week before she died, cutting out Phyllis altogether and leaving everything she possessed to Anne. Now Anne insisted on making a will of her own – naming Mr Pitt as her executor, and leaving the entire estate to 'my dearest and most trusted friend Abigail Valerie Hamish'.

Of course (as he later admitted to me) Mr Pitt suspected undue influence, a designing young woman preying upon her grief-stricken friend, but when he saw how shaken I was by the news of the bequest – the recollection of it still makes me feel dizzy and short of breath – his manner softened perceptibly.

Surely, he had asked Anne several times, she did not mean to perpetuate her aunt's injustice toward Phyllis? To this Anne would only reply, very despondently, that she *knew*, for reasons she would not discuss, that her sister would never accept a penny from her. He told her that she was in no state to make decisions (she was looking very unwell, he thought, and her face had come out in a rash) but she would not listen. He brought out every argument he could summon, but in the end she declared, exactly as her aunt had done a few weeks earlier, that if he would not do as she asked, she would go to another solicitor. 'I can't stay in London,' he remembered her saying, 'I have to get away, and I want you to look after things for me.' Very reluctantly, he agreed. She signed the will, and promised to keep in touch with him.

By the time I came to see him, Mr Pitt was already anxious about her safety. Even more alarming than her silence was the fact that no money had been withdrawn from her account. He alerted the police, and advertised repeatedly, asking anyone who knew the whereabouts of Anne or Phyllis to contact him, all without result. Of course we did not know that your mother had emigrated to Australia, which explains her silence. So much grief, as I have often reflected, sprang from that one quarrel between your mother and her aunt. Such a pity – but I must get on.

As the years passed with no news of Anne, I remained closely in touch with Mr Pitt. He was in his sixties when I first met him, and when ill health forced him to retire, he prevailed upon me to assume the role of executor. (There was no Pitt the Younger, you see, that was part of the joke.) After he died, I took my business to a Mr Urquhart, who proved unsatisfactory, and thence to Lansdown and Grierstone, with whom, as you can see, I have remained ever since. I was advised by Mr Urquhart that, as nothing had been heard of Anne for more than seven years, I ought to commence proceedings to have her declared legally dead, and take possession of the estate. This, of course, I refused ever to contemplate.

I should have mentioned that when the police came to search the house, they found nothing amiss, and concluded that Anne had simply packed her things, locked up the house and left. Mr Pitt, I know, was much troubled by the fear that she might have made away with herself; I have never allowed myself to believe that she would do such a thing, just as I have never ceased to hope that she is still alive. But I confess that not knowing has caused me much torment. I seem to have spent the greater part of my life waiting for news of

Anne. And now, quite suddenly it seems, I am an old woman, and must think about my own will as well as fulfilling my duty to the estate.

I am very tired – so much emotion revisited – and must make an end of this long letter. Writing it has stirred, once again, my passionate yearning to *know*, for certain, what became of my best and dearest friend, what really happened during those last troubled months before her disappearance: why she broke her engagement to Hugh Montfort, and what (if you will forgive my curiosity) precipitated the disastrous falling-out between your mother and Iris. My intuition has always hinted that the answers are to be found somewhere in the house by the Heath. In earlier years – after I had accepted the post of executor and could legitimately enter the house – I came up to town several times with the intention of making a thorough search. But the house is very large, not to say labyrinthine, and daunting, even by day, to a single woman who hears an intruder in every creaking board! It is many years – decades, indeed, since I last set foot in it. And of course I never liked to employ an outsider.

I wonder, therefore – since you will be in London very shortly – whether, before you come down to see me, as I very much hope you will, you would be kind enough to look over the house for me, just to see if anything turns up in the way of letters, notebooks, diaries and so forth. As a professional librarian, you will I am sure be interested in the Ferrier family library, which contains several thousand books. I am afraid the electricity was disconnected many years ago, and the garden is dreadfully overgrown, but it will be high summer when you arrive. Mr Grierstone will have the keys waiting for you at Bedford Row. And please feel free to follow your instinct wherever it may lead. Perhaps it is merely an old woman's fancy, but I feel there is a destiny at work here, and that if anyone is ever to uncover the answers, it will be you.

I am very much looking forward to meeting you.

Yours most sincerely,

Abigail Hamish

Lansdown and Grierstone
Commissioners for Oaths
14A Bedford Row
London WC1N 5AB
12 July 1999

Dear Mr Freeman,

We have received your letter addressed to our client Miss Abigail Hamish. I regret to inform you that Miss Hamish has suffered a slight stroke and is undergoing treatment in a private nursing home. It may be some weeks before she is well enough to reply to your letter, or to receive visitors.

In the meantime, however, we are instructed to make available to you the keys to the house at Ferrier's Close, 34 Heath Villas, Hampstead. These may be collected at the above address at your convenience, on presentation of appropriate identification, such as your passport.

Yours faithfully,

Giles Grierstone

From: Parvati.Naidu@hotmail.com
To: ghfreeman@hotmail.com
Subject: Alice is fine and sends you all her love
Date: Tue, 20 Jul 1999 20:12:46 +0100 (BST)

Dear Gerard,

Alice asked me to email you as soon as I could (I'm the ward sister) to tell you that the operation was a complete success. Mr MacBride says she'll have to lie completely still for the next forty-eight hours to let the sutures settle down. She says she'll write to you as soon as she's allowed to sit up.

I hope you don't mind me saying, but I think it's so romantic, the two of you having waited so long. Alice is so beautiful, we all love her. I'm sure you'll be blissfully happy together.

Must dash,

Parvati

FROM THE laneway outside, all I could see of Ferrier's Close was a mass of rampant foliage, towering above a weathered brick wall. The wall itself was at least ten feet high, shrouded at the top by overspilling branches, holly and buddleia and rampant blackberries. A solid wooden door, reinforced with iron straps, was the only entrance, just as Miss Hamish had said. Further along to my right, the lane was cut off by the stone wall of another house, with a third wall, painted white, running back behind me. Though most of the houses in the Vale opened directly on to the narrow streets, the occupants of this corner (somewhere on the western side; I had lost my bearings among the twists and turns and narrow passageways that had brought me, circuitously, to this cul-de-sac) clearly cherished their privacy. Luxury cars, stained with sap and bird droppings and humped up on the pavement, were the only evidence of occupation.

Just on two o'clock. The walk up from Hampstead Heath station had been uncomfortably hot, but here beneath the overarching canopy, the air was cool and damp. I had been in London just three days, and already I felt more at home than I ever had in Mawson. The transformation was extraordinary. On Saturday afternoon, after settling into my new, clean, high-rise hotel near St Pancras, I had wandered for hours through leafy streets and squares, breathing deep lungfuls of warm, diesel-laden air as if I had just arrived at a mountain health resort. People no longer avoided eye contact with strangers. The mountains of garbage had shrunk to a few isolated middens. Even the dogs seemed to have cleaned up their act.

I strolled up to the end of the lane and back, weighing the heavy bunch of keys in my hand. No one would know there was a house hidden behind the massive trees, some of them sixty or seventy feet high. I wondered how high they had been when Abigail Hamish had stood shivering here, just a few months short of fifty years ago, at the end of autumn. Most of the branches would have been bare.

Miss Hamish, as I had learned from Mr Grierstone's secretary a few hours ago, was now resting comfortably and would be in touch with me as soon as she felt well enough. She wasn't up to visitors, but I could certainly send her some flowers; they would be happy to arrange that on my behalf.

And for the first time in my life, I knew exactly where Alice was. In the National Hospital for Neurology and Microsurgery in East Finchley, less than an hour's walk across the Heath from Ferrier's Close. I had promised not to visit, or ring the hospital: Alice thought it would bring bad luck. She wanted to come to me, with no warning – 'it'll be too awkward and formal otherwise'. Like a bride and groom keeping apart on their wedding day, not seeing each other until the ceremony. 'I want to save everything from now until we meet,' she'd said in her last message. She was spending long hours in physiotherapy, gaining strength every day. 'My feet haven't forgotten how to walk. I'm aching all over, and it feels wonderful. Nothing can go wrong now. Enjoy your house' – Alice was convinced that Miss Hamish meant to leave the whole estate to me – 'and its mysteries, and soon – maybe sooner than you think – you'll hear a tap on the door.'

Secretly I agreed with her about the estate, but I didn't want to tempt fate by saying so: Miss Hamish might have another stroke and die before she'd met me. In which case the estate would presumably go to charity, or some distant Hamish relative; she sounded quite alone in the world. Tempting fate or not, I couldn't help imagining us arriving at Miss Hamish's place in the country – which had grown, in my fantasy, into a tall, rambling house with sweeping lawns and ancestral oaks – into Staplefield, in fact.

Though Miss Hamish hadn't replied to any of my questions about Staplefield, that might well have been out of delicacy – for the same reason she hadn't yet given me her address. The destruction of Staplefield would have been a huge and traumatic event; Anne would have talked about it. Whereas if the house had survived, it was quite possible that Miss Hamish, once she'd been appointed executor, had decided to rent Staplefield from the estate. Or simply to live there: as the sole beneficiary of Anne's will, her only legal duty had been to herself. She just didn't want to tell me, until the time came for us to meet, that my mother had lied about the fire.

Back in Mawson, reading and re-reading Miss Hamish's letter in the chilly hallway, a ghastly suspicion had leapt off the page. It had obviously never occurred to Miss Hamish – she could never have written so openly if it had – that Phyllis Hatherley might have murdered her sister. Everything fitted perfectly: Phyllis and her aunt quarrel violently; Phyllis is disinherited and leaves home in a rage; her aunt dies suddenly (and very conveniently) within weeks, leaving everything to sweet-natured Anne, who immediately makes a will leaving everything to her best friend Abigail. Why would a girl of twenty-one make such a will, unless she was afraid of her sister? But Anne doesn't know where Phyllis is, so she can't tell her about the will. Until, perhaps, it's too late. Phyllis discovers she's killed her sister for nothing, and that's the last we see of her until she turns up in Mawson a decade later.

It had seemed horribly plausible, until I realised that the same thing must have occurred to the police and the lawyer. It would have been their first line of inquiry. And they would have questioned Abigail Hamish about Phyllis: they would have wanted to see Anne's letters. So the police, and the lawyer – and therefore Miss Hamish – *must* have been satisfied that Phyllis was innocent. Otherwise Miss Hamish would never have trusted me with the keys to Ferrier's Close.

Or so I had persuaded myself. There were at least a dozen keys on the ring: three pitted gunmetal Banhams; two for spring locks, and several household keys, very worn and tarnished, for barrel-locks of various sizes. The door itself was curved at the top and recessed into the brickwork. It had weathered to a pale greenish grey, mottled with lichen; lines of moss sprouted between the vertical planks. A discoloured nameplate, a brass mailslot, locked or corroded shut, a latch and a keyhole. No bellpush or speaker grille; no way of making your presence known except to pound with your bare knuckles on the swollen timbers of the door.

The second of the Banham keys fitted the lower keyhole: the snap as it turned over was startlingly loud. I lifted the latch and pushed, against resistance. To my surprise the door opened silently.

I was standing at the entrance to a tunnel about eight feet high, formed by hooped metal frames over which branches of some kind had been trained. Dim twilight filtered through an arched roof of dense greenery; a few spots of sunlight glowed on the flagged stone floor. At the far end, some thirty feet away, I could just make out two steps leading up to another door. Vines and creepers and climbing roses had grown up amongst the gnarled branches; the metal hoops were heavily corroded. But the inside of the tunnel had been recently pruned. The clipped ends of vines and shoots were still sharply defined, the dark, lichen-stained flagstones bare except for a scattering of leaves.

I withdrew the key and let go of the street door. It closed behind me with a faint hiss. The spring lock clicked shut; suddenly fearful, I snatched at the knob to make sure I wouldn't be trapped.

It had been quiet in the lane outside, but you could still hear the faint hum of traffic from East Heath Road, the occasional howl of an accelerating motorbike, the distant whine of a jumbo from the endless queue descending towards Heathrow. With the closing of the gate, all of those sounds had ceased. The tick-ticking of my pulse was suddenly louder. I set off along the path, accompanied by faint rustlings and stirrings. Birds, I hoped, though I couldn't see any. The surrounding vegetation was impenetrably dense.

At the far end, the sides thinned out enough to allow glimpses of red brick and stonework, and the light was a little better. Though the tunnel – what was the word? – espaniered? – no, pleached – extended all the way to the porch, you could see where the original structure had ended and another section had been added, also many years ago, by the look of the gnarled vines overhead. I went up the two steps into a porch, only a few feet deep, with solid brick walls on both sides. It looked as if there had once been vertical windows on either side of the door, but the apertures had been bricked up. No glass in the door, either. Its dark green paint was cracked and peeling.

Three locks this time. After the snap of the second Banham, I had to wait until my heartbeat had slowed enough to distinguish it from approaching footsteps. I glanced back along the green, twilit alley and turned the key in the spring lock.

The door opened quietly, on to a dimly lit entrance hall. Dark panelled walls, an elaborate hall-stand immediately to my left, then a recessed wooden bench. Carpeted stairs at the far end ran up to a half-landing. Light filtered through a doorway to the left of the staircase. I stepped across the threshold, keeping hold of the front door, which like the street door appeared to be self-closing. I took another step forward, letting the door close behind me with the same faint, unnerving hiss.

The hall-stand was draped with hats and coats and scarves; there were several umbrellas and at least three pairs of Wellingtons. The sense of trespass was suddenly overwhelming.

'Is anyone here?' A muffled echo – I couldn't tell from where – sounded disturbingly like a reply. Then I noticed that the hats and coats – all of them women's – looked very old-fashioned indeed. Tentatively, I drew out one of the umbrellas. A small cloud of dust followed, and I saw that there were holes in the fabric.

I tried to move noiselessly, but the floorboards creaked at every step. At the far end of the hall, I found a closed wooden door to the right of the staircase. An opening to my left led into a passage running towards the rear of the house. Multicoloured light shimmered through a doorway opposite.

At first I thought I had stumbled into a chapel. Two tall, narrow stained-glass windows shone in the upper half of the wall to my left, an elaborate design of leaves and vines and flowers climbing over a plain, lead-lighted background. The moving shadows of actual leaves and branches outside made it look as if the pattern had come alive, greens and golds and brilliant crimsons rippling upwards into darkness.

Tall wooden shutters, latched on the inside, concealed the windows in the lower section. Humped shapes of furniture stood around a massive fireplace opposite the door. To my right, the lower half of the rear wall opened on to what looked like a dining-room. A gallery was built out above the opening, running the full width of the room.

Crossing to the shutters, I got the first one open and came face to face with a chaotic mass of nettles, buddleia and leaf litter, shot through with ivy and rising above head height. Sunlight filtered through the foliage overhead. The windows were protected by vertical metal bars almost eaten through with rust.

Apart from some archaic electric light fittings mounted on wall brackets, I could have stepped back into the 1850s. The brocaded chairs and sofas, mostly faded lemons and pale greens, the chests and screens and occasional tables, were all marked and worn by use. The polish on the woodwork had faded long ago; you could see the outlines of ancient stains on the huge, threadbare Persian carpet. And yet someone must be coming in from time to time to dust and air the place, and turn on some sort of heating in the winters, or everything would be rotten with damp and mould.

I moved on towards the dining-room, whose dark panelled ceiling, though still ten or twelve feet high, was only half the height of the drawing-room's. The opening between the two, I saw, could be closed off by a set of sliding panels which stood folded, concertina-fashion, against the right-hand wall. The gallery loomed overhead: it had a gilt rail at about waist height, with vertical rods below the railing, and doors at both ends.

Troubled by a vague sense of something missing or wrong, I moved on through the dining-room, between a long oak table with chairs for a dozen people, and a massive sideboard laden with tarnished serving dishes and candlesticks. With the drawing room closed off, it would be pitch dark in here. But when I got the shutters in the end wall open, daylight filled the room. I found myself looking down on to a flagged courtyard, surrounded once again by an impenetrable tangle of greenery.

The land on which the house was set evidently sloped downwards, for the window was at least ten feet above the ground, but the view beyond the courtyard was obscured on every side by rampant, towering foliage. Weeds sprouted between the flagstones. Below and to my right, a long, narrow conservatory had been built out along the rear wall of the house. From the far side of the courtyard, a path continued a few yards further, towards what looked like the remains of an ancient gazebo or summerhouse, half buried beneath a canopy of nettles.

I pressed my face against the glass, but could see nothing more. There were no bars on these windows, and no visible locks or bolts, but neither side would budge. I went on through a door to the right of the windows, on to a landing from which a wide staircase descended. A narrower flight ran steeply up to another half-landing on its way to the floor above. There were several other doors to choose from, but I went on down, hoping to find a way out on to the courtyard so that I could see the house from the outside.

I found a small parlour or breakfast room, immediately below the dining room, with shuttered French windows opening – or rather refusing to open – on to the courtyard. Behind the parlour was a small kitchen – 1920s or 30s, I thought – three-burner gas cooker, chipped porcelain sink, wooden cupboards and benches. Mixed crockery, also chipped and cracked, that looked like the remnants of expensive services. A few tins rusting in the food cupboard, labels long gone.

The main house door next to the parlour was painted a drab black. It appeared to be locked and bolted. To the right of that was another set of French windows, also locked, into the conservatory. Peering through the glass, I saw a long trestle table crammed with pots and seed trays from which a few desiccated sticks protruded. Garden tools leaned against walls and benches. An old wooden barrow stood blocking one of the aisles.

No other doors. The stairs continued on down, back in under the house. Daylight slanted down the stairwell on to a patch of stone floor. From where I stood in the entrance, the original kitchen extended out to my left. An ancient black range with a corroded flue; brick walls; a scarred worktable; canisters rusting along a wall shelf in descending order of size. The air down here was colder, and distinctly damp; the ceiling was only a foot above my head. I took a few uneasy steps into the gloom. There was a doorway in the opposite wall, opening on to darkness.

I retreated up the stairs to the landing, took the first door on my left, opposite the dining-room, and was greeted by the warm, faintly sweet smell of printed paper and cloth boards, dust and leather and old bindings.

The shutters – polished wood here, rather than painted – opened into a library as imposing as the drawing-room. Tall bookcases rose like pillars between four high, narrow windows in the rear wall of the house. Around the other three sides of the room, a mezzanine gallery had been built about seven or eight feet above the floor, giving access to a second tier of shelves, with cases built out like piers from the recessed shelves below, so that the books in the lower section were housed in a series of alcoves. There was an open spiral staircase at the far end of the room, leading up to the gallery; a chesterfield and two cracked brown leather armchairs stood below the windows. The centre of the floor was taken up by a massive table covered in worn green baize, with four high-backed library chairs ranged around it. Several large blank sheets of what looked like butcher's paper had been left at one end of it, with a folded chessboard and some sort of child's toy on top of the pile.

I wandered along the cases, pulling out volumes at random. Blue books, parliamentary papers, regimental histories, accounts of military campaigns and naval battles, gazetteers, clerical lists, law lists, county histories and so forth, occupied an entire wall. A nineteenth-century gentleman's library. Belonging to one J.G. Ferrier . . . and a G.C. Ferrier . . . then a C.R. Ferrier, in thick, greyish ink on the flyleaf of *A Narrative of the Operations of a Small British Force Employed in the Reduction of Monte Video on the River Plate, A.D. 1807. By a Field Officer on the Staff.*

I moved on to the next wall. Literature: Greek and Latin, all J.G. Ferrier; the standard English poets, mostly in nineteenth-century editions inscribed by J.G. and G.C . . . until I took down one of several disintegrating Byrons and found 'V. Ferrier/ Jan. 1883' on the flyleaf in a clear, spiky hand. And in the next alcove, in a well-worn copy of Balzac's *Illusions perdues*, 'V. Hatherley/ Oct. 1901'.

Half an hour later, though I hadn't even started on the mezzanine gallery, I knew that Viola Ferrier had become Viola Hatherley some time between 1887 and 1889; that she often marked passages in her books, but did not annotate beyond an occasional cryptic reference such as 'v. *P. de C, ix*'; that she, or someone with whom she shared her books, had been a heavy smoker – traces of ash and fine shreds of tobacco appeared between numerous pages in all her books – and that she read widely and eclectically in French as well as English. A system of shelving books by author and subject had been gradually subverted, so that a book by one Georges Lakhovsky, *Le Secret de la vie: les ondes cosmiques et la radiation vitale*, marked simply 'VH/ Aug 1930', appeared between Richard Le Gallienne and Alice Meynell on a shelf devoted to the poets and essayists of the 1890s. Percy Brown's *American Martyrs to Science through the Roentgen Rays*, which looked as if it had been dropped in the bath or left out in the rain, lay sideways across the top of Lakhovsky.

Suddenly overtaken by a lurching wave of fatigue, I sat down at the central table. Filaments of dust drifted in the light from the four great windows on my right. *Soon, maybe sooner than you think* . . . Perhaps Alice would simply appear in her white dress, leaning over the gallery rail, smiling down at me . . . *I'll come to your house.*

From my perspective, the gallery formed an elevated U, with the spiral staircase immediately to the right of the windows. At the corresponding point on the opposite side, just before the end wall, one of the bookcases seemed to have been set back into the side wall at a considerable angle. No; a dummy bookcase, disguising a low, narrow door, like the ones on the galleries in the old Round Reading Room. Odd that I hadn't noticed it before.

Idly, I reached over to the stack of paper and picked up the toy. It resembled a miniature tricycle, four or five inches long, with two polished wheels at the back of a boat-shaped platform of the same dark wood. But instead of a front wheel, the stub of a pencil had been pushed through a hole at the front, point downward, and secured with a rubber band.

I put down the toy and opened the chessboard. Only it was not a chessboard. Instead of squares it had YES in the top left corner, next to an image of the sun, and NO opposite, next to the moon, above the letters of the alphabet set out in two shallow horseshoe arcs, then the numbers 1 to 10, and below that, GOODBYE. The William Flud Talking Board Set. John Waddington Ltd, Leeds & London, permitted user of the trade marks Ouija, William Flud and Mystifying Oracle.

Now I knew what the tricycle was. I leafed through the sheets of paper, but they were all blank. After a little practice with the – plechette? – no, planchette – I could produce legible words. On a clean sheet of paper I wrote

WHAT HAPPENED TO ANNE?

in large, spidery letters, and set the planchette below the W, with my fingers resting lightly on the wooden platform.

I didn't – did I? – seriously expect it to answer. You needed at least two people, anyway. But I did have to find the answer myself if I possibly could. Because clearly Miss Hamish had given me the keys as a sort of test. To prove myself a worthy heir to Ferrier's Close and Staplefield. She had all but said so on the last page of her letter. *There is a destiny at work here . . . my passionate yearning to* know, *for certain, what became of my best and dearest friend . . . if anyone is ever to uncover the answers, it will be you.*

But suppose – just supposing – I were to discover that my mother really had murdered her sister? I would have to live with the knowledge for ever; it would poison my reunion (as I often found myself thinking, perhaps because of our shared dream) with Alice; and Miss Hamish certainly wouldn't leave me the estate.

Of course I didn't know that Anne Hatherley was dead. She might have . . . packed her things, suffered an attack of total amnesia, and started a new life under a different name? Joined a silent order of nuns and forgotten to tell anyone? Been abducted by aliens? All we knew for certain was that her body had never been found. Or at least identified.

The police found nothing amiss. But how thoroughly had they searched the house? Had they dug up the garden? What if the person who left with Anne's suitcases hadn't been Anne at all?

The old sick feeling of dread came flooding back. I released the planchette and tried to focus on breathing deeply and slowly. Unclench your hands. Concentrate on breathing. Repeat after me: if the police and the lawyer hadn't been certain that Phyllis was innocent, Miss Hamish would have known, because she was their principal witness.

And in the very worst case, if I were to uncover anything along those lines, telling Miss Hamish would be sheer, pointless cruelty. Whereas if I could come up with something benign – amnesia was, after all, a possibility, especially after so many traumatic events, coming so close together – or even a religious conversion, one of those blinding light experiences . . . really, I owed it to Miss Hamish to keep an open mind and not leap to conclusions that could only distress her. I hadn't even seen the upstairs rooms yet.

I had assumed that by the end of this first exploration, I would have gained a clear picture of the house and its surroundings. But the higher I climbed, the more disoriented I became. The air grew hotter and stuffier. I tried various windows on the upper floors, but none of them would budge: many above the ground floor were so thickly coated with grime that when blurred patches of the Heath began to appear amongst the tree-tops, I wasn't always sure which direction I was looking in. And yet there was something oddly familiar about the place.

The blurred views compounded the sensation of slipping backwards and forwards in time, for if it was still 1850 in the drawing-room below, the first-floor sitting-room had got as far as the 1940s: a large, light, comfortable room furnished with a sagging floral sofa, stuffed chairs, a massive cabinet radio to the right of the fireplace, and a bookcase full of novels: Galsworthy, Bennett, Huxley, early Graham Greene . . . Henry Green, Ivy Compton-Burnett . . . detective stories even I had never heard of, such as *The Public School Murder*, by R.C. Woodthorpe, inscribed 'V.H. Xmas 1932'. The window looked down upon the overgrown courtyard. A door to the right of the window led to the rear stairs – there seemed to be at least two different ways of getting from any one room to another – and to an L-shaped passage with doors leading to the mezzanine floor of the library at one end, and to the gallery above the drawing-room at the other.

Apart from the sitting-room at the rear of the house, there were only two other rooms on this level: another, much smaller sitting-room, and a bedroom, both opening off the front landing. The upper levels of the drawing-room and library and their respective galleries took up the rest of the space. The two front rooms, I decided, had probably been Iris's: the sitting-room bookcase held long runs of two spiritualist journals from the 1920s and 30s: *Light*, and *The Medium*, along with numerous volumes on theosophy, the tarot, Buddhism, astrology, astral travelling, divination, reincarnation, and more. I noticed a copy of *An Adventure* – which I had once skimmed – about the two women who claimed to have got lost in the gardens of Versailles and found themselves back in the eighteenth century. The closet was still full of clothes that looked as if they might have belonged to a tall, elderly woman; a rusting lipstick and several faded cardboard containers were neatly arranged on the dressing-table beneath a thick layer of dust.

I went on up the stairs to the second-floor landing. Ahead of me, a dim corridor led towards the rear of the house. Threadbare Persian runners over dark stained boards; William Morris paper, frayed and peeling at the joins.

I started down the corridor and tried the first door on my left. Daylight showed faintly below the curtains at the far end of the room, which shared a common wall with the landing. A musty old-dog smell rose from the carpet as I approached the window; for a moment I was a child again, trespassing in my mother's bedroom. I dragged the curtains open. Looking down at a blurred glimpse of laneway through thick foliage, I realised that this room must be directly above the drawing-room. Dust and fragments of the curtains – a dingy maroon – drifted down around me. To the right of the window stood a dressing-table with a swing mirror and a brocaded stool; on the left, an oak tallboy, and then a small bookcase. The bed, a single, draped in a bedspread the same colour as the curtains, stood with its head against the panelling opposite the window. The other three walls were papered: more fraying William Morris.

A closet had been let into the panelling beside the bed; the door was slightly ajar. Moving closer, I drew back the bedspread and saw that the bed was fully made up. A moth fluttered out from behind the pillow, trailing its own tiny cloud of dust as it whirred past my face. Inside the closet hung a single white dress or tunic; a yellowy, greyish white now. And on the floor below the dress, a tennis racquet, with ANNE HATHERLEY burnt in pokerworked capitals into the wooden handle.

The bedroom next door was almost a mirror image of Anne's, except that the window was in the side wall of the house. It too had a single bed, with its head against the common partition, and a closet built into the corresponding space to the left of the bed. The curtains and bedspread were dark green, made of the same heavy material. Nothing in the closet this time except dust and a few wire hangers. Just four books in a small case on the other side of the bed. *A High Wind in Jamaica*, *Rebecca*, *The Murder of Roger Ackroyd*, and *The Death of the Heart*. The Agatha Christie was unmarked. The other three had 'P.M. Hatherley' written in neat, slightly rounded script on the flyleaf.

For someone who had left home for ever with just a couple of suitcases, Phyllis Hatherley had done a remarkably thorough job of clearing out her room. Apart from the four novels, and a musty blanket in the bottom drawer of a chest by the window, the room was completely bare. Of course she might have come back later, when the house was empty . . . best not to think too far along that track. In fact it would make my task a lot easier if I were to think of Phyllis Hatherley and my mother as two quite separate people.

Which really, when you thought about it, they had been. And whatever Phyllis Hatherley might have done, Phyllis Freeman had paid for it with life in Mawson, no remission for good behaviour. I couldn't imagine my mother living in this house.

As I went to shut the door of the closet, it struck me that there must be quite a lot of unused space in the partition between the two rooms. I tried a panel above the bed and felt it give; pressed more firmly and it swung open. A cupboard, about eighteen inches square, the same depth as the closet. Empty again. Except that something heavy had evidently been kept in here: there were deep parallel scratches gouged into the wooden floor. A child could easily climb right inside; I imagined the girls tapping out messages at night, frightening each other with ghostly noises.

A loud clatter – or was it someone knocking? – sounded through the partition. I was out the door and half-way across the landing in a blind, panic-stricken rush for the stairs before I registered what I had glimpsed through the open door of Anne's room: curtains the colour of dried blood, heaped beneath the fallen curtain-rod.

I found I was holding my breath, straining to identify a faint rustling sound. A branch against the wall? Mice in the ceiling? Best keep moving.

Returning to the corridor, I saw a thin line of daylight, evidently coming from beneath a door at the far end. The room opposite Anne's was empty, unfurnished, and thick with dust; the next looked like Viola's. I opened a small jewelbox on the bedside table and found a gold wristwatch, engraved 'V. from M./ with love/ 7.2.1913'. 'V.H.' was inscribed in several of the books in the bookcase beneath the window, including, I noticed, a battered hardback copy of *The Sacred Fount*. Her clothes, or some of them, were still hanging in the closet, protected by the ghosts of old mothballs: everything from long tweed skirts to furs and several plain but very expensive-looking evening gowns, including one made of a material that shimmered like finely beaten gold, with shoes to match. But again no letters, no papers, no photographs.

The floor creaked more loudly at every tread, until boards were sounding up and down the hall as if invisible feet were moving all around me. I tugged at the end door, which opened inwards. Light from two high windows streamed into the corridor. There was one other door beyond Phyllis's: a boxroom, with only a small square window high in the wall. Trunks, cases, hampers, hat boxes, a golf-cart; more tennis racquets, croquet mallets, chairs with broken backs, a doll's house.

Two doors opened off the landing, on my right: a bathroom nearest the corridor. Bare board floor, porcelain washstand; an imposing claw-footed bathtub, darkly stained, with a greyish bath towel carelessly draped over the side. In the wall cabinet above the basin, a clutter of dried-up lipsticks, tubes, bottles, hairpins. Everything metal was heavily corroded, the labels unreadable.

I tried the other door. Not a closet, but yet more stairs, angling up to the left. I checked the door to make sure I couldn't be trapped, and clambered up. Two drab attic bedrooms, each with a single metal-framed bedstead; flock mattresses and pillows, tinder-brown with age, but no bedding. Plain wooden furniture, washstands with white china jugs and basins, bare boards. The windows were set like skylights into the sloping ceilings. Nothing in any of the cupboards.

Back on the landing, the sense of familiarity tugged at me again. Through the tall slit window in the stairwell I caught a blurred glimpse of the ruined summerhouse far below. The stairs came up on my right, with a railed balcony above the stairwell, extending about twelve feet to a dead end below the left-hand window. There was only one other door, immediately to my left, in the panelled wall that formed the other side of the balcony. Though there was nothing on the wall, I could see several slightly paler rectangles where pictures had once hung. The nearest of these was also the largest, at least five feet high and perhaps half as wide, just to the right of the door.

Pictures. The absence of pictures, or more precisely, portraits. That was what had troubled me in the downstairs rooms. The balcony was not the only place from which pictures had been removed. On several of the walls downstairs I had seen, without paying much attention, the outlines, and sometimes the empty hooks, where pictures had once hung, some of them very large indeed. A few small prints, mostly still lifes or rural scenes, remained. But so far no portraits, no photographs; not a single image of a human face.

I tried the handle of the door. Locked.

Like the door to the studio in *The Revenant*. With the portrait of Imogen de Vere beside it. The resemblance that had been tugging at me all the way along this floor. How could I have missed it? If the garden hadn't been so overgrown, I might have seen the resemblance from the lane outside.

Phyllis, Beatrice. Almost the same sound.

But that couldn't be right, because the typescript was dated December 1925, two years before Anne was born. Viola couldn't have known, then, that she would have two granddaughters. Or that her son and his wife would be killed in an accident. Miss Hamish had forgotten to mention when, or even what sort of accident; she must have assumed I knew.

The date could be wrong. But the story was set in 1925, seven years after the end of the Great War. And if she had been writing after the accident, Viola wouldn't, surely, have exploited her granddaughters' situation so closely. I already knew enough about her to feel certain of that.

And she absolutely couldn't have known that, four years after her death, her eldest granddaughter would become engaged to a man called Hugh Montfort.

Only I didn't know how the story ended. Or how many pages were missing. I had searched the house in Mawson all over again, even taken up the carpet in my mother's room, without finding anything more.

One came true.

What if this door opened on to Henry St Clair's pictures, 'The Drowned Man' on its lectern, the polished wooden cube with the carved rosette? What would I do then?

My concentration was broken by a faint rhythmic sound which seemed, as I became aware of it, to have been going on for some time. As I turned, a board creaked, and the noise ceased instantly. Birds or mice, no doubt – the walls must be full of them – but it had sounded unpleasantly like a nib scratching across stiff paper. Somewhere close by.

Suddenly I was stumbling down the rear stairs, glancing over my shoulder and trying not to run, all the way down to the massive black-painted door to the courtyard. None of the keys looked remotely large enough. Then I saw that the tongue, or whatever that part of the lock was called, was plainly retracted. Which was odd because I had – or thought I had – a clear memory of standing here a couple of hours ago and noticing that the door was locked. Jet lag, presumably. I dragged back the equally massive bolts and hauled the door open, letting in the scents of flowering creeper and warm stone.

The courtyard was about fifteen feet deep, and perhaps twice as wide; it was hard to tell because the surrounding wilderness encroached on every side. I crunched over dead twigs and leaf litter, past a rotting bench and several stone ornaments, cracked and flaking and pitted with lichen, to the path I had seen from above, hoping to find a way through to the boundary wall, wherever that might be.

The path, gravel with a stone border, had once been fairly wide, but the nettles had advanced so far that I had to clear the way with a fallen branch to avoid being stung. As I descended towards the wreck of the gazebo, I felt an odd prickle of recognition. It was a common enough structure: a wooden octagon, six or seven feet across, like a miniature bandstand, with a waist-high railing and entrances on opposite sides. Most of the roof had collapsed, leaving only a few corroded sheets of metal attached to the remnants of the frame. Traces of dark green paint still clung to the fallen sections.

Prompted by that elusive sense of recognition, I went on slashing and trampling the nettles until, at the cost of a filthy, sweat-soaked shirt and several painful weals, I had cleared a narrow circle around the gazebo. The slope here was quite steep, so that the entrance nearest the house was level with the path, whereas the one on the far side was at least two feet above the ground, with steps leading up to it. Wooden seats, enclosed like window-boxes, had been built around the sides.

As I was clearing away the debris of the fallen roof, I discovered that the middle sections of the seats on both sides of the gazebo were hinged. The lid on the right would not budge; the other one came up with a shriek of frozen hinges. Pale, bloated spiders scuttled away from the light. In the cavity below was a crumbling picnic hamper, black with dirt and mould and swathed in cobwebs. I used a stick to prise open the lid; apart from more dirt and spiders, all it contained was another, smaller box: an old-fashioned metal cashbox, I thought, about eight inches by ten, not very deep, with a handle in the centre of the lid. The rivets were so corroded that the latch came away in my hand.

Inside was a thick buff envelope, containing not jewels or banknotes, or the title deeds to Staplefield, but a mouldy paper-bound volume. *The Chameleon*. Volume I, Number 1, March 1898. Essays by Clement Shorter and Frederic Myers; poems by Ernest Radford and Alice Meynell; and 'The Pavilion', by V.H. As I turned to the beginning of Viola's story, a small printed slip fluttered from the pages. *With the author's compliments*. And in faded black ink, in Viola's clear, spiky hand: *for Filly if she can find it*.

The Pavilion

OF ALL places in the world, Rosalind Forster's favourite was Staplefield, a modest country house on the edge of St Leonard's Forest in Sussex, and the home, for much of the year, of her best friend Caroline Temple. Rosalind sometimes thought that wherever Caroline lived would seem the most desirable of all places, but there was no denying the beauty of Staplefield, with its light, airy rooms looking out over meadows and wooded hills to the south, and the sweep of the forest at its back. The two girls had been fast friends ever since their first meeting in town five years earlier, when Rosalind was fifteen and Caroline a year younger; they had been drawn together by a preference for solitude, strange as that may sound, over what usually passed for the delights of society, but were never happier than in each other's company. Both were only children, and both had recently lost beloved fathers—George Forster and Walter Temple had died within the same year—and their shared grief had further strengthened the bond between them.

Seeing them side by side you could almost have taken them for sisters, even though Caroline was fair and delicately featured, whilst Rosalind's complexion was quite dark, almost olive. They had a way of walking unconsciously in step, and of addressing one another, at times, as much through a shared language of gestures and facial expressions as through speech. But their situations were very different. Caroline and her mother had only a few hundred a year, but were content with a quiet country life and occasional visits to town; and the house, which since Walter Temple's death they had shared with his elder, widowed brother Henry, had belonged to the family for several generations. Whereas, though Rosalind's mother Cecily lived in Bayswater in much greater apparent splendour, it was all done on debt, as Rosalind was only too anxiously aware, to the point where their fortunes now appeared to hang upon Rosalind's answer to a proposal of marriage from one Denton Margrave. It was to consider this proposal that she had come down to spend a few days with her friend in the country, but though the two were usually inseparable, a severe headache had kept Caroline indoors on the autumn afternoon upon which we meet Rosalind setting out alone to walk in the surrounding fields. Caroline had positively declined to be read to, and insisted that her friend should take their accustomed excursion for them both, and for once Rosalind had allowed herself to be overruled, for she was restless and troubled, and felt that fresh air and movement would help dispel the cloud of oppression that hung about her mind and darkened her thoughts.

The sky was overcast and still as she left the house and made her way through the kitchen garden and across the lawns. She and Caroline had a favourite walk which took them through several fields and down to the riverbank with its canopy of willows, but today, on impulse, she turned right instead of left, in the direction of a steep, densely wooded hillside perhaps half a mile off. Even in the midst of her trouble, now that she was out in the open her old habit of dramatisation would not be stifled: she found herself mentally rehearsing scenes in which she rejected Mr Margrave's proposal, the first on the ground that she had firmly resolved to dedicate her life to Art, the second because she had given her heart irrevocably to Another. Such scenes were constantly presenting themselves to her youthful imagination with the utmost vividness; yet they would generally refuse to manifest themselves on paper when she sat down, as she so often did, determined to begin the work that would at last free herself and her mother from all financial anxiety. And on the rare occasions when she did manage to scribble down one of these dialogues as it passed, it would shortly reveal itself to be a thing of such hackneyed banality that she would hasten to destroy it.

There was another mode of composition, very much slower and more painful, in which she strove to capture the essence of certain events, real or imagined, as precisely as she could, and here she felt she might one day acquire a very different sort of facility, if only she could stumble upon some great conception, something that would absolutely distinguish her work from that of the hundreds of authors whose novels crammed the circulating libraries and bookstalls and jostled one another for notice in the pages of the reviews. At least half a dozen times she had launched herself with high hopes into "Chapter One", and felt her tale to be well under way, only to see a darkness fall across the page, blighting her carefully wrought sentences until her characters lay down, as it were, at the side of the road and simply refused to go on. And then persons from Porlock, usually in the form of her mother, would call just as she saw her way out of the difficulty. There were certain pages, composed almost as if from dictation, with which she was entirely satisfied, but they seemed like the work of another person altogether, and remained in any case unfinished. No; the life of an author was certainly not an easy one. Rosalind had variously accused herself of indolence, of an absolute want of genius, and of lack of experience, the last perhaps excusable at the age of twenty; yet here she was faced with a proposal of marriage from Denton Margrave, and upon her answer depended not only her happiness but that of her mother, for they were poor, and he was rich, and Rosalind was very much afraid she might be on the verge of accepting him for her mother's sake rather than her own. Yet even as she struggled to determine the true state of her own feelings for Mr Margrave, there was a part of her that stood back, and watched, and said that if only she could make fictional capital of her situation, real income might follow, to free her from the jaws of her dilemma.

Their difficulties had begun some two years earlier, with the death of her father. George Forster had been a successful illustrator, but his income had barely kept pace with his wife's expenditure. Cecily Forster lived only for Society, and it was the great disappointment of her life that her only daughter had turned out to be so entirely her father's child, for Rosalind would far rather stay at home with a book than accompany her mother to the endless round of luncheons and soirées and dinners that lent meaning and purpose to her existence. Father and daughter had conspired to spend quiet evenings at home together, whenever he could spare the time from his work; Rosalind had often wondered, as she grew older, whether it was altogether right for her mother to be out so often, but to any tentative inquiry along these lines her father's invariable reply had been, "Your mother must be amused." Though her parents had seldom quarrelled within her hearing, their example had not been sufficiently happy for Rosalind to be in any haste to follow it. And when her father died, there might still have been enough money left for a modest existence in the country, but her mother would sooner have died herself than live in the country, except in August, and had insisted upon keeping on the house in Bayswater. Rosalind had done her best to encourage economies, and an uncle on her mother's side had helped, at first, but the help was now exhausted (other than in the form of a standing offer to move to his rectory in a small Yorkshire village), and it had become clear to Rosalind that ruin must very soon follow. She would willingly have gone out into the world and tried to earn her living, and was secretly resolved to do so if all else failed; the problem being that working as a governess or schoolmistress might keep them from starvation, but would still require, from her mother's point of view, an intolerable descent.

It had also become plain to Rosalind, despite her own continued grief over the loss of her father, that her mother ought to remarry. A marked distaste for exercise and a liking for rich foods had not improved Cecily Forster's figure, but she had kept her complexion, and with the aid of strenuous lacing could still look more like an elder sister than a mother. Rosalind had, indeed, felt increasingly obliged to play the part of parent to her own mother, who seemed to have grown more childish since her husband's death. "Look after your poor Mama" had been amongst

George Forster's last words to his daughter, and to that end, once the period of mourning was over, she had begun to accompany her mother to various dances; besides, the house was lonely in the evenings now. Rosalind enjoyed dancing, but the young men in her mother's set seemed to have no conversation beyond riding and shooting, and to be positively unnerved by any mention of literature. She had, therefore, no great expectations of Lady Maudsley's ball, but in deference to her mother's anxiety to make the best possible impression agreed to have a gown made for her, though it was cut lower than Rosalind would have preferred, and she did not like the looks of frank appraisal she attracted, still less the feeling that she had consented to become a creature on display. It was on this occasion that she had met Denton Margrave.

Her first impression of him, in that initial glance with which we take in so much, was by no means favourable: he was fairly tall and well built, but his face was pale and slightly pock-marked; a clipped beard and moustache framed lips a little too red and moist, and a glimpse of discoloured, curiously pointed teeth; his eyes were a gleaming brown, but sunken, with dark circles deeply etched into the flesh beneath. His hair was almost black, shot through with greyish streaks, swept back and receding at the temples from a sharp peak at the centre of his forehead. Rosalind thought that he looked to be in his mid-forties, though he would later declare himself to be thirty-nine.

But all these reservations were, initially, swept aside by his being introduced to her as *the* Denton Margrave, author of *A Domestic Tragedy*, an "advanced" novel which she had recently read and admired, about the seduction, abandonment, and eventual suicide by drowning of a servant girl, and they were soon deep in conversation. She spoke, hesitantly at first, of her own ambitions; to her surprise he addressed her as an equal, seemed more interested in hearing her opinions than in delivering his own, and drew her out until she had quite forgotten her shyness. In answer to a question about the subject of his next book, he sighed deeply; his trouble, he confessed, gazing at her with an intensity she found both flattering and a little disquieting, was want of inspiration. He was, it turned out, a widower whose wife had died some years ago after a long illness, leaving him childless and alone. Rosalind's sympathy was naturally awakened by these disclosures, and by the end of the evening he had been introduced to her mother, and secured an invitation to call at the house in Bayswater, where he became a constant visitor.

Within a few weeks he had declared himself ardently in love with Rosalind, and asked for her hand, to which she replied that she could not possibly think of deserting her mother, and besides considered herself too young to marry. In that case, said Mr Margrave, he would ask only for her permission to hope, while assuring her that he understood their situation, and that her mother's fortunes would be as dear to him as her own. Rosalind thought that she had definitely refused him, but as he left he thanked her for giving him hope, and out of politeness she did not contradict him. That evening, her mother reproached her for trifling with the affections of such a delightful gentleman—and one, moreover, who possessed a secure private income. Cecily Forster would never ask her daughter to marry without love, but surely Rosalind could learn to love him, especially since the alternative was their leaving the house within the month and going to live on the charity of Rosalind's uncle in Yorkshire. Rosalind said she would think about it, but added rather intemperately that she wished Mr Margrave would propose to her mother instead of herself, which provoked a flood of outraged weeping, and ended in Rosalind's promising to reconsider her refusal. Denton Margrave renewed his offer within the week; Rosalind asked him for time to consider her final answer, and told her mother that she wished to spend a few quiet days alone with Caroline at Staplefield. Cecily Forster's expression had been like that of a prisoner awaiting sentence of death as she saw her daughter off in the cab to the station.

Rosalind was therefore compelled, as she climbed another stile under the placid and incurious gaze of the cows in the neighbouring field, to ask herself what exactly was her objection to Mr Margrave, for there could be no doubt of his ardour, and it was not fair to him to keep him in a state of uncertainty. To Caroline it was very simple: was Rosalind sure she loved him with all her heart? No, she was not. Very well then; she should certainly not marry Mr Margrave. The trouble was that Rosalind had never loved any man except poor Papa; she did not think she had any stronger aversion to Mr Margrave than anyone else, and his conversation was far more interesting than that of any of the young men her own age. It was very flattering to be told that with her at his side he could do great things, and that she would have as much time as she liked in which to write: they could divide their time as she pleased between his town house in Belgravia and a very pretty country house in Hampshire—she had not yet seen Blackwall Park for herself, but he had assured her that she would love it. Perhaps the force of his desire for her would overcome her reservations; and what, in any case, was the alternative? It was all very well to think of going out to work, but she knew she would hate being a governess or a schoolmistress, let alone a paid companion; she had had enough foretaste of that with her mother. The thought of being bound to some frivolous society woman to whom she had no connection beyond the monetary was intolerable to her; it would be like being sold into slavery, and besides, her wages would make no material difference; they would still have to leave the house in Bayswater and sell whatever was not already pledged to their creditors. Rosalind really feared that her mother would pine away, or worse, hasten her own demise, if confined to her brother's house in Yorkshire. She had had too much pride to ask Mr Margrave directly, but he had made it clear to her that her mother's future in London would be assured if they were to marry. Rosalind felt afterwards as if she had been negotiating terms with him, and did not like the feeling, for what, on his side, could he gain from marrying a penniless girl of twenty with, as it were, a dependent mother? That was what troubled her, if she was candid with herself: that, apart from his belief that marriage to her would bring him the inspiration he said he lacked, he so plainly desired to touch her, and lost no opportunity of doing so. There was something . . . he smelt of tobacco and spirits, but so had Papa . . . something else: she had no real sense of what "charnel" meant, but it was the word that came to her for—whatever it was that caused her to draw back from his embrace. Perhaps her imagination was overwrought; there was nothing visibly unclean about him; but the faint odour of decay had nonetheless continued to repel her.

But, on the other hand, could she really condemn her poor Mama to infinite misery because of an excess of fastidiousness on her part? So she framed the question as she set off through the last of the meadows separating her from the forest which now rose above her. For there was another thing she knew she ought to consider: that her expectations of love might be altogether unrealistic, and for a specific reason, which placed all mortal suitors at an absolute disadvantage.

It was a dream she had had not long after her eighteenth birthday; a dream unlike any other she could recall, in which she awoke to find an angel standing by her bedside. He—for so she thought of this seraphic being, though he seemed to her to combine in one body all of the perfections of male and female form—shone with a radiant light which filled the room, a light of such palpable sweetness that it brought to her mind "Jerusalem the golden, with milk and honey blest"; yet he was also visibly a creature of flesh and blood, who smiled upon her with such warmth that she sat up, entranced by the great white wings in their perfect balance of strength and softness, the curves of bone and sinew outlined beneath depths of snowy plumage so beautiful she felt she could gaze upon it for ever. He stretched out his arms to her and she rose effortlessly into them, as if he had given her the gift of flight, yet she could feel the floor beneath her feet, and the angel's heart beating against her breast as he took her up into his arms and kissed her. She could not, then or afterwards, think of him in any orthodox sense: just as he seemed to her both male and female, and more than either, so he seemed both Christian in the celestial light and radiance of pure goodness that shone from him, and pagan in his sheer beauty and the warmth of his embrace. As she kissed him in return, he folded his great wings gently about her, and she felt the light fill her whole being with sweetness until she cried out in rapture; and with that cry woke herself, alone in her dark room, with the taste of milk and honey fading from her lips.

Try as she might, Rosalind had never been able to relive the dream. She had never told anyone of it, not even Caroline, nor written it down, often as she had been tempted, and she had learned, painfully, not to strive to summon the angel in memory, but to wait for the rare moment in which the recollection came to her unbidden in all its strength and sweetness. Such a moment came to her now, in the quiet meadow, so vividly that she wept at the beauty of it, and knew for certain that she could never marry Denton Margrave. How, indeed could she ever marry anyone, for what man could love her as she had loved and been loved by the angel? Yet even if she were destined to die a maid, as the song went, in deciding against Mr Margrave she must still confront the immediate question of how she and her mother were to live; and she found herself murmuring a prayer, to whom or what she knew not, to show her the way out of her difficulties.

By this time she had almost arrived at the stone wall which divided the meadow from the oak forest above her. She and Caroline had sometimes walked this way, but they had never seen any path through the trees, and there were patches of nettles clustered thickly beneath the foliage, so they had always retreated. But today, Rosalind noticed a small wicket gate just at the corner where the two walls met, and upon making her way across to it saw that there was indeed a narrow path leading away into the wood. She tried the latch; the gate opened at her touch; and she was very soon out of sight of the meadow, following the path as it wound its way upwards in the dim light that filtered through the leaves overhead.

The path seemed to have been cleared quite recently, for the clumps of nettles rose up on each side, leaving just enough room for her to pass between them without catching her dress. As she made her way between the tall, mossy trunks of the oaks, she became aware that it was very quiet in the wood. Even the distant calling of birds seemed muted, and Rosalind began to wonder whether she might not be wise to turn back. What if she were to meet . . . well, someone who ought not to be here? A rabbit or hare darting across the path set her heart beating very fast, but curiosity drew her on until the slope began to diminish, and then to level and fall away and quite suddenly the path swerved around the trunk of a huge tree and brought her out of the cool, damp, bracken-scented air of the forest onto a green, sunlit hillside. It was, indeed, almost like a park, for the grass was clipped short and even, quite unlike the tussocky fields she had crossed before. Away to the south she could see distant fields and cottages, and the slopes of other wooded hills, and even fancifully imagine a glimpse of the far-off sea. The clearing below her ran for several hundred yards downhill before the forest began again; here and there a large oak tree had been left to shade the prospect; and as she stepped out into the sunlight, her attention was caught and held by something a little way down the slope and to her right, which had been partly concealed by the nearest of these trees.

It was a small pavilion, quite delightful in its proportions: a simple wooden structure, octagonal in shape, painted in soft blue and cream, with a dark green steeply pointed roof. A wooden rail ran around the sides at waist height, with latticework below that; above the rail it was open except for the posts which supported the roof. The ground where it stood was quite steep, so that the entrance at the back was almost level with the grass. As she came closer she saw that there was another entrance at the front, with steps going down from it. Below the rail on both sides, a sort of window-seat, heaped with cushions, ran right around; the floor was polished wood, and so were the sides of the window-seat boxes. It was all very new and bright; so much so that she could still catch the faint scents of fresh paint and polish. Strange that Caroline had not suggested they come here, and that her parents had never spoken of it. But perhaps she had wandered into the grounds of the neighbouring estate; even so, she knew that the Fredericks were kindly and hospitable people, and would not mind her stopping for a while in such a pleasant place.

Rosalind took off her shoes and settled herself along the window-seat at the left so that she was looking out across the slope and the hilltops. Now that the sun had come out, the afternoon was quite warm, and a gentle breeze began to play about her. She really ought to concentrate her mind upon the problem before her, but somehow it was impossible to be anxious here; she felt completely at home, and the cushions were wonderfully soft and comfortable. The pavilion was like . . . well, it was like that sunny dome in "Kubla Khan", though there were certainly no caves of ice hereabouts; and if she had a dulcimer she could play upon it, and perhaps catch a glimpse of the poet with his flashing eyes and floating hair, which reminded her that she too had once fed on honeydew, and drunk the milk of Paradise, so that she sighed deeply, and stretched out more comfortably and allowed her eyes to close, the better to hear the mingled songs of birds and feel the slight movement of air over her forehead, until after an indefinite time she became aware that the soft breeze was, in fact, a hand, gently stroking her hair. Its touch was so reassuring that she opened her eyes quite without anxiety; her first thought was that Caroline had followed her after all.

But though the resemblance to Caroline was plain, this woman who sat beside her was older, and thinner, and her face was drawn and pale and marked by illness. She wore, Rosalind noticed, an elaborate formal gown, in a fashion she remembered from her childhood. Despite the aura of frailty and ill health, the woman smiled down at Rosalind with maternal tenderness, and indicated that Rosalind should lay her head in her lap, which she did quite willingly, as if she had indeed become a child again. Somehow Rosalind did not feel the need to say anything, and the woman did not speak either, but continued for a little while longer to smile and caress her temples until, as if reaching a decision, she took something off the seat beside her with her other hand. It was a small volume, bound in brown and gold, and plainly new, for Rosalind caught the warm crisp scent of the paper drifting down to her. Still with that maternal smile, the woman opened the book at the title page, holding it so that Rosalind could read, without moving her head:

Blackwall Park

by

Rosalind Margrave

Rosalind knew exactly what these words signified, yet she felt no surprise and no anxiety, only curiosity as to what would follow as the woman turned the book away from her gaze, leafed forward a few pages and began to read aloud to her. But this was quite unlike being read to in the usual way, for the scenes formed themselves before her eyes, and the characters—principally herself, her mother, and Denton Margrave— moved and spoke as in life. Rosalind—the sensation was precise, though not easy to describe—was at first both within and outside herself as an actress in the drama, speaking the words and feeling the sensations, and yet also aware that she was safe in the pavilion, on a sunlit afternoon, with her head in the woman's lap, listening to a tale which, it appeared, she herself had written under her married name.

It began with her return to the house in Bayswater two days hence, quite determined to reject Mr Margrave. But she had reckoned without the extremity of her mother's response. When every other means of persuasion had been exhausted, Cecily Forster declared her intention of ending her life with laudanum that very night, rather than live another day with a daughter so heartless and unfeeling, so selfishly unwilling to surrender her foolish notions of love (which, unlike property and social position, could be guaranteed not to last), and to learn to like what she must otherwise learn to bear for the sake of her mother's and (did she but know it) her own future happiness.

There was an ominous quietness about this threat which awakened in Rosalind a sick apprehension of defeat, for she knew she could not live in the knowledge that she had, in effect, murdered her mother. In the strange double vision with which the tale unfolded, she witnessed her own capitulation, from her acceptance of her horribly elated suitor, through her vain attempts to suppress the repulsion that any physical contact with him inspired, to the wedding itself. There it became clear that Denton Margrave possessed neither friends nor family, for his side of the church was entirely deserted, whereas Rosalind's was packed with guests, many of them strangers to her, but all pale and mute. He had not even a best man; when the time came he produced a ring from his own pocket. The service somehow took place in dead silence; even the clergyman seemed appalled at the spectacle, and when Mr Margrave kissed her with his red, glistening lips, her senses were once again assailed by that charnel odour, whilst Caroline, as bridesmaid, wept soundlessly at her back.

There was no banquet. Mr Margrave led her out of the silent church, past the empty pews on one side and the thronged guests, still and white as statues, on the other, out to a small black carriage which was waiting at the door. This, he explained with an insinuating smile, would carry her to Blackwall Park for the honeymoon; he meanwhile had urgent business to attend to, but would be with her at nightfall. He handed her in; the door slammed; the coachman whipped up the horses and bore her away. So far as she could tell, the door had not been locked, but it did not occur to her to try to jump out; all volition seemed to have left her, and she sat devoid of thought or feeling through the hours it took the carriage to make its way out of London and down through the countryside. She looked out of the window, and saw what a traveller might expect to see, but the sights meant nothing to her, and the carriage never once paused in its journey until, after negotiating a long, deserted stretch of road through a series of empty fields, it turned in at a gate in a high wall and pulled up on an expanse of gravel by the front door of a large stone house.

Rosalind heard the coachman descend and come round to open the door; she alighted like an automaton; without a word, the coachman folded the step, slammed the door, leapt back onto his box and whipped up the horses, who clattered back across the gravel and out through the gateway. There they pulled up sharply; the coachman sprang down again, and swung the two high wooden gates closed from the outside, so that they came together with a thud and a clash of metal fastenings. The muffled sound of hooves and wheels resumed, receded, and died away to nothing, leaving her alone in the silent courtyard.

Sensation flooded back to her like cold water flung upon a sleeper. All consciousness of the pavilion was gone; she was here and nowhere else, the wife of Mr Margrave, and clad, she realised for the first time, in a wedding dress which was no longer white but a drab, rusty black. Perhaps it had always been black; she could not recall. The horror of her position grew upon her until she feared she would faint. She had been mad to surrender to her mother's threat—better to have swallowed the laudanum herself than come here. She looked frantically about the courtyard, but the smooth, high wall enclosed her on three sides, the front of the house on the other. There were no handholds anywhere along the wall, and nothing that she could use to help her climb. The house loomed over her, three storeys high, its pale yellowish blocks of stone too smooth and the mortared joints too flush to offer any purchase for hands or feet. At any moment they would be coming to take her inside; at any moment Mr Margrave himself might be here. Under a lowering sky, the day was fading fast.

Then she noticed that the shutters were closed on every window of every floor, and that the front door stood slightly ajar. Still nobody came out; there was not the slightest sound from within; the house looked and felt deserted. To enter was more than she dared; she would surely die of terror; but, as another survey of the courtyard indicated all too clearly, there was no hiding place here, and no way over the wall. Could she stand pressed against the wall near the gates until Mr Margrave's carriage entered, and escape while they were open? No; the coachman would surely see her, and then Mr Margrave would hunt her down. Trembling, she made her way across the gravel as quietly as she could, onto the porch and up to the heavy wooden door, and pushed without giving herself time to think.

The door opened upon darkness; the hinges creaked horribly. The house smelt of mould and damp. Rosalind's head swam with fear. In the dim light from the courtyard she could see the beginning of a passageway. Fighting off thoughts of being cornered and pounced upon, she gathered up her skirts and ran blindly through the darkness until she bumped against something flat and soft which moved away from her—a swinging door, she realised in time to bite back the cry that rose in her throat—and on towards a thin line of light which turned out to be, as she had prayed, another door, also ajar, that let her out into what seemed to be a kitchen garden, also walled, this time in crumbling red brick with jagged shards of glass embedded in the top. But this wall was lower, and it was possible she might get over, and anyway there must surely be a gate or door in it somewhere? The area, perhaps ten yards by thirty, was rank and overgrown with weeds: all except a plot away to the right below the rear wall. All of this she took in at a single glance, whilst trying to slow the terrible pounding of her heart which so confused her hearing.

Yes, there was indeed a door in the outer wall, in that far corner on her right, barely visible in the gathering gloom. She hastened along a weed-strewn path, feeling the hated gown catch and tear upon something as she approached the cleared area. But those were not garden beds between her and the door: they were graves, all quite new, and at the head of each mound stood a low tombstone. Even in the fading light the names upon the first six stones were plain: all women's names, and all the surnames his. The seventh grave was open, newly dug, with the soil heaped beside it and the stone already in place, and the name incised upon it was her own.

The smell of damp earth rose up from the pit; that, and another odour that drew her appalled gaze from her tombstone to the path behind her—to Denton Margrave standing not ten paces away. He was all in black, with what looked like a great travelling cloak draped over his shoulders, yet she could see the earth upon his clothes, for his face was lit from within by a pale blue light that shimmered and crackled in the air around him, glowing in the sockets of his eyes and in that terrible, insinuating smile. She began to back away; he did not instantly follow, but spread out what she thought were arms before the great black cloak revealed itself as wings, unfurling hooked and leathery as he launched himself upon her with a shriek that rose in pitch and volume until it tore at her throat and went echoing out across the hillside where she found herself in the pavilion, alone.

Rosalind was at first too much overcome by horror and relief to notice any change in her surroundings. But as her heart began to slow, and the fearful immediacy of the dream—as surely it must have been?—to recede, she became aware that the surface she was lying upon was very hard, and that the rail above her was weathered and cracked, like the posts supporting the roof, which was likewise no longer a lustrous dark green but drab and flaking and festooned with cobwebs. And something was crawling over her foot . . . She sat up abruptly, brushing various insects from her dress, and saw that the cushions had rotted away to shreds and tatters of brown fabric. The floorboards had warped and buckled, and grass was growing between them; lichen was spreading across the faded timbers of the window-seats. And the light was much dimmer, for the trees around the pavilion had grown, and new saplings had sprung up, and the lawn had vanished into a wild, overgrown tangle of long grass and nettles.

Bewildered, she looked around for her shoes, and was relieved to see that they, at least, were unchanged, for she was beginning to feel like one of those heroines in a fairy tale who wakes to find that she has slept for a hundred years. Where had the dream begun? She had only closed her eyes for a short while before the woman had appeared beside her . . . and before that she could distinctly remember emerging from the wood and seeing the pavilion new and shining on the sunlit slope . . . no, that had *not* been a dream, it was not possible, she had walked all the way from Caroline's room without stopping . . . and she was certainly awake now. Rosalind stood up and looked about her. Weeds and long grass and nettles encircled the crumbling pavilion in an unbroken ring; there was no path, and no sign of footsteps or trampling. She herself could not have got here without leaving a considerable trail; yet here she was.

Fear crept upon her, and a growing sense of loss and desolation; she had felt the woman's tenderness so strongly, in her touch, her smile; yet that gentle presence had forced her to confront the nightmare vision of Margrave, and left her alone with the ruin of what had been so beautiful. Rosalind looked up through the treetops overhead and saw that the sky was once again overcast; she realised that she was shivering not only from fear, but from the chill upon what was now late afternoon air. There was a fallen branch a little way off which would provide a makeshift staff to help her through the nettles. She knew she could not brave the forest path, even assuming she could find it again; not with that malignant apparition still hovering at the back of her mind. But how, then, was she to find her way back to the house? Her attention was drawn by a faint sound below, at the foot of the slope, which might be running water; if that were a stream, it might prove to be a tributary of the river along whose banks she and Caroline had so often strolled, and so lead her around the edge of the wooded hill to safety. Of course she might be led fatally astray, but she could think of no alternative, save waiting for darkness to overtake her.

As it turned out, there was indeed a stream at the foot of the hillside, marking the boundary between forest and fields, into which she emerged a good deal scratched, with her dress covered in burrs and grass seeds. And though it was a long way round, by following the direction of the water she did, eventually, reach a familiar point on the riverbank, and from there proceeded mechanically homeward. But the sense of desolation at finding the pavilion so despoiled would not leave her; she felt almost as if she were to blame for its decay; yet how could that be? Trying to recall exactly where the dream had begun was like unpicking a piece of work in search of a non-existent join; there had been nothing insubstantial about the pavilion as she had first seen it, new and brightly painted on the sunlit slope. She cast her mind back along the forest path, to the field in which she had remembered the angel; but found to her great distress that she could not now think of him without recalling the hideous bat-like figure with its loathsome smile; it was like watching black ink being spilt upon that pure white plumage, and feeling both responsible and powerless to prevent it. At least she knew for certain that she could never marry Mr Margrave . . . but then she recalled, with horrible clarity, her mother's threat of destroying herself, and the sick feeling that had grown in her; and the name upon the volume had been Rosalind Margrave: did that mean she was foredoomed to marry him? Yet the woman had seemed so kind, and smiled upon her so tenderly; and so her thoughts circled round and round until she arrived back at the house, very late, footsore and plainly distressed, to find Caroline, now recovered, anxiously awaiting her.

Rosalind had imagined herself falling into her friend's arms and telling her everything, but found that she could not. It had always been understood between them that

Rosalind's mother was "difficult", but loyalty, and perhaps pride, had constrained Rosalind's confidences on this score. Nor had she felt able to disclose to Caroline the full extent or immediacy of the financial calamity hanging over the house in Bayswater, for fear of seeming to appeal to the Temples' charity on her mother's behalf. The beginning of her dream—wherever that might have been—seemed too strange, and the end too horrible, to relate. And so, beyond the comfort of her friend's embrace, Rosalind confined herself to saying that she had definitely resolved to reject Mr Margrave but was a little uneasy about how her mother might receive this news, and had consequently taken a wrong turning and wandered further than she had meant. To which she found herself adding, at the dinner table, that she thought she had seen a small pavilion on the far side of the wooded hill over there, without being specific about where she had seen it from, or how close.

"How very odd," said Mrs Temple. "You must have walked a very great distance, Rosalind; and besides, when I last walked that way, the forest had quite swallowed it up—what remained of it."

"There was a little wind in the trees," Rosalind ventured, hoping her hands were not perceptibly trembling.

"Fancy—I had not thought of it for years. Dear Walter was always so distressed, I had got out of the habit of mentioning it for his sake . . . it was built for his elder sister Christina—before you were born, Caroline. Christina married very young, and most unwisely"—Rosalind thought she detected a glance in her direction—"and her husband treated her cruelly. He made her—that is to say, she became ill—and came home to her family here. Grandfather Charles had the pavilion built for her there because she so loved the prospect from that hillside—it was quite open then—and she would walk there every day to sit when the weather was fine enough, until she became too weak. Walter was so devoted to her, and so distressed by the manner of her—by her death, he could not bear to speak of it, or be reminded of her—grief takes some people that way, men especially—and when Grandfather Charles died, not very long after Christina, the pavilion fell into disuse, though I should rather have kept it up myself, but poor dear Walter . . ."

"Rosy, you are very pale," said Caroline.

The thread was effectively broken, but Rosalind went upstairs more troubled than before. Caroline, plainly sensing that more was wrong than her friend was prepared to acknowledge, did her best to coax Rosalind into further confidences, but in vain. Despite her exhaustion, Rosalind lay awake for what seemed hours, and when eventually she did fall asleep, it was to find herself back in the walled graveyard, staring into a newly dug pit from whose depths something that shimmered with a bluish phosphorescence was rising towards her, so that she woke with a cry of terror and lay trembling until a soft light came into the room. For a moment Rosalind imagined that her angel had come back to comfort her, until she saw that the white-robed figure was only Caroline bearing a candle, but her friend stayed with her, and she was comforted, and repented of the "only".

Two days later, Caroline and Mrs Temple saw Rosalind onto the stopping train to London; or so they assumed. In fact Rosalind had arrived at a desperate, not to say foolhardy resolution: to visit Blackwall Park privately and determine whether it was indeed the place of her nightmare. She knew that the house was currently closed up and deserted, for Mr Margrave was currently embarked upon a long stay in town (the better, she feared, to lay siege to her affections) and did not keep two sets of servants. She was well aware of the dangers, but the compulsion had grown upon her until she could no longer resist it. Her recollection of the dream remained as vivid as when she had woken in the ruin of the pavilion; she felt as if a dark doorway had opened in her mind, letting in a freezing draught from the nether world, and that she would never know peace until she had found a way to force it shut again.

The previous afternoon, she and Caroline had set out to find the pavilion. Rosalind had proposed they retrace her walk across the fields, without saying exactly what she expected to find: the wicket gate was, on close inspection, still there in the corner of the field, but quite overgrown and decayed, and there was no path leading into the forest on the other side, only a huge bank of nettles. Then they had made their way around the foot of the hill, back across the river and along by the side of the stream Rosalind had followed the evening before, but without success. She had neglected to mark the point at which she had emerged, and either the grass had sprung back up around her footprints, or . . . but Mrs Temple had said there was, or had been, a real pavilion; she could not have imagined waking in the ruin of it. Yet no matter how far they went, the wooded hillside presented a dense, unbroken aspect. Rosalind could feel her friend's anxiety on her behalf, and longed to unburden herself, but still the inhibition remained. She told herself she feared that even Caroline might doubt her sanity; in truth, the doubt belonged to Rosalind herself. No matter how often she cast her mind back over the dream—and she seemed to be able to enter and leave the memory of it at any point—the same bewildered confusion overcame her as to what had been real and what dream, or delusion, or apparition—a word she did not like to follow too far, for she could still feel the softness of the cushions in the brightly painted pavilion, inhale the fresh smell of new varnish, feel the weight of her head in the woman's—Christina's—lap; and if Christina could feel so palpably human and yet be a phantom, then why should the dark vision of Blackwall Park be any less real to Rosalind's perhaps disordered sight?

That was the question that most troubled Rosalind, and the one she felt she must resolve before she returned to London. She did not believe that she would find a row of tombstones; at least she was almost certain she did not. Yet, strangely, she half hoped that there would be *some* correspondence between the actual Blackwall Park and the place of her dream; some tangible sign, a thread to guide her through what was bound to be a painful and difficult confrontation with her mother. Rosalind knew, instinctively, that the slightest shrinking on her part might provoke the sort of display that had overpowered her in the dream; she did not, on reflection, believe that her mother would actually do away with herself, but was by no means confident of her own ability to withstand the threat. These thoughts preoccupied her throughout the journey to Bramley station in Hampshire, which passed without incident. The stationmaster at Bramley seemed puzzled, as well he might, by the young lady's assuring him that she was to meet her aunt and uncle at Blackwall Park, but nevertheless secured for her a dog-cart driven by a taciturn, grey-headed man who conducted her on the final stage of her journey—no more than a mile—in complete silence.

The day was overcast, as in the dream, but milder. Though the road was not the same, there was something about its atmosphere that reminded her of the dream: it was flat, and for the most part straight, and ran through a series of fields which appeared, from the glimpses through the hedges, to be quite deserted; but perhaps it was only the driver's silence that made her feel that she had passed this way before. All the while Rosalind was watching for a high wall of yellowish stone, so that when the driver turned down a short avenue of elms and she realised this was Blackwall Park, her first reaction was a curious mixture of relief and disappointment. There was no wall; the house was built of grey stone, not yellowish; the windows were shuttered, but it had two storeys, not three. They pulled up on gravel, but brown gravel was common, surely, as was a front door framed by a porch with stone pillars: it was not the same front door, and it was certainly not ajar; yet she was suddenly very apprehensive. What if Mr Margrave had come down after all? She had placed herself in the most compromising position; it would look as if she had secretly sought him out . . . how could she not have thought of this? She had been mad to come here; and with that thought the memory of the dream pressed so closely upon her that the smell of damp and mould seemed to rise from the gravel onto which she found herself alighting, telling the driver to wait for her.

Her intellect ordered her to retreat; but her feet carried her along the gravel to the left, around the side of the house, barely noticing an expanse of lawn and shrubbery, onto a flagged path which took her around a conservatory and back towards the rear of the house, where there was indeed a red brick wall, lower than in the dream, partly enclosing a kitchen garden. This garden was quite neat, and not at all rank or overgrown; yet there was a path leading diagonally from a door at the back of the house, through the garden beds towards the far corner of the brick wall, and her feet were again compelled along it until she could see clearly that there were no graves or tombstones anywhere here. Rosalind stopped, confused, and began to retreat. As she did so, the smell of newly turned earth floated up to her from a nearby bed; and something caught at her dress. She glanced down. It was a cucumber frame, and on the corner nearest the path was caught a long thin strip of material; not from the blue travelling cloak she was wearing, but a drab, rusty black. In the same instant she became aware that she was not alone.

At the edge of her vision—for she dared not move—she saw Denton Margrave standing exactly where he had stood in the dream, and for an instant it seemed to her that the sky darkened over. She waited for the ground to open into a pit; the dream rushed back at her with such appalling vividness that she saw the blue light crackle about him, heard the rustle of unfurling wings, and then . . . it was like looking out of a fast-moving train which had swiftly and silently reversed its direction: the Margrave-figure shrank back into itself; she seemed to be drawn backwards through the entirety of the dream, all in perfect detail but at such speed that she had not drawn breath before she was back in the sunlit pavilion with the woman showing her the title page of her book, hearing simultaneously the voice of Caroline's mother at the dinner table, and understanding, at last, what Christina Temple had come back to tell her.

The vision faded; the paralysis ceased; Rosalind's heart gave one dreadful jolt as she turned to face her pursuer, until she saw that he was not Margrave at all, but an elderly man in a frayed, grimy, threadbare suit of black and heavy workman's boots, leaning upon a hoe and regarding her with some bewilderment. They remained silently facing one another until Rosalind had recovered sufficiently to say, somewhat breathlessly but with a composure which amazed her: "Pray excuse me; I have come to the wrong house."

Staring out across the sombre fields as the train carried her back to London, Rosalind found her thoughts running beyond the impending scene with her mother. Yorkshire would be a kind of exile for her, as well, but she would have work to do. She had her tale to tell, and would find the right way of telling it. Much black ink would have to be spilt; the angel's pure white radiance might never be quite recovered; but she would remain Rosalind Forster, and would one day earn enough to set her mother up in London with a companion, and be free to return to Caroline and Staplefield. So she promised herself, imagining the pavilion restored and glowing with fresh paint and varnish, floating in sunlit air.

PART THREE

I SAT IN the wreck of the pavilion with *even Staplefield was a lie* and *Alice will be so disappointed* looping through my head. But my mother hadn't lied, not exactly: Ferrier's Close *was* Staplefield. And Ashbourn House; and others, perhaps, I didn't yet know about. So why had she brought me up on the story-book version – in the most literal sense – of her childhood?

Because she couldn't bear to let go of Viola altogether, said the Alice-voice in my head.

Then what did she do here that was so terrible?

The voice did not reply. From here, the house was invisible; the path curved away into the encircling nettles. When I first saw it, the ruined pavilion had had a certain romantic charm. Now it looked utterly despoiled. Rusting, twisted sections of the cupola roof littered the trampled clearing. The desolation was suddenly unbearable.

You're just angry, I told myself as I walked back to the house; angry she lied to you. She chose the story-book version because she'd been disinherited, not because she murdered Anne.

The anger carried me on up the stairs to the second floor and another search of the bedrooms. This time I made as much of a racket as I could, banging doors, slamming drawers, stomping across like a poltergeist. My noisy progress reminded me of something a colleague at the library had told me years ago, about a troubled boarding school, iron bedsteads flung across an empty dormitory. I looked again at the deep gouges in the floor of the cupboard above Phyllis's bed; they looked unpleasantly like the marks of paired claws. But I found nothing new.

I returned to the library, intending to begin a systematic search for papers, but instead was overcome by another wave of black fatigue, lay down on the chesterfield, and fell instantly asleep.

I woke – as it seemed – at dusk. The sky through the upper windows was still relatively bright. High above, the ceiling floated in a vault of gloom. My gaze drifted down rows of shelves towards the false bookcase at the end of the mezzanine gallery.

Only I couldn't see the false bookcase, because someone was standing motionless in front of it. A woman – for a horrible moment a headless woman, until I saw that she was veiled in black. And wearing an elaborate gown in some heavy material; I could see the flare of her skirt through the vertical bars below the railing. A dark green gown, gathered at the shoulders.

I thought, 'Viola', and then, 'Imogen de Vere', and then, 'This is one of those dreams where you dream you can see through your eyelids.' Usually I wake the instant I realise I'm asleep, a little disappointed to find that I can't see with my eyes closed, any more than I can fly. But the figure didn't vanish. Instead it appeared to shrink, receding into the shadow of the end wall. I closed my eyes resolutely, counted to three. The false bookcase had reappeared. There was no one on the gallery.

I slept badly that night for the first time since my arrival, spinning through interminable dreams of Ferrier's Close, stepping up to the front door over and over again, struggling half awake, then repeatedly demolishing sections of the pavilion, appalled at the damage I was doing but compelled to continue, round and round in a series of endless loops, up and down the empty passages and staircases until I was wide awake at dawn, watching the grey light slowly brighten across the miles of rooftops.

Of course the veiled woman had been a dream. I made myself a cup of tea and returned to the window. 4.37 a.m. I knew I wouldn't sleep again, and I didn't feel like reading. Breakfast wasn't until seven. I looked at the heavy bunch of keys beside my laptop. No one had said anything about keeping office hours – or any hours – at Ferrier's Close. I could sit here brooding for the next two and a half hours.

Or take a taxi up to the house and try to open the locked door on the second-floor landing.

The sky was brightening as I paid the driver at the entrance to the Vale of Health, but beneath the overhanging trees the lane was in deep shadow, and when the gate closed behind me it was so dark that I could not see the front door. I had a book of paper matches from the café I'd eaten in the evening before, but I didn't dare light one here; the whole thing might go up like a bonfire if the head of a match flew off. *Remember, remember, Miss Hamish is your friend.* The words came floating into my head and I started chanting them under my breath in a staccato rhythm that got my feet moving along the flagstones and helped mask the stirrings and rustlings and tickings that accompanied me all the way to the porch, where I used more than half the matches getting the front door open.

Floorboards popped and cracked as I passed through the drawing and dining rooms in near-darkness, and out into the comparative brightness of the landing above the back door. The whole staircase creaked when I set foot on it, as if the house were stirring in its sleep. Houses creak more at dawn and dusk, I told myself, climbing towards the second floor where the first rays of sunlight were angling in through the high windows, on to the ghost-shapes of vanished pictures and the locked door beyond the banister.

The smallest of the four household keys on the ring was the only possibility. It turned easily enough. I eased the door open, and a familiar blend of odours wafted out of the gloom. The same dusty-sweet smell as the library downstairs. A perfectly ordinary study. With a desk below the window: a walnut writing-desk, I saw as I drew back the heavy bronze-coloured curtains. Before the trees had grown up, there would have been a clear view eastwards to the wooded skyline on the higher ground beyond the Vale.

A covered portable typewriter sat on the writing-desk: an ancient Remington, with circular keys and a black, skeletal frame, worn to bare metal in places. There was a small fire-place in the centre of the wall opposite the window, with book-cases on either side of it. A low armchair, upholstered in faded green leather, in the corner behind the door. And to the left of the desk, a cedar cabinet like a half-size map chest.

The top of the cabinet was bare except for a single photo-graph. A head-and-shoulders portrait of a young woman in a dark velvet dress, with shoulders gathered like the wings of angels. The same as the one I had brought with me from Mawson.

This proves it, I thought: she can only be Viola. Put here as a memento, after she died. But then I remembered the inscription on the back of my copy. 'Greensleeves', and a date in 1949 . . . the 10th of March. I picked up the frame and removed the cardboard, but the back of this one was blank.

I looked through the trays in the cabinet: all empty. So were the drawers in the writing-desk, but when I closed the lowest one I heard a faint crackle of paper. I knelt down to look; the dusty, doggy smell of the carpet brought back a flash of Mawson on a hot January afternoon. I took the drawer right out of the desk and saw that several sheets of paper had been crushed into the space behind. A handwritten note to Viola from 'Edie', evidently returning some letters after the death of a friend. A few pages, presumably from those letters, in a small, spiky hand with a hint of italic, signed V. A length of rusty black ribbon. And a single page of typescript, evidently from the missing part of 'The Revenant'.

'The Briars'
Church Lane,
Cranleigh,
Surrey
Friday 26 Nov.

Dearest Viola,

I found these in the drawer of Mama's bedside table. I know you said to burn everything of yours but I couldn't bring myself to do it – hope you don't mind. I can't write any more now but I do so look forward to seeing you, soon I hope.

With all my love,

Edie

* * *

with Eva and Hubert to see The Cherry Orchard at the Lyric last Wed. It seems obligatory to admire Tchekov these days but I found it tedious and said so, which rather shocked H. I think. Then Wagner at Covent Gdn – the Valkyrie in German – I prefer opera when I don't understand exactly what they're singing, but I liked him more when I was younger. Before the war, I suppose I mean. I found myself thinking of Zeppelins, and that of course reminded me of George. Poor boy – charming as ever, though we see very little of him these days. I live in hope that he will settle to something.

Next week we go to the Fletchers (the Holland Park lot) at Hythe – C. becomes more tedious every year but I am very fond of Lettie – If the weather holds we shall get in some good walks.

Am reading The Sacred Fount again – don't quite know why – a perverse fascination. Sometimes I think HJ is simply Marie Corelli in fancy dress (you know what I mean), but then I remember the tales – The Way it Came, The Jolly Corner, The Altar of the Dead – no one else could have written those, let alone The Turn of the Screw –

yrs ever

V.

* * *

Ferrier's Close
25th July 1934

Dear Madeleine,

Relieved to hear you won't need another extraction. Teeth are the root of all evil (forgive the pun) – or so I feel whenever I have to face the dentist. I don't know why they call it laughing gas; I have never felt the slightest impulse to chortle whilst having my jawbone scraped. Enough of this.

The girls are doing well. Anne has got the whole of 'La Belle Dame' by heart (Iris thinks it unsuitable for a child of six, but I really don't see why). Miss Drayton is very good with them – they both adore her and I only hope she'll stay on. Yesterday we took them all the way to Parliament Hill – a long walk for Phyllis but she didn't complain. We met Captain Anstruther on the way home & he made a great fuss of them as usual.

Anne has been asking a good deal about the accident lately, but I don't see any sign that either of them <u>feels</u> orphaned or deprived or anything of that sort. If only people (mostly adults who ought to know better) wouldn't treat them as if they <u>ought</u> to be unhappy – the sad truth is that they have a better life with us than they would have had if George and Muriel had lived. I doubt the marriage would have lasted. Poor George . . . shell shock is such a ghastly thing. Though as he once pointed out to me, if he'd been a corporal instead of a lieutenant he'd have been shot for cowardice rather than invalided home. That actually happened to a man in his regiment and it preyed dreadfully on his mind. He said the humiliation of losing his nerve (that was how he saw it, no matter what the doctors said) was worse than the worst nightmares.

I don't think I shall be going to Scotland in August after all, so if you

* * *

for certain, but next week, if this wonderful weather keeps up, I shall go down to Devon to stay with Hilda.

You asked me what became of Alfred's 'infernal machine' – I kept it as a <u>memento mori.</u> I shall never forget that day at the Crystal Palace: I think of it whenever I read 'The Relic'. It destroyed the illusion of immortality, the feeling of infinite time that one enjoys when young. Alfred was obsessed – he had to have one. But it seemed to me pure evil, a thing of darkness. I think that was when I knew, irrevocably, that I'd married a stranger. (Though I suppose the obvious riposte is: who doesn't?)

Foolish youth – <u>illusions perdues</u>, indeed. But yes, I suppose it does fascinate me in a perverse sort of way. A few years after the War – I don't think I've ever told you this – I used it in a novella. All those years I didn't write – I seemed to have lost the impulse – and then the idea came to me, and went on nagging until I wrote it all down. Then a year or two later – it can't have been much more – George got married out of the blue. Though as everyone must have realised, he can't have had much choice: Anne was far too big to be a seven months' child. And then that dreadful smash. Sheer coincidence of course – literature is full of orphaned girls brought up by relatives – but there was something <u>unheimlich</u> about it. I felt that some sort of prognostic gift had been thrust upon me, and I didn't like it. So I put the manuscript away; I could never quite bring myself to destroy it.

Odd how one can write what one wouldn't say. I do hope Edie is quite recovered.

Yrs ever

V.

★ ★ ★

Harry flung up one arm as if to ward off an assailant. Beatrice cried out in fear, which turned to fury as she recognised her sister.

"What are you doing, hiding there?" she cried, advancing on Cordelia.

"I was on my way to meet Harry—"

"No you weren't, you were spying on me. You're so jealous, I can't even walk with him from the station, why do you think I never speak to him when you're around? Because you can't bear it, I only have to look at him to have you sneaking off to Uncle . . ."

"—I say, steady on," said Harry nervously.

"—I am *not* jealous," said Cordelia, backing away from her sister's tirade.

"Then why were you spying?"

"I wasn't—"

"Yes you were, or you would have waved as soon as you saw us."

Beatrice would not concede an inch of her ground, and soon Cordelia found herself apologising while Harry stood feebly by, leaving her no choice but to retreat. She did not

stop at the house, but kept on until she reached the river-bank, hot, humiliated, and confused. Being in love, she thought, has not made me a better person as it is said to do in novels. Beatrice is right; I am jealous, and distrustful, and clutching, and thoroughly miserable, and I hate myself . . . and if he does not follow I will break our engagement. The light was fading rapidly. A few moments later the still surface of the rock pool was broken by a large raindrop, then another, and then the heavens opened with a flash and a deafening thunderclap.

★ ★ ★

I read and re-read these pages sitting in Viola's armchair, distracted once or twice by the sensation, rather than the actual sound, of the faint rhythmic scraping or rustling I had heard the day before. The novella she mentioned could only have been 'The Revenant': the typed page in my hand was numbered '82', and the typescript back in my hotel room broke off at 81. So . . . I stared at the photograph, trying to imagine what must have happened: Phyllis running in here, perhaps, as she was packing to leave after the quarrel with Iris, wrenching the desk drawer open and snatching the typescript . . . which must, presumably, have been kept with the bundle of letters for these pages to be caught up together. But not the photograph . . . she must have had her own copy . . . well, obviously. Perhaps it really was Viola and the inscription had nothing to do with the picture at all.

And Phyllis must already have found and read the story. About two sisters growing up in this house. But where were the remaining pages? Where, for that matter, were the rest of Viola's manuscripts?

One came true.

I went on gazing at the photograph until I was no longer certain that the two pictures *were* identical. Different setting, different light, I told myself; and easily settled: I would bring my own copy up to the house on my next visit.

For the next two hours I searched the study. I leafed through every book on the shelves, took every drawer off its runners, moved the furniture, looked under the carpet. Nothing but dust and shreds of dried tobacco and an assortment of bookmarks, bus tickets, slips of paper with fragmentary jottings on them. But in several of the books, I found indentations where folded papers or envelopes had been crushed between the pages.

Someone had been through the house, not in a mad rush but carefully, thoroughly, removing letters, manuscripts, pictures, photographs . . . And it couldn't have been Miss Hamish because she had asked me to look for just these things.

It could have been Anne, in her last weeks alone here after Iris died. If she'd taken everything away, and died in an accident (yet another accident?) and somehow not been identified . . . but how could she possibly not be identified if she had all the family papers with her?

She could have made a bonfire of the lot – amnesia or breakdown again – and walked away from the entire estate to start a new life. Leaving behind just the one photograph on the cedar cabinet; which just happened to be the double of the photograph I had found in Mawson.

Again I became conscious of that faint rustling and scratching somewhere nearby, and again I found myself stumbling down the stairs, back through the dining- and drawing-rooms, fumbling with the front door locks in the semi-darkness of the porch, and out into the lane where I leaned gasping against the wall until I noticed an elderly woman with a dog, both of them watching me suspiciously. I attended ostentatiously to the Banhams, and walked away as casually as I could.

Breakfast, I told myself firmly. A solid English breakfast, and then some solid factual work in the Family Records Centre. I didn't run because I was afraid. I was afraid because I ran. I could always buy a large battery radio; but that would seem like sacrilege. Or a mobile phone, but who could I call?

Alice. The only person in the world I wanted to talk to. The only person I wasn't allowed to – had promised not to – ring. I started up the slope towards East Heath Road with a strange sensation of vertigo. How could I have accepted Alice's terms for so long? Or felt so sure, so much of the time, that we would fall into each other's arms one day and live happily ever after? Madness. Obscured until now, one day at a time, by the cosy routines of the library, the daily dose of worry about my mother. Tonight I would ring the hospital and ask for Alice and say, you're not the only one capable of surprises.

The new Family Records Centre in Clerkenwell was clean (except for the older registers, which stank even more than I remembered), spacious and, at opening time, relatively tranquil. The crowds built up as the morning wore on, but by then I had found most of the entries I wanted; and learned nothing, in essence, that I didn't already know from Miss Hamish's or Viola's letters.

Viola's shell-shocked son George – George Rupert Hatherley – had married Muriel Celia Hatherley, née Wilson in the district of Marylebone in the third quarter of 1927. Anne Victoria Hatherley had been born in the first quarter of 1928, and Phyllis May (just to make certain, though I didn't know why I was bothering, unless I suspected my mother of forging her own birth certificate), in the second quarter of 1929. And then George and Muriel had died in the third quarter of 1930, in the district of Brighton. George had been thirty-eight years old, and Muriel just twenty-seven when the accident happened.

They had died the same way as Alice's parents, it struck me as I sat in the basement tea-room amidst the roar of genealogical debate. Since our very first letters, Alice had insisted on writing as if she'd been born, rather than nearly dying, on the day of the crash. She rejected as too painful, or simply ignored, all my attempts to get her to talk about her family, until I gave up asking. Just as I had with my mother, which made Alice's attitude seem – if not normal then at least perfectly understandable. I didn't even know her exact birthdate, only that she had been born in March. We didn't do birthdays or Christmas, or send presents of any kind: all that had been left on hold, waiting for our life together to begin. Mad, mad, mad. But now I could find out.

I fought my way through the swelling mob in Births, from 1958 to 1970, without finding a single Alice Jessell.

Deaths weren't as popular as Births. It took less than twenty minutes to establish that no one called Jessell had died anywhere in England or Wales between 1964 (the year Alice ought to have been born) and the first quarter of 1978, when she first wrote to me.

Of course she could have been born – and the accident could have happened – in Scotland, which kept its own records.

At the counter they told me I could log on to the 'Scots Origins' website and run as many specific searches as my credit card would bear. I ordered my certificates and walked down Exmouth Market in brilliant sunshine until I found an internet café. But the Scottish system didn't allow searches later than

1924. I logged in my credit card number anyway and entered 'Jessell 1560–1924'. We have no records for this name.

I opened an email window to Alice but couldn't decide what to write. One of my favourite books, when I was about eight or nine, had been an old Puffin *Tales of King Arthur and His Knights of the Round Table*, by Roger Lancelyn Green. It had sinister illustrations in the style of woodcuts, which still occasionally came to life in my dreams. One of the stories was about a knight who married a beautiful princess under some sort of enchantment which meant that after seven years she would turn into something hideous . . . and there was another version in which they would live happily, so long as he never questioned her about her past. Of course the questions preyed upon his mind until at last he commanded her to answer, and then . . . I couldn't remember exactly what happened. Something dark and irrevocable.

I logged off without sending anything, finished my coffee and moved over to the payphone by the door. I had the number of the National Hospital for Neurology and Microsurgery in East Finchley in my notebook. It couldn't do any harm – could it? – to ring the desk and ask to speak to Alice Jessell. And ring off before she answered. But on the other hand . . . best leave it until this evening. Collect the photograph from the hotel, take a cab back to the house, start searching the library. Concentrate on the Hatherleys and try not to think about Jessells.

THE WINDOW of the cab wouldn't open. Every stretch of grass we passed on the way up was crammed with half-naked people soaking up the sunshine. I was dripping with sweat when I paid the driver at the entrance to the lane. Half-past one.

I had brought sandwiches, bottled water, a torch and spare batteries, three boxes of matches. But when the gate had closed behind me, there was plenty of light now that the sun was overhead. I tried again to swallow the sensation of something cold and metallic lodged in the centre of my chest, about where, I realised, my mental image of Alice habitually floated – an indistinct figure in dazzling white, glimpses of a face from several different angles, never quite in focus. As much a part of me as breathing. *As close to you as your heartbeat.*

I took my photograph up to the study and set it beside the framed picture on Viola's cabinet. They were indeed the same, but I was no closer to knowing who she was. 'Greensleeves', 10 March 1949. Just four days after Anne's twenty-first birthday.

Alas my love you do me wrong
To cast me out discourteously . . .
Greensleeves was all my joy . . .

I couldn't see a connection with anything I knew about her. It couldn't be to do with the breaking of her engagement to Hugh Montfort, because that hadn't happened until the summer of 1949. Could someone have written a play based on the song? A play for which she had auditioned?

Once more I read through the pages from Viola's letters, which I had left on the writing-desk. Something in the dusty-sweet smell of the paper reminded me again of that hot afternoon in my mother's room, where this had all started. Or so it felt. Were the missing papers crammed into some hiding-place I hadn't found, back in the house in Mawson? Of course I'd hardly begun to search this one; I hadn't even looked in the basement yet.

Hiding-places . . . the false floor in the top cupboard. Could my mother have got the idea from something in her bedroom here?

The house was completely still. I left the two pictures side by side on the cabinet and went on down the corridor.

Even with the curtains open, the light in my mother's room was unnervingly dim. I had already looked through the dressing-table and chest, but I searched them again by the light of the torch. I lifted the bookcase away from the wall, dragged the counterpane and bedding and then the mattress off the bed, stirring up a cloud of dust and several more heavy, slow-flying moths, deliberately postponing my last and best chance: the wall of built-in cupboards that divided this room from Anne's.

As I had noticed the day before, the beds in both rooms were centred against the common partition, with the space equally divided between the two, so that on either side of the partition there was fixed panelling to the right of the bed, a cupboard above the left-hand half of each bed-head, and then hanging space with a shelf above the rail. I shone the torch beam into the cupboard above Phyllis's bed. The gouges in the floor – long, wavering scars, about a foot apart – looked unnervingly fresh.

The shelf in the closet was indeed made up of two separate sheets of wood – I could feel them flexing – but both were solidly fixed. Silly idea in the first place. If it *had* been a hiding-place, Phyllis would hardly have forgotten to take whatever she'd hidden there. She'd remembered the typescript in the study, after all.

Just so I could tell myself – and Miss Hamish – I had left nothing undone, I moved on to Anne's room and repeated the search, with no better result until I took the yellowing tennis dress off the rail to see if there was anything in the pocket. It didn't even have a pocket. As I hung it up again, the shelf above the rail rattled slightly. I climbed on to the bed to get a better view. In the torchlight, I saw a faint dark line around the nearest panel.

In the cavity beneath lay a dusty quarto notebook. Lined pages, handwritten. A diary.

25 March 1949

Still freezing. I meant to start this on my birthday but it's nearly three weeks. Such a let-down, turning 21. The old suffocating feeling again, worse than usual. Something's missing and I don't know what it is. Like craving for a food you've never had but you'd know at once if you could only taste it, and then you'd never eat anything else. Or finding you can't breathe ordinary air any more.

I know what Grandmama would have said. Stop moping,

girl, smarten yourself up, get a job. Iris just smiles sweetly and says you must do whatever you think best dear and goes back to the seventh astral plane. Perhaps I'd be happier if I had a boring job like Filly, but then I wouldn't have any time to myself. I waste so much time and then I resent it when I don't have time to waste. I don't want to type and I don't want to nurse and I don't want to teach. But I know I could write if only I had something interesting to write about.

29 March

Went to a Labour Party meeting with Owen last night. In a horrible hall in Camden that stank. Of course it's awful, slums and all that, and I know I ought to care but I don't. The secretary, Ted somebody or other, tried to make me join. I said I'd think about it but I could see him thinking, rich girl slumming. Owen must have said something. And here I am queueing for neck of lamb and counting our pennies. I'm sick of Owen; he lectures me all the time and never notices what I'm wearing.

5 April

Had tea with Owen in the High Street yesterday and gave him the push. He went all doggy and pleading and I walked off despising him and feeling I'd been hard and cruel.

14 April

Iris got a summons from Pitt the Elder and insisted I go instead. You're twenty-one now dear, and I'm sure you've got a much better head for these things than I have. She's convinced herself she's going to die quite soon: one of her premonitions. Of course there's her heart, but she's only sixty for God's sake.

Felt very nervous about having to explain to Mr Pitt that I was there instead of Iris. But he was very charming and made a great fuss of me. Miss Neame brought us tea and a proper teacake and sandwiches, and I thought he just wanted to chat about how we were managing and all that, until I realised he was leading up to something.

I did wonder if Iris had been keeping something from us but it still came as a shock. He says our capital's run down and we're going to have to sell either the house or some of the pictures, furniture or silver or something like that. Apparently he's warned Iris several times but she hasn't done anything about it.

I asked him what he thought we should do and he said that depended on how much we want to keep the house. Now is a bad time to sell, apparently, because of death duties and supertax and all that, and with the housing shortage he said it would most likely go for flats and whoever bought it wouldn't want to pay much. But on the other hand if we know we want to leave, then perhaps the sooner the better.

Until now I'd never really thought about it. Somehow I'd assumed that Filly and I would get married and Iris would find herself a companion and everything would go on just the same. Even though we freeze every winter and the garden's going to pot I can't imagine not being able to come back here.

15 April

Iris more or less admitted she'd kept quiet because Horus or whoever came through on the ouija board had told her something was sure to turn up. I nearly said yes, the bailiffs, but I bit my tongue. Of course she doesn't want to move. And Filly doesn't seem to care either way; she says she just wants to get a flat of her own as soon as she can afford it. So we've agreed to ask Mr Pitt about selling some of the pictures or the good chairs.

18 April

Rang up Mr Pitt this morning. He asked if we had a copy of the inventory that Grandmama had made when she did her last will; if not he'll get Miss Neame to type out another one for us. Iris didn't know so I went up to the study to look.

Even with the morning sun streaming in the study always feels slightly haunted. Perhaps it's the leftover smell of her tobacco. And there was something rustling about in the ceiling. I don't think I'm afraid of mice but I shouldn't like it to be anything larger.

It wasn't in any of the drawers, so I started looking through the little cabinet, but then I got distracted and started reading some of Grandmama's stories again. And that made me remember her reading us 'The Pavilion' in the summerhouse before the war, at least I thought then she was reading but she made it into quite a different story, with nothing about Rosalind getting married or Mr Margrave being a vampire, or of course the angel; it was all about the way the pavilion changed whenever you went to sleep in it.

I didn't find the inventory, but at the back of the cabinet underneath a stack of typing paper I found an old leather music-case. Inside was another of her stories, a longer one I'd never seen before, called 'The Revenant'.

The creepy feeling started when I looked at the date. Three years before I was born, before our parents had even met. I wondered at first if she'd put 1925 for 1935, say, but I don't think she would have written it after the accident. Of course there must be lots of stories about orphaned sisters being brought up by aunts and uncles or grandparents. And it's not as if I've ever <u>felt</u> like an orphan. Just that so many things seem to fit.

It's this house for a start, though only this floor, really, and the lane and the garden. But why is it different from her turning the summerhouse into the pavilion? Because F. and I are the same age as Beatrice and Cordelia? Our rooms are side by side, and the studio is where Grandmama's study is. Beatrice goes out to work and Cordelia stays home, like me. And Iris has a weak heart. But so do lots of people, and she's not fat like Aunt Una.

And their not having any money, and having to do their own cooking.

And me just turning 21.

Still freezing.

19 April

Read the story again last night. It reminds me of the feeling when we used to play with Iris's ouija board: the way the glass seemed to come alive and tug. I'd never thought of Filly and me as estranged, just not terribly close. But now I wonder. Just as it didn't seem odd, before, that she and I haven't talked about our parents for years and years, and now it does.

28 April

Filly does remind me of a cat. And there *is* something guarded and distrustful about her. I notice it more and more.

But is the story making me see things that aren't there? Like walking on the heath at dusk, when you think there's a man watching you from the shadows and he turns out to be a treetrunk?

5 May

Mr Pitt says Christie's will send someone to look at the pictures. All I have to do is ring up and arrange a time.

This is silly. Lots of people have their pictures valued.

11 May

Mr Montfort – Hugh Montfort came this afternoon to look at the pictures. It was Iris's day with Mrs Roper's circle so I was here by myself. All morning I kept thinking, what if he looks exactly like Harry Beauchamp?

Of course he was nothing like, except for being young and quite good-looking. He's tall, and slender, with black hair swept back from the temples, pale skin, no moustache. And no corduroy trousers – he had on a charcoal grey suit, beautifully pressed. Very dark brown eyes, the corners crinkle when he smiles.

And he didn't make me feel embarrassed about our having to sell things. I wasn't going to mention it but he was so nice I ended up telling him all about us while I was showing him the pictures – although really he was showing me: he knew about almost every one we looked at. He thinks the Blake etching might fetch quite a bit.

He actually listens: such a change from Owen. His parents live apart and he has a married sister in Canada. He's sharing rooms in Piccadilly with a friend – they were in the army together but he didn't want to talk about the war. I don't think there's anyone special.

15 May

Hugh rang to say he'd like to have another look at the Blake. I asked him to tea on Thursday and he said yes!

19 May

Such a wonderful day: we took our tea out to the summerhouse and talked and talked. Afterwards I said I'd walk down to the station with him and we went on a huge detour, all the way to Highgate Ponds.

I asked how he got interested in pictures and he said he'd wanted to be a painter but realised after a while he'd never be very good. Apparently having a good eye for pictures doesn't mean you can do it yourself.

I said I liked Constable which was a mistake but he was very nice about it. And it's OK to like Turner though only the blurry ones, Hugh said they were done when his eyes were going and that's how the world actually looked to him. There was a painter called Fuseli who was colour-blind, he said, and had to choose his colours by remembering where they were on his palette. He told me about a collector he knows, very rich and eccentric, who buys every picture he can find by a man called Rees, because he hates his work so much he doesn't want anyone else to see it. Because he's a collector he can't bring himself to destroy the pictures, so he keeps them locked in a damp cellar where they're slowly rotting away.

That was the only slightly creepy moment, because it reminded me of Ruthven de Vere buying up all Henry St Clair's pictures. I won't think about it any more.

On Tuesday we're going to the Tate!

24 May

Went to Tate to look at the Turners but I couldn't really concentrate, I was so happy. Then walked for miles along the Embankment with the sun shining on the river. I want to live by water.

6 June

Cinema with Hugh. *The Heiress* – so exciting. Supper afterwards. He kissed me properly at last. And told me I'm beautiful. And I didn't mention Filly so it wasn't in the least like the story. I might as well admit I'm in love with him.

Somehow we got on to Iris. H. asked me whether she really believes, and so I told him about Geoffrey being killed in the last war, and how she never really got over it, and that led to our parents. He was very tactful and tentative, but I don't think he quite believed me when I said I'd never really missed them. Did Filly feel the same way, he asked, and I had to admit I didn't know, and that made me think of the story again. I wish I'd never found it.

9 June

Tea with Hugh in Mayfair: a celebration. The Blake has sold for 500 guineas!

I know we've only been out a few times but he's the man I want to marry. I've never felt this way about anyone. And I'm nearly sure he feels the same.

14 June

Hugh to tea here to meet F. and Iris. I couldn't put it off any longer. I didn't want to but he's been asking when am I going to meet them.

Iris was on her best behaviour – H. must have thought I'd exaggerated terribly – but when I introduced him to ~~Beatrice~~ – o my God Filly – I couldn't help noticing, she turned quite pale. Tea was awful. And when I said we'd go for a walk on the Heath F. asked if she could come too, and I couldn't very well say no. F. talked – I suppose he was only drawing her out, but why did he have to sound so *interested* in her boring job? – and I seethed, all the way up to Parliament Hill and back. And then when he kissed me goodbye at the tube he said how much he'd enjoyed it. I shan't bring him here again on a Saturday if I can help it.

F. behaved *exactly* like Beatrice in the story and I could see H. looking at her. But I was so tense and miserable, I can't help wondering if I brought it on myself.

17 June

Today I did a very stupid thing. I started searching the house for 'The Drowned Man'. To prove it doesn't exist. But not finding it only made me more afraid that it's hidden somewhere, lying in wait for H. Even Iris noticed. I didn't dare ask – one thing the spirits are quite good at is suggesting places to look. The last thing I want. I feel creepy enough as it is.

19 June

H. very busy – big sale coming up – won't be able to see me this week.

<u>No one is going to die</u>. I just mustn't think about it any more.

28 June

H. to tea <u>again</u> with Filly. He came to pick me up and Iris invited him before I could stop her. We had it on the terrace. H. talked about some Russian who only painted coloured squares. F. very quiet but hanging on every word.

12 July

H. started talking about money. Says he hasn't a bean – spends his salary before he gets it. I'm sure he was leading up to proposing. Tried everything I knew to encourage him without seeming to let on. I'm sure he will.

16 July

But he hasn't.

19 July

A perfect afternoon. Long walk with H. and then we lay down in the grass – really passionate at last. We were kissing and he was lying almost on top of me and I could feel the sun shining through his body into mine. It really is like going to heaven. He undid my dress and I thought we were going to make love properly. I didn't care about anyone seeing. I wanted him to. But then somebody's wretched dog came bounding up and H. got all embarrassed and started apologising for being carried away. I wish he hadn't.

25 July

H. asked me to marry him this afternoon. I'm so deliriously happy. I know I am. I wish we could keep our engagement a secret.

Later: I've locked the story in the study. I will never read it or think of it again.

28 July

Told Iris this afternoon. I hadn't meant to, so soon, but it just came out. So when Filly got home I had to tell her too. She said all the right things but I felt she didn't mean them.

8 August

H. here <u>again</u> for tea with F. We had it in the summer-house and then he wanted us all to play tennis. I said I couldn't remember where the net was, but Filly went and dragged it out of the conservatory. If I say anything he'll think I'm jealous.

I should tell him about the story and how it haunts me. But then he'll want to read it, and he might

<u>I must not think about it any more</u>.

12 August

Alone with H. at last. He asked me if something was wrong and I said no, just a bit of a headache, which was exactly the wrong thing to say, because he insisted on taking me home.

I keep thinking he's not as passionate as he was a month ago, but I'm so tense and miserable I don't know if it's him or me. I'm sure he loves me. <u>I will not read the story again</u>.

20 August

Filly is acting very strangely. I keep <u>watching</u> her – about Hugh I mean – I can't help myself. Sometimes I think I must be going mad.

25 August

Hardly slept at all. H. very busy again at the saleroom. Tried again to tell him about the story and couldn't.

10 September

Very close and airless. H. stayed late again playing Scrabble. Kept willing Filly to go to bed but she wouldn't, even though I could hardly keep my eyes open – just played on and on until H. realised he'd missed the last tube. He said not to worry about making up the spare bed, he'd sleep on the couch in the library. I wanted to go downstairs with him but he said good-night on the landing in front of Filly.

By then I was too angry to sleep. I tossed and turned for hours until I gave up and went and stood at the window and looked at the moon. And I thought, I'll go down to the library and have it out with him.

Filly's door was locked and it was deathly quiet. Until I got to the landing outside the study and heard the noise. A squeaking, creaking sort of noise. Coming through the ceiling.

I tiptoed up the attic stairs and there they were, on Lettie's old bed, stark naked in the moonlight. He was sprawled along the mattress with his head hanging over the foot of the bed. She was riding him like a horse, straddling him with her hands on his shoulders, lashing his face with her hair. I couldn't move and I couldn't look away. Then her whole body arched and shuddered and she threw back her head and looked straight at me.

(*The rest of this page, and all the remaining pages in the diary, had been torn out.*)

* * *

I read through the diary by torchlight, sitting on Anne's bed with the faded white tennis dress floating at the edge of my vision. I could not associate the mother I had known with the woman in the attic, and yet the final scene left me with a nightmarish sense of having witnessed my own conception. It was also disturbingly like one of the fantasies Alice and I had shared. I remained staring at the torn page until a very faint rustling somewhere overhead set the hair on the back of my neck bristling.

Downstairs in the comparative safety of the library, in an armchair beneath the four great windows, I read through it again. I had known, really, since I first read Miss Hamish's letter. Why else would Aunt Iris have turned so violently against Phyllis? (I would not think of her as 'my mother' any more.)

Phyllis had found the diary; had probably been reading it all along. 'Filly is acting very strangely': I saw what must have happened, set out as clearly as an endgame at chess, with Phyllis always one – no two moves ahead . . . *One came true*, indeed. Anne's record of the closing trap had gone with the torn-out pages. But why had Phyllis put the rest of the diary back in its hiding-place after – whatever she had done to – had done *with* Anne? It made no sense: after all, she had taken 'The Revenant'.

And there was something else . . . something that didn't fit. I took out Miss Hamish's letter to check the dates. Somewhere around the middle of September, Anne had written to say the engagement was 'all off'. But the 'dreadful set-to' between Phyllis and Iris hadn't happened for another fortnight or so. Anne clearly didn't tell her friend *why* she'd broken off with Hugh Montfort. Then Iris had changed her will and died within days of learning the truth. And Anne had last been seen alive in Mr Pitt's office on 26 October.

Miss Hamish. The diary did not once mention Miss Hamish.

How could this be? Unless she hadn't been nearly as close

to Anne as she imagined . . . but no, Anne had left her the estate. For a few wild moments I toyed with the notion of Miss Hamish and Phyllis conspiring to murder Anne, but that was idiotic. Every detail in her letter fitted exactly with my own discoveries, and with Anne's diary, including Mr Pitt the solicitor. And the police would have investigated Abigail Hamish, as the sole beneficiary, very carefully indeed.

No: the only obvious answer was that Anne simply hadn't included the friendship – and presumably whole other dimensions of her life – in the diary. Odd, all the same. I leaned back in the armchair, staring up at the gallery where the veiled woman had appeared in my dream.

A woman in a dark green gown. Greensleeves.

The back of my neck prickled. *Of course* it had been a dream. I didn't – did I? – seriously believe in ghosts. Any more than I believed in spirit messages from beyond. I looked over at the stack of butcher's paper on the table. Something about the planchette had changed.

The squeak and scrape of the chair rose into a high, drawn-out note as I stood up. There was my question:

WHAT HAPPENED TO ANNE?

but the planchette had moved on. In faint, spidery letters, an answer had appeared:

Filly murdered me

* * *

From: ghfreeman@hotmail.com
To: Alice.Jessell@hotmail.com

Subject: None
Date: Wed, 11 August 1999 19:48:21 +0100 (BST)

. . . later I rang Mr Grierstone's clerk and asked her if the cleaners, or a security patrol had been in the house last night, and she said no, certainly not, no one else has keys, Miss Hamish was most insistent about that. She said the only way anyone could have got in was if I hadn't locked up properly last night, and I know I did.

I felt angry when I first saw the message. A defensive reaction, I suppose. Someone's playing games with me, I thought, but I'll show them. I wrote down another question, something no one else could answer, thinking, that'll prove you're not a ghost. It seemed perfectly logical at the time. But I knew really, even before I went out to phone, that it couldn't have been a cleaner or anyone like that. Who could possibly know that my mother was Filly to the family?

Maybe Mr Grierstone lives a double life, creeping out at night to frighten his clients. I wish I could believe that.

The only other possibility – the only one I want to think about – is that I wrote it myself, when I was sitting at the table yesterday afternoon, doodling with the planchette. But I KNOW I didn't do that. I can see myself sitting there yesterday, trying to convince myself that Mother couldn't have killed Anne, and the planchette doesn't move.

So either I'm turning into one of those 'missing time' people with alternate personalities, or Anne's ghost is telling me what I already know from her diary. I don't know which is more frightening. If I did write that message, what am I going to do next? What if it's inherited? – the condition, whatever it is? Am I going to turn into a murderer too?

I know what you'll say: I'm letting my worst fears run away

with me. If only. It would actually be a relief, now, to believe what I've just written. Because I don't. I keep getting flashes – like the shadow of something truly monstrous creeping up behind you. Your mind keeps saying no, no, but your skin and your spine and your hair and the pit of your stomach know what's coming. In that house, anything is possible.

Alice I know we agreed to wait but I really need to talk to you right now. I've never felt more alone in my life. This morning in Family Records I looked you up, or tried to, I just couldn't help myself. You weren't born in England, so why have you always let me believe that you were? And that the accident happened here? After the shock of losing Staplefield, and finding out my whole childhood was a lie (I mean my mother's, but it feels like mine) and now this, you must understand why I need to hear your voice now, not 'very soon' but now.

I'll wait for an hour to see if you've read this before I ring the hospital . . .

From: Alice.Jessell@hotmail.com
To: ghfreeman@hotmail.com
Subject: None
Date: Wed, 11 August 1999 20:29:53 +0100 (BST)

I didn't tell you because I wanted it to be a surprise, but I've already left the hospital. I'm having a last lot of physiotherapy, in a clinic in St John's Wood, and I'll be with you in three more days, maybe sooner. There's nothing I want more in the world than to pick up the phone and pour out everything I feel. But we might regret it later. We mustn't have a conventional beginning, hi how are you, nice to speak to you at last. I think of you as my questing knight, facing his last ordeal.

And it is a terrible ordeal, but you mustn't lose hope yet, about your mother. I think you did go into some sort of trance and write that message, but it doesn't have to be either/or, either you wrote it or Anne did. I think Anne was trying to speak through you, only the fear that was preying on your mind took over the pencil. Houses, especially old houses, hold the impressions of people very strongly, and you're so attuned to her.

We'll be together very soon

Your invisible lover

Alice

As soon as I had read Alice's message, I took the lift down to the foyer and joined the crowds heading west along Euston Road towards the last of the sunset. The roar and stench of traffic was comforting; it stopped me from thinking. Just beyond Tottenham Court Road I found an entire street full of restaurants. I chose the noisiest, ate something vaguely Middle Eastern and drank a bottle of bad but expensive red, a thick metallic wine heavy with sediment. On the way back to the hotel I stopped at an off-licence and bought a bottle of whisky.

I woke at ten the following morning with a slow, thudding headache, which accompanied me down Kingsway to Somerset House on the Strand, where I intended to look up Iris's will, only to be told that wills were no longer kept there. I was sent back up to First Avenue House, a featureless modern building with airport-level security, in High Holborn. There were only two other people in the registry, and it took me all of three minutes to establish, from the probate registers, that Viola's estate had been valued at £12,989; Iris's – she had died on 6 October 1949 – at £9,135. I applied for copies of the wills, was told there would be an hour's wait, and went back to the registers.

George Rupert Hatherley, my grandfather, had died intestate in Prince Alfred Hospital in Brighton on 13 August 1929, leaving effects to the value of £724.13.9. Viola's husband, Alfred George Hatherley, had died not at Ferrier's Close but at 44 Ennismore Gardens Knightsbridge, on 7 December 1921, leaving just under six thousand pounds. So Viola had presumably inherited money, as well as Ferrier's Close, from her own family. Then I thought I might as well search forwards from 1949, just to make sure that Anne Hatherley hadn't died without Miss Hamish's knowing about it; I had got as far as 1990 before I remembered that as Anne's executor, Miss Hamish couldn't *not* have known. A coffee break was clearly overdue.

My copies arrived just as I was leaving. Viola had made her last will on 10 August 1938, leaving everything to Iris with the proviso that if Iris should die before the will was proven, the estate should be divided equally between 'my granddaughters Anne Victoria and Phyllis May Hatherley, both of Ferrier's Close Hampstead in the County of London'. Her executor was 'Edward Nichol Pitt of 18 Whetstone Park Solicitor'. Iris's last will, signed on 4 October 1949, two days before she died, was even simpler. It left everything to 'my dear niece Anne Victoria Hatherley'. Pitt the Elder was again the executor; Phyllis wasn't even mentioned.

Surrounded by people shouting into mobiles through the clatter of cups and the hiss and roar of the coffee machine, while the traffic outside negotiated High Holborn in a series of kamikaze rushes, I felt almost certain I didn't believe in spirit messages. Of course I had written those words myself. If only I could *remember* writing them, I wouldn't have to worry any more about alternate personalities, or missing time. Or ghosts. I picked up my pen and sat with the tip resting lightly on a blank page of my notebook, trying to will myself into recalling the moment. But the memory would not come, and instead I found myself thinking about Alice.

Some time later I realised I had been doodling. Above a heavily inscribed 'A' I had drawn a small pig with wings, an imbecilic smile, and a halo.

At least it showed I could have written that message.

At seven that evening, I was sitting in a vast beer garden at the foot of Downshire Hill. Evening sunshine slanted across the grass. Still plenty of daylight left.

From Holborn I had walked slowly back up Southampton Row, intending to call in at the new British Library and try another search for more of Viola's stories. Instead I had gone straight back to the hotel and slept until half-past five. The headache had gone when I woke, but the knot in the pit of my stomach was still there. Hunger, I told myself. A good meal will settle it.

Yet in spite of the roast lamb, and the beer, and the roar of several hundred conversations, the knot had refused to unravel.

I think of you as my questing knight, facing his last ordeal. In a couple of days' time I could be sitting here with Alice. *Trust me.* I tried to imagine her, in her white dress embroidered with small purple flowers, her thick copper-coloured hair loosely tied back, smiling at me from the empty chair opposite. She would be wearing that dress, she'd told me, when we met; it still fitted her. *Alice is so beautiful, we all love her.* Parvati Naidu, the ward sister at Finchley Road, had said so. I'd forgotten about Parvati during this last attack of doubt. I should learn to be more trusting.

And what would we be talking about, sitting here on the terrace, watching the sun go down? Whether Phyllis had murdered her sister as well as sleeping with her fiancé? I loved Alice for defending my mother to the bitter end, but I couldn't agree with her. On the evidence of Anne's diary alone, Phyllis May Hatherley was guilty unless proven innocent. And to prove it either way, I would have to find out what had happened to Anne.

I found that I was on my feet and heading for East Heath Road. The shadows had lengthened noticeably; the sun was only just above the treetops on Rosslyn Hill. All I needed to do this evening was check the library and confirm what I already knew: that the planchette would be sitting exactly where I'd left it, beneath the question I'd scrawled on my way out, in a moment of nervous defiance – if you're so smart, answer *this.* To make certain nobody was creeping into the house at night, I had fetched a reel of black thread from a sewing basket upstairs, tied a length of it across the hall a few paces from the front door, and another half-way along the path to the gate. I hadn't told Alice.

I took the path that ran past Hampstead Ponds, now crowded with swimmers, and across the Heath towards the eastern end of the Vale; the path I had taken on that wintry day thirteen years ago. Half of Hampstead seemed to be out walking or cycling. My mother and Anne, and Iris and Viola had walked these paths hundreds of times – all those coats and scarves and boots and galoshes by the front door – they would have been a familiar sight. Anne must have had friends; she'd lived here all her life. The life excluded from the diary. Apart from Miss Hamish, I didn't have a single name to pursue.

Except Hugh Montfort. I'd been so preoccupied with my mother and Anne, I'd hardly given him a thought. Had he and Phyllis run off together? Wouldn't the police have wanted to question him as well? He might still be alive, in fact – he'd only be in his seventies. It would certainly be worth trying to trace him: if not through public records – and I hadn't even checked the London residential phone book yet – I could try another advertisement in *The Times*.

As I approached the pond that lies between the Vale and the open Heath, I kept trying to identify Ferrier's Close. There were several possible candidates lurking behind dense stands of trees on a rise away to my left, but the geography of the Vale was so deceptive, I wasn't even sure I was looking in the right direction. Back in Mawson, I had skimmed through a massive history of Hampstead and the Heath: in the 1870s, the Vale of Health had been a rowdy pleasure-garden with its own gin palace; before that, it had been mainly cottages and a handful of larger houses, of which Ferrier's Close must have been one. I wondered how the bachelor uncle had felt about the gin palace.

Now gentrification had triumphed: the only remnant of commerce was the fairground on the eastern fringe of the Vale, an incongruous stretch of wasteland crowded with run-down mobile homes, derelict cars, mounds of salvaged timber and broken stone, rusting pieces of machinery.

A puff of wind sent dust eddying across the yard. Last time I saw this, it had been a sea of mud. Dank and dripping; as Miss Hamish had said, the gloomiest corner of the Heath.

Something in that swirl of dust, or perhaps a rowan tree on the far side of the fairground, dripping with scarlet berries, reminded me of Mawson, sitting with my mother in the back garden, the morning of my return. She had been so joyful, so *relieved*, to have me safely home. Consumed with misery and self-pity, I hadn't taken much notice. And then I'd mentioned the Vale, and she'd broken out in a cold sweat. *Anything could have happened to you. You might have been murdered.* No one could fake a reaction like that. Murders must have been committed on the Heath from time to time; perhaps she'd been warned, as a child, never to wander off alone. *I had to keep you safe.*

Meanwhile the sun was dipping below the trees on the skyline, and I had better get a move on.

In the gloom of the pleached walk, I had to use my torch to locate the first line of black thread. It was unbroken, exactly where I had left it, at knee height. Along with the torch and matches I had brought the bottle of whisky, and in another attempt to loosen the knot in my stomach I swallowed a couple of mouthfuls in the porch before tackling the Banhams.

The thread in the hall was intact too. But it wouldn't hurt to check the back door before I went into the library. Torch in hand, though there was still plenty of light from the stairwell, I turned left into the drawing-room. Overhead, the stained glass shone crimson and gold, casting a faint sheen over the humped sofas and chairs and the faded rectangles on the walls where pictures had once hung. Once again I caught myself trying to move noiselessly. A board squeaked. Whisky sloshed in the bottle. I swallowed another mouthful of Braveheart, left the bottle with my bag of provisions on the dining table and went on through to the rear landing and courtyard door. Which was again exactly as I had left it, firmly bolted.

Cold air brushed my neck. I turned and shone my torch

down the stairs to the flagged floor of the kitchen below. This was one of the reasons I had bought the torch. It would be dark down there at any time of day. Or night. *I think of you as my questing knight.*

The drop in temperature was much more noticeable this time. I went down the stone stairs with the sensation of entering a pool filled with chill, invisible water. The beam of my torch wavered across the black range and around the shelves to the doorway opposite. A tunnel, or passageway, about ten feet long, leading to a low wooden door. Rough stone walls, a flagged floor. Two massive joists running crosswise overhead; floorboards above the joists. A little unsteadily, I crossed the floor and shone my torch into an opening on the left, just inside the entrance. Two massive tubs, a copper, mops, buckets, fireplace in the wall opposite. A hint of stale soap, starch and cold metal, mildew.

I turned the torch beam to the door at the end of the tunnel. My hair brushed against a joist: I guessed I might be somewhere beneath the dining-room. Grit slithered underfoot; mortar flaked and crumbled when I steadied myself against the wall.

The door was very like the one in the front wall: heavy vertical planks, massive hinges. The black metal straps spanned more than half the width of the door. Timber architrave, flush with the stonework. Latched by a solid metal bar, which evidently slid up and over a metal tooth projecting from the architrave, and dropped into the slot behind, where it was now secured by an archaic padlock. A heavy pull-ring, black metal like the other fittings, was bolted to the centre of the door.

I reached into my pocket for the keys, then hesitated, glancing over my shoulder. The last of the daylight was fading from the basement steps.

Tomorrow morning, if the weather held, the sun would be shining directly down those steps. The door could wait until then. But I would sleep better tonight if I checked the planchette first. I hastened back up to the dining-room for another – well, two more healthy slugs of Braveheart and strode purposefully across the landing to the library, taking the bottle with me.

The stack of butcher's paper on the table was exactly where I had left it. There was my question:

WHO IS MY PENFRIEND?

But the planchette was no longer beneath the 'W', and even without the torch, the faint, looping reply was clear enough:

Miss Jessel

⋆ ⋆ ⋆

I was still in the tunnel, trying to find the basement stairs, but I couldn't see where I was going because someone was shining a light in my face. The light grew brighter until it hurt my head, which was propped at an uncomfortable angle. And someone was calling – no, whispering – my name.

I was lying on the chesterfield below the library windows, with a full moon shining down into my eyes. And a blurred recollection of having drunk too much whisky much too quickly.

'Gerard.'

A slow, insinuating whisper, making two long syllables of my name. It seemed to hang in the air above my head. The moon was painfully bright: everything else was in darkness.

'*Ger-ard.*'

I lifted my head slightly, trying to locate the sound. Pain shot through my forehead; the moon wavered and lurched.

'Close your eyes, Gerard. You're dreaming.'

I had had dreams before in which I dreamed I woke up, but never as real as this. My throat was parched; my tongue felt sore and swollen.

'I wouldn't try to run if I were you. You're dreaming; you don't know what you might meet.'

The voice was coming from the direction of the gallery.

'Who are you?' It came out as a hoarse croak; I hadn't meant to speak.

'You know who I am' – intimate, caressing – 'but you can call me Alice if you like.'

I must wake up. I must wake up. I heard a cry that might have been 'Alice?' and realised it was me.

'I know everything about you, Gerard. You're dreaming, remember; I'm inside your head. Closer than your heartbeat, you might say.'

Another incoherent sound.

'Why don't you ask me something? I'm dead, you know. The dead know everything.'

This is a terrible hallucination. I must wake up.

'Wouldn't you like to ask me about Anne?' the whispering voice insinuated. 'She left you a message last night. She's dead, of course, but you know all about that. You've seen the scratches in the cupboard.'

'*Who are you*?'

'That would be telling, wouldn't it? I might be you.'

'Me?'

'That's very good, Gerard. I might be you. Or Hugh. I might be Hugh Montfort.'

The whispering lingered on the last two syllables. There was no sound of breathing, only soft, insinuating words floating in darkness.

'We're all dead, you see. Filly killed us all, one by one. Hugh too. She killed Hugh too, Gerard, you just don't know it yet. And soon, very soon, we'll be together for ever and ever.

'You can go back to sleep now Gerard. Sweet dreams.'

The moon still shone through my eyelids. A barred shadow touched my face. I shot bolt upright with a shriek that rang and reverberated around the library and died to a slow drip, drip, drip somewhere beneath the couch. I had lost control of my bladder.

The barred shadow had been thrown by the casement halfway up the window. Slowly, the library beyond the small moonlit area around me began to materialise. I stumbled the few steps from the couch to the table and snatched up the torch.

There was no one on the gallery.

Following the quivering patch of light through the darkness to the front door, with a hundred malignant eyes playing up and down my spine, was almost as terrifying as listening to the voice in the dark. I walked all the way down through Camden to the hotel and arrived at three in the morning, smelling like an incontinent drunk but cold, shivering sober. Even the headache had gone. I showered and made tea and stood at the window, staring down at the yellow vapour lights ranged along the bleak expanse of Euston Road.

I had been awake when I heard the voice. No point pretending otherwise. And no one could have got into the house; not even, to be totally paranoid for a moment, Alice. She didn't have keys, and I hadn't told her about the black thread.

Either my mind was coming apart, or I'd been listening to a real ghost. Though when you thought about it, there wasn't much difference. The voice was part of me; it had said so; it knew everything about me. It knew about Alice; it knew about Filly. It was the embodiment – the disembodiment – of all my worst fears, an escaped nightmare, loose in the house.

You don't know what you might meet. The veiled woman on the gallery. I'd been awake then too.

When we first began writing, Alice had often said that her parents were watching over her, that they appeared to her in dreams, not just as memories but as actual beings. Every emotion, she thought, left some trace in the material world. Ghosts appeared wherever those traces were concentrated, but only certain people could perceive them, and only when they were alone and quiet.

Ghosts or hallucinations – did it make any difference what you called them? The whispering had certainly *started* in my head. It had been lurking there most of my life; ever since that hot January afternoon in Mawson when I first saw the photograph and Mother stopped talking about Staplefield. And now it had got out of my head and on to the gallery, and I had nearly died of terror, and there was absolutely no limit to what might happen, or what I might meet, if I went back to Ferrier's Close alone.

A police car went tearing west, no siren, red and blue lights flashing wildly.

So far the – manifestations – had been confined to the house, but if something truly monstrous appeared, how did I know it wouldn't cross the threshold? Or walk into this hotel room and send me running head-first through the window rather than meet it face to face?

And supposing Alice came with me to the house, would she hear what I heard, see what I saw? I might believe I was trying to save her from some nightmare creature when I was actually strangling her. All of my doubts and suspicions about Alice might be symptoms of incipient madness.

I remembered the story of the iron bedstead sailing across the empty dormitory, the appalling crash when it hit the wall. The image was still as vivid as if I'd been there myself. If a roomful of troubled adolescents could generate that much psychic energy, why couldn't one very troubled thirty-five-year-old man cause a planchette to move by itself: when he was somewhere else in the house, perhaps, upstairs in another room? I liked that even less than the idea of whispering voices escaping from my head.

How could I be sure Alice would ever be safe with me?

Filly killed us all, one by one. Hugh too. Filly killed Hugh too, Gerard, you just don't know it yet. Or had it said 'you too'?

The dead know everything. No: these were my own worst fears running wild, not the words of an omniscient ghost, and to prove it, maybe even to save my sanity, I would have to prove the voice wrong. Search the deaths in Family Records this morning for Hugh Montfort – as well as the searches I'd already planned for him. Renew my reader's ticket and search *The Times* on microfilm in the new British Library for any mention of Anne Hatherley or Hugh Montfort. Find out where lists of missing persons were kept. No more speculation.

Another police car hurtled past, heading towards King's Cross.

The police had searched the house; Miss Hamish had said so. I knew her letter almost by heart, but I got it out anyway, to check her exact wording. 'They found nothing amiss, and concluded that Anne had simply packed her things, locked up the house and left.'

I wondered if they had opened the padlocked door in the basement.

I stayed up until well after dawn writing to Alice, telling her as dispassionately as I could manage everything that had happened since my last message, and what I feared might be happening to my mind. Meeting at the house, I said at the end, would be a very bad idea; I would go anywhere she chose, but not Ferrier's Close. I lay down on the bed, not expecting to sleep until the alarm dragged me out of a black, dreamless void.

Passing Coram's Fields playground, breathing diesel and cut grass and the dusty farmyard smell of the miniature zoo, I found myself wondering whether Alice would want to have children now that she was healed. Neither of us had ever raised the question. I felt certain I didn't, and probably shouldn't, but supposing she did . . . what would we tell them? 'Your grandmother? Oh, she murdered her sister; the police never caught her.' No: I would lie to them, as my mother had lied to me.

In fact the best thing I could do for everyone involved – for the living, at least – would be to walk down Doughty Street, which I was now approaching, to Gray's Inn and along to Bedford Row, and return the keys to Mr Grierstone's secretary. Because I still didn't know, for certain, that my mother *had* murdered Anne. And so long as I didn't discover anything more, I need never know. Already I could almost believe that the whispering had been a drunken nightmare. 'Miss Jessel' would fade from the sheet of butcher's paper on the library table. Tell Miss Hamish I had searched the house thoroughly and found nothing at all.

Only I would have to go back once more because Anne's diary was still on the library table. Along with the planchette and the messages and half a bottle of Braveheart. And a bit of a mess on the chesterfield.

I could whisk the butcher's paper off the table and crumple it without looking. Clean up, lock up, restore Anne's diary to its hiding-place, and take the keys straight back to the office. The shutters were open; the ghost would not walk in daylight. I hailed a cab, changed my mind as it pulled up, and told the driver to take me to the Family Records Centre instead. First set my mind at rest about Hugh Montfort. I realised, as we hurtled along Calthorpe Street, that I didn't know his middle name, and that it would have been better to start by searching *The Times* in the British Library for an engagement notice, but then if I didn't find one I'd have to come back here anyway. Besides, it wasn't a common name; and anyway why was I doing this search at all? At four in the morning it had seemed overwhelmingly urgent to prove the whispering voice wrong. Now it just seemed mad.

The doors were opening as I came up the front steps. A small eager crowd surged in ahead of me and dispersed among the registers, leaving me alone with Deaths 1945 to 1955. All I wanted was not to find anything.

Nothing for the second half of 1949. Or the first, second or third quarters of 1950. But in the register of deaths for Oct.–Dec. 1950, I found my own name.

Montfort, Gerard Hugh   Infant   District of Westminster

Filly killed us all, one by one. You too. She killed you too, Gerard, you just don't know it yet.

I filled out the form for Gerard Hugh Montfort, Infant, with the sensation of ordering my own death certificate. By express, £24 for a guaranteed twenty-four-hour turn-around; they might have it by late afternoon. Then I went over to Births, where I found him in the second quarter of 1950, also District of Westminster.

There was no entry in Marriages for either Phyllis May Hatherley or a Hugh Montfort. No Hugh Montfort in Deaths either; I searched both registers all the way through to the end of 1963, the year my mother married Graham John Freeman in Mawson.

Under her maiden name, it struck me as I was leaving the registry, prompting a sudden crystal-clear memory of my mother's drawn, anxious smile, already middle-aged in the wedding photograph on the mantelpiece in Mawson. And then of the picture I had found in the study, my amazingly youthful mother with an infant on her knee. Gerard Hugh Montfort, Infant. Deceased.

From an internet café I wrote to Alice, telling her what I had just discovered, in the spirit of a castaway consigning a message to a bottle.

I spent the rest of the day in Humanities Reading Room Two in the British Library searching *The Times* on microfilm, first for an engagement notice for Anne Hatherley and Hugh Montfort, which I didn't find, and then from 1 October 1950 for any mention of Gerard Hugh Montfort, Infant, Deceased. After twenty minutes of that, I realised I was wasting time: the death certificate would give me an exact date. I went back to 6 October 1949, the day of Iris Hatherley's death, and began working through the home news pages, looking for any small item – it would have to be small, as neither Hatherley nor Montfort appeared in Palmer's Index. When my shoulder began to ache, I went out on to the gallery and leaned over the sheer precipitous drop to the marble concourse far below, thinking how little it would matter if I slipped over the edge.

At 3.30 I rang the FRC; the certificates hadn't arrived and

wouldn't until Monday morning. I decided to carry on for another hour – the mechanical concentration at least kept me from thinking about Gerard Hugh Montfort, Infant – then have something to eat and go up to the house for the last time. There would still be plenty of daylight left.

Back at the microfilm reader, I remembered something from Miss Hamish's letter: Pitt the Elder – Edward Nichol Pitt of 18 Whetstone Park, Solicitor – had advertised repeatedly for news of Anne. Whom he had last seen on 26 October 1949. I might as well know exactly how his advertisement had read. Starting at the end of November, I began scrolling through the personal columns, day by day. And in the column for 16 December 1949 I found

> Would anyone knowing the whereabouts of Hugh Ross Montfort, late of 44 Endsleigh Gardens WC1, please communicate with Pitt & Co. Solicitors of 18 Whetstone Park Holborn.

The same advertisement appeared twice more, at fortnightly intervals. I went on through February and March, expecting any moment to see a parallel advertisement for Anne. I had worked up a steady rhythm by now, picking up the columns in fast forward, five days a minute, six minutes to the month. At the end of June I stopped to check Miss Hamish's letter. Mr Pitt had been anxious when she went to see him in February 1950. 'He alerted the police, and advertised repeatedly'. Surely he wouldn't have waited another four months. I was working fast but carefully, checking each date to be sure I didn't miss any; I knew I wouldn't have missed even one advertisement. I went all the way through to December, but I didn't find one.

* * *

Light from the stained glass flowers fell like splashes of blood across the drawing-room, spilling from chairs and sofas into the darker red of the carpet, around the fireplace, in great elongated streaks along the wall towards the dining-room. Ten to seven on yet another improbably perfect evening. I carried my bag of cleaning materials on through to the library and set to work.

Scrubbing at the stains beneath the chesterfield reminded me of childhood humiliations in Mawson, things that happened while you were asleep, but were still your fault. I felt very strange indeed: something akin to the disembodied sensation of severe jet lag, as if my physical and emotional selves had parted company altogether, but my mind seemed perfectly clear. At the moment – when not brooding on the disappearances of Anne and Hugh – it was simply refusing to accept that the whispering voice could have been anything other than a nightmare.

So far I had kept well clear of the planchette: from where I knelt I could just see the vertical stub of pencil, above the edge of the table. The sight induced a mental log jam: I *know* I didn't write those messages; it *couldn't* have moved by itself; the messages *did* appear; no one else could have written them . . . round and round, jumbled together with thoughts of Alice, and missing persons, and Staplefield, and Gerard Hugh Montfort, Infant, deceased in the borough of Westminster. My half-brother, you could say, except that I had only been born because he had died. I still didn't know what he had died of. I was his ghost; or he was mine, I couldn't quite decide.

I packed away the cleaning things and stood up, looking around the alcoves at the thousands of volumes I had scarcely begun to examine. When Miss Hamish died, Ferrier's Close would presumably go to some distant Hamish relative. The library would be sold and dispersed, the house bought by some commodities broker, or converted into luxury flats. Judging from the agents' windows along Hampstead High Street, it would fetch several million pounds as it stood.

This could have been my inheritance, said a small rebellious voice. I recalled my fantasy of taking tea with Miss Hamish on the terrace at Staplefield, its sweeping lawns and formal gardens ranged before us. Which had once been the view from here, I thought, staring at the undergrowth encroaching on the dry, desolate courtyard, the wreck of the pavilion beyond. *I feel, young man, that you are the rightful heir to all this . . .* She had actually said something like that, in her letter. Yes: 'I am an old woman, and must think about my own will as well as fulfilling my duty to the estate.'

I sat down at the table – as far as possible from the planchette – and re-read, yet again, her account of her visit to Pitt the Elder in February 1950. By then he had already placed three advertisements seeking news of Hugh. Anne had last been seen in Mr Pitt's office on 26 October 1949. How could Miss Hamish possibly not have known that Hugh Montfort had also disappeared, at almost exactly the same time? The disappearances *must* have been linked; the police would have been working on that assumption.

'Phyllis would never accept a penny from me,' Anne had said. Not in anger but 'very despondently'. As if she'd tried to persuade Phyllis, and failed. Extraordinarily generous, especially if she already knew that Phyllis was pregnant by Hugh. Which could well have been the reason for Hugh's disappearance: fleeing his responsibilities. Just as it could have been Phyllis who got Mr Pitt to place those advertisements; he was the family lawyer, after all. But again Miss Hamish would surely have known about it.

And if Anne thought Phyllis should have her share in spite of everything, why not will it to her anyway and let time decide? Leaving an entire estate to an outsider, even 'my dearest and most trusted friend Abigail Valerie Hamish' was a huge decision for a girl of twenty-one. Maybe Anne just couldn't bear to admit – even to herself – that she *hadn't* forgiven Phyllis.

Nothing about Miss Hamish's letter suggested confusion, or failing memory.

Except that she wasn't once mentioned in Anne's diary. And on Miss Hamish's own account, Anne had written just three short notes to her dearest and most trusted friend during those last crucial weeks of her life. Why hadn't she, at the very least, written to say, Dear Abby, I'm going to leave everything to you? The lawyer would certainly have asked. 'How do you know this young woman will accept your bequest? What is to happen if she doesn't? Who is to inherit if Abigail Hamish dies before you do?'

'My dearest and most trusted friend Abigail Valerie Hamish'. They had shared the same initials. Abigail Valerie Hamish. Anne Victoria Hatherley. That was how they'd met, of course. The alphabetically minded schoolmistress who believed in order in all things.

I was reading with a pencil in my hand, as I often did when concentrating. Now I saw that I had been doodling variations on the two names at the foot of Miss Hamish's page: AVH ANNE VICTORIA HATHERLEY ABIGAIL VALERIE HAMISH MISS A V HATHERLEY MISS A V HAMISH

The last set of letters rearranged themselves into

MISS HAVISHAM

I almost laughed. Great expectations, indeed. A two-million-pound bequest, courtesy of Miss Hamish-Havisham? This message comes to you direct from your subconscious.

Like 'Miss Jessel'? And the whispering from the gallery?

That was a dream.

But how had it – the whispering voice in the dream – known about Gerard Hugh Montfort, Infant? That had come as a complete, paralysing shock.

Coincidence. The register entry interpreted the dream, not the other way round.

You've seen the scratches in the cupboard. You know all about that, the voice had whispered. But I didn't. I glanced up at the gallery. Though it was still almost full daylight outside, shadows were gathering in the alcoves.

There was one other possibility. Apart from a choice between ghosts and hallucinations. Miss Havisham. Hamish. Ridiculous, of course. But at least rationally ridiculous, unlike escaped subconscious minds writing messages on butcher's paper.

Purely for argument's sake: she could have lied about the stroke. She had access to keys. She knew the house. She might have seen the black thread. And as the sole beneficiary of Anne Hatherley's will, she even had a motive for murder.

Ridiculous, nonetheless. Aside from everything else, she could have had Anne declared legally dead after seven years, taken possession of the estate, and either moved into Ferrier's Close or sold it.

Unless she was afraid the process might spark a fresh investigation into Anne's disappearance. Such as a more thorough search of the house and grounds.

Which Miss Hamish had kept unoccupied and overgrown for fifty years.

Ridiculous all the same, because if Miss Hamish had

murdered Anne, she would never have answered my advertisement. Let alone given me the keys to the house. Besides, Miss Hamish couldn't have answered my second question, or whispered those words from the gallery, because I hadn't told her about Alice. So not only ridiculous, but impossible.

Unless Miss Jessel and Miss Havisham had joined forces.

Alice is so beautiful, we all love her.

Terminal paranoia beckoning. Time to leave. I picked up Anne's diary, again with my eyes averted from the planchette at the other end of the table, and headed for the front stairs.

Though sunlight was filtering in through the trees above the stairwell windows, I could not help glancing over my shoulder every time a board creaked. I realised as I approached the second-floor landing that I couldn't even recall what I was doing here. But if I turned back now, I might lose my nerve altogether; and I still had to get the downstairs shutters closed and make my way out of the house by torchlight. Forcing myself not to tiptoe – or run – I moved swiftly across the landing and into Anne's room.

A patch of light fell across the floor. The closet was still open. I replaced the diary, slid the panel into place and closed the door firmly. As I did so, the cupboard above the bed swung open.

You've seen the scratches in the cupboard. But the floor of the empty cupboard was unmarked, and for a disorienting instant I thought I had simply imagined them. Then I remembered that the scratches were on my mother's side.

I had a sudden horrible vision of some monstrous creature concealed, scrabbling loose in the dark, dropping on to Anne's bed. But the side panel separating the two cupboards was entirely solid; so was the section of wall which formed the back of the cupboard in Phyllis's room. And the cupboard floor was firmly screwed to the frame below; I tried one of the screws with a small coin to make sure. The cavity below, directly between the two beds, didn't seem to be accessible from either side of the partition. There was no loose panelling, and certainly no door. Only a tarnished electrical socket, still connected to a lamp on the bedside table. The lamp, I noticed, had no switch of its own: to turn it on, you had to reach down to the power point.

I think of you as my questing knight, facing his last ordeal. What would Alice think of me if I didn't see this through? The question, which I had managed to suppress until now, propelled me along the corridor to my mother's room, which was much darker, because the overgrown window faced north.

Again I shone the torch on the deep gouges in the cupboard floor. Too straight for claw marks, surely: more as if something very heavy had been forced into the cupboard. I noticed, too, that the heads of the screws that secured the floor were burred.

It's only the wiring, I told myself, some long-ago electrician, making repairs. The bedside lamp and socket were identical to the ones next door, but there seemed to be a lot more cord. Crouching beside the bed, I drew out a dusty tangle. The cord from the socket ran to an ancient double adapter: from there, one lead went to the bedside lamp. The top of the light bulb was blackened; broken ends of filament glinted in the torch beam.

The other lead vanished through a hole in the panelling just below the frame of the headboard.

She's dead, of course, but you know all about that. I tried the coin on one of the screws in the cupboard floor and felt it give. Too fearful even to look over my shoulder, I removed a second screw, and then a third, tugged at the edge of the panel and the rest flew out as it came loose. Darkness and floating dust, and then, in the torch beam, an extraordinary piece of apparatus. A bulbous glass tube about a foot long, draped in cobwebs, appeared at first to be floating in a black void. Then I saw that it was suspended above a wooden base-plate by an arrangement of slender rods and clamps. The tube had nipple-like protrusions at both ends, and another emerging from one side, all three with fine silver rods running through them and soldered to what looked like electrodes, small concave sections of silvered metal. Insulated wires connected the tube to an imposing black metal cylinder mounted on the wooden base.

I had seen a picture of something very like this – and recently. Here, in the library downstairs, in the book about martyrs to radiation that looked as if it had been dropped in the bath. Just a glimpse as I'd flipped through the pages: the glass tube clamped vertically on a stand, the black cylinder on a bench nearby, presided over by two bearded Victorian gentlemen.

'Alfred's infernal machine.'

'I used it in a novella' . . . that was it, 'The Revenant': the glass tube Cordelia broke in the studio when it slid out of the green dress. The dress Imogen de Vere had worn in Henry St Clair's portrait.

I understood at last how my mother had murdered her sister without attracting the slightest suspicion. Viola, all unwittingly, had drawn up the plan for the perfect murder, and Phyllis had executed it ruthlessly. Anne had died without ever knowing who – or what – had killed her.

Three minutes later I was back in the library with Viola's letter in my hand, staring at a picture of the first X-ray photograph ever taken: the skeleton of a hand shrouded in ghostly flesh, the black band of a wedding ring stark against the fingerbone. The hand of Anna Röntgen, wife of Wilhelm Conrad von Röntgen, discoverer of Röntgen rays, as they were then called, taken in December 1895. The machine upstairs was called a fluoroscope; the vacuum tube that generated the rays had been named after its inventor, Sir William Crookes. Like several other distinguished Victorian scientists, Crookes had divided his energies between science and séances, especially the séances conducted by an attractive young medium named Florence Cook.

In the spring of 1896, thousands of people had queued at exhibitions throughout the United States and Europe to place their hands, even their heads, in primitive X-ray machines and see the skull beneath the skin. Thousands of fluoroscopes had been sold in that first year: to physicians, engineers, prospectors, amateur scientists and cranks of all persuasions. One of them must have been Alfred Hatherley.

> I shall never forget that day at the Crystal Palace: I think of it whenever I read 'The Relic'. It destroyed the illusion of immortality, the feeling of infinite time that one enjoys when young. Alfred was obsessed – he had to have one. But it seemed to me pure evil, a thing of darkness.

Viola had been right: the machines were appallingly dangerous. A Viennese doctor subjected his first patient, a five-year-old girl, to 32 hours of radiation in an effort to remove a mole from her back. All her hair fell out; her back burned and blistered horribly. Thomas Edison's assistant Clarence Dally was the first to die, in hideous agony, at the age of thirty-nine, with both arms amputated in a vain attempt to stop the cancer from spreading. An early radiologist described the pain of X-ray burns as 'worse than the torments of hell'.

And this was what my mother had knowingly inflicted on

Anne. There was no question of concealment any more. I would have to tell – I wanted to tell – not Miss Hamish, the truth was too appalling – but the police. Fifty years too late, but they could close the file.

As I moved around the table to replace the book on the shelf, the planchette caught my eye. I had meant to scoop up the sheet of butcher's paper and crumple it without looking: that way I would never be certain that I hadn't dreamed the messages. But the idea now seemed childish; I knew perfectly well that 'Miss Jessel' would still be there.

As indeed it was, but the planchette had moved on again. From the tail of the final 'l', a faint pencil line meandered back towards the left-hand edge of the sheet, then downward in a sudden decisive swoop into thin, spiderish script:

Try the cellar

* * *

In the smoky, flaring candlelight, the tunnel was alive with shadows thrown by the branched candelabra in barred crisscrossing patterns over the timbers of the door, multiplying my own gestures in monstrous dumb show. I felt the heat of the flames as I set down the candelabra and turned the beam of the torch in my other hand on to the black padlock.

Here in the tunnel it would be just as dark at midday. And I would have spent another sixteen hours imagining what I might find on the other side of this door. With a certain fatalistic dread, I saw that the keyhole in the padlock had a short central pin, just right for the barrel of the one key I had not yet identified. The lock scraped and grated; the body of the padlock dropped away from the hasp. I lifted the latch and opened the door a fraction.

Nothing came out. The torch beam wavered down a narrow, precipitous flight of steps on to another flagged floor, dark with moisture. There was a handrail attached to the wall on the left of the stairs, but no banister on the other side, just a sheer drop to the stones below. A raw, urinous odour drifted up to me. Racks and shelves, mostly empty so far as I could see, extended along the walls. Patches of lichen flickered in the torch beam. The cellar was long and narrow. Beneath the end wall, I could just make out a mound of something that looked like earth.

The more I played the torch over that mound, the less I liked it. The candles gave far more light, but the flames dazzled me no matter where I held it.

I had been kneeling with the open door propped against my shoulder. When I moved away, it swung closed of its own accord: the bar slid almost to the top of the catch. I tried it again, letting the door go from hard against the side wall. This time the bar slid up and over and dropped, unnervingly, into place. One of those massive Victorian irons in the laundry would wedge it securely open. But then I noticed a small metal eye in the top of the door above the latch. At the corresponding point on the wall, in the vertical gap between two blocks of stone, a hook had been mounted so that it hung inside the recess. I dropped it into the eye and shook the door hard to make certain it was secure.

As I did so I noticed that the inside of the door was scarred by numerous vertical gouges, especially along the joints where the planks met, as if some savage animal had tried to claw its way out of the cellar. I remembered the deep scratches in the floor of the bedroom cupboard.

* * *

Down here the air was colder still: chill and damp and stale. I had the torch in my right hand, flames trailing from the candelabra in my left. A cobweb flared along the shelves – mostly anonymous tins and bottles, labels long gone – as I approached the dark mound. Not earth: a black tarpaulin shrouding an irregular form about five feet long. I stretched out a reluctant foot and twitched the covering aside.

Something scuttled from the heap. I recoiled, shuddering, and bumped against the shelves. The whole end section came crashing down, shattering glass and sending cans rolling and clattering into the dark. By a small miracle I kept hold of both the candelabra and the torch. The flames guttered wildly but did not go out, and as the light steadied I saw amidst the debris a small yellow package tightly tied with string.

As I bent to pick it up I heard another, softer sound from above. The creak of hinges. I had not even reached the foot of the steps before the door swung shut. The click of the latch dropping into place was audible even through the heavy planks.

By the end of the third hour I had exhausted every avenue of escape. The timber was like iron; the door closed flush on to a broad lip of stone, so that the edges were inaccessible from inside. I might have forced a blade between the planks, or prised them apart with a crowbar or even a heavy screwdriver, but there wasn't a single implement in the cellar. The entire construction of the shelving was wooden, much of it rotten, none of it strong enough to make an impression on the door. There were no tools, no knives; nothing bigger than a rusty nail. I tried scraping at the timber with broken glass, and cut my hand badly without making any impression. I tried the keys themselves: most were the wrong shape for gouging, and those that were thin enough had bent and then broken.

I thought of prising up a flagstone to use as a battering-ram, but I had nothing to prise with; they were all immovable. I had even overcome my dread of what might be hidden beneath the black tarpaulin, and found only a pile of rotting sandbags – left over from the Blitz, perhaps. I tried hitting the door with one and it split on the first blow, showering me with damp sand.

Now, as I sat on the top step with my back against the immovable door, the torch was noticeably dimmer, though I had used it as sparingly as possible, and the first of my four candles – I had put out the other three as soon as the first wave of blind panic subsided – was almost gone. On one of the intact shelves I had found a pool of long-congealed candle wax, with an empty matchbox beside it. The corroded tins had all held paint or household cleaners. I had no food, no water, no jacket: only a filthy, sweat-soaked shirt and trousers, a box of matches, almost full, a fading torch, and three more candles.

I had read somewhere that you could survive for many weeks without food, so long as you had plenty to drink, but only four or five days without water. My mouth and throat were already parched. *I'll be with you in three more days, maybe sooner,* Alice had said in her last message. Tomorrow was Saturday. But even if it occurred to her that I might be trapped here, she had no way of getting into the house, and Mr Grierstone's office would be closed all weekend. So even if a very long chain of 'even ifs' came out my way, there was no hope of rescue before Monday at the earliest. And would anyone hear through the floorboards whatever sound I was still capable of making by then?

My frenzied efforts at escape had given the panic an outlet. Now it was rising like water up the steps towards me. *A force that could use a planchette to write 'Try the cellar' could just as easily unhook a door.* Exactly the sort of thought I mustn't think. I would be crouching in the dark soon enough. Use the last of the torch to search the cellar again.

I had left the candelabra at the foot of the stairs. Beyond the circle of light, I could just make out the wreckage of fallen shelves and broken glass, and a faint gleam of yellow: the package, which I had dismissed as simply a folded section of waterproof cloth: there appeared to be nothing solid inside, and the knots were too tight to undo. But I might as well be sure.

Only about an inch of candle remained. The flame swayed as I passed, spilling molten wax on to the floor. I used a piece of broken glass to cut the string. In the centre of the package I found several sheets of typescript, also tightly folded several times over, with the typewritten side outwards.

Within seconds she was drenched, and though Harry met her with an umbrella as she approached the house, the roar of the thunder drowned every attempt at speech.

Towelling her hair dry in her room, while thunder rolled and reverberated overhead and the electric light flickered after every flash of lightning, Cordelia was seized by a reckless impulse to put on the emerald green gown. Earlier in the week, she had spent several hours brushing and sponging and pressing it, and airing out the musty smell. But how would she explain its sudden appearance in her wardrobe? and besides, it would upset her uncle. She chose another dress, also green but in a lighter shade, and went down to the kitchen, where she found Harry helping Beatrice assemble a cold supper.

"I'm sorry for what I said in the lane," said Beatrice,

as soon as she came in. "You startled me, that's all; I didn't mean it. No"—as Cordelia reached for an apron—"you've done everything all week; Uncle has a glass of wine waiting for you."

"Yes, you put your feet up, old thing," said Harry. "I'll be in in just a minute."

Though Cordelia had grown used to being "old thing" in company, she had not realised until that moment just how thoroughly she disliked it. But after insisting that she was not jealous, she felt obliged to accept. Harry's minute stretched to what felt like ten, and when he did join her and her uncle and aunt, she could not decide whether he was simply being his usual self, or behaving like someone determined to pretend that nothing whatever was wrong. The hiss of rain and the constant rumble of thunder made conversation difficult, and then, after an especially fierce flash of lightning, the electric lights went out, leaving them to dine by flickering candlelight, which made it impossible to read anybody's expression, even when you could hear what they were saying.

Gradually, the thunder receded and the rain diminished until there was only the drip drip drip from the eaves onto the gravel outside. The wind, too, had died away, and when Uncle Theodore opened the window, cool damp air wafted into the dining-room. Aunt Una retired to her room; but still Harry, Beatrice (who had evidently taken the confrontation in the lane as sanction for casting off her reserve with him) and Theodore chatted on, until Cordelia could bear it no longer, and more or less ordered Harry to accompany her upstairs to the studio.

The air was so still that, rather than light a lamp, she simply took one of the candlesticks from the sideboard.

"Anything the matter, old thing?" Harry asked, as they approached the stairs.

"Don't call me that any more! I'm not old, and I'm not a thing." And, she almost added, I'm not yours, either.

"Sorry, old—I mean—er—sorry," he said, sounding aggrieved, and they ascended in silence while she choked back one angry opening after another, so preoccupied with her suspicions in regard to Beatrice that they had reached the second-floor landing before she remembered "The Drowned Man".

It came to her as she went to fetch the key of the studio from her room, leaving Harry to wait in darkness on the landing. She could not say anything about Beatrice without sounding jealous, and putting herself even further in the wrong, for he *might* be perfectly innocent on that score. But she could set him a test: she would place a strand of her hair between the covers of "The Drowned Man", and leave the door unlocked that night; if he lied about it in the morning, she would know, and break the engagement regardless.

Though it had been cool on the landing, the day's heat was still trapped in the studio. She lit the candles on the table, and placed her candlestick in a holder on the lectern. When she knelt on the bed and opened the window, the candle flames barely wavered. There was no moon, but the sky had cleared and she could see starlight glimmering on the wet grass beyond the flagstones below.

She stood up and turned to Harry, who was standing beside the easel, and, it seemed to her, ostentatiously ignoring the lectern.

"What's the matter, old—sorry, I mean, what's up?"

"Nothing," she said coldly, thinking, how could you possibly not know?

"Not still upset over that little spat in the lane?"

Too angry to reply, she tugged at the ring he had given her, meaning to fling it in his face, but it would not come off.

"Good, I knew you wouldn't be. Look here old—sorry, I'm quite done up, I think I'll turn in. Don't worry about a candle. 'Night."

He dabbed a perfunctory kiss on her cheek and retreated to the doorway. In silence, she extinguished the candles on the table and retrieved her own from the lectern.

"Er - aren't you going to shut the window?"

She shook her head, and removed her key from the open door as she left. Dazzled by the flame of her candle, she could not see his expression, but her own was surely unmistakable.

"I see—leaving it to air—er, good idea. 'Night." He set off down the stairs in his irregular, slightly crab-like fashion, while she watched, still speechless, until he had vanished into the dim, starlit recesses of the flight below.

Back in her room, she removed the offending ring with soap and sat on her bed rehearsing what she would say when she returned it to him in the morning. Or should she go down to his room and have it out now? No; that would only upset her uncle, and give Beatrice something more to gloat over. She would wait until she could get Harry alone in the wood. For an hour or more she paced up and down her room, sustained by the heat of her fury. But as it began to cool, doubts crept in. Harry hated scenes, and would go to any lengths to avoid a quarrel; perhaps he would have apologised if she hadn't been so hostile. And what—supposing he was innocent where Beatrice was concerned—

was he supposed to apologise *for*? Calling her "old thing"? She had never protested until tonight. For being chronically unpunctual? She had never objected to that, either. For his lack of ardour? Again, she hadn't complained of it. Was he supposed to read her thoughts? Yes, said a rebellious voice, because I know I can read his. But how could she be so sure? He had been ardent enough, last Sunday on the riverbank; her headache had put an end to that. A wave of self-loathing rose up like bile; she buried her face in her pillow and wept for a long time.

She must have fallen asleep, for after an indefinite interval she woke in darkness, with the impression of having heard a door close. Or had she only dreamt it? She slid off her bed, still fully dressed, and crept out into the corridor. No light shone beneath her sister's door, but the door to the landing stood open, and as she came nearer, she saw a faint glimmer of yellow light on the polished floor outside the studio.

Candles burned in the sockets on either side of the lectern. His hair was dishevelled, his feet bare, his shirt half-unbuttoned. He had also lit the triple candelabra on the table; its light shone full upon her face as she stood with her hand on the handle of the half-open door, but he did not see her. His forehead gleamed; she could see the reflection of the flame moving over his temple as he swayed slowly back and forth. Once again she waited, willing him to look up, her anger rekindling as the seconds passed. A stirring of the air set the candles flaring; the portrait of Imogen de Vere, which stood just to the left of her line of sight, caught her awareness, and she knew exactly what she wanted to do.

She closed the studio door softly and returned to her

own room, where she lit another candle, and changed into the emerald green gown. It was a little loose around the bodice and shoulders, but that would not matter; and her hair was still pinned up. She took out the veil, and for the third time drew it over her head.

The mirror showed only a flame floating in black mist, but that did not matter either; she knew the way blindfold. Her sister's room was still dark and silent as she made her way back along the corridor.

Even through the veil, she could see that his gaze remained fixed upon the lectern. She took a step into the room, then another. Still he did not see her. Three more paces, and a hooded shadow fell across the portrait as she came between it and the candelabra on the table. He looked up, and though his face was little more than a blurred impression of features, it seemed to her that he smiled. Then he began to speak, but so softly that she could not hear him through the muffling folds of gauze. She raised both hands and threw back the veil.

The smile faded; the words died on his lips. For several seconds he stood petrified. Then, very slowly, his expression changed to one of disbelieving horror. She began to back away, her shadow growing larger as she retreated until she bumped against the table. The room suddenly brightened; something moved upon—no, *in*—the bed, at which she had not even glanced before. In the flaring, crackling light she saw Beatrice's head upon the pillow, a bare arm and shoulder emerging from beneath the sheet, eyes opening wide as Cordelia tore off the burning veil and beat at her hair with both hands.

The flames around her head went out, with a horrible smell of singed hair; the blazing remnants of the veil floated across the room and settled upon Henry St Clair's palette-tray. Cordelia stood paralysed, watching her own narrowly averted fate enacted upon the canvas. A tongue of fire darted up one bare arm and across the shoulder of the emerald green gown; the beautiful face seemed to rise up in flight; and then, with no memory of an interval, she was stamping with her bare feet at the smouldering ruins of the portrait, with acrid fumes burning her throat, and a thousand tiny red sparks floating and settling and crawling about the floor.

She had knocked over the candelabra on the table; it too had gone out, but the two candles on the lectern still burned. Someone had been screaming; she did not know whom. Harry had not moved; he stood gripping the lectern with both hands, his mouth half open. Beatrice had wrapped herself in the sheet and was shivering on the edge of the bed, staring at her sister with glazed, uncomprehending eyes. Cordelia's hands and the back of her neck were beginning to sting painfully. Aside from the stinging, she felt perfectly numb; her mind had frozen in mid-thought, somewhere between Harry and Beatrice and what her aunt and uncle would do now that Ashbourn would have to be sold.

But now Harry was folding away "The Drowned Man". Meticulous as always, he fastened the clasp, took up the black volume and placed it under his left arm. He might have been walking in his sleep, or perhaps the dream was hers, for it seemed to take him an age to cover the few paces that separated them. She thought he would pass her without speaking, and knew that she ought to be angry, angrier than she had ever been in her life, but the feeling would not come, nothing would come; until he stopped between her and Beatrice and muttered something that sounded like "Sorry old . . . sorry." And then, quite clearly, "I must, you see."

The open window was directly behind him; one good push would send him reeling backwards past Beatrice, across the bed and over the sill. Something must have showed in her face, for he flinched away from her, hugging the black book to his chest. Beatrice, now with her clothes clutched against the sheet, held out her free hand as if inviting him to help her up. But he did not see her; his eyes remained fixed upon Cordelia, to whom he repeated, "I must have it, you see." Then he turned and made for the landing at a horrible hopping run.

Cordelia followed, not knowing what she meant to do. From the doorway, she saw him silhouetted crabwise against the starlit window as he reached the head of the stairs. Then she was thrust violently aside. A pale figure darted across the landing and flung itself at Harry. His arms flew up, and he lurched violently forward, clutching at the black volume as it sailed over the banister. One foot caught on the rail, and for an instant he seemed to hang motionless in the void. Whatever sound he made in falling was drowned in Beatrice's scream before she vanished, wailing, down the stairs.

A lantern gleamed on the landing below, followed by the sound of Uncle Theodore's hurrying footsteps. Cordelia turned towards the light, but then, remembering what she was wearing, and what he had seen before, she retreated into the darkness of the corridor, to prepare herself for all that she had yet to face.

* * *

One came true. I had found the missing pages of 'The Revenant'. Crouched beside the guttering candle, I turned over the last page and saw that there was writing on the back.

My name is Anne Hatherley and my sister Filly – Phyllis – shut me in here. I heard the front door slam hours ago. I'm afraid she's left me here to die. I mustn't waste time, there's only half a candle left. And half a pencil.

I'll try and write in the dark.

Filly slept with Hugh. Hugh Montfort, my fiancé. I heard them in the attic. They were making love on Lettie's old bed. It's all in my grandmother's story – the pages I'm writing on. No time to explain. I thought it was haunting me but Filly was making it come true. She's been reading my diary – I don't know for how long.

I posted Hugh's ring back the next day with a note saying, you know why, I never want to see you again. He didn't reply. And then for a week Filly behaved as if I'd done something unforgivable to <u>her</u>. She was daring me to speak and I

The pencil just broke. I had to light the candle to sharpen it on a stone. Only nine matches left.

A week after I saw them in the attic my face and scalp started burning. Exactly what happened to Imogen in the story. And then it all blew up. Iris heard the row and Filly started screaming at her too. Next thing she was walking out the door. She must have had her cases packed and waiting, I think she went straight to Hugh's flat. Iris was so angry she cut Filly out of her will and left everything to me. She died that same week, I know it was the shock.

Every day my skin's got worse. It burns like fire and I feel sick all the time. The doctor said he'd never seen anything like it. Just like the story again. He gave me some ointment but it didn't help.

She didn't even come to Iris's funeral. I had the locks changed so she couldn't get in. I was staying with friends in Highgate, coming back here to pack when I could face it. I was afraid of her, I even made a will yesterday, but I didn't tell

The pencil just broke <u>*again*</u>*. Seven matches left.*

Nobody knows I'm here. Except Filly. I hid this and my diary in the study where I thought she wouldn't find them again – I wanted to leave them behind but I couldn't. I came out of the study and saw her coming up the stairs with a carving knife in her hand. She smiled when she saw me.

I threw the diary at her and ran, but she didn't follow. If only I'd kept going. Instead I stopped to listen, and got caught in the most terrifying game of hide-and-seek. I slipped the story down the front of my blouse to protect me from the knife. The floorboards kept giving me away, but Filly never made a sound. I knew she was lying in wait. In the end I went down the front stairs to the first floor, making sure I trod on the boards that creak, and then crept through to the back stairs and down to the courtyard door. I managed the bolts quietly but the lock

Hours later – I've tried everything I can think of and I can't get out. It's so cold down here. I could burn the rest of Grandmama's story but it would only last a minute or two. I'll hide the pages I've written on in case

The last of the candle's going

Dear God help me

Anne had been braver than me. Far braver. I still had the last of the torch, and a full box of matches. My second candle was more than half gone, and I hadn't once dared sit in the dark. It would swallow me soon enough. Like Anne I had given up scraping at the granite-hard timber; I wondered whether she had sat where I was sitting, huddled on the top step with her back against the door. I was shivering in August; she must have frozen to the bone. Perhaps she had died of cold. It was supposed to be painless at the end. Better than radiation poisoning. You felt warmth stealing over you, and a great desire to sleep, and in the last moments of consciousness you might see brightly coloured visions, blossom and hedgerow and birds singing when you were actually freezing to death on the ice. One of the Antarctic explorers had written about it. Though he couldn't have died that time. I thought of the bottle of sleeping tablets beside my bed in the hotel room and wished I'd brought them with me. I wished they had caught Phyllis May Hatherley and hanged her. Though she was already pregnant by then; they would have had to wait until Gerard Hugh Montfort was born. He at least might have survived if they had.

I thought of Phyllis coming back to dispose of Anne's body. If I was going to die here I wanted to die before the last candle dripped away to nothing and the whispering began again.

I had set the candle about half-way down the steps. The flame burned steadily, motionless except for the faint pulsing of the shadow around the wick. Darkness lurked behind the wreckage of the shelves, biding its time.

I could burn the shelves, I thought. Pull the rest off the wall, build a fire in the middle of the floor and burn them one at a time. It would hold off the darkness for at least another hour, maybe several. If I kept it low there should be enough air to breathe. And if enough smoke got past the door, there was a very faint chance that someone might see it and call the fire brigade.

The door was made of wood too. I could build my fire at the top of the steps . . . but if it got into the floorboards directly above the door, the whole house could go up, and me with it. Horrible but quick; I'd probably suffocate before I burned. No water to control the fire . . . but I could empty those damp sandbags and use them as beaters.

Breaking up the shelves and building a pyramid of fragments at the base of the door was easy enough; the hard part was getting it to burn. The wood was too damp to catch. After twenty matches had yielded only faint yellow flames that crawled and turned blue and died, I was beginning to panic again. Two sheets of newspaper would have set the whole lot blazing, but I had no paper to burn.

Except ten sheets of typescript, proof – the only decisive proof – that my mother had murdered her sister.

The second candle was almost gone. It had burned much faster while I was trampling pieces of shelving. If I get out of here, I promised Anne, the whole world will know what happened to you, proof or no proof. I arranged five sheets, loosely crumpled, at the centre of the pyramid and got the other five ready to feed in.

The whole cellar lit up for a few seconds; the heaped wood caught and hissed and died with the blazing paper. I added another sheet, then two more in quick succession. The wood flared again and dwindled; now the flames had a small hold, but they were turning ominously blue as I fed in the last two sheets of typescript. The fire blazed and dimmed for a third time, but now the wood was crackling and catching and licking at the scarred planking. Fragments of Anne's last message floated around me, glowing and fading and sinking to the stones below.

For a couple of minutes, the fire seemed docile enough. The burning patch on the back of the door crept upwards. I was beginning to cough, but the draught was clearing the smoke and bringing up fresh air for me to breathe. Small tongues of flame began to lick over the edge of the stone lintel at the joist and floorboards above. I beat at them with the sack, and the fire leapt back at me. Smoke burned my throat. I turned to retreat, missed my footing and fell in a burst of pure white light that exploded inside my head and went sailing away into the dark.

The pain came first, then the head it was pounding in. Throat and lungs, a shoulder, an elbow and a hip materialised, burning, throbbing and stinging in chorus. Somebody was moaning in the darkness nearby. Me. I began to cough instead. Slow dripping sounds; a sour, acrid reek of ash. I was lying in a pool of water.

The fire brigade had arrived in time. But where were they? Apart from the drip drip drip of water, the cellar was deathly still. At least I hoped it was water I was lying in, and not my own blood. I discovered I could move, and then prop myself in the angle between two walls. I coughed for several agonising minutes. Everything hurt, but nothing seemed to be broken.

How long had I been unconscious? Had the firemen simply not seen me lying below the steps? I felt in my trouser pocket for the matches, and remembered putting the box down on the top step, along with the torch. I stood up, wincing, and felt along the wall to my left until I found the edge of the steps.

As I began to feel my way upward, it seemed to me that a rectangular patch of the darkness above was fractionally paler, an impression that strengthened step by step until a gleam of silvery light appeared in the distance. Moonlight at the top of the basement stairs. The door must have burned right through.

I felt around for the torch, but couldn't find it. There was surprisingly little debris on the steps; the floorboards overhead seemed quite intact. I stepped into the tunnel, put out a hand to steady myself, and the door rattled against its hook. My foot struck something metal that went clanging and clattering across the flagstones. A bucket. There was water on the tunnel floor.

Definitely not the fire brigade. Someone had opened the cellar door within seconds of my fall and flung a bucket of water over the blaze on the steps. Someone who was already in the tunnel when I lit the fire. Listening – for how long? – to my frenzied efforts to escape.

Beneath the distant gleam from the landing, the tunnel was in darkness. Whoever – or whatever – had let me out could be waiting in the black cavern of the laundry. Where perhaps it had been waiting when I first came down here. I backed against the end wall and crouched down. If anything moved, I should see it against the band of moonlight.

Until the moon passed over the roof of the house and the darkness became absolute.

My mouth and tongue were coated in thick black glue; I was appallingly thirsty. Better to make a dash for the stairs now. And then? Out by the courtyard door, clear a path through the nettles to the back wall. I felt for the keys and realised they were lost in the cellar. Useless anyway: I had bent or broken every one.

But the courtyard door was only bolted shut. I strained to listen over the blood pounding in my ears until the effort brought on another fit of coughing. Panic sent me lunging forward, straight into another clash and clatter of rolling metal. *I've kicked the bucket again.* The echoes pursued me through the kitchen and up into the moonlight. I had drawn the two bolts, and twisted and tugged several times at the handle before I realised that the door – which had certainly been unlocked three days ago, and which I could not possibly have locked, because I had never found the key – was not going to open.

No one else has keys. Miss Hamish was most insistent about that.

Pale light shimmered down the basement steps, over the empty seed trays in the conservatory. The latticework in the French windows was solid metal. On my right, the door to the breakfast room stood partly open; those windows too were barred. Above the pool of moonlight, the stairs leading up to the dining-room landing were shrouded in darkness. The house was completely silent.

One last bruising rush up those stairs and along the dog-legged corridor that ran between the library and the drawing-room would carry me to safety. If I could face the dark. And if whoever was waiting somewhere in that darkness hadn't also deadlocked the front door.

But if I ran I wouldn't be able to hear. I crept across the flagged floor towards the stairs, and began to climb. In the stair-well overhead I became aware of a faint yellow light, which could only be the moon shining through the stairwell windows. Odd, because the moonlight in the basement was a stark, silvery white.

Three more steps brought me on to the landing. Staircase on my right; dining-room beyond that; library to the left; corridor straight ahead. I felt certain I had left those doors open; now all three were closed. In the hall it would be pitch black. Here at least, I could see; the yellow moonlight seemed to be shining directly down on me.

I looked up and saw that it was not the moon, but a light bulb suspended above the half-landing.

I am afraid the electricity was disconnected many years ago.

I tried the switches on the wall beside me. More lights came on, none of them very bright, in the stairwell, beside the dining-room door, in the basement below.

Miss Hamish had lied to me. Though there might be a perfectly innocent explanation: she had changed her mind and got the electricity reconnected before the stroke put her in hospital. The power could have been on the whole time I'd been searching the house.

But someone had switched on the stairwell light while I was in the cellar.

I stood irresolute, glancing from one door to another, trying to decide which way to go. The murky yellow light only accentuated the shadows all around me. I felt the pressure of unseen eyes; the feeling of something monstrous waiting behind one of those doors mounted until the dark stained timbers seemed to bulge towards me and I found myself retreating up the stairs to the half-landing and on to the first floor, where again the door to the passageway was closed, as it surely had not been before.

The stairwell lights burned steadily. I could wait here, I thought; daylight can't be more than two or three hours away. But my thirst had become intolerable, and the craving for water dragged me upwards, towards the bathroom on the second-floor landing. *Bathrooms have locks*: the thought carried me all the way to the top of the creaking staircase. As below, the door to the bedroom corridor was now closed.

The bathroom door was ajar, as I felt sure I had left it, but the door to the attic stairs stood wide open, and those stairs too were lit from above. *The attic where I was conceived*, I thought stupidly, and then, *no, that was the other Gerard.*

I pushed open the bathroom door. But the light did not work, and the bolt had rusted solid. I wedged the door shut with my foot and gulped down handfuls of cold, metallic water.

The pane of glass over the door gave just enough illumination . . . but what if the lights went out again? – and then if something began to push against the door, a slow, stealthy, irresistible pressure . . . Outside at least I could run.

A floorboard popped and snapped as I stepped back on to the landing. Whoever had turned the stairwell lights on *must* know I was here. What were they waiting for? Why had they closed the connecting doors? Why let me out of the cellar at all?

Perhaps they really had gone for help.

From where I was standing, I could see all the way up to the attics while keeping the main stairwell and the door to the bedrooms more or less in view. Something about the attic stairs – no, the landing above them – looked different. I moved a step closer and saw that a doorway had appeared in what I had thought was a blank panelled wall at the top of the stairs.

With the same disembodied, sleep-walking sensation that had propelled me into the cellar, I went on up the stairs. A section of panelling had opened into a low, cavernous room, dark except for a glowing crescent a few paces to my left: a reading lamp, with its shade swung right down on to the surface of a large desk. An upright chair stood in front of the desk; heavy curtains were drawn across the wall behind it. Bookcases along the opposite wall; an armchair and chesterfield like the ones in the library; various chests and cabinets. The floor was thickly carpeted; the air smelt of dust and worn fabric and decaying paper and a faint, archaic medicinal odour: something like chloroform or formaldehyde. Nothing moved; the stillness remained unbroken.

Drawn by the light, I moved towards the desk. A humped shape beside the lamp resolved itself into a computer monitor.

The screen was dark. Glancing fearfully around, I raised the lampshade and saw that the desk drawers were partly open, as if someone had been disturbed in the act of going through them. In the top right-hand drawer lay a thick bundle of typescript, its title obscured by a band of black ribbon. *A novel. By V.H.*

The dusty animal smell of the carpet rose and filled my nostrils, and I was looking down on my ten-year-old self, crouched beside my mother's dressing-table on that stifling January afternoon, staring directly over his shoulder at a large manila envelope addressed to P.M. Hatherley, the row of English stamps with their heavy black cancellation marks along the top of the envelope, the slit in the end, the creases formed by the typescript of 'The Revenant' . . .

It was gone in an instant, leaving only the conviction that I had missed something vital, something that ought to have been blindingly clear. I tried the left-hand drawer and it rolled smoothly outwards to reveal a long row of folders, all crammed with papers . . . no, letters . . .

From: ghfreeman@hotmail.com
To: Alice.Jessell@hotmail.com
Subject: None
Date: Wed, 11 August 1999 19:48:21 +0100 (BST)

Something very weird has happened. I've discovered a diary – Anne's diary – hidden in my mother's room – I'll tell you about that in a second – but in the library this afternoon I found . . .

My own letters to Alice. All of them. Running backwards in time, from the email printouts at the front, back through the laser and the inkjet and dot-matrix printers, down to the next tier of cabinet, the electric and the manual typewriters, all the way back to my lumpish, sprawling, thirteen-year old handwriting and 'Dear Miss Summers, Thank you very much for your letter. I would very much like to have a penfriend . . .'

This can't be happening. I must be concussed; I'm hallucinating; I'll wake up in a minute, back in the hotel. It felt exactly like the moment in a nightmare when you realise you must be dreaming. I stood staring numbly at the folder in my hands until the contents slid out and scattered over the keyboard. Lights flashed green and orange; the fan whirred; the screen lit up.

From: ghfreeman@hotmail.com
To: Alice.Jessell@hotmail.com
Subject: None
Date: Fri, 13 August 1999 11:54:03 +0100 (BST)

I've just made the most appalling discovery in the Family Records Centre . . .

'Gerard.' A slow, insinuating whisper at my back. From the shadows at the far end of the room, an indistinct figure, shrouded in flowing white, detached itself from the wall and glided to the door. Draperies swirled; the door closed; a key turned in the lock. As the figure moved towards the circle of light I saw that she was tall and statuesque and veiled like a bride; a long white veil, floating above a great cascading cloud of chestnut hair that flowed on down over her shoulders exactly as it had in so many dreams of Alice. Her arms were entirely concealed by long white gloves, and her gown, too, was white, gathered high at the waist. Small flowers showed beneath the fringes of the veil, between coiling strands of hair; small purple flowers, embroidered across the bodice of her gown.

'My questing knight,' she whispered. 'Now you can claim your prize.'

'*Who are you?*'

'I'm Alice, of course. Aren't you going to kiss me?' It was the voice I had heard from the gallery, intimate, lingering, with an icy hiss on the sibilant, and an eerie after-echo, as if two – or several – voices were whispering in unison.

The figure moved towards me. I retreated around the desk until it halted a few paces away. No trace of features showed through the veil.

'You don't seem very pleased to see me, Gerard. Is it because I'm dead?'

I made an incoherent sound.

'I died, you see – perhaps I forgot to mention that. In the accident with my parents. But I still want you, Gerard. Body and soul. For ever and ever.'

The floor dipped and swayed. I gripped the edge of the desk and tried to will myself awake, but the veiled figure refused to dissolve. *This isn't real.*

'Oh but it is.' I did not think I had spoken aloud. I wanted to run for the curtains behind me, but I knew I would fall if I let go of the desk.

'You're not thinking of *leaving*, Gerard? That would be so rude. We haven't even made love yet. And you've always said you wanted me so much.'

She moved a little closer.

'Shall I take off my veil, Gerard? Or don't you like dead women? No? Would you rather run away? There's a balcony behind you: you can throw yourself over.'

The veiled figure began to circle around the desk towards me. As it came closer still, I saw that it moved with a strange, jerky rhythm – glide and halt, glide and halt – as if it had stepped from the screen of a silent film.

I backed away, keeping the desk between us until I bumped against the open drawer containing Viola's manuscript. For an instant I saw my mother's Medusa face in the bedroom doorway, contorted with fear and fury. The formless suspicions of the past four days flared like the papers I had burned in the cellar.

'You're – you're Miss Havi – Hamish,' I blurted. 'You found Anne's body in the cellar and then –' *went mad*.

We had come full circle around the desk. The veiled figure halted.

'It's you that's mad, Gerard. You've been mad for years. That's why you can see me.'

'No! You loved her – Anne – you wanted revenge. You traced my mother to Mawson, posted the story – the pages you found in the cellar – and then – why didn't you go to the police?'

For the first time, I heard the hiss of breathing.

'It's your story, Gerard. Your bedtime story: you finish it. And then we'll play *here comes a candle to light you to bed*.'

She was at least as tall as I was. The veil rustled and stirred: clichés about maniacs having the strength of ten came horribly to mind.

'But I never hurt Anne,' I said desperately. 'I didn't even know she existed until you wrote to me.'

'We all have to pay, Gerard. Unto the third generation. You know that.'

'Then why did you spare my mother? Why *didn't* you go to the police?'

'You know what they say, Gerard, about a dish best eaten cold. There you both were, rotting away in Mawson, wasting your lives . . . and what would poor Alice have done, without her lover?'

The room lurched and spun. She must have been insane from the start: had she dragged Anne's body out of the cellar and buried her in the back garden instead of dialling 999?

'How did you know where to look for Anne's body?'

Silence. She was no more than six feet away, almost near enough to lunge across the top of the monitor.

'Anne didn't die in the cellar,' she said at last. 'That was for *your* benefit.' The voice had taken on a deep, rasping note. 'She had nine operations and seven years of radiation treatment. Radiation, for radiation burns. Therapy, they called it. Worse than the torments of hell. You saw where your mother hid the machine. She left it on all night, six inches from Anne's head. They skinned her alive, trying to stop the cancer. And then she died.'

'But – but you said in your letter,' I began, and stopped dead. Most of what I thought I knew had come from that letter. All false, all fake; all bait for the trap she had set. Like that last desperate message in the cellar. Like Alice.

'All fake,' I said numbly. 'Everything I found here.'

'No, Gerard; only the message in the cellar. Everything else is real.'

'You stole my life,' I said.

'Your mother stole mine. But at least I know – thanks to you – that she lost the baby – *his* baby, the one she *really* loved . . . And remember, Gerard, you enslaved yourself. I didn't force you. Think of the life – all the girls you could have had. Instead you chose to be my eyes and ears, my puppet. My adoring puppet.'

I shuddered, swallowing a wave of nausea.

'Why did you let me out?'

'You set fire to my house; one has to improvise. And now it's time to put the puppet back in his box. The machine still works, you see.'

'You can't mean . . . you can't make me –'

'Can't I?'

She made as if to circle the desk again. My knees shook wildly; I realised I was gripping the desk with both hands. Through the shrouded layers of material, I caught the outline of something dark and formless: it did not look like a face.

'You really don't like dead women, do you, Gerard? Shall I take off my veil now?'

'NO!' The word echoed around the room.

'That's not very flattering, Gerard. I think I'd better see you off to bed now. In Anne's room. You can crawl, if you like. And then in the morning, I might even let you go.'

I became aware of a low, muffled keening. It sounded like wind in the trees outside. Somewhere a small, distant voice was saying that beneath the veil was an elderly woman called Abigail Hamish who, however crazed, could not actually stop me if I could find the strength to run. But I knew that my legs would not carry me; and that if the veiled figure caught me, I would die of terror.

And if I obeyed her, I would die as slowly and hideously as Anne Hatherley had done. I thought of the fluoroscope waiting in its lair below, and in that instant – as in the instant before a car crash, when time stalls and you seem to slide ever so slowly toward the point of impact – I saw the tangle of cords hidden beneath the bed in my mother's old room, the ragged edges where the pages had been torn from Anne's diary, and understood at last how I had been *led*, every step of the way. I had assumed that my mother had torn out those pages, carefully preserving the evidence of her affair with Hugh Montfort, and then restored the diary to its hiding-place. I had seen, without understanding, that whenever my mother switched on her bedside lamp, the fluoroscope would have come on too. Flooding *both* sides of the partition with X-rays from the unshielded tube . . .

But the lightbulb was blown. The thought hovered for an instant, but made no sense. Just as I had stared at the advertisement for Hugh Montfort, late of Endsleigh Gardens, without once considering that my mother, alone and pregnant, might have asked the solicitor to place it. Thinking that Hugh had abandoned her when he too was already dead. Under the cellar floor, perhaps.

Along with Anne.

And no record of Anne's death, and not one mention of Abigail Hamish in Anne's diary.

I tried to keep you safe.

'You killed them both,' I said. 'Anne and Hugh.'

I could hear my pulse ticking like a demented clock.

The veiled figure stirred.

'He came crawling back here . . .' she whispered. I couldn't catch the rest, only something that might have been 'accident'.

'And Anne,' I repeated. 'You killed her too.'

'In a way,' she said, and raised her gloved hands.

'Filly slept upstairs in the attic that night. Where she slept with *him*.'

And then, almost inaudibly, 'There was no light under her door, you see. I thought I was safe.'

The veil floated free; the cloud of chestnut hair slipped from her shoulders and fell at her feet with a soft thud. Lamplight gleamed upon a bald, mummified head, skin stretched like crackling over the dome of the skull, with two black holes for nostrils and a single eye burning in a leprous mass of tissue, fixing me, half a life too late, with the enormity of my delusion as I saw that Alice Jessell and Anne Hatherley and Abigail Hamish were one and the same person.

For a moment neither of us moved. The wind had grown distinctly louder. The sound seemed to be coming from beneath the floor. A rushing, *crackling* sound. She swirled around, glided to the door, and unlocked it. I saw, as I came up behind her, an orange glow in the doorway at the foot of the attic stairs. The air was shimmering with heat.

She stood for a moment with one hand on the doorknob, then moved calmly on to the landing. I thought she spoke, but the words were lost in the noise of the fire. Then she took hold of the banister and started down the stairs. I felt the heat on my face, and could not move. She had almost reached the landing below when a great gust of smoke came boiling up the staircase. I heard myself cry 'Alice!' and fell to my knees, choking. A blast of hot air followed; the smoke cleared, and I saw through streaming eyes that there was no one on the stair.

Then the smoke boiled up again, and I was forced back into the room, slamming the door as I went. The desk lamp shone blue through the smoke; blind instinct sent me crawling towards the curtains behind the desk. I dragged them apart and saw French windows, a narrow terrace, the night sky; and beyond a low parapet, a faint flickering gleam on the nearest treetops. I threw open the doors, breathed fresh air. The trapped smoke began to clear.

But where was the fire brigade? All I could hear was the muffled rumbling of the fire: no sirens, no voices, no alarms. Vertigo seized me; I crawled across to the parapet, a plain brick wall barely two feet high. Even lying almost prone behind it, I found myself gripping the top of the wall with all my strength. Gravity seemed to have altered; I felt the outward pull, the impending headlong plunge to the glass roof of the conservatory far below. Lit by the pulsing glare of the flames in the stairwell and the four great windows of the library, the encircling wall of vegetation looked more than ever like jungle. Despite the ferocity of the blaze, it was evidently still concealed from the neighbouring houses and the Heath. None of the glass appeared to have broken yet, but it could not be long now.

And there was no fire escape. The terrace ran the width of the house, bounded at both ends by the steep descending angle of the roof. The only possibility would be a wild leap from the corner to my left, where the jungle along the edge of the courtyard came nearest to the house, into the crown of the nearest tree. I tried to imagine myself doing it, and the terrace seemed to slide from under me.

Still no sound of sirens. The fire must still be confined to the back of the house; it would have raced up the rear stairwell and spread outwards from there. Perhaps there was another way. I retreated from the parapet, managed to stand, stumbled back into the room. The air was hotter, the roar and crackle of the flames much closer; a line of orange light was flickering beneath the door to the landing.

The desk lamp still shone. I looked at my letters to Alice, my wasted life; thought of Viola's library blazing below. There was one thing I wanted to save. I seized Viola's typescript and thrust it inside the front of my shirt, thinking, *this is what Anne did*, and then, *but that never happened either.*

Which way? Oily black smoke was seeping under the landing door. I had no idea what lay beyond the other door, in the darkness at the far end of the room. Better to fall than burn. I ran back through the French windows on to the terrace, to the brink of that dreadful plunge. I saw the wreck of the pavilion, bathed in flickering light. I thought of Alice, Miss Hamish, Staplefield, everything I thought I'd known: all phantoms, all gone. With nothing to hold me to the earth, and no life to relive, what was there left to fear? I could simply close my eyes and dive, and vanish in a flash of light.

Then the world breathed fire and my feet carried me, not over the edge but along the terrace and up and over into a dark confusion of tearing branches and a jolt that left me winded and sprawled backwards, but somehow attached to the tree. Through the hole smashed by my fall, I saw flames rising above the parapet. Small tongues of flame began to detach themselves and soar above the main fire, more and more of them, like flocks of fiery birds, flaring and rising and vanishing into the night sky. I felt the weight of the manuscript tugging at my shirt, and began precariously to descend.